THE DRAUGHTSMAN

Robert Lautner

THE BOROUGH PRESS

The Borough Press
An imprint of HarperCollins*Publishers*
1 London Bridge Street
London SE1 9GF

www.harpercollins.co.uk

This paperback edition 2018

1

First published by HarperCollins*Publishers* 2017

Every effort has been made to trace and contact copyright holders.
If there are any inadvertent omissions we apologise to those concerned and will
undertake to include suitable acknowledgements in all future editions.

A catalogue record for this book
is available from the British Library

ISBN: 978-0-00-812674-2

This novel is entirely a work of fiction.
The names, characters and incidents portrayed in it, while at times based
on historical events and figures, are the work of the author's imagination.

Set in Perpetua by Palimpsest Book Production Ltd,
Falkirk, Stirlingshire

Printed and bound in Great Britain by
CPI Group (UK) Ltd, Croydon, CR0 4YY

MIX
Paper from
responsible sources
FSC™ C007454

This book is produced from independently certified FSC™ paper
to ensure responsible forest management.

For more information visit: www.harpercollins.co.uk/green

'It is not so much the kind of person a man is as the kind of situation in which he finds himself that determines how he will act.'

Stanley Milgram, *Obedience to Authority: An Experimental View* (1974)

Prologue

Erfurt, Germany,
February 2011

The site had become a squat for the disenfranchised, for anarchic youth. They even formed a cultural group. Artists and rebels. Appropriate. Perhaps.

Over the bridge, across the railway that once moved the iron goods from the factory to the camp at Buchenwald, Erfurt still maintained its tourist heart, its picture-book heart. A place where romance comes. Where carriages drawn by white horses still mingle with trams and buses and young and old marrieds hold hands crossing the market square. Rightly fitting, just so, that the industrial quarter on Sorbenweg ignored, left to rot, to be forgotten. A despised relative a hurt family no longer calls upon. Its only colour in the graffiti, signs and spray-paint portraits that only the youth understood.

The squatters removed, the land and remaining dying buildings reimagined. Erfurt ready to remember that history, no matter its shade, had something to pass on.

Myra Konns ran the morning tours of the museum risen from the ruins of the Topf administration buildings. She guided school-children through the original ISIS drafting tables they had found scattered and vandalised over the years by the transients, guided them through the director's rooms still furnished with the wide cabinets that once held drafts for cremation ovens. Labels still sitting in their brass handles. The impression of ink soft and leaving. The drawers empty. Yawning only dust and memory. All restored now.

Myra would show them the small canisters with the clay plaques that the factory made to store ashes to be collected by relatives; a legal requirement until someone decided that it was no longer required. Hundreds of them found abandoned and empty in an attic in Buchenwald. These and other smaller items all on the third floor, where the drafting tables were repaired and displayed, where the chief designer's office had been recreated, where the tours could still see from the window to Ettersberg mountain as the draughtsmen at their tables would have done and Myra would point out that the smoke from the Buchenwald ovens could be seen crawling over the mountain all day. All day.

The oven doors, removed from Auschwitz and Buchenwald, the most sombre items of the tour. No need to highlight the prominence of the company plaque set above them. Topf and

Sons exhibited now as the 'Engineers of the Final Solution'. A brochure saying so.

In one display cabinet Myra would put her hand to a drawing of an experimental oven, never employed; for the allies had closed in before its realisation. Beside it a letter from a director to Berlin explaining the function of the new design. And Myra would always choose her words with care.

'It works on four levels over two floors, one of which is the basement, where the morgue would traditionally be, replaced by the furnace. The deceased would be put in at the top and a series of rollers over grates would convey them to the furnace. The letter confirms the effectiveness of the design at being able to work continuously. Day and night. Reducing the need for coal as the oven was intended to be fuelled by the deceased themselves. Hundreds, possibly thousands of corpses a day. No intention to distinguish one from the other. A machine. An eradication device criminal in nature and design. Thankfully never introduced. The Allies having liberated Auschwitz some months before.'

A hand went up in the midst of the group. Myra took a breath. An old man. Always a sparse group of old men and women dawdling amongst the children. In her induction, just the month before when the museum opened, Myra had been informed to be especially aware of the aged visitors. The air about the place theirs. The tomb of it theirs.

'Yes, sir?'

'Excuse me, Fräulein,' he bowed slightly. White, pomade-brushed hair and grey-blue eyes that smarted from the cold

February wind outside, made worse by the radiator warmth of the halls. He wiped his eyes behind his glasses.

'That correspondence does not refer to the design of the continuous oven. Of that oven.'

Myra's breath released. Always one.

'Sir. This letter has been donated from the Russian archives. It has been verified by many experts.'

He moved forward, his age more apparent in his careful step, in his politeness in moving through the young elbows that might bruise him as he passed.

'Forgive, Fräulein. That oven – the continuous oven – was patented in 1942. *That* letter was for a circular design. From Herr Prüfer. From one of the engineers.' He tapped a finger on the glass. 'This drawing was for a new annotation of the previous patent. Ordered to be redrafted in May 1944.'

Myra looked between him and the glass display. Always one.

'I'm sure it is not a mistake, sir.'

He wiped his forehead.

'We have all made mistakes, Fräulein.'

He bent to the cabinet, lifted his glasses to peer at the fading paper within.

'This is only an error. This article comes from the Americans, does it not?'

'It is paired with the letter from the Russian archive.'

'No.' His lips thinned. 'I can assure you.'

'How is that, sir?' As respectful as she could.

He moved towards her, as if he did not want the children to hear, as if he wished no-one but Myra to collect his whisper. She could smell the pomade in his hair, looked down at the expensive shoes as she moved to not tread on them.

'Because I gave it to the Americans.' His hand back to the glass shielding the exhibit. 'Because I drew it.'

*

Myra found him sat outside. Cap playing in his hands, eyes at the ground. Sat beside him without invite. He began as if the conversation had started minutes before and he finishing it off, rounding it off politely so he could put on his cap and leave.

'We were married in Switzerland. In '41. Her parents had moved there. Run there. Etta's father – Etta was my wife – was wealthy. Wealthy for those days. A property man. I thought I had done well to marry a woman of means. Poor all my life. Where are you from, Fräulein?'

'Munich.'

'Ah. Just so. I was born in Erfurt. You know the Merchants' Bridge? That was my childhood home. An ancient place. The people ancient. Me – a boy – an intruder on the bridge. When my father needed to tan me I would hide all about the stairs and gutters. The little paths. Right under the bridge. He would never find me. Old cities full of hiding places. They are built around the hiding places.

Modern cities are not like this. They are built straight and plain. Wide. Open. It is because the people do not need to hide as much. Old cities. They cringe around the churches like children to their mother's skirts.'

Myra watched him look about the walls. Breathing them.

'I was grateful to work here. No-one will understand. My Etta did not even understand. And she knew everything.' The wink of German humour.

Myra leaned closer, had to speak over the noise of a new arrival of children.

'What happened here?'

He put back his cap. Not to leave. Against the cold.

'Nothing. Nothing happened here.' Sat back against the bench. 'Always the problem.'

He rubbed the salt and pepper grey of his stubble. Grunted at the disapproval of it.

'Left early,' he said. 'To get here. I need a shave.'

PART ONE

Chapter 1

Erfurt, Germany,
April 1944

I shave every other day. The new blade already dull when purchased, yet twice as expensive as the year before. Steel for higher order than grooming. But I will shave tomorrow morning as I am not the man I was yesterday. I have work now. My first since I graduated and married.

There is the man you were the last year, without work, and then there is this day. And nothing is the same. The clock ticks down the hours to your *first* day, not just to the *next* day. A man has signed your name alongside his own. A contract. Real work.

And you begin.

I always stand by the curtained window looking over the street three floors below when Etta and I have these serious talks. I have a cigarette and she lays on the chaise-longue that her mother gave her for our wedding. The window half-open to exhale my evening smoke and to watch the street pass by and listen to the trains bringing workers home. Our voices never raise. We have become dulled. Like the blades of my razor that were never sharp. I am too weary from not working and she is tired from me not doing the same. Only couples understand such malaise.

'It is a job, Etta. Forty marks a week. We owe two months' rent.'

'A skilled draughtsman. Forty marks a week.' Tutted her disdain.

I draw on my cigarette, blow it against the curtain, just to annoy.

'It is a start. A beginning.'

'A low one. You start from the bottom. Four years of study and you gain the lowest rung.'

'I have no experience. Herr Prüfer has selected me because he came from the same study. That is a good wage for a new man. You want to stay in these rooms forever?'

A one-bed apartment with a kitchenette off the living-room. Etta put up new curtains which made all the difference. The curtains I was blowing smoke on.

She is draped over the chaise-longue like Garbo, her breasts accentuated through her dark dress, the one with the small red roses the same colour as her hair, the evening sun painting them further. I go back to smoking through the curtains and the window. A man below removes his homburg to wipe his sweating pate. Even at six o'clock it is still warm, warm for April, but all the businessmen are still in full dress, except that waistcoats seem to have vanished. Either a lack of textiles or some American trend. The harder grimier worker in cap, cardigan and jacket. That will not be me. I will be with the businessmen. I can feel Etta seething behind me.

'I did not expect to be the wife of a man who makes pictures of grain silos for a living.'

Pictures. Pictures she says. Belittled with a word. Austrian women do this well, even the ones born in Erfurt like Etta. Austrian by proxy.

'It is a start.' I draw a long, calming drag. 'They do other things. Crematoria. They do dignified crematoria.'

'How is that "dignified"?'

She said this in that cursing inflection that Austrian women perfect along with their curtsies. Swearing and not swearing. Her mother's voice.

'I spoke to Paul about it last week. Before my interview.'

Paul Reul, an old school friend of mine. He had made a name for himself as a crematorist in Weimar, a successful businessman. A thing to be admired in wartime. We did not see him so much since the jazz club where we used to meet had been closed, since we had married. Always the way. Your single friends become strangers.

'He told me Topf invented the electric and petrol crematoria. Changed the design so you could have a dignified service, like a church, with the oven in the same building. Topf did that. Made a funeral out of it.'

'It is all disgusting.'

'Before that the dead were all burnt out the back, a different place. Like hospitals. Just incinerators. Like for refuse.' I punctuate smoke into the room. Etta revolted. Not at my smoke.

'Stop talking about it. It is horrible. Why would you talk on such things?'

The cigarette goes out the window. Her disappointment a mystery. Real work. My first contract to draft plans since leaving the university. Silos or not. A start in wartime. Not an end. Not like so many others. But Topf and Sons were hiring. Everywhere else in Erfurt closing. I guess the army had need for a lot of silos.

She swings her legs from the lounger.

'I have to get ready for work. There is some ham and pickles you can eat.'

She goes to the bedroom removing the pins from her hair as she sways, her voice over her shoulder.

'I am pleased you have work, Ernst. I am just in a mood. And I shall probably miss you during the day.'

Etta's café job started at seven. Three nights a week if we were fortunate. Kept us fed when my subsistence ran out and she could always bring home leftovers, sometimes unfinished wine if the diners could afford it. It was long work when it came. Often she would not return until past one, the café closing at ten for the blackout, but the work goes on beyond the leave of guests. Only staff know this. The hard work is after the bill has been paid.

She closed the door to change. Her mystery always maintained by how many doors she could close. Fewer now than in our old place that we could no longer afford. Here I would put my fingers in my ears when she made her toilet, her insistence, the rooms that small. In our bedroom we can hear our neighbours flushing their broken cistern. You don't find that out when they show you the place.

She puts her make-up on before I wake. We sleep in separate beds, pushed together when desire desires. Three years married and I had never been permitted to know that she washed her undergarments, or seen them drying. As far as I knew she hung those silks out for faeries to attend to.

This her upbringing of course. Better than mine. My confidence in my good looks gave me no doubts why Etta Eischner should fall for a boy from the bridge. My grey-blue eyes and blond hair enough. But not to her parents. No reason for Herr Eischner to see why his daughter loved a penniless student, despite the blue eyes, despite the groomed blond hair. A boy from the bridge. Herr Eischner had plenty of suitable young men she could meet, rich stock like his, good stock. A boy from the bridge. Nothing in his pockets but dreams. Dancing in the clubs. Too much drinking, too much walking late at night. Too many dark alleyways for him to pull her into. The red look on her face when she came home far too late. She refused to join the bridge club or the Rotary, before they were outlawed of course, where good young men with connections and families could be found. The flame hair of her not the least of her fire.

Eventually he settled. Remembered even when little his daughter had always been looking for something she could never find, that even he could not satisfy, not when she was little and not when she had grown and argued with him on his politics and business. And that was why the blue-eyed boy came. She cooled after she had him. Poor boys from the bridge more capable than he where daughters are concerned. 'Curiosity killed the cat,' they say. To dismiss and persuade the young to seek. To tut, and warn them to not question. But they forget the final line: 'But satisfaction brought it back.' The poor boy from the bridge brought it back. The best the father would get.

I sniff my black tie that needs washing. All ties thin now. Again, either fashion or a textile shortage. I preferred them this way. Less like a noose. Tomorrow it will be a working tie. Odd to be starting new work on a Thursday. You assume Monday. They must be busy. Good. Though I will miss that serial play they put on the radio at lunch time. I suppose only housewives should listen anyway.

Working men do not need the radio.

Chapter 2

Our apartment is on Station Street, a grey shrivelled building next to the largest hotel in Erfurt and we share a double-front door with the radio shop below us. I wink to Frau Klein, our landlady, sweeping the porch. She has not seen me outside the door before nine until now and she eyes me like the Devil.

'Work to go to, Frau Klein,' I tell her. 'I start a new job this morning. Work at last! Won't you be happy for me?'

She grunts, as those of her profession do when they have been widowed and forced to let out their rooms to young married smiles.

'I will be *happy* to be paid.' And the broom beneath the bosom drags on. But still I whistle as I step by. To add to her disdain of me, of all youth.

My name called from above. Etta with a kiss, a wave.

How fine it still is to have someone you love call out your name, past the time when it was necessary to do so across a fair or a crowded square in courtship, for now you do not need to meet, are always a hand's reach from each other, and the echoed call of your name is rare. But going to work on your first day a time to hear the call again. And envious men look up with me to the pale shoulder slipped from the gown and the red tussled hair. And then their heads go back to their feet as I stride. Taller than them. If only in pride. I look at their passing fedoras. Eyeing those I may one day pick and choose to purchase. My own poor replica winter-beaten.

I had sold my bicycle, for who needs a bicycle in winter when there is only flakes of tea in the cupboards, so now I would walk to my employment in April sun following all the other black coats and hats to the station. But I am still grinning because I am not like them. I am one better than them. I will not be cramped and stifled in a smoky carriage. I am not an hour or two from my office. I will go through the station and over the footbridge to my work with Etta's warm body still glowing on me. A mile walk. Just enough time to clear your head and good enough exercise for all the working week to keep off the fat which I will soon be putting on our Sunday table.

I thread through the crowds shuffling to buy their tickets, shuffling to their transits and trucks, and take the iron-capped stairs two at a time. Puffed when I reach the top. In two weeks that will change. In two weeks I might have worn-out shoes but by then be able to buy a pair without care. Or perhaps not. It has been a long time since I looked at the price of shoes.

Over the bridge the landscape changed, you could not even see the dominating cathedral. As you walk to the station the city becomes a gradual grey, as work beckons, but you are only minutes away from the pretty doll's houses of our medieval streets and the statues always looking down, pitying those walking beneath them. The city I have lived all my life, the city of study, of Martin Luther, of grand culture uniquely German, and mercifully not bombed. We still had two synagogues, one the oldest in Europe, one a burned-out shell since 'crystal night'. But no-one now to use them of course. That had happened. The same as everywhere.

All my life in Erfurt and I had never seen this part of town. Tall old buildings, last century and more. Crumbling now.

I would have been thirteen when these homes became the ghettoes. Empty now, or the homes of the adamantly unemployed and destitute drunk. Fine homes upon a time, judged only by my looking to their pediments and stone-work. Still it is only a short walk, and I have nothing worth stealing, no bicycle, not even a watch – also sold – for who needs a watch with no work to go to. But sure I will be at the doors of Topf and Sons in good time, and time enough for one rolled breakfast cigarette, not knowing if Topf subscribed to the government's ban. Trains you could still smoke on but not the trams and buses, not in public buildings.

When I was first at Erfurt University you could smoke

in class, and then the rules came and soon after that my first professor, Josef Litt, was removed from class, by the Sturmabteilung, the SA no less, the chalk still in his hand as he was carried out by his elbows, half a word written on the board, never finished. Jews now not permitted to teach, to do anything in public work. We got the week off. Then we got an American professor, his German as bad as his breath, and my second year a struggle.

A right into Sorbenweg, chimneys along the skyline, already smoking, and then the long wall of Topf, a clutch of city-style houses opposite, not slums.

The administration building hides the construction factories and workshops that cover almost half a square mile. A neat front, three storey, concealing the heavy and dirty work boiling behind it, the manual workers coming in through another entrance. The smart wooden gate for suits not overalls.

A black chimney in the centre of the roof, the white letters of Topf encircling. In my eye, my draughtsman's eye, I see the one-dimensional plan of stoves heating the floors all connecting to this chimney, the furnace in the basement, but no need for it now, not in April.

I am not nervous. My first opportunity in the workplace yet I am confident. Perhaps bolstered by Prüfer's admiration of my qualifications, perhaps by Etta's admiration, enthusiastically bestowed that morning, in that blue light before April dawn. Always the best time. Or perhaps confidence always wears a suit.

The woman at the desk wishes me good morning. She looks like she has been up for hours, fresh and beaming, and I am sure not the same woman I saw last week. My eyes weeping from my walk, worse because they are such a pale blue. Almost an old man's eyes. An annoyance all my life. Too sensitive to sunlight and wind.

From the clock behind her I am five minutes early. Good, but I realise this is probably where my employers and directors also enter for their work. An anxiety about this. I would rather meet them at my desk in white-coat than in my shiny suit and worn hat.

'Can I help you, sir?'

She asks so delightfully that I almost do not understand the words. I give her my employment letter.

'Ernst Beck,' I said. 'Hired by Herr Prüfer.'

She asks me to take a seat and presses a telephone. The chairs are modern. Sweeping chrome and fine leather, more comfortable than my armchair at home. I leaf through technical magazines laid on a low glass and chrome table, one eye to the door to get ready to stand if an expensive suit approaches. But I suppose, with relief, that maybe directors and owners do not get into work so early.

I hear the clack of smart shoes coming from the marble staircase, hurried but rhythmical, like the wearer is dancing down not to meet me but Ginger Rogers.

The gleaming black wing-tips appear, then a suit I do not think I could ever afford. The cloth so black he seems fluid, floats to me like a wraith.

He held out his hand as I stood and bowed, lower than I intended.

'Herr Beck. I am Hans Klein. So pleased to meet you,' he ushered me to the stairs. 'I should get you a pass for your car so it does not get mistaken.'

I do not mention that Klein is also my landlady's name.

'No need, Herr Klein. I only live across from the station. I walked.'

'Oh. Really? Good. I live in Weimar myself. Not in the city. In the country. I apologise. It is my fault to assume that everyone drives to work. I suppose we have many local people here. This way, please.' He led me up the stairs, talking effortlessly as he went with his dancer's feet and I struggled to keep up.

'Come to my office, Herr Beck. I will acquaint you with the nature of things. No need to worry on your first day. No-one is to expect much of you. Just relax and enjoy. This is why we start you on Thursday. Today and tomorrow you are to familiarise yourself with the department, meet everyone, and we can start you in earnest on Monday.' We reached the third floor and he smiled as he waited for me to gain. 'In earnest . . . Ernst.' He laughed. 'Earnest Ernst. Quite a quip, no?'

His talk as smooth as his suit.

'Yes, sir.' It was then I saw the lift, and he noticed, seemed pleased with my crestfallen look He was not much older but assured in exactly the same way that I am not. If I enter a bar or café I wait patiently until I am attended to. He is one who snaps his fingers and calls.

'Ah. I forget the lift. I always take the stairs. I drive so much. I take the opportunity to exercise whenever I can. No need for you, of course, walking everywhere as you do. I am envious of you for that. Come.'

He walked beside me, his arm against my back. I tried to place where I had seen his face before, and then it came. It was in his smile. All teeth. It was Conrad Veidt, an actor, in a film I had seen as a boy. Veidt had left for America with his Jewish wife. He had terrified me as a child in a film. A man who could only grin, ear to ear after a horrible torture to his face. A Victor Hugo book. I thought it would be an adventure, like his other books. It was not. The film ran through my mind in an instant. A silent film. The first card of speech in front of me again:

'Jester to the king. But all his jests were cruel, and all his smiles were false.'

I was to ask him about his position when we came to his frosted glass door with the gold lettering.

'Hans Klein. Director of Operations. D IV.'

*

He reached across me to open the door and waved me in before him. 'Please, Ernst. After you.' Herr Beck now left downstairs.

He was behind his desk before I reached a chair and I

stood beside it while he popped open a metal orb on his desk and dozens of cigarettes fanned out from underneath its top. He took one and an onyx table-lighter and I stood and waited for him to light it and he let me stand while he did so. Three strikes of the lighter and three puffs before he noticed me again. Camels. I could smell they were Camels. Not our cheap German Kamels but actual American. I was not sure if American Camels were black-market. Surely not. Just rare now. Expensive now.

'Oh. Excuse my manners, Ernst. Please take a seat. I am so often on my own here – excepting meeting with Topf – that I sometimes forget myself with my staff.'

He said, 'Topf'. Not 'Herr Topf'.

'Cigarette?' He waited until I was seated to offer. I would have to stand to take one.

'No thank you, sir.' He closed the orb, the cigarettes drawing in magically.

'Please. Call me Herr Klein. No formalities on my floor. Do you not smoke? I can smell it on you? Or maybe it is just from walking through the station and the streets?'

'Yes, but I did not know whether . . . I did not know the rules for the building. I am so used to the ban.'

He took his black leather chair, his suit disappearing within.

'Fortunately we are not a public building yet. I do not travel publicly so I suppose the smoking ban does not bother. Although we have many contracts with the SS so I would not smoke around them should you see them, or around

Prüfer or Topf who are Party members. And you are not permitted to smoke on the draft floors or public areas.' He leaned back, put his feet up on something I could not see and exhaled hugely. 'Coffee?'

'No, thank you. Unless you are having one, Herr Klein?'

'I never drink coffee.' He waved his cigarette. 'I find it disagrees with my Martinis!'

That grin again. I did want coffee. I was lucky if I could afford three cups a week. To be offered it free and to turn it down. Still, my first day. Be a polite fool. These were successful men. Confident men. Not in war. Ernst Beck the young one amongst them. The apprentice. These were not people I knew, not my world.

As a boy I played football – my father's encouragement – before the first war that was all the entertainment he had. Football a German invention to him. A game that marked towns above each other more than harvest.

I played on the wing, but would always want to be a striker, every boy did. Sometimes we would play against the boys from Weimar, the richer boys. Weimar paid for us to play. Bought our footballs, bought our kit.

'Let them win,' my father would say. 'Ernst. Play the game.' His finger stern above me, bent to me, breath like stale meat. 'Do not be the hero. We are not here to always score goals. To win. If we always beat them too much less money they will give. Do you want to play next year or win today? What is for the better?'

The polite fool. Know what you will gain. And what you

will lose. The democracy of the football match. Sometimes you cannot afford to be the best team. But you will play next year. I could have scored five times against those Weimar boys. Sometimes a goal is just a goal. Two posts without a net.

'It is polite,' my father would say. 'You win by making it better for next year. By losing today. By abiding.'

I became a good German because of that. Got new kit the next year. Played the game.

'Do you have your identification card?' He put out his hand. I fumbled inside my jacket, gave across the rough cardboard we all hated to carry. Not obliged to carry. Preferred. It would go back in a drawer that evening. I had been asked to bring it. Normal to be copied for employment purposes.

'Thank you, Ernst. I'll have it back to you today.' He did not put it away, placed it on his desk, and then it sat between us like a brick. 'You'll be given a worker's pass as an alternative to use.' He blew his smoke towards me. 'I have looked over your qualifications. Prüfer and Sander are sure you will be competent. Understand that we have lost a great deal of men to the service over the years. We have to make do with less experienced men, but it is a great opportunity for yourself. I hope you understand?'

'It is the opportunity I seek and am grateful for, Herr Klein. I will do my best.' Polite fool.

'You will have to. These recent months we are often using prisoners from the camps, from Buchenwald, so the plans are ever simpler and of cheaper construction for them to comprehend. Still, the labour is cheap.' He put out his stub that I would consider not done. 'I believe that Sander – you will meet him tomorrow – is most looking forward for you to work on his new designs. They are patented but need . . . clarifying. To be presented to the SS. His originals are too complicated for the layman. We need someone to present them efficiently and more simplified. With our shortened workforce all our best draughtsmen are working on the malt works and silos and they have been with the designs for years so that is where our best men need to be. Which is why we have hired yourself, Ernst.'

I straightened in my seat.

'Am I not to be working for the silo department?'

'No. Sander is our chief designer for the crematoria. My department. "Special Ovens." Our smallest department. The smallest part of our business. But we are one of the foremost in the world. And getting ever busier, thanks to the SS. The more camps they build the more ovens they need. And because they want them so cheap they are always wanting repairs. Repeat business. The best business. Prüfer and the engineers are always fixing something at Auschwitz or Buchenwald and beyond. I limit myself to Buchenwald if I can.' He stood and I followed. 'Come. I will show you the floor. Not the floor with the skylights I'm afraid. That is for our top draughtsmen. But the second floor is pleasant enough. There is a fine view of the hills. All day you can see the smoke from Buchenwald rising to them. It is a pleasant room.' His hand on my back again, his other already on the door.

Chapter 3

I did not know how to mention the ovens to Etta at dinner.

Bern sausage, sauerkraut and swede. Etta put the meal on the table with pride. Pride for me.

'Ernst, we should see your parents this weekend. Celebrate your good news now it is official.'

I found an orchestra on our 'people's radio'. No long-wave any more and you paid two marks a month to listen to Wagner or Kraus. As a boy we used to have these great jazz stations. My mother and father danced then. Waltzed around the floor amid my electric train set that never truly worked but that I pretended did should my father punish me for breaking it. All other music gone now, all too degenerate for our sensibilities. The kids still listen somehow. A black-market in music they record on their Tonfolien machines and share. Swing-kids. That is what we call them. You cannot keep kids from music, no matter how black you think it is. Our leaders forget that's how they came to be. Older people told them 'no' once too. They should be proud of the youth emulating them. And I have to listen to Wagner.

'My parents? You want to put that upon us on a Sunday?' I sat at the table. Wished I had wine.

'It's been months since we saw them. At least now we have something to see them for instead of just borrowing money.' A snipe at me? No, she was smiling. I do not think she meant to offend. Just married talk. 'Don't you want them to be proud?'

'Hardly proud.'

'And why not? You are in a company in wartime. Would they rather you were at the front?'

'Which one?'

I was at university, had missed conscription. And Erfurt had no military attachment or demand for young men to serve. Too deep in the country for administration then. The first war different. Men had come from the forests to fight, my father amongst. Someone considered that if the enemy were faced with these giant axe-wielders they would drop their guns and run. Not now. These were the places that needed to be protected. We were the Germans of Germany. The heart that the rest fought for. The war distant from us, protected by mountains of pine bastions like a great wall. During the summer those who were students in Berlin or Munich would be deployed as medics to the front. Imagine being shot and having a geography student patch you up? I guess stabs of morphine would be their limit. Pat his chest in sympathy and then move on to the next. It was what those students saw at the front that began the protests when they returned to their universities. Their last protests.

Our city almost distinct from the war. The war heading east. A Russian war. The West done now. Africa and the Mediterranean ours. Victory assured. Normality coming back. My job a sign of that. Normality. New cars on the streets and the trains running on time. Klein had shown me his new Opel before I left. I do not know why. To me a car is just a car but I suppose these things are important to certain men. He lifted the engine's cover.

'Look at the plate.' He had placed his hand on the engine to introduce it. 'A General Motors engine! Ford and General Motors supplying German cars. We cannot all afford Mercedes! And we have their American engines in our army trucks. I wonder how the Yankee soldiers feel when they discover this. They bomb a supply convoy and find American engines in the trucks. That must be a kick! And we even sell them our ovens for their own prison camps. Topf are the largest exporter of crematoria. Not that we ever had any Jewish business. The Jew does not approve of crematoria.' That grin again. 'The body is only borrowed to them. It must be returned as given. Enjoy your walk home. Tomorrow you will meet Sander so shine your shoes better.' He slapped my back. 'Soon you will have your own car, no?'

*

'Etta, I must tell you something.' My cutlery still on the table. Her face became too concerned or maybe it was the look on mine.

'What is it, Ernst?'

'It seems that for the time . . . for the moment . . . as I am the new man . . . I must begin work on the second floor. Under Herr Klein.'

'The second floor? What is that? You are not working on the silos?'

'No. The second floor is for the Special Ovens Department. Special designs.'

'Special? How are they special?'

I took my fork, ate into the mash, the meat too steaming to eat for a while. We often eat one after the other, Etta first. I have to let my food cool, like a child, otherwise my night will be just heartburn and milk.

'Furnaces and incinerators for the prison camps. I'll know more tomorrow when I meet Herr Sander.'

'Aren't the prisons run by the SS? You don't have to work with them, do you?'

'Herr Klein says I might meet them in the building. They are only officers, Etta.'

She ate slow.

'I know. But it is just when you say SS you think of Gestapo. It is so quiet here. To think that just across the tracks there are SS. Here.'

In the single bulb light over our table her face had lowered as she ate, as if reading the tablecloth like a book in a library.

I had never heard her mention the SS or Gestapo at our table before. This not dinner talk. A husband's duty to ease his wife's concerns.

'I am to make the designs simpler for them to understand. Label everything. They won't understand the Alphabet of Lines so I must make it clear.'

'You do not think of the prisons needing ovens.' Her voice almost too quiet for me to catch.

'It is just like hospitals and schools. You need ovens for refuse, for heat, for the dead. No-one likes to think that hospitals have crematoria. Anywhere you have large numbers of sick people you need crematoria.'

Her fork rang against her plate.

'Ernst! I am eating! Why are you always using that word?'

'Etta, I am working for a company that makes crematoria. For all the world. I am going to be using that word often if you want me to talk on my day. If you consider it correctly it is probably one of the most important subjects. Paul almost holds it as a religion. It has laws.'

The mention of Paul, our crematorist friend in Weimar seemed to lighten the air. I had an ally. Not a conspirator. Paul's business could not exist without furnaces. This she would have to concede. Just a business. That's all.

'Well . . . use a different word. Say "oven". That sounds better. And stop talking about the dead. There is no place for that in this house. And certainly not at my table.'

I apologised. Moved the talk to visiting my parents. Agreed to it. They lived on the Krämerbrücke, the

Merchants' Bridge, in the medieval part of the city. The house I was born in. The houses on the bridge itself. On stormy nights I was always terrified in my bed that we would collapse into the river. Etta's parents had moved to Switzerland with her sister when the Americans joined the war. They feared invasion. We travelled there to get married. Etta insisted that her mother should see her wed and her father should take her arm. My own parents not attending. They do not travel. My father does not leave the bridge. All the stores he needs are there, he says. All his friends are there, he says.

'Why do I have to meet strangers?' he would shrug. 'I have met and outlived everyone I ever need to.' And he laughed at the passing of his friends.

We finish our supper, turn down the radio and the light. Tomorrow I meet Herr Sander. Too anxious to make love and we go to sleep just holding each other, the beds pushed together. My brain will not sleep and I try to imagine what Sander will look like.

'Ernst?' Etta whispers above my head under hers. 'I am glad I did not have to work tonight. It was good to eat together.'

I sighed into her chest and pulled her tighter. Her hair on my cheek. Red hair smells different. It blooms of youth somehow, like newborns in their close perfume.

'Ernst? The SS wouldn't look into us would they? If you are working with them?' A tension in her hold of me, as if I was about to be pulled out of bed and away. I touched her hand, felt it calm.

'I'm not working with them. I work for Topf.' I lifted my head. 'Why? Do I have a criminal I should worry about?'

She pulled me back to her breast. 'No! Do *I* have a criminal to worry about?'

'I have a receipt from your father for you. I could ask for an exchange.' She held me closer.

'You wish you could afford me.'

And the night came, the blackout, the sleep of couples.

Chapter 4

Raining the second day. Not the best walk. Raincoat and umbrella at least and Topf had a cloakroom where they might dry by the end of the day, as long as the day were longer than yesterday; not much more than a tour of the floors, the factory and barrack buildings where the workers from the camps ate a meal before the transport back to Buchenwald.

I had thought of Herr Sander all night. He the chief signatory of the design departments. Outside of the owner-ship of the company — the Topf brothers — the man in charge. I wondered what he might be like. A good boss or a hard one. I was sure all men only rise if they were the latter. My father would come home from Moor's pharmacy every night and be quiet for the first half-hour. Some wine and a sandwich before dinner and he would begin to talk and smile again. Sundays he would spend sighing and devouring the newspaper. I do not think he enjoyed his work. The pharmacy had to sell up in '35 to German buyers, the Jewish owners no longer permitted to be part of the community. I remember before then going as a boy with my mother to take my father his lunch one Saturday. We came out and a young man handed us both a leaflet. My mother paled as she read and the young man tipped his hat at us, went along with a whistle. The leaflet Gothic in script and tone.

'You have just been photographed while you have been buying Jewish. You are going to be shamed in public.'

We had not bought anything. We were bringing my father his meal but the man did not know. My mother whisked me away in the opposite direction. Spat her words.

'These bastards.' She was pulling me along now. 'Never trust a man in a suit, Ernst. He only wishes to lend you money or take it from you.'

I recall that my father was just as unhappy with his new employers as the old ones.

Prüfer I perceived to be a good man. He smiled, made jokes, he asked after my university. He was an engineer, had started at the bottom with Topf and determined his way to become a head man. He was pleased I had no children.

'They interfere with a man's career,' he said. 'Wait until you are a director! Children are a vice to a man's promise when he is young.'

Fritz Sander did not offer a handshake. He nodded when Herr Klein introduced me in his office and I returned the nod as proficiently as his own. I had my white-coat now, my blond hair smoothed back with Etta's pomade. It felt like I was at work. That I almost belonged.

'Has Herr Klein detailed your work here?' His answer already known.

'Yes, sir. The Special Ovens Department.' They were both standing, hands behind their back and I put mine the same.

'It is important work, Topf has secured the contracts for all ovens for the prisons.' I saw his skin was raw around his moustache and neck. A shaving rash like all of us except for Klein's talcum smoothness. Even the wealthy had trouble getting good blades I supposed. But Sander's grey hair was closely cut, precision sharp around his ears. He did not get his cut by his wife in a kitchenette with sewing scissors. A waft of Bay Rum as he moved.

'The regular muffle ovens have become inadequate. They break. Operated by inexperienced men. And they are over-worked. We are able to supply mobile counterparts and engineers to repair but new ones must be built. I have hired you to help me prepare the drafts.'

I opened my mouth to speak but he anticipated.

'You need not know anything about crematoria. I just need you to replicate the drafts from the designs. For SS approval. Any aspect you do not understand can be put to Herr Klein or Herr Keller on the third floor for annotation. The designs are to be as clear as possible for a layman.'

I had prepared questions as I slept, in my dreams. Questions that an ambitious man might ask.

'These new designs will improve the process, sir?'

His eyes now smaller through his glasses.

'How do you mean?'

'That Topf is superior throughout the world for crematoria. I'm sure we are improving all the while. I am honoured to be a part of such endeavour.'

Sander half-turned, hands opening and closing at his back.

'These contracts were won on price not quality.' He turned back to me sharply. 'You know our closest competitor?'

'Kori of Berlin, sir.'

'Quite so. We beat a Berlin company because of our price and location.'

Klein lifted his hand for my attention. Spoke proudly.

'And that when the call came we installed mobile systems into Mauthausen within a day. *That* is service,' he said.

'Mobile systems, sir?' I had heard this word previously, jumped on it now.

'Stock items,' Klein said. 'For farmers, small abattoirs and such, who do not need their own scale furnace. Petrol fired. The incinerators had broken and they needed an emergency replacement. We fulfilled where Berlin could not.'

Sander raised a finger to me and then to Klein. 'That reminds. Herr Klein is going to Buchenwald. A site visit. Monday. It would be useful for you to attend.'

I inhaled, stalled.

'To the prison?'

'We are measuring for new muffles,' Sander said as reply. 'It would be useful for you to see our work first hand. It is important for an architect to see the fulfilment of his task. You will learn much.'

I would like to say that I feigned enthusiasm. But I was curious in that pedestrian way people stare at accidents or listen to a neighbour's fight or as a child you try to peek a look into the butcher's back room as he emerges when his bell rings, wiping his hands and beaming at your mother.

And this my work after all.

'That would be most interesting, sir.'

'Good,' Sander nodded again. 'Be sure to bring your identification.'

Chapter 5

Before supper Etta and I went for a walk. The early evening dry and warm, my coat only a little still damp from the morning's rain. We went arm in arm by the river, towards the bridges and the old quarter. Etta had asked what Sander was like, how my day had been. I volunteered the walk. Easier to tell her outside.

'The *camp*!' Etta stopped walking, pulled her arm away. Stragglers coming home scowled from beneath their caps.

'The *prison*, Etta. Buchenwald is well established. Topf has hundreds of workers from the place in the factory.'

'Slaves you mean.'

'Labour for their crimes.'

'But Ernst, it is a *camp*. People die there. There is disease. Dangerous men.'

I took her arm again and strolled slower.

'Klein and the engineers go there often. I am sure it is safe.'

'I don't like it. Why did you say you would go?'

'I could hardly refuse on my second day.' We walked into the cobbled streets, a walk around the block to take us back to Station Street. Quiet here. The Jewish businesses closed and sold to develop into apartments, but that had stopped. The developers no doubt waiting for the war to end any month now and the prices to rise. But even with the boarded-up windows a nice peaceful stroll in April.

'Do you like this Herr Klein?'

'I do not know him. Does it matter? He's the head of the floor. When the war ends a few of those who used to work there may come back. Part of their service is to retain their old jobs. I must do well before then. Everything I can.'

'Will you have to join the Party?'

'No-one has mentioned. Prüfer wears a pin. A standard one. Herr Sander did not. Nor Klein.'

'Would you? Would you join?'

I do not know why I did not think before answering. It seemed natural to say it.

'If it helped my career. For you. For us. All other business ties are gone. No Freemasons or Rotaries. How else do you get on?'

We said no more on this.

If you live near to your parents you walk slower to meet them for Sunday lunch than if you had to get on a train where at least you can pretend that something enjoyable is happening. The slow walk, lingering around shop windows, all to avoid the dreaded hour. The walk enlivened by the Sunday street all looking to the sky as a squadron of Heinkels flew west overhead. Our skies normally silent.

Etta shielded her eyes to watch.

'Where do you think they are going?'

'I don't know. England? Early for a raid. Where from is more interesting. I did not know we had bases in the east.'

'Perhaps the Russians have surrendered. And we have taken their bases.'

'Do they even have bases to take? I thought them all farmers?'

She slapped my arm. 'Ernst. They are an army. I'm sure they have planes.'

'We conquered France didn't we? And *they* have toilets inside their homes. The Russians?' I cocked my thumb over my shoulder. 'Toilet behind the house with chickens in it. That is all you need to know.'

The streets animated again and we came to the old bridge. You may know the Merchants' Bridge from songs or pictures from a Christmas butter-biscuit box. A fairytale place. One of the last medieval bridges in Europe that still had the colourful houses and shops built right on its stone. Paris and London had lost theirs hundreds of years ago. Erfurt maintained. We know our history. It is still here. England does not know us to bomb. Their bridge fell down, as the song would have it. Because they did not care enough for history.

I was born on this bridge. The vaults and steps above the

Breitstrom waters were my hiding places as a boy or where I crouched concealed from the wrath of my father's open hand.

I thought we were poor to live here, our house so small and ancient, but no, despite the small leaning buildings looking into each other's lives we were privileged. I would be happy to inherit it, as my father had from his father, if only to sell it and buy a proper home for Etta and our children. *My* son would not live in a box of a room with straw-packed walls and no window. Our front door would not open onto stairs to take him to a floor above a camera shop.

My father opened the door, his once blond hair now yellow and grey but still thick with vitality, like the whole of him.

'Ernst! Etta!' He hugged Etta and scolded me. 'Why did you not let us know you were coming? What boy does this?' Neither of us had a telephone. I suppose he wanted me to shout from our window. 'We have nothing in.' This my fault, and not true. When my parents died there would be two small plots for them and a mausoleum for their food. They were of the great war. When there were real shortages not just rationed ones. The habit of hoarding jars and cans, pickling everything, not given up. Just in case. I was born the year my father came back from the war. I stacked tins like other children stacked blocks.

The creaking stairs, my mother's voice howling from the kitchen.

'Etta! Ernst! Why you not let us know! My hair, Willi!

My hair!' She clutched at her head. It was in exactly the same clipped bun it had been since my youth.

I took off my hat and Etta's coat as my mother fussed and my father reminded me that I had not joined the church football club for yet another year.

'I am hoping I won't have time for football soon enough.'

My mother clasped her face. 'Oh Willi! She is pregnant! She is pregnant!'

Etta waved her down. 'No, no, Frau Beck! The news is all for Ernst.'

'Let them sit, Mila,' my father pulling out glasses and Madeira. 'What is it, Ernst? You have not signed for the army?'

The glasses to the white paper tablecloth with the cherries decoration. The same tablecloth as when I lived here. My crayon marks still on it.

'No, Papa. Better. I have a job.'

He took our coats. 'A draughtsman? A real job. You hear this, Mama?'

Her hands had not left her face. 'Oh, Ernst! My boy!' And then the hands were on my face. 'My clever boy! When did this happen? How?'

My father poured wine. The Madeira meant it was Mama's pickled pot roast for dinner. I cannot drink more than one glass of the sickly stuff but I would wait to see if a beer would come. Sunday after all.

'So, you can start paying me back at last!'

'Willi!' My mother dropped my face. 'Let the boy sit. Give them some wine. Let him talk.'

The wine in the thin glasses was already in our hands, Etta's knees against mine on the small sofa, the same seat where I once put my little cars to bed before myself.

'Topf and Sons were hiring. A junior position but—'

'Of course. Why not?' My father lifted his hands as if bargaining for a rug in a bazaar. 'That is how men start. A year or two and you will have your own department.' He slapped my knee.

My mother sat and tightened her shawl. 'Topf, you say? My, my. Such a fine company.'

Father saluted his glass.

'The oldest firm. The proudest. The world will open to you now. What are you working at, Ernst? Or is it secret?' Eyed me in a way I had not seen before.

'Why would it be secret?'

He shrugged.

'Maybe they have some war works or such.'

I drank my syrupy wine.

'They have contracts with the prisons. And for military parts.'

Etta touched my hand. Patted it.

'Ernst is, unfortunately, only working on new oven designs for the camps.' Not looking at me. At my mother. I took my hand away. 'Unfortunately,' she had said.

My mother's shawl tighter.

'The camps?' Her voice as a whisper. 'Buchenwald?'

'All of them,' I said, let Etta's disparaging of me pass. She had suggested this visit. I thought because of pride in

43

her husband. Maybe she had hoped a different reaction from my parents about the camp. 'I am to work on new patents.'

'New?' My father nodded sagely over his glass. 'You see, Mama? They give him new projects to work on.' And then straight to it. 'How much does it pay? Salary? Not week?'

'Forty marks a week. No trial. I have already started. May I smoke, Mama?'

She stood. 'I must get to my roast.' I took that as yes and brought out my tobacco, and father's pipe came from the drawer by his chair.

Etta stood.

'Let me help you, Mila.' And the men were alone.

An age for my father to suck his pipe into life. The sound of my childhood.

'Ernst.' He shook out his match into the glazed ashtray I made him at school. 'Tell me about the ovens?'

I exhaled with him.

'Topf created crem—' Etta's ear turned. 'Created *ovens* for use in chapel, in ceremony. They invented the petrol oven and the gas fuelled. They export all over the world. But the prisons use coke for cost. As such I understand they need repairs. Often.'

'Why so?'

I watched the cloud of him reach to the yellow-stained ceiling.

'Overuse. Brick ovens. Typhus is in the prisons. Coke ovens and brick are not able to cope with the demand.'

'So why use coke?'

'Cost. Petrol is too expensive. Too crucial to waste on ovens. The SS are all about cost I gather.'

He leant forward.

'The SS?'

'You know they run the camps?'

'I did not think they bought the ovens?'

I drew long on my cigarette. 'Nor did I. I have learnt that much already.'

'That is what you must do. Learn every day. Ask everything. Show that it is more than just a job. And then when they are looking for the next top man they will look for the one who shows the most interest in the company. He drummed his words out on the arm of his chair. 'That is the way.'

'I am doing something on that tomorrow. I am going to Buchenwald with my department head to inspect for a new oven.' I looked to Etta not smiling at me from the kitchen.

He put his pipe on his knee.

'You are going inside the camp?'

My mother's voice. 'Who is? Who is going to the camp?'

'Ernst is, Mama,' my father called over his shoulder. 'Ernst is going to Buchenwald. Tomorrow.'

She came into the room, drying her hands. Always drying her hands.

'Why? Do you have to work in the camps? That is not so good, Ernst.'

Erfurt not far from Buchenwald. The prison almost ten years old but known for disease now, for more than

45

criminals. To my mother even the air of the place would be corrupt.

'No, Mama. It is just to view on-site the work that we do. It will be good experience.'

Etta gone from the kitchen doorway. I heard the tap running. Running louder as my father spoke. His pipe neck pointing at me.

'And it will show how keen you are to learn. When I worked for Littman, at the pharmacy, that man would teach me *nothing*. Nothing I tell you. Everything was a secret to him. I was too old to apprentice so to him I was worthless. When Quermann took it over, when a German took it over, he showed me true respect. A gentile cannot work for a Jew. You just become their chattel. I have always said it. Now it is Germany for the Germans we all look after each other. Nothing to gain but a better country for us all. Working together for the good. Not for the purse.'

Mother slapped him with her cloth that was always attached about her.

'It was Littman who gave you that job, you old fool! Me running around scrubbing floors with Ernst in my belly and you with holes in your pockets. Quermann did not hire you. You were stolen.' She groaned back to the kitchen. 'That man, that man.'

I finished my wine and the bottle came back, which was a first for him.

'All the same,' he went on. 'You *learn* from these men, Ernst. They are doing well. Government contracts. Always there is work there. When we conquer Stalin think how much work will be needed.'

'The ovens is a small department, Papa. But they design silos and malting equipment. And gas jets and aeroplane parts. That is what I want to do.'

'And why not? Mercedes you could work for. Build me a car for my old age. This country is for the young now. My war gave us a broken country. The Bolsheviks and the Jews conspiring to destroy us. Nothing but unemployment unless you were in *their* families. And now it is Germany for the Germans, the best men for the jobs, not just for the good connections. And my son has a career with one of the largest companies in the land.' He thumped his chair. 'This is how good life begins. I am proud of you, Ernst.'

He had not said these words since I had graduated.

Women were laughing in the kitchen, and the waft of steaming food came from rattling pots, and I would not have to ask awkwardly to borrow ten marks. I realised it could be good to visit parents.

*

We walked home arm in arm through afternoon light burnishing the wet cobblestones. I waited until the river's rushing was behind us to ask Etta why she had called my work 'unfortunate'.

'I only meant that you should be doing higher things.

Not drafting ovens. For the SS.' Her head down now, moved close into me. 'Not what I want for you.'

'I'm sure it will not be for long.'

She stopped, looked about and took my hand.

'But what if it is? What if it is for long? Do you not think of the ovens, Ernst? Why they need so many?'

'The typhus. The disease. The sick. Prisons need ovens, Etta. I've told you this. It is unpleasant but it is fact. Would you question Paul buying a new oven?'

'Coal ovens. Yet you tell me they order gas jets from Topf. What are they for if not for the ovens, Ernst? Do they not heat with coal?'

'I don't know. It is not just Topf, Etta. What company does not work with the SS now? Would you be concerned if a hospital wanted gas jets?'

She dropped my hand, put hers to my back as Klein did when he wanted me to understand something, guided me along.

'But hospitals aren't run by the SS, Ernst. Why are the camps run by them? Shouldn't that be a government thing?'

The beer and wine flushed on me. A temper at defending my work. Now. Before my first pay.

'Do you not want me to work? You were the one who wanted to go to my parents to celebrate. Now you want to deride my employers? Nothing happens in this world, Etta, unless someone sells something to someone else. Nothing.' I walked on, left her behind me until her voice came.

'I'm sorry, Ernst,' she said. 'Ernst?' Like a charm. Holding me to the street.

I turned back to look at her framed in the sun. She walked out of it to me. Took my arm again.

'I'm very proud of you. For you. Maybe it's that you are going to the camp tomorrow. I'm worried. For you. I am being foolish.'

We walked on.

'I promise you,' I said, calm now, 'I won't do anything for you to worry.'

Chapter 6

'Here. Put this on.'

Monday morning. We were in Hans Klein's black Opel on the main road outside Kleinmolsen, the groan of the wipers unable to cope with the sheets of rain but Klein did not slow his speed. I could feel the water on the road hitting the panelling like waves. The tyres almost skating along. He had taken his hand off the wheel to pass me a Party pin.

It was plain tin, not enamelled. I did not question and put it on my lapel. His was enamelled and, again, as we slid along the road, he put it on with one hand.

'It does not hurt to wear it,' he said. 'Gives a good impression. I am personally not political. Yourself?'

'No, sir. I have not given it much thought.'

'Prüfer is of course. And the Topfs. But then they would have to be dealing with the SS. Are you a union man?'

My interview had contained this question. The usual

standard. 'Are you now or have you ever been a member of the communist party?'

Who would say, 'yes'?

'Are not unions banned?'

He nodded, managed to light a cigarette with one hand.

'I'm sure that some of our workers are members of the KPD. Communists. And the SDP. There was a faction of them at the factory in the 30s. I think the Buchenwald workers are influencing ours. The camp is nothing but communists. I'm sure Sander is on top of it. But keep your own ear out and let me know if you hear anything. I will make you my top boy on the floor!' He shifted a gear down at last. 'I cannot trust the old ones.'

The countryside blurred past. Twenty minutes in the roaring car, a super-six, and Klein showed it off. Twenty minutes. A camp a short drive from Erfurt and Weimar. I had only been in taxis before and probably only half a dozen times in my life. I did not appreciate cars, or watches, shoes and suits, but I was beginning to think that Klein thought such things impressive.

'It is a nice car, Herr Klein.' I looked around as if it was the Sistine Chapel, trying to admire it as we rolled across the railway line, the rail that led to the camp.

'Twenty-five hundred marks,' he said for reply. I imagine that is how he judged the world. The price of things. He pivoted the car between a gap in the forest with just a gear change, no brakes, and I was braced against the door.

A good gravelled road, the beech forest cut back from it

with maintained grass all along. Buchenwald. Beech Tree Forest. A name for holidays. As the camp came in sight, set in a clear plain, the rain slowed, I wiped the condensation from the window, sure that I had seen men outside, outside on the grass. They were cutting the grass, had stopped to watch the car. Mowing in the rain. Their garb unmistakeable.

'There are prisoners out there?' I looked at him. My professor now. 'Outside the prison?'

Klein did not even check.

'Of course. Why not?'

'But might they not escape?'

'Where would they go? What would they do? Escape to starve? To be shot? Not everyone is the Count of Monte Cristo, Ernst. Some men know they belong in prison. Some men know they do not like work. Career criminals. Why escape one prison for another? Why buy your own bed and food when we can buy it for them.' He put his arm across me to point to an outcrop of rocks not far from the barbed fence. 'They even have a zoo. Bears, monkeys, birds of prey. You could take kids here. Although the zoo is for the guards of course. The prisoners have a cinema and theatre. A brothel for the non-Jews.'

He closed the car down the gears as we approached the gated walls. All the roads leading off the main marked by decorative wooden signs, this one, the road to the main gate designated 'Caracho Road' – Caracho Spanish for 'double-time' – decorated with four swarthy-looking men hunched and hurrying close together in prison clothes.

Some of the prisoners here would have been from the Spanish war. The building like a factory except for barbed wire instead of walls. A red-timbered building like a Swiss chalet sat atop the entrance, a balcony all around, a clock above, a flagpole rising out of it. The flag just a red swathe. Beaten by the rain. Taller than this I could see the square tower of the crematoria, to the right of the gate, almost opposite the odd zoo. Not far from the main building. Good. We would not have to go deep into the camp.

Klein reached to the back seat, passed me his briefcase as we waited for the guards to come.

'You take the notes. I will measure and photograph. I have my own Leica. Better than Sander's Zeiss he would have you use. One hundred it cost me.'

The latticed door in the gate opened. Words were written in the iron tops but I could not make them out. They were reversed. To be read from the other side only. A black-painted slogan on the stucco wall above the gate read to those who approached:

'RIGHT OR WRONG THIS IS MY COUNTRY.'

A grey uniform and box-cap stepped through, his jacket instantly dappled with the rain.

Klein stubbed out his cigarette.

'You have your identification, Ernst?' His window opened. I passed the card and Klein gave the guard his grin with our papers.

'Good to see you again, Simon. Pity about the rain, eh?'

Simon smiled back but became stern when he looked at

our cards. This was his purpose. His moment. It would be his hand that waved the gate open.

'We are here to meet the Senior-Colonel,' Klein said without being asked. 'About new ovens. Another breakdown, eh?'

'All the time.' Simon handed back our cards. 'Build a better one for us.'

'Pay us more money, eh?' Klein winked.

A circus going on around me. A joviality incongruous to what was about to happen. I was outside a prison. About to go within. I had never handed a soldier my identification before. I could only see his holster from my view in the car, another guard watching from the gate with a rifle slung. To see them so close. The shape of a gun hidden by leather a few feet from my eyes. I was in a dream. Klein knew an SS soldier's name and had asked him for more money. An anxious dream. A little nausea, from this scene or the chicory coffee of my breakfast. Not even an oat biscuit in the house to settle my stomach.

Klein's window closed and the gates opened. The Opel into gear. As usual he noticed or sensed everything.

'Don't worry, Ernst. It is quite natural to be nervous around soldiers. And prisons. You will get used to it.' He leaned over, grinned. 'As long as you are not *forced* to get used to it, eh?'

We parked on the left. There were trucks beyond the gate, waiting for their work detail and then another strange sight to add to my dream.

There was a full band in the courtyard, an orchestra almost, dressed in red trousers and green vests. Tubas and horns, even a man with a great drum on his chest like a circus parade. We got out and Klein grinned at me over the roof of the car.

'Ah. We are in time for the band. This is good, Ernst. Every morning and evening they sing the camp song.'

I could not stop myself blinking, waking from my dream. 'Camp song?'

'Of course. Pride in *their* camp. Good for morale.'

The rain gone fully now and the brass of the band glistened from it, some of the band conscientious enough to wipe their instruments with their sleeves, proud of them, did not wipe their own faces. Their box-caps flat on their heads where they had stood in the downpour.

I flinched to the sound of loudspeakers along the fence crackling into life, the distinct sound of needle scratching record.

Trumpets and oboes blared, a fast drum beat. I would almost call it a 'swing' tune as the crash of cymbals came in and Zarah Leander's voice came tinnily out.

'To Me You're Beautiful' the song. I did not know if the colonel in the red-framed building knew it but this had originally been a music-hall Yiddish song. No. Maybe he did know.

The jolly song used instead of a klaxon. Hundreds of men were coming from huts like bees from a hive. The mass of them terrifying and I stepped back to the security of the steel car and Klein laughed at my reaction.

'This is just the main camp-men. The work details. With the sub-camps there are almost sixty thousand here. Filthy.

Diseased. Typhus. Do not worry, it is clean here. This is the good side.'

I could only stare. The only word for it. Stared. For such a sight. There was something familiar in it. Something I could not place. In the bones of us perhaps. Such sights.

The song came to its end, the men accustomed to timing themselves to assemble in the square before the finish, packed in the square, not an inch between them, and then a prisoner stepped from the band, came to the front. The conductor.

I was watching a conductor at eight in the morning in a prison. A captive audience of hundreds, a choir of hundreds. I began to smile myself, with Klein, to smile as at elephants or bears performing for handfuls of nuts. In absurdity. To not think how the elephants or bears are trained. It was if this were for us, for Klein and myself. But no. This happened every day. Twice a day. Their roll call. They did not even know we were here.

The band began. A martial tune, not like the record, a rousing powerful song, the type used as food for starving soldiers to forget their holed boots and damp socks. But the voices were not rousing, they were dulled and low like a warped record winding down, exactly as Zarah Leander's wasn't. The counter of her voice.

'Here,' Klein said. 'They like this bit. Watch them stand straighter.'

It was the chorus. One line in it that came stronger than a mumble. Something on once being free from prison walls.

'They wrote the song themselves,' Klein tapped the roof

of his car. 'Ten marks to the composer. A competition. That is quite impressive, no? Every camp has a song. And they beat those who do not sing well enough – which is bad, but it is their song. They should sing it proud. They voted for it. Come.'

We walked away from the car and I remembered to look at the gate with the backwards writing, for those facing it on the inside.

'TO EACH HIS OWN'.

Klein watched me read it. Saw everything. Always.

'It means, "You get what you deserve." And don't we all, Ernst? At the end. And at the beginning, if you are lucky enough. And work well.' He waved me to the stairs, to the wooden building above the gatehouse. Guards and their machine-guns walking around the balcony.

'This is the main guard tower. We passed the commandant's quarters along the road but Pister likes to breakfast with his men. Likes to hear the song. Walk smarter, Ernst. You are to meet a colonel!'

The marching tune ended. The roll call begun. Zarah Leander again, quieter this time for the guards to hear the names.

This like my first day at school. Bewildering, fearful. I could only think of telling Etta of it, as telling my mother of my first day with my teacher and the strange new children. The strangeness, my clothes even out of place against the stripes of prison suits, stripes of barbed wire and the gates. No walls, electric wired fences. Green freedom just beyond, in sight all around. Bears tumbling each other in a zoo. My first day.

Chapter 7

Senior-Colonel Pister opened the chalet door himself. I did not know what I expected but not the portly, white-haired man in red sweater and red braces above his SS trousers. If it were not April, if not for his lack of beard, I might have just met St Nick.

A wood stove, the smell of coffee and bacon warming the room. I was jarred for a moment, almost hiding behind Klein as Pister welcomed us against the sound of names being barked in the square below.

Pister's arms opened wide as if to embrace.

'How are you, Hans?'

'Very well, Colonel.'

Klein negated, defeated, Pister's open arms with a handshake, his left hand on Pister's arm, drawing Pister's hand into the shake. 'I am so glad we managed to catch the song.'

The 'we' directed to me and that was how I was introduced and how I realised Klein controlled rooms. He did not wait for Pister to ask who he had brought, he did not reciprocate Pister's embrace but initiated his own and I tried to recall if he had done the same to me, and then I saw that his hand was on Pister's back, gently, and this I recalled, and the pace up the stairs on my first day. Keep up, keep up.

Keep up. Klein's way. Keep up with me. Or I will leave you all behind. A trick. You could not keep up. He would not let you, and he did it so naturally you would never notice. My only insight. Seeing him do it to someone else.

Pister took my hand. 'Welcome to Buchenwald, Herr Beck.'

Klein spoke for me.

'Herr Beck is new to Topf. Our new draughtsman. He has never seen a prison before. I am pleased he can see it under your command, Colonel. Rather than before.'

Pister's face saddened.

'Ah, yes, Herr Beck. I inherited a sorry place I can tell you. Now, to business, gentlemen.' He bid us to sit, offered the percolated coffee. Klein had told me in his office that he did not drink coffee, and, in truth, he did not touch it other than to dip a biscuit Pister had given as the names still came loudly from outside and men with guns walked past the windows.

Pister bemoaned the ovens.

He wanted a six-muffle oven, six doors, to increase capacity. The reduction of matter too much for the old set. A new oven. The old three-door model broke down too often. Was never meant to work so hard. It would have to be replaced.

'I will not return to using just pits like my predecessor. That is animal work.'

I was taking the notes. Needed clarification. Klein's jaw clenched when I spoke.

'Why do the ovens break, Colonel?'

Pister sat back in his red leather armchair. With his black boots and red sweater his Christmas look almost completed. I waited for him to pat his knee for me to sit upon.

'We have a high death rate here. The other camps send only their sick and old to us. We are more morgue than prison. The healthy stock comes from the Sinti and Roma, and the POWs. When I can get them.'

Klein snapped his biscuit.

'Building a new oven, Colonel, will take a month. Herr Prüfer will have to build it and Herr Sander would have to sign it off. And I can tell you, Colonel, that Prüfer will not build a new oven for less than sixty thousand marks.'

'That is preposterous,' Pister said. 'Nonsense.' Christmas no more.

'Nevertheless. We could replace some of the bricks in the existing oven, add one more three-muffle, which would only take two weeks, and provide you with mobile ovens in the meantime to maintain your conversion rates. That we could do for forty thousand marks.'

'Bah!' Pister shooed his arm at Klein. 'I have had these mobile ovens before. They are too slow in the open. I am not burning pigs.' He leaned forward. 'I do not think any of you ever understand. There are more than sixty thousand prisoners here. A third of them are sick.' He raised a finger.

'And do not forget this is a prison. We have thousands of criminals here. Real criminals. This is where the murderers come. They are controlled by the ovens.'

'How are they controlled by the ovens?' I spoke without thinking. Idiot. Fool. Pretended not to see Klein's glare.

Pister tapped his temple.

'In the head, Herr Beck. You control them in the head. When you have broken ovens they know they cannot be shot. They see no smoke. Or even if only one is working they know you are not going to add to the pile of dead you already have with a couple more. So, murders and thefts increase. Every day the ovens are broken there is more crime, more disorder. And when they rob, they kill, because again that will add to the pile that they know you will not add *them* to. It is exasperating.' He looked hard at Klein.

'That is why I need a six-door oven. But, reluctantly, I will take the mobile units. To suffice. They have good presence. In the fields. The prisoners can see them.'

'Excellent.' Klein gave his grin, kept it going. 'We can install three mobile units tomorrow. I will take your concerns to Herr Sander personally, Colonel. He will telephone you direct. We will measure for the six-muffle and I will inspect the others. See if they can be repaired quickly. As I said, the difference between building new or adding

61

two more will be twenty thousand marks and two more weeks. By what you have said I understand that is unacceptable. I will advise Herr Sander that we need a better price and I will send out a repair team today. So as you may reduce your crimes.' He smiled broader, like a ventriloquist's dummy. 'By reducing your criminals, eh?'

He stood, his hand out, and I followed. 'Thank you so much for the coffee, Colonel, and for your valuable time.' He declined an escort and, as we stepped the stairs, handed me a surgical mask from his pocket.

'Here,' he said. 'You will need this.' He stopped on the last step, blocking me. 'And I would think it better if you did not speak directly to men like the colonel again. You are new. You could make unintentional mistakes. You understand, Ernst?'

'Yes, Herr Klein. I am sorry.'

'No, no. No need to apologise. It is my fault for not helping you. Come now.'

We passed the gatehouse again to reach the crematoria, the trucks being loaded with the prisoner work details behind us. Some of them for our factory, for Topf. To work to make the muffles that would find their way back here.

*

We smoked outside the crematoria beside a wooden fenced area taller than us. A cigarette for the work finished. The smell. The mask not helping, but I had expected it, readied for it.

'It must be full,' Klein said. 'That stench. The morgue is below the ovens. They used to use pits.' He waved towards the forest. 'They still do. But the land is too marshy. The bodies rot into the water table. They discovered that early. It is the same problem at Auschwitz and Birkenau. The ground is like a swamp half the year. But good for us, eh? Less pits means more ovens, no?'

All this a revelation to me. Perhaps bringing me here my induction.

'How will he react to speaking about bodies as commodities?'

'He must understand we furnish ovens for the camps. Must have the aptitude. The attitude.'

'And if he doesn't?'

'Plenty of unemployed men.'

I consoled that my friend Paul's work was harder. In his crematoriums. He actually worked with the dead, worked the ovens. I only drew them. Someone else designed them, someone else installed them. Prisons need ovens. Cities need sewers. Unpleasant, but the way of things. Every hospital has a tall chimney somewhere along its skyline. Children will be born in the happier wards but far away from them will be a tall chimney. Make it as efficient as they could. The camps rife with disease, with sickness and the damned. A necessary service. This surely my induction to such.

*

I had taken down Klein's instruction and measurements. He had taken photographs. We had finished for the day, passed lunch.

'Two o'clock, Ernst. We should go. What do you say? Home early. I can develop my film at home. I have my own darkroom.'

'Are we not going back to the factory? To send a repair team for tomorrow, sir?'

'I organised that this morning. Before we left. I knew he would have to go for the repair. Senior-Colonel? Ha! You know he came from Himmler's motor-pool?'

Keep up. Keep up.

He threw away his cigarette in an arc and I watched it fall and saw an officer in a peaked cap approaching. Klein did not wait for him. He strode toward, away from me, and I watched him put out his hand and intercept, converse out of my earshot.

I stood on my cigarette and watched them go back and forth, happily back and forth, and Klein turned his back to me. I shifted nervously, waved when the officer looked to me as Klein spoke. He did not wave back. I flushed at the glance, bent and pretended to fumble through Klein's briefcase. Their shadows came over me.

'Ernst,' Klein said, and I stood up clumsily in the mud. 'This is Captain Schwarz.' We shook hands, his in leather. He bowed and I did the same, not as naturally. 'I want you to do me a favour, Ernst,' Klein said. 'My house is only a few miles from here. It seems pointless for me to travel back to town only to come out again, no? I wondered if you would mind riding back to Erfurt with the captain?'

A gratified look from the SS captain.

'I am going to Erfurt. To pick a gift for my wife, Herr Beck. At the Anger. It is her birthday. It is no trouble for me to take you home. I would welcome the companionship.'

Klein took his briefcase from me. 'Would you mind, Ernst? I would appreciate it.'

'Of course. Yes. Of course. But, Herr Klein? I think you still have my worker's pass?'

The captain snapped out his gloved hand. My pass between his fingers like the reveal of a magician with my chosen card.

'Here it is, Herr Beck. We will leave by the east gate.'

'I'll get your hat and coat from the car,' Klein said.

Chapter 8

The Daimler-Benz was not as grand as Klein's Opel. Klein's car for pleasure. This was austere, quieter, more noble. The first mile in silence and then as the farmhouses became manse houses the captain's fingers became looser on the wheel. Removed his cap to my lap.

'Too warm. Hold that for me would you, Herr Beck. I do not like to put it on the floor.'

I looked at the grinning silver skull.

'Klein tells me that you have only been at Topf for a few days now?'

'Yes, Captain. Since Thursday.'

'What did you do before?'

'I was at the university. Studying to be a draughtsman. Then no work until this.'

'So you got the work you studied for? That is good. Well done.'

He was maybe ten years older than me but seemed

ancient in comparison as if he had already lived one life and come back and remembered it all. I was the boy next to him. His uniform pristine like a wedding table, my clothes hanging around me with the wet morning. I could smell them above the car's leather.

'I never went to university. I envy you that. I could have. But I valued my duty more I suppose. But your duty is just as important. Your education will be a great asset to your country. We value that.' He looked at me kindly. 'When did you graduate?'

'41.' I added nothing else but he was ready to go on.

'And you have only just found work?'

'There was not a lot of work about.'

'Ah. That is true. Did you not think of joining the war? For the time being? That is duty too, no?'

'I married that year. I thought I would get a job sooner. I thought I would be helping the country by planning fighter craft by now.'

'As did your wife I'll bet? Women, eh? Look at me. I am going to the Anger and using up a day's relief to buy something I do not want. And when I have to work Sunday to make up for it she will complain, eh? Women.'

'I have only just started work and she has already spent my wage.'

He slapped the wheel and I jumped at his laugh.

'That is it! That is just so, Ernst! We married men only understand! Look at Klein. No wife, no children. What does he know? Something we do not for sure.'

I did not know Klein was not married. I had assumed so. It bothered me. Unsure why. I thought everyone wanted to be married. Fool. Poor fool in a damp suit again. Riding in a car with an SS captain while Klein was at home fixing himself a bath and a Martini.

'So, when did you join the Party, Ernst?'

I had forgotten the pin, the proud pin still stuck to my lapel. I looked at it as if a scorpion had appeared there.

I could say that Klein had given it to me. Given it to me for the reason he had said. To make the right impression. But that might get him into trouble. And myself. I had thought of Klein first. I was sure I should not treat a small tin badge with such flippancy. But if I said a year, a time, committed to it, there would be a paper somewhere to confirm. Everything, even my subsistence chits, were stamped with an eagle.

'Oh. That would have been '42. I think. To be honest, Captain, I am not political I must confess.' I tried to say it the way Klein had done. 'My wife insisted. Thought it would help with my career. They always know what is best for us.' Now I was being more than the fool. I was playing it. I did not believe such sentiments about Etta. It is just what you say when you ride with an SS officer in his car. Your opinion his opinion.

He laughed again.

'That is the way! That is the way! Do you have children, Ernst?'

'No, Captain. But when we have won the war we should think of it.'

'Exactly. Just so. I have a son. My proudest gift. I envy him the country he will inherit. What is your wife's name?'

'Etta.'

'A good name. My wife's name is Emma.' He grimaced. 'I think it is too English.'

'Not at all. Where are you shopping in the Anger, Captain?'

He leaned his ear to me. 'Hmm?'

'The Anger. For your wife's birthday.'

'Oh. Yes.' He shrugged. 'I have not thought on it. I have a few hours to waste.'

'We do not see many SS officers in town. You will be stared at no doubt, Captain.'

He nudged me with his elbow. Like a friend.

'But I bet I get good service, eh? Now, where do you live for me to drop you?'

I had not thought on this. An SS car to my door. The black and silver pennants flying, the runes on the licence plate, the twitch of curtains along the street. Etta watching from the window.

'If you drive to the Anger I can walk from there. I do not want to trouble you, Captain.'

'Nonsense. It is no trouble. None.' Turned his face to me, eyes off the road. 'Where do you live, Ernst?'

*

I did not mean to slam closed the door of the apartment. Etta, alarmed, staring at me from the sink as I stood with the door braced at my back.

'Ernst? Are you all right?'

'I'm fine.' I went to the window, threw my hat and coat to the chair.

'You are home early? Was there a problem at the camp?'

'No. No problem.' I looked through the net curtain. The black car still there. 'But I missed the cafeteria lunch.'

'That is why you look so pale. I will make a sandwich. What are you looking at?'

The car sat there. No blue smoke from the back. Just sat there. Its flat roof looking up at me.

'Frau Klein. Landlady patrol again. I had to run in. She was hovering around the door.' This was partly true. Frau Klein had seen the captain open the car door for me from her ground-floor window. He bowed to me as I passed back his cap.

A slam of a plate, the yell of my name like my mother's scold.

'Ernst!'

I spun from the window, sure a rat had run out of a cupboard.

'Why in hell . . . why are you wearing that pin?'

I went back to the window. My eye up the street to the Anger, down to the station corner.

The car gone.

Chapter 9

I rapped on Klein's office door. The polite two-tone tap. A congenial pat-pat.

He called me in, sat behind his desk with pen and journal.

'Good morning, Ernst. You have my notes?'

'Yes, sir.' I put the pad to his desk. Eight-thirty and I was already in my white-coat. I think he approved.

'Sander will bring to your floor some plans for today. I will be chained to my desk, on administration for my labours. Prüfer is back from Auschwitz so we must all jump.'

'It will be good to see Herr Prüfer again. If I get the chance, sir.'

'I doubt it.' He closed his pen. 'He is in such a mood when he returns.' He saw that I was waiting. 'Is there anything else, Ernst?'

I brought out the pin.

'I return this, sir.' I placed it on his journal. 'But I may have created a problem.'

The pin was gone, to his hand, to a drawer.

'Explain.'

'Captain Schwarz asked me when I had joined the Party. I did not want to lie . . . but I fear I have. I did not want to cause you any difficulty.'

'Ah. I see. No. It is my fault. I did not think on it. A natural question. But it is fine that you concerned yourself, Ernst. About me. But do not worry. I have been a Party member since '38. Schwarz knows this.'

'But I thought . . . You said you were not a member? The pin just for impression?'

He went back into his chair.

'No. I said I was not political. The badge is useful. Being in the Party is useful. I thought it would help you to wear it.'

'But I have lied to him?'

'I appreciate your concern. But do not think, Ernst, that SS captains spend their days trawling over paperwork checking up on junior members of staff of a factory. I should hope he is far too busy. As am I.' He opened his pen.

'I thought to let you know. He did ask. And I did lie. To an SS officer.'

'I thank you for that. Your motives were for me and the company. Very good, Ernst. I am sorry you were inconvenienced. Please forgive me. I acted in your interest.'

'I will not get into trouble?' I changed my angle on that. 'I would not wish to embarrass the company.'

'No. You are right to tell me. If Schwarz should call I
can explain.'

Call. If Schwarz should call.

'I told him that I only joined at my wife's insistence. That
I was not active.'

'So you are being too concerned. Get to your desk,
Ernst. Do not worry. I can control my own department.
Thank you for your help yesterday.' His pen to his journal.

I bowed and left. Sweat in my palms.

*

Yesterday, explaining the badge to Etta, had not gone well.
I tried to pass it off. As nothing. A small thing.

'Herr Klein gave it to me.' I plucked the pin from my
jacket, pocketed it. 'To make a good impression in the
camp. For appearances sake. It is nothing.' I moved away
from the window.

'It *is* something. You wore that in the street?'

'No. I came from the car and straight in.'

'Car?'

I needed a cigarette. The papers and tobacco pause enough.

'Herr Klein gave me a lift. He was going to the Anger.
For shopping.' Only half a lie.

Etta enraged as she lit the hob for the kettle.

'He should have taken back his badge.'

'I'll give it to him tomorrow.' I switched on the light.
'Do we have money for the meter?'

'Don't do that. Don't change the subject. If you want to join the Party to get on that is up to you.'

'What difference does it make? A party is a party.' I lit my cigarette, resumed my position by the window. To deposit my ash. To watch the street. As usual. Trying not to look up and down the road. 'It does not mean anything any more.'

'It means you are old-fashioned. That you belong in lederhosen. That you are an old man shouting at the dark. I am sure your father would approve.'

I left the window. 'Would it change your opinion of me?'

She pulled cups and tea from the cupboard. Her face away from me. 'It is your choice. If you want.'

Not the words she wanted to say. Not in their tone.

'I didn't think we were political,' I said. The same tone.

'Our country is at war, Ernst. Everyone is political. Even this damned tea has a swastika on the box. Why should my husband wear it less? Who am I to object?' Slammed the tea back to the cupboard. 'Now. Do you want to tell me about the camp?'

I waited for the whistling kettle. It would be easier to talk on my day over tea.

Chapter 10

I went to my board, the last one on the right, the others
smiling or ignoring me as I passed. I was the only one who
did not wear glasses, the only young blond man. Everyone
else with black slicked hair and thin moustaches. The old
men that Klein had said he did not trust. These men had
unions once.

We did not have stools, we stood all day, and that would
take getting used to but no matter yet. Today was Tuesday
and since Thursday last I had maybe only spent three hours
at my desk. I stared at the blank white paper of my board,
checked the wheel of the ISIS by moving it from corner
to corner.

'Those are yours,' the voice of my colleague from the
row beside me. He nodded to the table between us and to
a grey bound folder almost the same size. 'Herr Sander
brought them. I told him you were not here yet.' That
meant he had told him I was late.

'I was with Herr Klein,' I said, in exactly the timbre to declare that he was not in such company.

I sat on the edge of the table, slipped off the corner ties and took out the first sheet. A note attached.

'Furnace designs for Auschwitz – Birkenau II & III. Translate Alphabet with annotation in ink. F. Sander.'

This was a ground plan. An enormous room divided into several others. The ovens in the furthest room, complete with detailed trundles for putting the bodies in. Five triple-muffle ovens. Five in each drawing. Two crematoria. Thirty iron and fire-clay oven doors. For two crematoriums. Thirty doors. And there were still three more crematoria in this prison.

I was incredulous. Voiced it.

'How many people die here?'

My colleague never stopped scratching his pencil.

'Hundreds a day. The typhus is everywhere. And they execute criminals all day long. Did you see that fenced area at Buchenwald? By the crematorium?'

I did not know they were aware of my visit. Perhaps nothing to be hidden between floors. I would note that.

'I smoked there.'

'The execution yard. That is why the fence is so tall. The prisoners cannot see into it. Beside the morgue so you do not have to drag them too far to the chute.'

Hundreds a day, he said. How many camps the same? Thousands a day. Another front to the war. A war of disease. Did not want to think of it. Pictured the brass band instead.

Every camp had a song Klein had said. Think of the better picture.

I took the paper to my board, clipped it up. I would only have to explain the dashes and breaks of line, the shaded areas and what these meant to the viewer in terms of constructing the building. The names of each room plain enough. But I decided that speaking to Paul would help me understand what I was looking at. What if I found a mistake? What if I could help improve? Make an educated difference. To get to the third floor. I would take a trip to Weimar at the weekend.

'How have you been, Ernst?'

I jumped at the friendly voice. Kurt Prüfer at my shoulder. His smile like a shy boy's. A chubby face behind round spectacles, grey and white hair cropped close to the bone to camouflage his baldness as men who have a roll of fat above their collar are wont to do. Grey suit to match his hair. He did not seem as moody as Klein warned.

'Very well, sir.'

'I see you have Sander's new designs.'

We looked at the plan side by side.

'I was wondering, sir — if it should help — I have an old school friend in Weimar who runs two of the crematoria there. I thought I might pay him a visit at the weekend. So that I may better understand our work.' I thought this would be a good thing to say, to show my interest in the company's products, and in my own time, but Prüfer's mouth went thin.

'The Special Ovens accounts for less than three percent of our output, Ernst. If you want to learn more about Topf the malting equipment and granaries would be a better study for a graduate who wishes to get on.'

'Yes, sir. It is my ambition to do so.'

He rapped the plan. 'Can this be done today?'

'Yes. I understand it.' I pointed to the stylised sig-rune heading at the top of the print that corresponded to the eagle and stamp in the right corner, signed by Sander. Not a double 'S' at all. An ancient Germanic rune reversed. It now stood for 'victory' instead of 'sun'.

'This is for the camp commander? I am to make it plain, sir?'

The cherub came back. 'But do not make it look as if the reader is a novice. You understand?'

'Yes, sir.'

'If you can get this done by this afternoon bring it to my office. I have come from Auschwitz with new requests that must be drawn up as soon as possible. Sander is working on them now.' He pushed his glasses back where sweat had slipped them. I noticed his hands were rubbed almost raw from washing. Sanded almost.

'Before five, Ernst.'

'Yes, sir.' And he left me, as simple as he had appeared. My colleague opposite pretended to hear none of it, as if our desks were in a different universe, and I hummed to myself at his flush of face and set to work.

The new boy taking his work direct to Prüfer's office.

*

78

By four-thirty I had finished the annotations. I had started my walk to Prüfer's office confidently but with each step I realised this was my first completed task.

Suppose I had not done well? Suppose my notes were obtuse? Vague? It was a deconstruction of the plan. We had done such things at the university many times but perhaps I had been too succinct, perhaps not enough. I would be judged by my first work in the real world and I slowed as I passed Klein's office and onto Prüfer's, appropriately the door that ended the corridor. I knocked twice, waited. An age. The shutting of filing cabinets echoed through the corridor.

'Come in, Ernst.'

Prüfer's office did not have the draughtsman's board when he had interviewed me. It dominated the room, appeared strange in the room that I remembered. The room that now demanded something of me. He gave me no instruction as he stood beside it and I bowed, automatically, set the plan to the grips and stood back.

He removed his glasses, one hand to his back, a sea captain studying a course, and his spectacles roving across the plan like a magnifying glass.

'Excellent, Ernst. Excellent.' His eye moving along the paper from corner to corner and then he stepped aside, his spectacles' arms pinned with difficulty behind his ears again.

'This will do well. Sander will be pleased. Well done. Now, tell me what you might think of something.'

He went to his desk and with anything that came to hand weighted down another plan. I crossed the room, looked down at the paper spread as large as a tablecloth, a cog-like mechanism its centrepiece. Prüfer did not wait for any query.

'The problem with the camp ovens, Ernst, is that they run on coke. It is inefficient to run and damages the ovens quickly. It takes much longer to reduce the matter than our gas ovens – such as your friend probably has in Weimar. One of ours no doubt.' He was pleased at this. He may have installed them himself.

'The SS will go for nothing less than coke. For cost. Yet they want more efficient ovens every year. They are wrong of course. Although more expensive to build, a gas oven is more economical. But they think like old men. Coal, coal, coal. Coal is cheap, the oven must be cheap. But now it is not so cheap.' He tapped the cog on the drawing. 'But see here, see here. The problem is that an oven must be a regulatory size if it is to work correctly. And they simply do not have the space for anything larger than the eight-door muffle oven in any building in Auschwitz. I know. I built them. If they build another crematoria, again no more than an eight-door, otherwise the heat will be too great. The men operating it would burn. By the end of the year there will be fifty-two ovens in these camps. They don't listen. That will take enough coal to run a railway. But see here, see here.'

I turned my head to the diagram, like a dog trying to comprehend another's bark coming from the radio.

'Is this one of Herr Sander's designs, sir?'

'No. It is my own. It is a circular oven.' He indicated the protrudes of the wheel that made me perceive the drawing as a cog-piece. 'These are the muffle doors. Instead of having ovens in a line, each creating its own heat, you have a central furnace. Eight doors all around.'

I could see it then. Pictured the special unit of prisoners, a trundle, the sliding bed for the body, for each, standing in front of their oven door, trying not to look at each other across Prüfer's central furnace as they loaded their burden.

'They would have to remove the old ovens of course but it would double the capacity and – with a single larger furnace – it would be more efficient. The problem with each muffle having its own furnace is it negates the savings of using coke. If they had gone with gas jets from the start it would be cheaper overall. But they have made their bed.'

I saw the single massive furnace roar before me.

'But how would you determine the ashes? From each other, sir? To send to their relatives? For interment?'

He stared at me, and then back to his crude design.

'I don't think you understand, Ernst. Do you think Kori of Berlin are not working on furnaces to improve efficiency? Marketing such to the SS? How are we to compete if it is not by better design?'

I had disappointed him. Could feel it. All design, all invention falling to the same adage:

Build a better mousetrap. It did not say build a bigger one.

*

'Thank you for your efforts today, Ernst. Your plans must be brought to my office every night,' he ordered, 'for security. One of the reasons for hiring you is that many of the older men are ex-union men. They still hold socialist ideals. And there are many communists amongst them.'

I kept hearing these words. They were being drilled into me from every office in the building. I began to think that I was not so talented or wanted. Just local. And young. New.

'And we have communists on the factory floor. Sure of it. From our own workforce and from the camps. But without knowing who they are we do not get rid of skilled men when we have need of them. We could not fulfil our contracts without. But we have been instructed by the SS that the men who work on these plans must be totally trustworthy. Must have no communist ties. It is easier to use new men.' He took the plans from the board and folded them into his safe.

'The new ovens are . . . important . . . to the SS. Not for communist eyes.' He winked his cherubic smile. 'You will have them waiting for you every morning. Good night, Ernst.'

I bowed and left, cursed myself. I should not have opinions. A man should admire everything from his superiors, not question. I passed Klein's office, the sound of him laughing down the telephone at my back as I walked.

My ISIS machine was the last one on my row, no-one behind me to see, my co-worker beside me too engrossed in his own work and I was sure he would not know what I was permitted to do and not do, but still, I waited until he took a pipe break to copy the Auschwitz plan from memory. A scaled version in my pocket. Take it home. To show Paul at the weekend. Working at home a good habit for an ambitious man.

Chapter 11

When I first met Etta she was that entrancement of a typical zaftig Austrian woman. Curls and curves. City life and style had near straightened her red curls and she maintained them religiously. I imagined that as a child her auburn hair had set her out when all her classmates would have been as shining blonde as the brass in an orchestra.

Her figure too gone the way of a city girl walking to work, and the privations of war had slimmed her so that her nightwear no longer clung but draped, flowed like water about her. Every year she became a new woman before me. Every year a new bride. I envied even myself over my fortunes with her. We argued because we were so similar. We made up because we were so similar. I had known women before her but all I learned from them was how to erase the errors of arrogant youth so I could correctly love this one. I met her at an Erfurt fair, she had tripped, and I caught her and her soup bowl over my shirt. It was dark, the only light from the bulbs of the market stalls selling pretzels and hot chocolate. I never saw she was a redhead until the next day when we met for lunch. I never looked at another woman after that. My youth had been only training to get to that point, sure that some higher power had closed his book and said, 'I'm done with this one. Next.'

We married in Switzerland, where her parents had moved to in '39. We were twenty-one. I was ending my last year at university. Etta had been coming to the library there for years. We had never met.

Her parents had rented her an apartment and I advantaged on that to leave my parents, to leave my small box room where I had grown up. This was not a sudden thing. We had courted for months. Needed more time together. It was like playing at house. Decorated the place like a child's birthday party. Never made the bed up. No point. Ate meals on our laps. Listened to the radio that grew worse every week. Even the music controlled. Everything on it decades or centuries old or just shrill speeches from names we did not know. They took the long-wave from us, took music from us. We shrugged. The country shrugged.

Etta had married a poor Erfurt boy. No reason to. She could have had anyone. Any of those rich boys her father knew. Sometimes the bafflement of this needed reassurance and she would touch me, would smile as at a child.

'There's no such thing as a good rich man, Ernst. No-one ever got rich being a good man. I would rather trust a poor honest one. One without a mistress.'

'And how do you know I don't have a mistress?'

'Because you can't afford one.'

We moved into that one-room apartment next to the hotel that summer. Her father no longer able to pay for hers from Switzerland as the banks consolidated under government control. Only internal transactions permitted. I signed on for the married man's subsistence. She took a waitress job. But we were never happier. Until a month became three years. Until the war became three years. People wore it on their faces. The people in their maps that they pushed their tiny markers of planes and battalions over like croupiers dragging away your losses. Thin as paper maps. The bed got made. Ate at table.

Marriage is for the young. Yet the old men you invite to your wedding scoff, the women cry, the divorced drain their glasses, talk behind hands. But there is red hair under a white veil, a boy in a loaned suit and everything is possible. But you have to go home. The larder has to be filled. You take a job drafting ovens for prison camps. The bed got made. Ate at table. Turned off lights only to save the meter. Early. Before the blackout.

When Etta and I returned from our marriage in Switzerland we had a celebration for all our friends which at least my father had got off the bridge to attend. A real Erfurt celebration with Bach and beer. The women in white and the men in green felt and caps. A gloriously ludicrous display. Probably the last time I have been truly drunk. It was Etta's friends mostly, Paul Reul the only one of mine, the only one we shared, the only one other than my father I let dance with her.

Paul left school at fourteen to work as a stonemason with his father, and from there, from the headstone commissions, he managed to get himself in with the undertakers of Weimar and Erfurt and studied the almost religious sanctity of the crematoria.

Paul had carved his own headstone, as his father had his own. An eerie tradition. The last date missing. He was proud of it, mentioned it to people he had only just met as an ice-breaker after he had introduced himself and his employment and the laughter would come awkwardly as he explained.

'I won't get to see it else. And who knows what they will write about me!'

Before '34 and the Nuremberg laws cremation was not popular, and for Jews it was against their beliefs entirely, but once the deportations began and German families moved into Jewish homes, and the camps began to bring them their trade, business increased from miles around.

The Nuremberg regulations made cremations as religious as burial. For Paul and his colleagues this legitimacy made them as respected as priests. They built chapels of rest, held services, and Topf's petrol and gas ovens made the process contained, not vulgar, as distinguished as funerals, like the white-smocked clergy by the grave and dust to dust, and no widow would have to brush ash from her black sleeve when she took a walk outside, for a breath of air, for the private dab of tear.

Paul was a close friend at school, he was in classes below me but a good stalwart at play and with an older sister a constant source of female mysteries. He had not attended the university but his profession could aid me in mine I was sure.

Etta had wanted to come but I explained that this was work, not a day-trip. Besides, I could enquire on another matter in Weimar which would be easier without her.

*

It is only fifteen minutes and ten pfennigs to take the train to Weimar. There are five crematoria for the city. Paul owns two of them. He is on the steps of his chapel in Jacob Street in his black suit waiting for me like he must wait for his hearses or the wagons from the camps. He sees me, and his dignified stance changes to an animated rush as he runs to greet me like the boy in school again.

'Ernst!' He waves, clasps my hand. 'So good to see you!'

'Thank you for seeing me.'

'Of course, of course! Come. I make you coffee. How is Etta? How can I help you?'

I needed my friend's advice, his opinion. Colleagues and family, even wives, sometimes reflect only your own.

Old friends the mirror that you cannot see yourself in.

*

'What is this, Ernst?' Paul studied the paper, the plans across his coffee-table in his private rooms. A comfortable place. Nicer than my home. Not an office. No paperwork here. If working men had rooms where they could retire to during the day I am sure they were doing well. He had left school at fourteen. I went to university and rent a gas cooker with one working hob.

'These are replacement ovens for a few of the crematoria at the Auschwitz camps. The place is enormous. Its own city almost.'

Paul sat back to furnish his pipe. I would not show him that I still smoked rolled cigarettes. His speech lisped as the pipe hung from his mouth. He sounded like my father judging my school-work.

'You know, Ernst, the camp at Buchenwald used to bring wagons of corpses to us for disposal. Not so much the last year. And we used to get deliveries of ashes from the eastern camps to return to families. Not now. The camps have dispensed with formalities. Ignored the laws of their own government. By law the remains are supposed to come to people like myself. We formalised the paperwork and contacted the relatives. We store them here for them if they cannot pay for their release. The SS charge them for the cremation. We have cupboards full of them.'

'The typhus means they are having to burn more deceased. I suppose in times of emergency laws must be bypassed.'

'But we get no ashes now. None. They cannot all die of

disease. The Party are the ones who regulated. Would you not wonder what hand decided that the rules no longer mattered? That the dead do not matter?'

'I have been inside Buchenwald,' I said. 'There are sixty thousand men there. They have one crematorium. Six ovens. They are overwhelmed. The morgue is below the ovens. The stench was incredible. They cannot cope. Topf is trying to help them. Auschwitz must have the same problems.'

'And what is so different about *this* crematoria. What am I looking at?' He went back to looking at the plan and I pointed the rooms out to him.

'Instead of the ovens being on the ground floor they will be on the same level as the morgue, the mortuary and pathology. All underground. They use hand-drawn lifts currently.'

'So do I. And what is this large room between?'

'The delousing room. This annexe next to it is for the clothes.'

'They delouse the prisoners next to the mortuary and the ovens?'

'They delouse,' I indicated the showers in the ceiling, 'and then they shower them. This is for the new prisoners. Straight off the train. The track is close by so they do not mingle with the rest of the camp.'

He sucked on his pipe and it rattled on his teeth.

'And what are these lines here, to the morgue?'

'Gas pipes.'

'Gas for what?'

'I do not know. Exactly. Heating?'

He sat back. 'You do not heat a morgue, Ernst. You do the opposite.'

'For the hot water then?'

'I doubt they give them hot water. What is the building above?'

'I do not have that plan.'

He studied for three puffs of his pipe.

'This building makes no sense to me.'

I watched his hands navigate the drawing.

'You have five triple-muffle ovens behind a delousing room the size of a school hall. The dead would have to be trundled through this hall making it inoperative at those times and – if it is to be as busy as you say it is – that is useless. The morgue and pathology also in this room? There is also only one entrance. These are steps leading to it, yes?'

I agreed, but unsure of it.

'Well, I do not see any chutes leading to the morgue. So they carry the dead down one by one? By these stairs?'

I looked hard at the plan.

'There was a chute at Buchenwald. To the morgue.'

'There does not seem to be one on this plan. Are the dead expected to walk down?'

I had not noticed, felt foolish in front of my friend. Fool. Idiot.

'Perhaps it is missing?' My first thought glinted. I had found an error, an oversight I could highlight. To my superiors. Ernst Beck. A designer. 'They have missed the chutes.'

'Do you think Topf would make such a mistake, Ernst?'

'Maybe it is a cost issue? From the SS.'

'Cement stairs rather than a couple of chutes or a lift to the morgue? I could not operate a morgue underground without a platform lift or a chute. With this design I would be carrying the bodies through the chapel. That is illegal, Ernst. This design is illegal.'

I could no longer refrain from pulling out my sweepings of tobacco. His observations needed a deliberating smoke. Paul watched me roll a cigarette before he went on. I do not think he judged my cheap simulation of smoking, as Klein would have done.

'I would like to copy this plan, Ernst. I could maybe help with its improvement. Make suggestions. One friend to another.'

'You *have* helped, Paul. I did not notice there were no chutes. And you are right. It makes no sense to wheel the dead through a shower room.' I struck a match and lit up, to think on my next words as I folded the plan away from him. 'I'm sure that it is an SS request rather than an error of our engineers. No need to trouble yourself further.'

The plan would stay with me. Paul had once been a stonemason. In my innocence, my naivety, I could only think of Freemasons. Of unions and communists. And I had been warned often enough. And I had copied this plan without permission.

'It is no trouble, Ernst,' he said. 'Perhaps you and Etta could come to supper one evening? Catch up properly.'

'I would like that. We would like that.' I stood. 'Thank you, Paul.' We shook hands.

'Is there anything else I can help you with, Ernst? A long way to come for so short a visit.'

'Actually there is. While I'm here.'

'Of course. Anything.'

'Could you direct me to the Party office? We have none in Erfurt.'

Paul's hand dropped from mine, went to hold his pipe in his mouth.

'An office? Headquarters, Ernst. Weimar has an NS head-quarters. The Gauforum. A whole square of them.'

I think he wanted me to react, to check something in me. As if our handshake had been a secret sign.

'Just an office would do. Thank you.'

Chapter 12

The office in Rittergasse, behind the Herderplatz, had both the Party flag and the yellow and black-eagle standard of the Republic, the Weimar Republic, for Weimar was the city, the heart, of constitution. All but gone now, a memory. The red, white and black flag was twice the size, ridiculous on the small medieval building, the bottom of it almost stroking people's heads as they passed underneath. Reminding them as they passed. This was the small face of the Party. Where ordinary citizens could pay to join. Weimar's Party headquarters and buildings not for the public.

'*Ernst!*'

That familiar call again. The one from across a square, from a crowded fair while courting, from a balcony as you go to work. That courting call. The red hair loose about her shoulders, not curled. Etta only ever walked in public with her hair curled. Curled and warmed as if she had paid for it and had not spent the morning making it so. She had hurried. A green woollen hat hiding the care she had not taken.

'Ernst!' she cried again, waving, and stopping with her hand to her face as a bicycle bell cut her path and the rider cursed as he swerved from her. And then she was at my shoulder, her gloved hand upon me, green, like her hat, no matter her hurry Etta could match her clothes from the pile that fattened in the bottom of our wardrobe before washday with ease. I could not match socks.

'Ernst. Don't do this,' she said. A hoarseness as if she had screamed this a dozen times on her way here.

'Etta? How are you here?' All I could say.

'Frau Klein came for her rent. I knew you had ten marks in your old cigar box. Your papers were missing from it. Your birth certificate and mine.' Her hand to her mouth again. 'Please don't do this, Ernst.'

'You followed me here? I was only seeing Paul.'

She looked over my shoulder to the flags. 'And coming here. I knew you were coming here.'

'You said I could. If I wanted. For my career.'

'I thought you wouldn't. If I said I didn't mind, I thought you wouldn't.'

The minds of our women. The hand left my shoulder.

'Buy me a tea,' she said, took my hand. 'We have to talk.'

*

95

A teapot for two in the restaurant of the Elephant Hotel. Weimar had a hundred places we could have gone and I would have preferred the Black Bear Inn next door, but I guessed that Etta thought the hotel would be quieter during the day. This was a grand place on the cobbled market square, the Party's favourite adopted hotel. They had it redesigned several years ago and built balconies front and rear where our leader and other dignitaries could give speeches to the multitudes that gathered in the square or privately behind the hotel; for speeches that were not for the public.

There was an amusing rumour that the leader himself had called for the remodelling as his regular rooms did not have their own WC. This meant that every time he left to visit the one at the end of his corridor he would re-emerge to rapturous applause from the throng that had heard that their leader was up and about. He would have to salute as the toilet flushed gratefully in the background while he walked back to his rooms in his pyjamas. Not so many parades this year. Everything now centred on Berlin.

I thanked the waitress for the biscuits she placed beside the tea. The biscuits welcome for we could not afford to eat here. Etta thanked her warmer and the girl smiled back as she bowed away. Etta also a waitress. People who worked in service always warm to each other. They know the rest of us are the worst.

'Do hotels have rationing?' I asked no-one, looking

around, feeling awkward in the company of my own wife. As if we were both someone else's partners.

'I don't know, Ernst,' she said, patting the back of her hair. 'Does it matter?'

'No.' I smiled, hoped she would meet me with it. 'Why did you not want me to go in, Etta? To the Party office?'

She tried to dab at her eyes without disturbing her make-up. I waited for her to finish and for the teapot to cool. The handkerchief and compact away to her handbag, its clasp's click punctuating her talk.

'I have to tell you something, Ernst. But promise me that you will not think that I have lied to you. Please don't feel that. It is not personal.'

All the dread thoughts that husbands have when this conversation comes ran through my heart before my head. A flutter in my chest. She saw my consternations and her face became gentle again.

'Ernst. My birth certificate is not my own. My parents paid for it years ago. When I was a girl. To change my name and theirs.'

'What?' I exclaimed this more with relief than surprise. 'Why?' Relief that it was not another lover. That I had not been betrayed. 'Is your name not Etta?'

'Of course it is. But not Etta Eischner. It is Etta Kirch. And now Etta Beck so probably none of this matters anyway.' She poured the tea, the chime of china as she trembled.

'I have three Jewish grandparents. My mother and father are Jewish. But they do not practise. But I do not think that matters any more. Jewish by birth is still Jewish. But – under the law – you are married to a Jewess, Ernst. Our marriage is invalid.'

My thoughts and words stumbling. 'But we were married in Switzerland? Does that not count for something?' Gibberish. 'You're not Jewish. You were born here.' Nonsense from the boy.

'Do you think that concerns any of them now? They still take you away in the night. Camp first. Questions later. That is why I had to be married at my parents' villa. Safer for us all. And I'm sure there were plenty of Armenians in the last war that were married Protestant in Paris. Do you think that mattered to the Turks?'

We sipped our tea as other guests went past our little table, our little tableau.

Strange how the most shocking things are revealed in congenial places and moments. I imagine it is God's amusement. Everything we touched cool white. Everything above us gold plaster. We apart from it all.

'What does this mean?' I said. The room empty again.

'Our marriage would be annulled. That would be the least. But . . .'

'But you are married to a German?'

She looked hard at me.

'I *am* German, Ernst.'

'You know what I mean. You were concerned that if I showed an official your birth certificate they might notice it was counterfeit. Or they would check up on it.'

'I'm sure they would.'

'So we are safe. Nothing has changed. No-one needs to know. No harm to us. I do not care. Your parents only did what they saw right. To protect you.'

'But they left for Switzerland. I stayed here and met you. We cannot afford to leave.'

I no longer noticed if the mention of money was a slight at me. Just fact.

'Why should we leave? I have a career now. These are our roots here. Germany is the capital of the world.'

'Perhaps my father could pay for us to get out? Would you consider that?'

I leaned forward.

'I have a job, Etta. For us. For our children to come. Travel is too restricted now. You have a forged passport as well.'

She sipped, shrugged, and it curdled me.

*

'Ernst? It changes nothing with us, does it? But no-one official should see my papers. You agree? Not now?'

I reached across and our hands touched for the first time since we had sat. I saw the staff at the bar wink and whisper. We must have looked newly in love. All the more sweet on a Saturday in wartime when no-one knew what tomorrow dawned on.

The door crashed in. Four grey uniforms came laughing

and slapping each other to the bar and the staff snapped up like rods, the laughter echoing louder off the high ceiling as if there were fifty of them. I withdrew my hand and Etta looked to them, back to my pale face.

'What is it, Ernst?'

Their appearance had reminded me of Captain Schwarz. The black holsters at their waists, still startling to me. They laughed louder as their drinks came, caps to the bar. I recalled a death's-head cap on my lap. His face leaning towards me.

'What is your wife's name? Where do you live, Ernst?'

'Etta.' I said her name as if for the first time. 'I also have something to confess. And it might matter now.' I pushed my cup away.

'Etta. I did not get a lift home from Herr Klein the other night.'

Chapter 13

We returned to Erfurt station. Almost six, the west sun came through the glass of the concourse in golden shafts, motes of dust shimmering along them like rapturous lanes to a better place. From train-lines to throne. We walked through them, Etta's body close into mine shivering like a child rescued from a river. The shimmers glowed on us. Chose not to take.

We spoke when our door closed.

'Do you think he . . . they will check on us?' as her coat fell to the floor.

I repeated what Klein had said.

'I would hope the SS are too busy to examine one minor employee of a factory.' I picked up her coat, hung it with mine. 'My references from the university would have already been assessed. I'm sure everything is fine. I have no work records. No union history, no political preferences from the university. That is why I'm the one working on these drafts. It has been mentioned enough.'

'But your wife is a Jew. They have not known that.'

'You knew I was taking this job, Etta. And even I did not know that you . . .'

She sat, pulled off her hat like it was a rat, flung it to a corner.

'I did not know you would be working for the SS. I thought you would be drawing silos. Not ovens for Jews.'

I sat beside her and she edged from my arm about to comfort.

'They are ovens for the camps, Etta. Tools for the camps. Necessary. Buchenwald has a theatre. Cinema. Even a brothel.' All Klein's words again. 'They need furnaces.' I said this as factually as I could, but I thought on Paul's words. He said he used to get the ashes to send to the relatives. That the government would charge the relatives for the cremation. I could not concede that they no longer needed the money. They did not even want to afford the coke for the furnaces.

'Don't, Ernst.' She touched my hand. 'Don't be so . . . Do you remember when there was the Zionist plan? When we were younger? The Party and the Jewish leaders joined together to have them relocated to Palestine? The *Attack* newspaper – Goebbels' paper for Christ's sake – even gave away that souvenir medallion. Star of David one side, swastika on the other. And then the war came. The government could no longer pay for such a plan. Now it was a cleansing instead. My family went to Switzerland. By then I had met you.' She held my hand tighter. 'But who would have imagined this? Years of this.'

'You are not Jewish, Etta. And imagine what? We are at war. We do not know what enemies we have or from where. The Americans imprison Germans, the Italians and Japanese. We are only doing the same.'

'It is not the same.' She let go my hand. 'This is different.'

'How?'

'The conference the rest of the world had about the refugees. Remember that? No-one would take them. Every civilised country in the world refused them. Forced them to stay. The Party said they'd put them on luxury liners if another country would take them. You know who said yes? The Dominican Republic. The bloody Dominican Republic! They wanted to take one hundred thousand and everyone else just turned their backs. Ernst, you had to get my father to send you that Lotte book. A book set in Weimar about Goethe. A book set in our own cities. For Germans. He sent it in two pieces because *they* had banned it. They burn books, Ernst. What do you think they do? To Jews? If they ban even German books?'

I stood, went to the window and my tobacco. The motion and method of making a cigarette a catechism. To steady thoughts. To distract with our own hands. How often does one do that in a day? Concentrate on our hands. The smoker knows this. The rosary of it. The lighting of the paper the lesser part. It is the retreat that matters.

'I do not know,' I said. 'The ovens are being increased to stem the typhus. The diseased dying. Imagine if that spread to the cities? What then?'

'Ernst.' She paused as my match struck and my hands cupped and drew life. 'Why build more ovens, spend more money, in the *expectation* of more disease when that might not happen? Is not that money better spent on prevention? Is that what scientists do? Only find better ways to kill the infected? Would you go to the dentist whose only tool was a hammer? And does not the forced labour workers from the camps spread that disease? The ones in your factory?'

I blew my smoke into the room.

'What are you saying?'

She seemed to grow small, her body retracting.

'I don't know. I do not know enough. You are building . . . you are working for a company that builds ovens for the SS. You say that Auschwitz is almost a city. And you have had no work until this . . . so . . . I don't know.' She looked at me. 'It is just fear, Ernst. If you were drawing planes I am sure this feeling wouldn't be . . . but . . . I don't know.'

'So if I annotate a bomber that kills thousands that is fine. But an oven is wrong?'

'You were driven home by an SS captain. The car outside our home.'

'What difference does that make?'

She grew larger again, the colour back to her face.

'I'll tell you, Ernst. I will tell you what difference such

things make. I saw how you shut our door when that car brought you home. The car you did not tell me about. When Frau Klein came for her rent, when I had only ten marks to give her and I found our papers missing and us owing her forty marks. She took the ten. And she *apologised*. I have never seen that woman sweeter. She told me not to worry on the rent. Pay her when we can. Whenever we can.' She crossed her arms. Found interest in the corner where her hat lay.

'That is the difference such things make, Ernst Beck.'

The cherry of my cigarette was the only light in the room as I drew on it, turned it away from her to look out on the street alone. My usual pose.

Chapter 14

April became May. The radio and newspapers reported our army's successful strategic redeployment from Rome, from Cassino. But we knew what that meant, had all become used to reading between the lines. When children played with wooden guns in the street they had American accents. They could not be blamed for such. They had picked this up from the Party's own cowboy movies. Our leader an avid Western fan. It had a symbolism to him. Films about claiming land, on overcoming and conquest and Christian victory. He did not perceive that the only thing the children would pick up would be the guns and the drawl. There was more Tom Mix in them than Siegfried.

Here did not feel like a place of war, surrounded by it, yes, but only as much as we were surrounded by forest and so did not take part in the wars of the birds either. We, Erfurt and Weimar, still our country's Christmas card paintings.

There was a foreboding around Etta and I in the first days after our revelations. But nothing happened. No knock on the door. Just that fog of dread. Waiting for it to come.

I did my work. Did not ask questions. And we became calm again. I had been paid. We went to café lunches at weekends and paid our rent and Frau Klein even curtsied to me. I bought wine in bottles not closed with a beer stopper and no label. I signed off from subsistence. Etta quit her waitress work. I provided.

And then Hans Klein called me to his office. On a Friday morning. The favourite day to fire an employee I had heard. The way of business.

I had to wait before my knock on the door was acknowledged. Seconds only. Enough time to think of every horror behind the door. From yelling to gunshot, all extremes and everything in-between, and every one of them ending with Etta's sobs. But there was only the sound of cabinets closing. The usual sound in Topf's corridors. The sound of muffle doors closing ovens. Only people without imagination do not doubt and fear.

'Ernst!'

Klein blew out my name happily with his smoke. I could almost see my name form in the cloud. He pushed his orb of cigarettes to me. I bowed and took an American Camel. My first in three years. I ran it under my nose. It did not smell as well as expected, hoped. Perhaps they were never good. Or nothing was how it was before.

'I am pleased with your work, Ernst. We all are.' He passed his onyx table-lighter to my hand. 'And I have grand news.'

'Thank you, Herr Klein.'

'You have not heard it yet.' He gave me that grin. 'You may not like it.'

He was in grey today. A Hugo Boss. The couturier for the SS. I had begun to notice such things. Begun to notice shoes in windows beyond the sureness of their soles. I looked at their stitching now. Owned my own pair of black wing-tips.

We sat, the desk between, and shared an ashtray, which Klein pushed to favour my side.

'Your name, lately, Ernst, has caused even Herr Topf to take notice of you.'

I coughed on my cigarette. Harsher than my tobacco.

This? This the knock on the door?

He watched me cough. Waited for me to settle.

'Your name stood out to him. It would. Would it not?'

My mouth too dry from the cigarette to speak. Drawing on it again the automatic solution. I must have seemed sick to Klein. A parental concern on his face.

'I mean your *names*, Ernst. Your names are the same. Ernst Topf. Ernst Beck.' He studied me behind his cigarette. 'Why? What did you think I meant?'

I apologised.

Fool. Idiot. A kid coughing on his first cigarette.

I sat back with him. Copied his pose and he grinned. 'Don't you want to hear my grand news, Ernst?'

*

'A *house*, Etta!'

I had run the stairs. She had panicked at the rushing sight of me, not heard what I said, only the door crash, her hand on her chest.

'Topf has given us a house!'

'What are you talking about? What house?'

I held her shoulders, gasped for air, grinning like Klein.

There were fine houses opposite the Topf factory, I had seen them on my first day, on my first walk to work. They were near the ghetto, but the ghetto was not there when they were built and the ghetto empty now anyway, not there now. Open suitcases left in doorways, in the streets, along with the single shoes as if the rapture had come here. A decade of rain and dust breaking the shoes to corruption.

Topf senior had bought these houses for his workers during the Great War, for his top men. A benefit. He had his own villa nearby. He could walk to work. And he wanted his best men to do the same; did not want them to have an excuse to be late. And they would have no excuse to not be early if he so chose or work as late as he so chose. Topf the juniors kept the same ideals. Keep work close to home. Early and late. The benefit of no unions.

Klein had shaken my hand. His other passed a set of long keys. An aged paper tag.

'These are yours, Ernst. The house has been profession-ally prepared. I will have one of our trucks move you in whenever you are ready. Congratulations.'

*

'But why, Ernst?' Etta's hands flat on my shirt, against my chest, and I could feel my heart beneath.

'My work is to increase. The SS have been pleased with my explanations of the designs. My work has gone to Berlin! And Topf have more of them every day for me to work on. I have become their preferred man for the task. Klein says I will go the top floor once this job is done!' That was an exaggeration. But it was a time for such.

'But a house?' She stood back, a hand to her face. 'Why would they do such?' Concern on her face more than elation.

*

Klein had said it straight enough, as if it was his good work, his plan.

'Topf has expressed to Sander that a workman such as yourself, one in demand, approval from Berlin, should not be exploited by having to pay the rents of the common. These houses used to be for the top-floor only. Rent free.

You are too new to be promoted, to pay you more, but your work is important enough that you should gain some benefit. As good as promotion. This from the Topfs themselves. Six weeks you have been here. Well done. I am proud to have you on my floor. It makes practical sense to have you closer to the factory. And in a place of comfort where you could work from home. Sander and Prüfer agree. You could work in privacy.'

'You said I might not like this, sir? Herr Klein! You have changed my life!' I blushed at my exclaim. Foolish words, no matter how honest. Childish.

'I meant,' he said, 'that I like to go far away when I leave work, Ernst.' He went back to his desk. 'You are across the road. You will be first in and the last out. An eye upon you all the time. That might dampen your spirit.'

I could not pocket the keys. I was weighing them in my hand. I am twenty-four years old. I have a house. Rent free. My wage doubled simply by walking through its door. Maybe short term, maybe not. You do not think like that when someone puts keys in your hand. The top floor had been mentioned. That was enough. If Klein and Topf had me in their pockets I could justify that scrutiny.

'I will not let you down, sir,' I said. Foolish even as I said it. But I did not know how to express such worth bestowed. I had done my work. Rewarded now beyond it. It was a prize. A prize unjustified. Like finding a winning ticket to a draw you had not entered. Found in an old suitcase abandoned in a doorway in a ghetto.

Klein opened his pen. His signal for his office to be vacated.

'Take your wife to her new house, Ernst. And, no: You will *not* let me down.'

Chapter 15

I could not wait until the Saturday. It did not get dark until after ten and so with coat and shawl Etta walked on my arm. To a house. Her concern dissipated as my enthusiasm wooed. I had seen it already, the outside, when I left work. But the inside should be shared together.

It was a terraced house, on the street, no front area, a few steps to the basement and two steps to the great front door. Six windows. One large window on the ground floor. All overlooking the wall and chimney that said, 'Topf' written in white around it.

I had a key to a lock that I did not rent.

Etta walked in, away from my arm. She opened every door with a gasp for each as I watched her from the doorway. She halted at the stairs.

'Who lives up there?' she asked.

'You do, Etta. We do.'

She ran them like a child at her first beach sprinting to

the sea and I heard more doors opening. I came after
her, the solid echo of an empty house. Promise in that echo.
It was impossible not to see it filled with children and I
even thought of Christmas. Thinking of Christmas in May.
Lights came on as I ascended, Etta met me at the stairs.

'We do not have enough furniture, Ernst. There is another
floor. Two bathrooms.'

'And a small garden. We'll buy more furniture. We'll
have a bathroom each.'

She touched my hand on the balustrade. Our hands on
our wooden balustrade.

'Is this true, Ernst? We can live here?'

'Klein will loan us a lorry to move in. Maybe Tuesday
we could work it out.'

I reached for her but she walked away and into the
bedroom at the front of the house. I followed. Held her as
she looked out to the factory. Felt her body tense.

'It's all so sudden,' she said, 'to take in. And you'll be
right next to them. You might not get time away from them
now.'

'They want me to work from home. That's why we get the
house. It'll be like I'm not at work at all.' Kissed her neck.

'Or always at work.' Her eyes still on the factory. 'Why
so generous? To a new man?'

I had hoped this paranoia had left us. Standing there, in
the near dark, my arms around her, it was still as if a blanket
of guilt was the only blanket we had. Like the gambler says,
'If I didn't have bad luck I'd have no luck at all.'

'My plans are for Berlin. They want me to have privacy.'

'Private. To work in secret they mean.'

I let go of her.

'Are you not pleased for me? For us? A home, Etta. This is not a common thing for me. I grew up in a room without a window. I only want you to be happy.'

She smiled, held me close, but her body still tense.

'I'm sorry, Ernst. I am just tired. That's all.' Kissed me. Her double-tap kiss.

I said nothing. Wrapped her into me.

*

On Sunday we went to my parents again. I had to tell someone. Over the years – and it did not seem something I had noticed with the passage of the war – our friends had dwindled down to a precious few, like that Walter Huston song. That September song. Jewish composer, gone like all of them to America, but it still made it on the radio. Someone must have missed that. I wonder if anyone was aware the cultural bereft we would have with the writers, composers and artists that had exiled themselves. A land of labour. A cemetery of culture. *They burn books*, Etta had said. What would they do to the people that wrote them.

Partners had gone to the army, their wives to their parents. Others had moved for work or had left Germany altogether, sometimes without a word. But we could guess what the word would have been. I was still the boy. Living in the town where he was born.

Etta had her friends from the café but I had never met them. They would still meet once a week to catch up but during the day now, which I preferred, instead of after work, as it had been. Sometimes, after hours, they had gossiped and drunk until the day became tomorrow, in a blacked-out café.

I was usually asleep when she returned and was pleased that she maintained society besides myself. I have always been a loner. More than four people in a room and I become withdrawn. Etta always the more gregarious of us and I would use her as a shield at times for this nature. She insisted this was because I had no siblings. I grew with only my parents as guides and parents prefer quiet children if they cannot pass them off to an elder brother or sister. I can spot a man who was a lone child in an instant and probably he I, but we do not talk for the same.

As long as Etta was laughing and talking at a gathering no-one minded the quiet husband in the corner pretending to peruse the bookshelves and drinking too quickly. And I would always hate the question, 'So what do you do, Ernst?'

'Nothing,' I would have to say. 'Nothing.'

I would be quiet and let her to it. That might change soon. I was a career man now. And no brothers or sisters meant that all my parents' pride could be for mine alone. I did not have to hear how well my brother might be doing.

The opposite also true. All their shame could be mine also. But not now. Not today.

*

My mother had made her Jaeger Schnitzel with spaetzle but only one pork fillet, so spread thin between the four of us, but with more than enough of the pasta to make up. I would not have been able to get hold of a pork fillet. It helps if the butcher is your neighbour on the bridge and your father went to school with him. That is how people get through war.

I was given the cut in the middle, the thickest, and my father brought out his Bavarian beer.

They were more ecstatic than us with our news but quickly my father came down to odd practicalities, as fathers do.

'You will have to have your post redirected. Who pays for the light? You will have to be careful with that. Your coal ration will probably not heat such a place.' But this was his way of showing he was pleased, and my mother could only talk of grandchildren.

I wondered if it was my father's stubbornness to stay in his father's house on the bridge that had kept them to only me as their offspring. I had never thought before that perhaps my father could not afford to move. He was forty years older than me but lived in a house that was already hundreds of years old. The walls bulged with age and no part of it was straight and this antiquity had spread to its occupants. The knots in their hands the same as the knots in their house's corners. Everyone on the bridge was ancient. Their bones creaked with their stairs. They say people come to resemble their pets. I say they grow to resemble their homes. Look for yourself. You will see this now I have said it so.

We left after only a few hours, Sunday lunch with one's parents always an hour too long, the evening for us. And I felt tall. Admired and loved. I was not like my father on his Sundays of my youth. Grinding his teeth and dreading the alarm clock to be set.

I would run to work if the stragglers in their homburgs would not object so.

And then *he* came.

There before me, before I arrived on Monday morning. With Prüfer and Sander when I was summoned first thing. I had not had time to change my coat from black to white.

Chapter 16

I had never seen a man with one leg before. He did not move as if he had only one. Moved as if it was merely invisible, that only we could not see it, his crutch a decoration for us to admire along with his uniform. His cap on Prüfer's desk. Klein not in the room.

'Ernst,' Sander said, 'this is Senior-Colonel Voss. From Berlin.' Only Voss seemed pleased with the introduction. He came at me before I had finished my respectful nod of acknowledgement and his hand went out for mine.

You expect one-legged men to hop. You have imagined it. I had seen Wallace Beery in *Treasure Island* do so. Voss swept across effortlessly in a single movement.

'It is good to meet you, Herr Beck.' And our hands shook. The second SS man I had done this with. You expect flash-bulbs to go off; they do it so emphatically. 'I will say how pleased Berlin is with your . . . deciphering.'

'Thank you, Senior-Colonel. I have done my best.' I began

to blush, from nervousness rather than modesty and his thin lips crawled into a sympathetic smile. I am sure he was used to the effect of uniform and rank to the citizen. The pinned flap of his right leg provoked less. Only children do not know to resist gaping at such things.

He was balding, fine grey hair above his ears only, and the sharp intelligent face that one might find on a philosophy professor.

'I understand you were a student before here, Ernst?' he said. 'Graduated almost three years now, yes?'

I nodded. His eye watching mine. To show he knew me.

'Good. Excellent. Erfurt such a fine university. None of the hubris of that "White Rose" nonsense we had in Munich. True Germans here.' The thin smile again. His hand dropped mine.

Students elsewhere had protested against the Party, against the regime, as students always do. But those that were of the 'White Rose' were almost a party in themselves. In number and passion. The movement ended, crushed, last year. The main protagonists beheaded. *Guillotined*. In the twentieth century. Guillotined. If they were married their widows were sent a bill for the execution. We did not hear much of protests from then on.

Sander and Prüfer looked at me. I was expected to reply.

'Yes, Senior-Colonel. We are happy only to be studious in Erfurt.'

He swung away, his crutch inaudible on the floor. His

boot made more noise. He set himself on the edge of Prüfer's desk.

'You are married, Herr Beck?'

'Yes, Senior-Colonel.' I felt uncomfortable in my suit. Without the white-coat it did not feel that I was at work. And now it began to feel that I was not to start work today. Waited for the other shoe to drop. But then he did not have one to do so.

'And Topf have given you a house? Your wife must be pleased, yes?'

'Extremely so. We are both very happy. We have not moved in yet.'

He wagged a black-gloved finger at me.

'But we will expect you to work hard for it. That is the new way. It is a good world for men with clean backgrounds such as yours. Those who have studied to achieve rather than rest on union cushions. Is that not so, gentlemen?'

Prüfer and Sander agreed.

'We have great hopes for Ernst, Senior-Colonel,' Sander said. 'We have suffered with unions in the past.'

'As has all Germany.' Voss took his cap, twisted his body to get it. His crutch never moved. 'Their nature is revealed in their secrecy. But we get ever better at finding them, no? Now, we should not deter this young man from his work. I would like to inspect the barracks that you have for the Buchenwald prisoners.' He stood from the desk. The death's-head cap screwed to his head and Prüfer and Sander followed his stride. He stopped at me as I opened the door. Prüfer handed me my plans for the day without a word.

Voss bowed his head. To me. 'A pleasure to meet you, Herr Beck. Having seen your work I wished to see your face.'

See my face.

'I hope you and your wife – Etta, is it not? – are most happy in your new home.' And he brushed past, Prüfer and Sander waiting for me to go through, to lock the door behind.

Klein was in the corridor, smoking a cigarette outside his door.

'Hans,' Voss said for hello to Klein as he bowled along with us at his heels. Heel.

'Helmut,' Klein's grinning response, tipping his cigarette to his forehead. He winked only to me as we passed. Did not seem to worry about smoking in front of the SS. Knew a colonel's first name. Deferred the title.

I did not tell Etta of the colonel. She had been upset enough by my ride with Captain Schwarz. I did not want to spoil our new home. Not with talk of men from Berlin. A city even we had begun to fear.

Chapter 17

I had a dream. Of when I was a boy. A memory. No, not a boy, a youth, not yet thirteen surely. But in my dream I was younger. Seemed younger.

We were only allowed to take two books from the school library, but Dumas was too tempting for only two. I was D'Artagnan in my school-yard. My fist my sword. And there was Swift and Stevenson and Burrough's Tarzan, and we had no bookshelves at home.

I, like all boys, was a natural smuggler, and with my satchel I strode out of the library every week with my dutifully stamped two books and another two hidden in my swimming towel. Oh, I returned them. I was not a thief in the traditional sense. A smuggler, as I said. And are you not supposed to borrow from libraries? Other children forced to take two books. Such limitations a rationing to me.

'Will you show me your satchel, Ernst?' Frau Meikel,

our librarian, asked as I was leaving one day. She had become faded in my dream of course. She was now a blur of my mother and Etta but her glasses were the same.

Like all smugglers I had become complacent and gave up fair when the hand of justice came. Caught as sure as the pirates in my books.

She frowned as she pulled out the green- and brown-backed volumes.

'I always bring them back,' I said. 'We have no books at home. I meant nothing. I just wanted . . . I am sorry. I—' I had to stop. She had begun to cry.

She took a handkerchief from her cardigan, that cardigan that all librarians wear. She was a small Jewish woman, ancient to me and fearful. She, after all, controlled the books. To me they were hers. I had taken from her and this was why she was crying and I began to cry also. For the harm I had done her, and for my shame. She sniffed into her linen. Wiped her eyes under her glasses.

She slammed the books back into my satchel as if we were both late for something.

'Take them, Ernst,' and her voice was pleading. 'Don't bring them back. Be a good . . . a bright boy.' And she stopped looking at me, pushed the bag from the desk and forgot I was in front of her. I did not dream of walking away.

I came back next Thursday as usual, to borrow and return my purloined books, sure that Frau Meikel had not truly wanted me to keep them. She was not there. I never saw her again. Half the books gone also. I do not think she took them with her.

I woke up with that memory. It was Tuesday. And Etta and I moved into our home.

*

Klein had arranged a lorry for us. I did not expect it to come with a soldier but then I did not expect it to come with three prisoners from Buchenwald either. But how else was Klein to move us? His attitude was if Topf paid the camp for the prisoners then they could do what work they required to be done. The soldier told me I was not to help but Etta insisted on carrying her own secret bags to the transport. You cannot begrudge a woman her privacy. No matter how smart your uniform.

It was not a difficult or long job anyway. Pitiful how little we owned. The beds and Etta's lounger and my old armchair the most of it. The rest we could probably have walked round like refugees, like we had watched from our windows years before.

The soldier drove the lorry. He shook our hands in the morning but did not talk or look to us after we had thanked the prisoners for their help. Fortunately a short ride beside him. Etta and I huddled together away from his stern sinewy form. A perpetual anger about him. It came off his coarse uniform like static. The prisoners sat on our belongings in the open bed of the lorry and held back our mattresses from falling over the side as the soldier pummelled the gears around Erfurt like a train about to wreck. I do not think he was pleased with his task. After it was done Etta and I could only offer the prisoners a jug of water. The three of them shared only a cupful before nodding their thanks and being pushed back onto the lorry.

'You should say something to him,' Etta whispered. 'Look how he treats them.'

'They are prisoners, Etta.'

'Imprisoned for being alive.'

'You do not know that.'

'And so you think your Klein would have sent murderers and thieves to help us?'

My Klein. He was of me now.

She walked away with the jug. Up her steps that she had already cleaned.

I waved to the soldier as he pulled away to go into the main gate across the road. I do not think he saw me. The prisoners did. One waved back and then the others joined. The gate opened and closed and they were gone. Back to making the muffles for the ovens.

There was a darker mood inside the house than I would have wanted, expected, for our first day in our home. The distasteful nature of the help that had assisted us. The word you did not want to say attached to their labour. The instinct to pay something to them meaningless. Worthless. We had become those that do not pay for worth. It was throttling me somehow and I had bowed my head in appreciation whenever I could at the men in caps and striped clothes who had helped us move into our home.

Etta was unfolding her curtains when I came into the parlour, her lounger and my chair the only furniture. They were cramped in our apartment. Now they were miniature. She nodded to a small table under the window.

'We have a telephone,' she said. 'That was not there the other day.'

I walked over and picked it up, the receiver to my ear. Like an idiot. The number written in pencil inside the rotary dial. I had never had my own telephone before. It hummed in my ear and I put it down, terrified, before someone across the world picked up at the other end. It looked new, its black shone. My fingerprints the only mark on it. I had never possessed a new piece of machinery. I felt a sense of power, of maturity. A telephone had made me feel important.

'Klein must have put it in,' I said.

'That is so you are on call. For him. And it means he has keys.' She took her curtains upstairs.

I made tea for us and cleared dead flies from the window-sills. The house had been cleaned and swept. *Prepared,* Klein had said. But I suppose no-one had seen these little corpses. Not important enough for concern.

PART TWO

Chapter 18

I did not expect to see the colonel again on the
Wednesday. But I would imagine one does not come
from Berlin for just one day. I started my day as always.
In Prüfer's office. Eight in the morning now I lived
opposite – my decision. But Prüfer already there. The
colonel not present. Klein was. He sat, clipping his nails
in an armchair I had never seen anyone sit in. Prüfer
standing when I entered with my knock. Klein only
looked at me with his grin as greeting. Prüfer and himself
wearing their Party pins.

'You have finished the plans for Auschwitz-Birkenau,
Ernst,' Prüfer said.

I missed this was not a question.

'Not entirely, sir. There are some—'

'You have finished the plans, Ernst. We have something
more pressing. For you.'

I put my hands behind my back, straightened, still tired

from rebuilding the beds in our new home last night. I thought only of the coffee pot on my floor.

'Yes, sir.' I looked to the sound of Klein catapulting one of his chips of nail. He put the clippers away, brushed his knees. Prüfer ignored.

'Myself and Herr Sander are to Auschwitz today. Herr Sander himself would work on this otherwise. But we both deem you competent to the task.' He unlocked his safe.

'It is not your usual work. This is a patent only. You must draft this one. Yourself. Alone. Scale from the patent drawing. And annotate it as usual.'

'*My* draft, Herr Prüfer?' My voice leapt. I coughed my exuberance away as if it were just an accident of my body not yet awake.

'The patent is crude,' he said, 'it has the Alphabet but it is not correctly scaled. We designed it two years ago. Patented at the request of the SS. It has now become a priority.' He handed me the single sheet of paper. One drawing and the patent. Stamped by the patent office in Erfurt. The drawing not a good one but the detail was in the script beneath. I had worked on such translations at university. You needed to turn the writing below the drawing into a draft. Textbook. Final year. I had dreamt of this moment. The drawing did not look like an oven. It looked like a building. A tall, narrow building.

'There is some urgency to the draft.' Prüfer picked up his briefcase. 'I will return Monday. Herr Sander will expect it by Tuesday. You will have to work from home.'

I agreed. Glad to. I had always hoped to be the man working under a lamp in his own comfort. His wife bringing him tea and sandwiches, hushing the children because Daddy is working. And then pulling the bevelled gold chain of the green lamp, to darkness, when the job was done. Pencils and tools away. And satisfied to bed.

But only imagination. Forward in its thinking. The house empty. I do not even have the lamp. Not yet.

'Tuesday,' Prüfer reminded. 'And, Ernst.' He was firmer now. 'Show that plan to no-one.' He left Klein and me alone, did not close his own door on us. It was the first time I had ever seen him not lock his door. Klein saw my thoughts as always.

'I have the keys,' he said. 'Come. Sit, Ernst.'

He in his armchair, me in the wooden swivel in front of him.

'How is your new home?' he asked.

'Very good, sir. Thank you. You have no idea what difference this makes to Etta and I. She is used to richer homes but I have never lived in such a large place. We have so little to fill it.'

He brushed at his lap again.

'I hope you will have many years to make it yours.'

'We do not seem to have any neighbours?'

'Topf owns most of that street. Homes for our best workers. A lot of those families have been gone for years. Early casualties. We do not give them to widows.' He looked over my shoulder to the door and beamed. 'Helmut! So good to see you again.'

I turned my head and then stood at the sight of the one-legged colonel filling the door-frame. Klein did not stand until the man swung into the room.

'Hans,' he said, looking at me. 'And Herr Beck. It is good to see you are early to your work.' His uniform was crumpled, not as pristine as the day before. That is what hotels in Erfurt will do to princes. He took the seat at Prüfer's desk. Kept his cap on. We sat after him.

'You moved in successfully, Herr Beck? Good, good. I hope Hans has not been calling you day and night yet, eh?'

The telephone. Did he mean that? Knew of that?

'Does he have the plan, Hans?'

Klein confirmed for me. Voss approving.

'So. You will commence directly on it, Ernst. Good. I must meet with the Topfs this morning at their villa before I return to Berlin. With the plan.' He looked at me. Confirmed. 'It is to be back here for Tuesday.'

'Yes, Senior-Colonel,' I said.

He leaned back.

'Have you looked at it yet?'

'No, Senior-Colonel. I will study it at my table.'

Voss looked to Klein.

'He means he will work on it at home. Not on the floor,' Klein corrected.

This was now my understanding. I did not comprehend that Prüfer had meant that. To totally work from home.

Show that plan to no-one.

Fool. Idiot.

'I understand.' The paper in my hands.

Voss comfortable in Prüfer's chair. His crutch beside him, taller than him, and his hand never left it, like it was his bride as they posed for their wedding-day photographs, pretending to sign the register as they make you do.

'*Do* you understand, Ernst?' He drew me to look at him. 'Let me explain something to you. Something that I hope will help. How you will save lives.'

I raised in my seat. The coffee pot still in my thoughts, my throat dry. I was the only one still drowsy. I blinked and sniffed to concentrate. This was significant. I could tell. Could tell that something of great importance was about to be imparted. And I was about to be departed from the norm of my work.

These moments are rare. The knock at the door late at night that I still feared. A policeman and his handcuffs, a soldier's open holster through Klein's open car window. The stand in a courtroom. When a new life starts. A physical feeling. And you change in a heartbeat. I was between them. One in an armchair. Relaxed as listening to a radio. The other in cap and uniform in a leather chair that was not his.

'Ernst,' Voss said my name. Almost dubious of it. His use of it like a gunshot to me when it did not come with the formality of 'Herr Beck'. I think he knew this when he spoke to civilians. The uniform does this.

'Some years ago it began to concern the Party that our internal work was having a detrimental effect on our soldiers. The police have managed many successful cleansing operations of criminals throughout the Reich, but our soldiers were not bred to be . . . monsters. They are German sons. Good men. With experience we have learned that soldiers do not appreciate being burdened with the execution of criminals. We are slowly making brutes. Did not anticipate this. We cannot send men home to their families so. We did not perceive that there would be so many criminals against. And who could have foreseen the typhus to its extent? And that leaves us with a problem.' He could read the questioning in my face, as if it were a question he had already expected to answer not from me, a draughtsman in a factory, but from on high, from other chambers.

'One would think that the typhus is so virulent we would quarantine those infected into their own camps. And that would be the way. But camp commanders hide the numbers of the infected. We move prisoners based on age, race, religion. Those that can work, those that cannot. To put them where they can be of most use and where they can be with their own. The disease becomes secondary. No commander wants to admit that he has typhus in his camp. But they move them anyway. And then it is the other's problem. But we are trying to prevent this.' He paused to remove his cap to the desk, made sure I was paying attention.

'So. We have the problem that we require our soldiers to be executioners. Force this upon them. To kill the sick and the criminal. A good soldier would accept that he might, in his duty, have to execute criminals. But nothing like in the numbers now. It is our concern for the mental state of our men, for now, for the future, that alternatives must be sought.'

I looked at them both.

'But this is an oven, yes?' I said. 'It has nothing to do with . . . as you said . . . executions . . . I mean—'

Voss finished my thoughts.

'Yes. It is an oven. The SS would never consider involving any of its contractors in internal procedures. What we need is something to help us dispose of the consequences of our increased output. Something which does not put further strain on our men.' He looked to Klein then back to me. His lips tight. Words held back. New ones forming. Ruminating on what to tell a civilian.

'We should all be concerned for our young men's well-being. We cannot afford the time, the distraction, to shoot every criminal. The morale, and the morals, are not good.' He swept his hand across the table, sending an imagined mess to the floor. 'If you find the Devil you must kill him quickly. I believe that is an old Russian saying. Hans can explain further.' Done with me. 'I know nothing of ovens.' He sat back. Looked at neither of us. Klein cleared his throat.

'You see the drawing, Ernst?'

I opened it out. Klein held it with me, leaned forward so that I could smell his cologne and his cigarette breath.

'This is a four-level oven design. It will require a major construction or adaptation. For Auschwitz first of all. You have a friend in Weimar who is a crematorist, yes? He will understand that when you have an oven,' he started to use his hands to visualise, 'if you put more bodies in the same oven they burn not as one, but as many. If it takes one hour to burn one unfortunate it takes four hours to burn four. No matter the fuel. That is just the rules. What we have here, what *you* have here, is a design that will revolutionise the process.'

We went through it together. Voss watching.

A brick-built oven. Still using coal. Single furnace. Four stations above the furnace, a single muffle. One door. One door in.

Beyond that door grates going downwards, angled, would convey the corpse to the next section and the next conveyor, and free the muffle for another corpse to enter and, when that was cleared, another would go in. And then another and another.

By the rollers under their backs the bodies would trundle down all four floors, being consumed all the while by the raging furnace below and, using their own bodies as fuel, the heat could be maintained. Reducing the demand for coal.

The burning bodies moving down each level would begin the cremation of the body that entered above and so on. One door in. One furnace at the bottom filled with ash and the fuel of the burning fat. One door out. Dozens, maybe hundreds an hour. The rules vanquished.

'They will be cremated by the motion of them, Ernst,' Klein said. One special unit at the top. One special unit at the bottom. They will not have to wait for the bodies to be cremated and removed before they can enter more. It will be a continuous oven. The only problem I conceive is one of blockage. But that is why it is on four levels. Each station will have a door accessible by ladder. One floor at the top, ground level, so no chutes, and then the furnace in the basement. All other access is by ladder. Make that clear.'

'Do you understand now, Ernst?' Voss said.

I took the draft, my draft, from Klein's hands and smiled. My possession.

'Yes, Senior-Colonel,' I said. 'I understand.' But not true. I understood the efficiency. But also understood what Paul had told me about all the ashes. About how he no longer received the urns with the clay plaques. One furnace. Ashes mixed. The ashes of a bonfire. An oven to consume hundreds a day. A conveyor belt of the dead producing a mass of limbs and torsos and heads with no memory reduced to a sludge. A slag pile of teeth sifted as if from a tremendous beast.

'Excellent,' Voss said. 'But you will need to visit Auschwitz to understand the scale of your work.' He stood, replaced his cap. His morning and lunch with the Topfs to come. My visit done. Checked off.

'We will arrange for yourself and Hans to visit Monday. At Auschwitz you can see the building for which it is intended. A surveyor will attend. If you see any problem with the plan you can discuss it with him.' A smile as he shook my hand. 'At least you will not need a coat, Ernst. Auschwitz is quite pleasant at this time.'

*

I had my tools from university, my portable set, and I could work on the kitchen table. The kitchen almost larger than our whole living-room in our old place and I would not get in Etta's way. So no matter that there was no desk or green lamp in a study with children at my feet. That would come. This work the first step to that. I had passed my studies in the shrunken rooms of my parents' house. A kitchen table was a plain in comparison.

'It is good to have you at home to work.' Etta touched my shoulder as she passed to fill a jug with water and lemon slices. 'I get lonely in this big house.'

'Or broody,' I said, not lifting my eyes from the paper. 'But I must have this done for Monday, Etta. I will stay in for the weekend.'

'Could you not join me in the garden for an hour today though? It is such a beautiful day. You have not been in the garden.'

'You mean you want me to work *on* the garden.'

'It is very overgrown. It could be so nice out there.

What are you working on anyway?' She came to my shoulder.

Show that plan to no-one.

But she would not understand it.

'It is for a new oven. For large abattoirs.' I drew my finger down the sliding levels. 'It works on a conveyor system. In at the top. Out at the bottom here. Much more fuel efficient and faster.'

'How is it faster?'

'You do not need to have to wait for one animal to be cremated before putting in the next. They burn as they move down each stage. The one below is fuel for the one above.'

She screwed her face. 'That sounds gruesome.'

'Everything more efficient usually is. That is all engineers do. Improve on the gruesomeness of the generation before.'

'You must finish this by Monday? Can you do that?'

One of our courses at university was to estimate work in advance and calculate your charge on hours taken to complete. I had done this the moment I had seen the patent.

'It is only eight hours' work in all. But my best work. So I am aiming for three o'clock Sunday. With annotations.'

She leaned by my ear, still looking. Covering it, hiding it would be unfaithful. There are husbands like that. Not I.

'This is not for the camps? Is it? Ernst?'

I took my hands away from it. Pushed it and the table away an inch. Just to make space to reach into my waistcoat for my cigarette pouch.

'It is an improvement. Over the current system. I am just drafting it, Etta. I have no say where it operates.'

She straightened, her hand off my shoulder. Put down her water jug.

'It is, isn't it? You're drafting this thing for corpses. Not for pigs. For hundreds of corpses. Aren't you?'

'The typhus, Etta. An epidemic. The old ovens can't cope.' Did not mention the colonel. His speech about the soldiers not returning home as brutes. That they did not want to shoot or hang people any more.

'You still believe this? That typhus is the reason? Or dysentery? Or criminals, or whatever it will be tomorrow.'

'What do you want me to believe? I work for a company that makes ovens. For use. What if I designed light bulbs for political prisons, would that be wrong? Am I to be out of a work for . . . for choosing what I am to work on? Do you think those lemons in your water are free? That's a day's wage for some.'

'Then lemons should not cost so much. Whose fault is that?'

She slammed down the jug. Went to the cupboard for some peanuts. Bird peanuts and crumbs. For pigeons in the park. A beggar on the street sold them for any coin given, for a paper bag of sweepings from the bars. Legal begging. Like the match-seller, or the shoelace man. No-one needed the half-empty match boxes or the frayed shoelaces plucked from the lost shoes of the ghetto, sold from an old cigar-box tied around the neck with string. You bought a licence to sell junk on the street, licence to beg. The way some people in the maps lived now. Most people ate the nuts themselves. Etta bought them for their original purpose.

She had made a table for the birds in the garden. Just a wicker tray on a post. I followed her out, apologised. Apologised for nothing. What was right in her was wrong in me. A man doesn't work if he does no wrong. I watched her as I smoked. Spoke across the garden. To ease. To be us again.

'You like feeding them, don't you? Even in spring. They can feed themselves in spring.'

She sprinkled the food.

'They've fed themselves for millions of years. I don't do it for that. It's like I'm God.' She closed the bag, stepped back from the tray, watched the finches twitch in the bushes, eye her suspiciously.

'I can watch them eat. Or I can leave. It doesn't matter that I'm here. They'll do the same. Hoard the food, fight over it, feed their families or just themselves. They'll never eat from my hand. When it's empty they might wonder where I am. Stand on the handle of the door. Tap on the window. They do that. Either way, whether I watch them or not, the outcome is the same. They eat whether I watch them or not. Impartial as God. And he is. Impartial. He has to be. Or none of this would happen.'

She smiled, as if in a mirror at her reflection, walked past me, put the bag to the cupboard and took up her jug. 'If I died tomorrow they would go somewhere else. Would not miss me. I don't do it for them.' Took her water and sat in the garden, her back to me. Watched the birds.

I went back to my work. Did not tell her I would be taking the design to Auschwitz. I would wait until she went shopping tomorrow, then tell her I had received a telephone call from Klein while she was out, that way it would only be one night for her to concern herself. Wives never understand we lie only to protect. All work, and all marriage, has little, little lies alongside huge truths. Every beautiful serene painting hides the noise and coarseness of hammer against nail behind its frame.

*

We had taken the exit for Klettbach. Klein could open up his super-six. Get rid of some frustration. He was not happy to be going to Poland, to the camp. He had expressed such before, preferred to allow Prüfer and the engineers such opportunity.

'We will luncheon in Dresden,' he said. 'Another two hours.' He had to shout over the engine's roar or he just wanted to shout at me for dragging him into this rupture from his country house. Eight o'clock he had picked me up, intending to get the work done at the camp before nightfall and then overnight in a hotel in the town. I had packed my bag with Etta cursing.

*

'Auschwitz now is it? What next? Berlin? For Christ's sake, Ernst!' She paced the bedroom. The sparse bedroom gilded by only her curtains stained with my tobacco.

'It is my job, Etta. What else can I do? Colonel Voss insisted.'

I did not tell her about the one leg. The conjured image of the comedic pirate not suited. Or the horrific one of a body without form below. A body that never had two legs. How could I give that image to my wife sleeping alone tonight?

Was it fact now or rumour still about the lorries of disabled and mentally affected in the basements of manse houses or never leaving the covered vans while the slow carbon monoxide came? How many other SS officers were there from the first war and this one with one leg or one arm, one eye, limps and stutters, metal plates over their skulls? Clearly not disabled enough.

'What else am I to do?' I repeated. 'What choice?'

She slammed the door. She had other bedrooms to sleep in now. Even if there were no beds in them.

*

Klein mellowed with the eating of the road by his Opel. He pointed to the towns as we sped.

'See, this is the problem, Ernst. We have so many cities, such a population. We do not have the land or resources to feed us all. It is the fault of the treaties forced upon us from the last war that has driven us.' He nodded to himself, approved his own words. 'It is only economics. A fellow wrote a book about it. The same year our leader's book came out. And the other sold more than his.'

'Sir?'

He rapped the wheel, rapped out his words.

'We need more land. The only way a race can expand is to expand its frontiers. Like the Americans, no? They displaced the Indians, the Mexicans, pushed the French and English up north to freeze. Everyone accepts that as history. Are we doing more? Wait until you see Poland. Endless fields. We could feed for a thousand years. We are at war over carrots and pigs. They want us to starve out of existence. So we turn the tables. We will starve them instead. No bullets. And then we will win. And it has always been about the east. Every war for a thousand years. It starts with the great cities but it always ends in the east. That is where the land is, the ports, the middle hub everyone wants. For trade. Oil. That is why the Jew chooses it as his promised land. No-one has ever wanted to trade with the West. All the world wants the East and where it leads. Everything is there. It is all there. Where civilisation comes from. That is where you conquer. The rifles will become shovels. You cannot farm Paris and the only oil is on their bread. The Russians want the same. They do not want to beat us. They want what we want. Thousands of years and the world has not changed. We are all following the emperors before us.'

I looked out the window. I had studied the wrong books. Goethe not a farmer. Klein's wing-tips clearly farm boots and I had only observed them wrong. His Opel a tractor. Or someone else was to till his fields and bring him his bounty. Who would that be? But this not a discussion for a junior draughtsman.

I could not wait to reach Dresden. One thing it is impossible to explain to the man who will drive hundreds of miles in his automobile rather than rub shoulders on a train is that at least a train has a convenience, an eating car that will sell you a tea or a soup. But then it would not be under his own power. His control. I still did not see the need to own a vehicle in a city other than for show.

I checked my old university satchel at my feet. Managed to pack a nightshirt and some bathroom things in it. Only one night. And then it hit me. Only one night for sure but it was the first night I had spent away from Etta since . . . since ever. Since we lived together. I had our telephone number pencilled on a ripped envelope in my wallet. I would call from Dresden.

The road became longer. Distant as I thought on Etta being alone, as I looked through the glass at the infinity of the lane stretching to the horizon of mountains. And an infinity of it already behind me. Taking me further away from her. From our locked door. The anxieties I thought gone with the security of my first salary back in a rush of blood to my ears. To be paid meant trust, meant security.

Going to Auschwitz. And securing me away from Etta. Alone for one day and one night. Klein dreaming of planting potatoes in Ukraine for Germany. Me enclosed in his car. Never more than inches from him.

Chapter 19

This was not the Dresden I imagined. It was how I envisioned Paris to be. Grand stone buildings of several storeys, turrets and spires. We drove through the square and under an arch with a leaded glass passage above us joining what seemed likc palaces together. Saxony defined. A colony of kings and princes making even Weimar seem young and modern.

Klein parked the Opel past the glass passage, outside one of the palaces.

'Luncheon,' he said and opened and closed the door behind him before the word was finished. I stepped out, carried my coat and hat. Klein left his raincoat and he did not wear a hat which was unusual to me. Even the swing-kids wore hats; although with their brims the wind was fond of them. I suppose Klein's was a fashion I was not aware of. He always looked likc he was in a ballroom simply waiting for a lucky girl to blush at him.

He did not wait for me, and my back was crippled from sitting so long. I stretched, which did nothing to ease and waddled after him like an old man, an old man from the Merchants' Bridge.

The courtyard full of tables under parasols and despite the mottled cold sky there were those I should call sophisticated sitting there with waiters flowing between them. Coiffured courtiers laughing and gossiping and eating salads from small plates. I looked as elegant as a postman as I hobbled past.

Klein was in the centre of the lobby when I entered. He lit a cigarette from a silver pocket lighter and blew a plume of blue and judged a palace.

I saw the three wooden boxes of telephone booths.

'Herr Klein,' I said when I reached his shoulder. 'I must telephone my wife. I will be a moment.'

'Nonsense. They have a Parisian bistro here and we are early for a seat. We cannot waste time or they will be gone. Come.' He took my arm. I resisted just enough. For politeness.

'I must call, sir,' I said. 'I promised I would.' His hand moved to my back to usher me on and I took a step away, his hand off me. 'Go ahead, sir.' I faked embarrassment. 'You know wives and their worry.'

'I am gladdened that I do not, Ernst.' He patted me to the telephones. 'Go. Go ring the little woman. I starve. I will get us a table.'

I watched him leave. I should have said that I needed to use the convenience, which was true and would have needed less debate, but I did not think of it. Etta my only thought.

I closed the concertina glass door of the booth, picked up the receiver and took the number from my wallet. The operator came on before I had unfolded the number.

'What number caller?' The female voice urgent, like our past landlady at the wrong end of the month.

'One moment.' I gripped the lump of receiver to neck and shoulder, opened the number only to find the last two figures smudged and blurred from the sweaty cheapness of my wallet. I had never telephoned it before. Did not know it to recall. I had taken it down hurriedly. One of those last-minute things you do when your manager's car is honking outside your window and your wife asks you to telephone her when you can. And we had never called each other before. Our calls were across market squares. From balconies. This a new communication of love to me.

'Erfurt,' I said to the Bakelite. I almost said, 'Etta,' as if that would be enough. I had never had my own number to call before. This was probably the second time I had ever used a pay telephone in my life. Just holding the thing made me nervous.

'I think it is 4703. Or 4708. Or it could be 4768. I cannot read it very well.' I fumbled for change and put it on the tin tray. I had two coins. Because I am a fool.

'Please deposit two pfennigs, caller.'

I had a five and a one. I put in the five. There was a ratcheting noise in my ear.

'What number, caller?'

'I am not sure. If I get it wrong can I make another call? I have put in five.'

'Please, what number, caller?' This woman I could not see was in a room miles from me. A bank of red and white tabs and switches distanced us and she did this for hours a day, hundreds of times a day. I was not even a voice to her. A sound in her headphones. My being a twist of wire and a plug. A red flag in a bank of others that indicated a call. My tremulous voice only that.

I closed my eyes. Pictured my hand writing the number from the dial of our shiny telephone on the little table. I discarded my coat and hat to the black and white tiled floor of the booth.

'Erfurt, 4703, please.'

'Thank you, caller.'

The telephone hummed, electricity in my ear, then what I hoped were the clicks of success. I waited. Watched the lobby empty and fill again. Klein appeared in the corner through the throng, studied me with two puffs of his cigarette, one hand resting in his jacket. I jerked a smile to him, rolled my eyes to signify the problems of all married men and he turned, vanished among the suits and polka-dot dresses. Then the wrong voice came.

'There is no answer, caller.'

'Can I try another number?'

'Please deposit two pfennigs, caller.'

'I have put in five. Can I not make another call? I may have the wrong number. Can I try again?'

'Please deposit two pfennigs, caller.'

'Can you try Erfurt 4708, please? I am sure that is the number.'

'I am sorry, caller, you must deposit two pfennigs to make another call.'

'But I did not get through! Please, operator. I am trying to call my wife. In Erfurt. I am in Dresden. I do not have any more coins. I have a one and have put in a five. If I put the one in can I try again?'

'I am sorry, caller. You must deposit two pfennigs to make another call.'

'But I have not made a call! Can I try another number, please. It is important that I speak to my wife. Please. I have put in five!'

'It is two pfennigs to call, caller.' Like a crow now, with the repetition of the sounds.

'Two, to, kaw, kawller.'

'Thank you, caller,' she said, another red flag in front of her I imagined, and her world clicked and left me. Etta never there. Hundreds of miles away down a wire and never there. I put the bony receiver back, hoping that the return well would grant me change. I heard my coin rattle down and a bell chime in the machine's heart and I fingered the giggling drawer looking for a prize, like we all do. Nothing.

*

'I have ordered for you,' Klein said when I found him in the crowded bistro. The room was trying to look simple inside its palatial walls. Square tables with blue or red gingham tablecloths laid out like a chessboard. Us on a red one, our dining partners on a blue. Klein in the centre of the room like a raking bishop chess-piece in middle-game. He did not ask me about my telephone call.

'I have ordered you something I am sure you have never eaten. The most expensive bill of fare. If a man does not have an expense account by the time he is thirty or his income does not exceed the first digits of his age in hundreds he is not a man, Ernst. My father taught me that. So we eat on Topf's dollar.'

I said nothing. Water on the table and I drank. Dry from the road and the exasperation of the telephone booth. Klein tapped another cigarette on his engraved case. This supposedly settles the tobacco. I had seen Bogart do it. He did not offer me and lit up as if I was not there. Smokers often do this. Drop out of the world while they concentrate on their ritual. And it gives us time to think. The smoke in my face. The lighter placed on his case matching perfectly the silver tableware beside it. I could afford my own pack now but had become so used to the art and satisfaction of rolling cigarettes. But still I could not do it so comfortably in company.

'This oven design could be revolutionary for Topf. We could all be rich. Richer. The first genuine twenty-four-hour cremation oven. It is like inventing the automobile all over again. Your friend in Weimar would be most interested.'

'I do not think he could accommodate something that needs such height, sir. I thought this oven was designed only for the camps?'

Klein dragged long on his cigarette, his eyes left and right of him.

'You are in public, Ernst. No business in public. Please.'

'My apologies, Herr Klein.' Fool. Idiot.

'No. You are still learning. My mistake. I should have told you beforehand.'

I noticed that every time he admonished me it would always be given as an apology. My fault was his error. His error in not teaching me better. And I realised how very easily he had set me as his pupil when the position of professor was not given. But now that I had realised it, the trick of it, his power waned. No matter how expensive his cigarette lighter, the shine of his cuff-links. The tail-coated magician on the stage just a box of tricks beneath a false-bottomed table. He rested his elbows on the gingham, smoked faster.

'You know it is only the degenerate races that contract the typhus? You do not see their guards or the officers getting sick. It is their weakness that belies them. And we are providing a service to dispose of this problem that their race has created.' He waved his cigarette hand as if all of this was a past historical event, an act of Genghis Khan, that no longer mattered.

I mirrored his pose. His trick.

'You told me that Jews do not allow cremation. My friend, my crematorist friend, and his colleagues have almost become sanctified. Cremation is a religious process now. But not one for Jews. They are for the same process?'

'They do not allow tattoos either. As I told you: the body must be returned as given. At Auschwitz the prisoners have their number inked. Tattooed on their arms.'

'They *tattoo* them?' He did not acknowledge the shock in my voice.

'Only at Auschwitz. It used to be on their chest but the arm hurts less. And the ink is their own fault. They gave them numbers on their clothes but the Jews would take the clothes from their own dead to wear for themselves. It messed up the records. That is how much respect they have for each other. Robbing the dead for one more shirt. They complain that they cannot have tattoos. They cannot be cremated. Even in prison *they* need to be special. So they get marked and cremated anyway. That makes them realise they are not so special. One country has finally said "no" to them. Displacing Poles and Roma is not the same. The Jew is the immigrant of the world. They're not even Semites. They have stolen even that. What rights do you give a people without a country? They trade passports and daughters like cards. For profit. Each one of them has more than one passport. No sovereignty. What pride is there in that? They marry German women to gain our lands.' He sat taller. 'Let me tell you how a Jew works, *Ernst*.' My name ground out like pepper.

'A Jew enters a golf club. He begs to join and the owner concedes because the Jew offers two years of membership upfront. For a year the Jew attends. Plays a little, eats a lot. Slowly more Jews join. Recommended by their friend and gradually they become the majority. Other members leave because they cannot get the best times, and evenings in the clubhouse are taken over with mitzvahs. After a time the owner cannot attract new members and has lost too many of his old. This is because the Jew knows how unpopular his race is. He takes advantage of it. To turn good neighbourhoods into ghettoes and crowd in his own renters living like rats. He does not care what hovels his own people live in.'

His stub had gone out, rare for him to let it so and he tutted at himself and immediately lit another.

'So the Jew, and his friends – they never do anything alone – make an offer to the owner to buy the club, at a reduced price naturally now that the club has become unpopular. And the owner buckles and sells. And the golf club goes. And a ghetto comes up. And more Jews come in. Not fine houses. Slums. Did you ever hear of a Jew building a mansion? That is their way. That is what Europe has become. That is how it was done.'

'That does not sound good economic theory, sir.' I smiled, but only to be polite. We were businessmen at lunch. You could say such things out of hours; sure that was the way. I went to put my napkin to my lap but paused; still needed to relieve myself. 'I studied economics.'

'Ah, yes. Erfurt University. Theory. But I was a member of that golf club, Ernst.' He sipped his water. 'Not theory. Remember, Ernst, we are only making ovens. As Topf has ever done. Should the man who makes the clock decide which wall it hangs? We are only pushing and pissing paper. To make profit. We eat here today because of it. Supply and demand. I am sure that was day-one economics at Erfurt University was it not? Where are you going?'

I had started to rise.

'I need to use the bathroom, Herr Klein. Excuse me.'

'Do not excuse yourself to another man, Ernst. Only when there are ladies present. The napkin goes on the table and you stand up.'

'Yes, sir.' And I did just that. And left him. Talk of new ovens not appropriate in the Paris bistro of the Taschenberg Palais. The Jewish 'problem' apparently natural for discourse.

There was a man in the facilities better dressed than I. He was by the door and greeted me as I entered and pretended not to hear me in the stall. After I had washed he gave me a towel and sprayed me with a cologne without asking and I flinched as if he was striking me. He pretended not to notice. I was still thinking of tattoos.

I gave him my last coin. The coin I could not use to dial my wife. He stroked my collar ineffectually, dusting me with a camel-hair brush. I had notes in my wallet, but you cannot make a telephone call with those or tip a cloakroom attendant. I had a hotel to get to. Did not know what money I would need for that. I had never stayed in one before.

The food was at the table when I returned. A good sight for the starving traveller.

'Speciality of the bistro, Ernst,' Klein said. '*Angemachetes Rindertatar.* Eight marks. That is expenses for you.'

I could eat on eight marks for a week.

'Fried cut potatoes also,' he said. 'The Belgians can do something right. Enjoy.'

I copied him and took up my fork only. But it did look as if one should eat it in the hand it was that small. A potato cake above and below. A fat pink meat between. I scooped a little, as he did, and it came away like ice-cream as I now know that expensive food does. It pulls away and melts. That is how you know it costs eight marks.

When I took it in my mouth my instinct was to spit. It was raw. The meat raw. If my mother had served me such I would have called a doctor for her. Klein watched me as he chewed. He wanted my surprise. Wanted my reaction. I swallowed without giving him such.

'You have ate tartare before?'

'No,' I said, and cut another piece. 'It is good. Thank you.'

He chewed hard. His eyes to his plate. I could tell he was disappointed with my reaction. He had a lesson primed no doubt. A lesson for my ignorance.

'I hope that you do not mind that we have no wine. Topf's expenses will only stretch so far. And the beer is terrible here.'

This remark, about the beer, as so many of his, dropped,

slapped to my face to show his familiarity with a world larger than mine. But I had begun to take his measure. I had university in my past and from his lack of boasting on the subject and his irksomeness of mine I suspected he did not. No wife. He spoke of cars with the same devotion. He talked of Martinis at his country home as if my having a wife prevented me from doing so. I began to think that he was lonely, or, if that word was too strong, a man who did not understand that he was lonely, or the perception of it. A man not aware that he had missed something and defended it with lessons to impart his superiority. Everything *you* had done in your life was foolish. You were still in short trousers if you did not have a black Opel.

'Do not eat it all, Ernst,' he said. 'Only peasants lick their plates.' He put his fork down. Waited for me to do the same. 'We have four hours to the camp. We should go.' He snapped his fingers for the bill. I kept eating, as unpleasant as it was. His mouth down-turned at the scrape of my plate.

He got his receipt and waited impatiently for my hat and coat.

'That is why you leave them in the car,' he said. 'You need a vehicle, Ernst. You will gather these things eventually.'

It was only as we left Dresden that he asked me about the telephone. I sighed my frustration at not having got through. Relayed the whole débâcle to him.

The charger of his engine growled with his first stroke into its last gear as the road opened.

'You could have asked the desk, the reception, to make the call. They would have done it for free. You should have asked me. I know the number. How else would I call you if I needed you?'

I wanted to slam the dashboard in front of me. Scream at him for not telling me so. But this was still my boss, the head of my floor, the director of the Special Ovens Department.

I laughed instead, because it was not what he expected me to do at his great reveal. I spent four hours looking out the window at a country that had become Germany while I was at university. The road signs still in Polish. The call to Etta would wait until I was at the hotel. Klein did not volunteer the number as we drove. He would hold that back. A gleam of power until I said 'please' and 'thank you' to him for giving me my own number that I was too childish to know myself. I could have taken out pencil and paper and asked directly but I did not want to show him my concern. It had waited three hours. It could wait four more even if Etta was looking at the clock wondering and worrying. And if I did not press he had no hold over me. He might stew on it. On the fact that I did not seem to care. He could feed me with gems or breadcrumbs as he saw fit, as I now knew he did to all. But if I did not trouble with what or when he chose to divulge I was confident he would drain like a battery lantern. And I would glow the better. At least to myself.

Chapter 20

I had said it often without thinking of it. Auschwitz and Birkenau almost a city combined, divided by a railway. I did not comprehend until I saw it for myself.

We did not know the scale. People must forever understand this. We did not know. This was Poland. Another country. A prison larger than Erfurt. And what I could not see Klein mapped out to me.

'You will never see it all, Ernst. It would probably take two days to take it in. They demolished a town to build it. Right here by the river. They have water. A coal mine near. Just this month they have completed the railway spur from the mainline. Before that they had to use lorries. Wagons. Very inhumane so they built a railway spur instead. The deportations exchange at the main station. From the whole empire. Then here. They can now process much faster. From train to ramp and in they go.'

And in we went.

*

We were checked twice. Once outside the redbrick edifice, from Klein's car window, as at Buchenwald, and then after we had parked the car at the Birkenau block supervisor's office. None of this area looked like a prison. It was acres of office buildings just like the Topf factory. Street signs to direct. Our oven was destined for Birkenau, for Auschwitz II, as it was designated. That was where it was needed. I never saw a prisoner. Just the brick or wooden barracks. It was as silent as a prison should be imagined. The only noise came from the endless parade of secretaries and officers from building to building. I heard no howls or screams or the rattle of chains, if chains there were. It felt safe. Assured. I had not known what to expect after the mud and bleakness of Buchenwald. I left my coat and hat, my jacket also, in the car. You could not see any difference from myself and Klein in our shirtsleeves. Only my worn satchel and his smart black briefcase distinguishing.

We were walked to the Construction Board by a young secretary along toy-town paths. Birkenau had seven SS departments. An administration as complex as any city and probably as corrupt. Klein nodded to several faces. I do not think he would have known them given his reluctance for such a journey. It was just his way.

Our Party pins on our ties. Mine, not being a member, meaningless as a child's tin sheriff badge. It was past three o'clock. My early lunch of small raw steak empty in me now and I eyed the beef sandwich on the major's desk in the Construction Board with envy.

Klein put out his hand first. Introduced himself and I, but confused by the face behind the desk.

'Major Bischoff is no longer here, Major . . . ?'

'Norin, Herr Klein. Major Norin. Major Bischoff left us just this month. He has been rewarded well for the creation of the second camp. He built it from nothing except the drains of the old town. I am pleased to assist Topf and Sons in our new endeavours. Please be seated, gentlemen.'

'It would be better for us to get on, Major. We do not want to take up your valuable time. If you could just introduce us to the surveyor and where the oven is to be installed. We would not wish to impede on yourself or your staff.'

The major approved this attitude. I could have told him that Klein was only thinking of the room service and bath in his hotel.

'You have the plan?' he asked.

Klein snapped his fingers at me. I handed it over from my bag and the major held it in both hands. Ogled it.

'How tall is this thing?'

'Ernst?' Klein to me.

'It has four levels. But it will require only a two-storey building, Major.'

'We do not have time to build another structure,' this said to Klein. 'It is to fit into the current oven area. Dig below if needed. But I would rather that the triple ovens are not taken out of operation.'

Klein did not hesitate. 'We will not interfere unduly I am sure, Major.'

The major content with this.

'I am told such an oven, based on our current rate, could consume over four thousand on a twenty-four-hour shift.'

'That is paper figures, Major,' Klein said. 'I am afraid that Berlin's estimations have always worked on the basis that an oven can work all day and night. That is why we have to repair them so often. They are overworked by inexperienced men. Accountants' figures are always gleefully given. I am sure you have experienced the actuality, Major.'

The major laughed. 'Quite so! Quite so! Every morning a man with a sooty face tells me so! Is there a way to overcome the repairs?'

'Gas, Major. We should have always gone with gas. But that is accountants for you also. If we converted your ovens now it would cost one hundred and forty thousand marks, even with the other contractors of the SS's help. So coke it is. Even so you are looking at sixty-five thousand marks. But this oven advantages that the consumption of coke will be reduced. It relies on the bodies themselves for fuel.'

'I have heard this. It is true?'

Klein took back the plan with a bow.

'I am the head of the Special Ovens Department, Major. If I present myself at Auschwitz that is even greater than my word.'

The major shook his hand again.

'You will find Koller, the surveyor, at the railway. That

is where the oven will be. Beyond the processing area. Straight off the train.'

'My assistant will attend, Major.' The plan passed back to my hands, passed from behind. Never looked at me. 'I should take a seat. I have been travelling all day. Ernst?' He sat opposite the major. 'I am exhausted.' He took out his cigarette case and offered it to the major. 'Go back to the railway and main gate. See Koller. I will discuss with Major Norin. Meet me back here.'

I bowed and left, had only spoken once. I had drawn that plan. What went into the oven and what came out nothing to do with my pencil, should not be my concern. My work. But I had heard the figure of sixty-five thousand marks. And the other one. The other figure. The one that related to the fuel for the new oven. *Over four thousand on a twenty-four-hour shift*, the major had said. I did not want to calculate what I was being paid for by the hour. On such a figure. By the hour, by my pencilled lines. I walked to the railway.

*

'Herr Koller?' I asked. My hand out. But who else could it be? Every other body in grey with club or rifle or ragged cloth and cap with hoe or paintbrush.

'Steven,' he said, shaking my hand. 'Call me Steven.'

'Ernst. Ernst Beck.' We were between the train 'station' and the brick of the pediment and long wall of the main entrance. The smoking chimneys from the ovens beyond this wall above all. Plain as a bakery.

'Are you new?' Koller asked. 'I usually only see Messing and Koch here.'

He was a short man, his hair wiry, untidy. Glasses like all surveyors. He held my hand as we stepped over the tracks. Leading me like a boy with a secret.

'I have been with Topf for two months. We are installing new ovens. And a newly designed one.'

'I know. Prüfer and Sander spent the weekend here. It must be important. Although I cannot see what a new oven here will accomplish.' He breathed deep and looked about. 'A bird has only enough feathers as it needs. You would think forty ovens would be enough. Maybe fifty. I do not know. I've not seen them all. Twenty percent of the whole camp is devoted to them. They have more of them than water tanks. Show me this plan. Inside.'

We moved to the processing antechamber, right inside the archway where the short walk from the train cars ended. No door was locked. There were chairs and desks for the invisible secretaries and a table large enough for us to use. Koller unfolded my paper and spread it on the table.

'At present the train comes in and the processing is done here. Through the opposite door, in the arch, all the belongings go for searching and confiscation. A pile of suitcases to the left. The "relocated" to the right.'

I looked about the room. There were no inkwells, no typewriters on the desks. Shelves which should hold paperwork and box-folders empty. Empty water jugs. Cobwebs on them. Koller went on.

'It is intended that this new oven can be installed beside the current triple muffles. The ovens are beyond here. The new train tracks are designed so that three cars can come in and the prisoners are taken straight to the delousing chambers and the ovens are in the same place. This ensures that the infection is quarantined to this area only. Ovens inside the camp would be futile. To move the infected and dead through the camp futile. The SS have finally made efforts to contain.' He stood back from the plan. 'I am not seeing how this oven would not require a new building. But there is no time for that. So we are told.'

'No time?'

He folded up the plan.

'War, Ernst. The war is not about building now. Bischoff left this month. He built this place. Himmler imagines this city to become a true city. An actual place for people to live. For fine people. After the war. I have seen the plans.' He looked around as if he could not see such a dream happening.

'Come. I will show you where this is supposed to be constructed. I cannot take you into the actual building. Just the outside.'

'Why not?'

'It is in use. All the time. Until the brick fails. As it always does. Only the SS and the special commandos are permitted near.' He pointed to my tie-pin. 'You might get closer. If

you wished. I forgot mine. No-one seems to care I find.'
He smiled. 'But you never know.'

We walked to the crematoria. Four of them. The heat
already felt from a hundred yards away. One of them
closed and undergoing the reconstruction I had drawn
previously. A workforce digging out the ground for
the concrete steps. I had not mentioned to Prüfer that
the plans had no chutes. Koller informed me that one by
one all the crematoria would be adapted so. To delouse
and to cremate in the same place. To keep the typhus and
its lice from walking through the camp.

'But there's a new urgency now, Ernst.' We walked on.
To the last building. 'You know Hoss? He was the comman-
dant here three years ago. He came back last week. That
is an SS you do not want to have look at you unfavourably.'
He lowered his voice. 'He learnt his trade in the East.' East.
A word for Hell in wartime. 'Your oven is part of his remit.'

'Remit?'

He breathed deep, studied me.

'I am only a surveyor, Ernst. And I talk too much.' He
indicated the brickwork of the last building in the block.
'I think this building is appropriate for your oven.'

I saw the black seeping into the mortar.

'Christ! The whole thing is burning!'

'They all are. I do not think there is enough time to
build an extension. But it will need another floor below.
This one is the best grounded. But that should still take
two weeks. And no-one will be happy about that. They pull

their figures out of their arses. By the time they replace all the old ovens this thing must be operational. It must be working by July. Topf has fifty-six days I'm told.'

'That is impossible,' I said, and looked at the small area with my architect's eye. From paper to brick. But no trees to be cleared. The ground good and level. You could toe into the foundations of the crematoria beside it. But still . . .

'Impossible to not build another structure,' I said.

Koller passed me his tape. 'The SS do not understand that word. You should have gathered so in your two months. I have listened to them for years. They expect and deliver miracles. Infinite labour. No unions. Nothing has been impossible to them. They can think of a dam and it will be up next week. As long as they don't have to pay for it.'

We set to work. No guard or officer questioned. Two men in white shirts and suit trousers with measure and notepads. Unquestioned. In a prison. There were two lorries waiting along the path. Covered and guarded at the sides, rifles all around them, their drivers watching us.

'What are they doing?'

'Waiting for us to leave,' he said.

'So am I.'

He laughed. Agreed.

'Do not look at them. They wait for eyes to look at them.'

We were done. Nothing pegged into the ground. All on paper. The manual work would be for Prüfer and his men.

'Do you smoke, Herr Koller? Steven?'

He did not, told me to go to the railway. The SS did not approve of smoking he reminded. Major Norin had smoked Klein's Camels with him in his office. Lawmakers' immunity.

'I must wait here for an officer,' he said. 'Lucky me.'

He called me as I left.

'Ask your boss about the fifty-six days, Ernst. Then you will understand what I said about pulling these figures out of their arses. Fifty-six days.'

He waved me away. Not in a friendly manner, dismissive, and I thought on that wave as I rolled my cigarette.

I was in braces and white rolled sleeves. A warm day. A wave of heat shimmering above the smoking chimneys. I followed the rail spur, smoking contemplatively as tobacco sometimes permits. My head light, thoughts like a poet's. The best cigarettes. Those when you are alone and walking slow, looked to the sound of a train coming in to the camp. A diesel engine pulling cattle trucks not carriages. I could see the driver. Not a man in army uniform. Just a regular train driver. A man doing his job. Like all of us. I could feel the ground shake with the approach. Koller had said the station was made for three trucks. There were seven.

Guards were running from behind me, as if the train had caught them by surprise.

I could hear the jangle of the straps of their rifles in unison, so not running. A quick march. The train not a surprise. Scheduled.

I had not noticed the dogs until they barked. No rifles for the men restraining the dogs. They had clubs like table legs. I smoked and watched. I knew this was something rare. Again, Ernst Beck, experiencing something rare, as in Prüfer's office when Voss had explained. Told me how important my work was to the SS. Rare sights now becoming common to a man who had never left Germany. Now standing in the field of a prison camp in Poland. No. In Germany.

The yelling of the guards and the barking of the dogs as the doors of the cars rolled open brought goose-flesh on my bare arms and I brushed them. Ash rose from my skin. Not from my cigarette.

I had come closer without noticing. All of the soldiers were moving. Not one of them guarding, rifles on shoulders. They were all pulling people from the trucks, from both sides, barking with the dogs. Headscarfed old women trying to get down gracefully. Children in coats and caps too big for them, their father's clothes, the men in vests and braces and shirts like myself. The only sounds above the shouts and the dogs were the children's cries until their mothers covered them into their coats.

They were marched down the platform or dragged and barged if they were too slow or weak. My poet's smoking respite broken with the curses and the straining dogs leaping at children's arms. Children that had once known dogs as pets.

I saw a girl fall, her mother or aunt pushed along away from her screams. Their hands reaching, mouths wide, and then the girl's pleading arms crushed by bodies walking over, being pushed over her.

I threw my cigarette, left my bag, yelled as I ran. Was running without thinking. Was running at guns. I could not see her any more with the press of them. I ran at the image of her fall.

A young man with shorn hair picked her up at the same time I reached her. We checked her together. She beat at us, her face dirty and damp, her eyes closed. He spoke to her in their language and thanked me I thought, but he pushed me away gently, took her with him.

I was in the midst of them when I stood. I tried to push back, back to the side, but they were too close together. I looked behind for a guard, saw the suitcases being piled up from the train. I had got in the crowd without resistance but now only saw the helmets and the clubs all along the mass. The mass of us.

I yelled at the nearest helmet, clawed toward him, held up my tie with the pin. He heaved my chin back into them. I was carried. In the current. The current that would break only past the arch.

I fought but they pushed me along, the prisoners pushed me along. And I saw the arch of the redbrick building loom. Looming like a cathedral door. I was going in. My identification back in my jacket, back in the car.

I kicked at the dirt, back-pedalling and knocking heads with my elbows but still the arch came on. I was a man in an ashen shirt and braces like hundreds of others. And there were hundreds of others. And me in the middle of them. The arched mouth yawned above me.

'Wait!' I yelled. 'I am not a prisoner!' I pushed myself up on an old man's shoulders. 'I am not a prisoner! My name is Ernst—' My body dragged down. By the motion of them. My voice drowned by barking dogs and spittle-covered cursing, the clubs swinging at backs and heads and I ducked like all the rest. We moved each other. Impossible to stop the swell. Those at the back pressing us together by rifles pressing them until we were no longer even walking. We carried each other in.

I elbowed more, kicked more, and then I saw a group of peaked caps, of officers to our right nodding at clipboards. I saw a face I knew. Captain Schwarz. One of them was Captain Schwarz from Buchenwald I was sure. Hoped I was sure. The captain who had given me a lift. A lift home. Weeks ago. He may not know me at all.

I punched now. Struck out at eyes and faces without seeing them and hurled myself over the wave of bodies to reach his earshot. I would ignore the guards at the sides. Hoped my German would carry. No-one else was calling to an SS officer. I would be noticed. Or I would be shot. But I did not think of that. Panic was all I had. A bullet beyond concern.

'Captain Schwarz!' I bellowed. 'Captain Schwarz! It is Ernst Beck! From Erfurt! From Topf! From Topf! Help me!'

I repeated this call again and again as his group went past, as we travelled on and I swam and pleaded out of the sea.

His shoulder finally turned. He seemed to sniff the air.

Left and right to his name called in such a place. Oddly his first instinct was to smile and wave in recognition and I did the same, as if we were only acknowledging each other across a crowded dinner ball. Then he saw, realised.

And an SS officer was running to me.

Rifles separated the crowd, miraculously, impossibly halted, and Schwarz cursed at the guards and dragged me as if from quicksand and I was on the grass. The cool grass. I sprawled out on it thankfully, tugged at it. He knelt beside me, his leather boots creaking at my ear. A smile as he patted my shoulder.

'So,' he said. 'A rum thing, no? A close thing. We almost lost you there, Herr Beck, didn't we?'

He rolled me to sit. I could not speak for catching air. I watched the crowd move on through the arch. Turned away from their stares.

'Thank you, Captain,' I said. 'Thank you. It was a mistake.'

'It very nearly was, Ernst. You are lucky I was here today. I am only taking numbers. I visit all the camps. What would Topf have said to me about this, eh?'

He patted me again, laughed, stood and left me sitting, returned to his fellow officers.

The track empty now. The train withdrawing. The gates under the arch closed. The guards gone. Only the suitcases remained. Piled in a pyramid behind.

I stayed sat. Made and lit another cigarette. It took three attempts. Tobacco collecting in my trouser-cuffs as I trembled. Fingers bruised and shaking. These are the worst cigarettes. When they are most needed. To try and return to normality. For that is the trick about smoking. The confidence trick. A smoker is only trying to feel how a non-smoker does all the time. To return to clarity. I clawed my hands through my hair. Stopped as I heard Schwarz and his officers' laughs as he explained about the young man sitting on the grass. I kept my back to them. Smoked as I watched the train pull away. The driver watched *me* this time. With my different cigarette. A pooling of cold sweat on my back.

Chapter 21

I made my way back to the car. Slowly. Eventually. I headed there rather than the office with the laughter and the smoking and the brandy that I imagined happened between men like Klein and SS officers. I smoked and waited. Kept my eyes low to the pleat skirts carrying clipboards, and the uniforms carrying their arrogance and scorn aimed to young men not at the front. I lit up again and Klein appeared the way trams do when you light up waiting for them, and the cigarette goes beneath your foot.

'Ernst,' Klein put his briefcase to the roof, 'you were to come to the office when you were done. I waited.' He looked over the sweat and ash on me. 'Are you all right?' My face of a pallor for interest.

'I'm fine, sir.' I opened my door. He raised a palm.

'No, no, Ernst,' he said. 'You are not to come with me now. I have decided with our time constraints you should stay here longer and set to work. Major Norin has an office and a desk for you. You can make a copy of the plan for him. So it does not have to go back and forth.' He cursed at his briefcase, slapped dust from it and his shirt. 'Damn this ash! It gets everywhere. Worse than sand at a beach.'

I held onto the door. 'What time will you come back for me, sir? For the hotel?'

He tossed the briefcase to the passenger seat.

'Topf's expenses do not stretch to multiple hotel rooms, Ernst. I have arranged with the major for you to spend the night here. A guards' barracks. A cot in their kitchen. You will be quite safe.' He was in the car, reached across to take the door from me and looked up. 'I will pick you up in the morning. You will probably eat better than I!' He pulled the door closed from my hand, the starter motor growling instantly. I rapped on the glass. His arm across and the window rolled down an inch. I put my head to the gap.

'But I must call my wife, sir. Can I use one of the camp telephones?'

'They are secured lines, Ernst. I doubt the SS allow personal calls. You can ask the major if you want, if you wish. That is what I would do. If you were me.'

If you were me. Not, 'If I were you.' Even in his advice he would be the centre. He looked to the path ahead.

'I will tell you what. I will call her myself and explain for you. It is no trouble. Will you let me do that, Ernst?' He rolled up the window before I could reply, took off, and I had to step back from the spinning rear wheel.

I still did not have the telephone number for my own house. Etta watching the black object. The silent machine. Mocking her concern with its inaction, its dust. Etta taken from her garden to wait to hear her husband's voice. The sun setting as she fretted. No neighbours' noise to distract her silence. No neighbours. Alone. Klein's car a cloud of dust already.

The telephone number in his wallet, not mine.

Alone. The bag by my feet my only piece of home. I thought of all the suitcases piled outside the camp. I bent and salvaged the crushed cigarette from the sand and ash. Klein had not even passed me my jacket with my wallet and worker's pass. My hands still trembled as I lit up again.

I was set. By him.

To a night in Birkenau.

*

Major Norin was generous with his coffee over the afternoon. I was at least grateful for that. He looked over my shoulder at my copying of the plan and nodded to my answers to his questions with a practised sagacity. The sun was setting in the one window of his antechamber and I was still nibbling at the doorstep tuna sandwich one of his secretaries had made for me. She had put pepper in it. Something local to her I assumed.

The late afternoon and the loosening of ties that comes with it and the major's endless questioning of the plan made me feel confident that I could raise the subject that the surveyor suggested. Fifty-six days. Fifty-six days to have all the ovens converted and the new one, the continuous one, functional. I put down my pen.

'Why such a hurry for all this, Major? If I may ask? The surveyor said something about fifty-six days?'

'Hmm? Oh, yes. You do not know? Prüfer should have told you. If you are to work on it.'

'I have not been at the office for a while.' Not untrue. A small lie. A 'while' is subjective. I had not seen Klein for a 'while' so what harm?

'Our scale of work has increased. Or is it work of scale? Never mind. It is simple politics, Herr Beck. The Hungarian ministry fears a Soviet invasion, as Italy did, and so wishes to turn to the enemy as did the Italian cowards. It has become imperative for that not to happen and to remove the Jewish influence. We have installed our own rule in Hungary. The deportations have started to arrive.'

'I saw the train today,' I said. 'I had wondered on the language I heard.'

He laughed.

'Quite so! You remember when you walked into *their* shops and they spoke in tongue around you to each other? You would pass them in the street and they would not tip "Good morning" to you. But now you see how rats squeal when they are cornered, eh? That is the urgency.'

I could only think of the Jewish businessman who had employed my father when no-one else would. I looked up at Major Norin from my stool and he pitied my lack of understanding.

'In fifty-six days we will transport over four hundred and thirty thousand Hungarian Jews.' He studied the four-level oven with the conveyers and furnace that would never go out. 'We cannot fit them all in here, Ernst. In the camp.' He took a bite from my sandwich, spoke as he chewed. 'And imagine Poland with millions of Jews? We would almost be giving them their own country after the war. What would we have achieved then, eh?'

I picked up my pen and pencil, put them away with my rule.

'I have finished, Major,' I said.

Chapter 22

I approached the guards' barracks as one could only do, probably as a civilian should only do. Heavily. Low in heart. These were soldiers not at the front. Had probably experienced worse for being here. Voss had told how Himmler worried about the soldiers of the camps becoming brutes, becoming monsters. And I would be their age. And not in uniform. I had begun to realise that regardless of race the man in the suit was despised by the soldier in war. I raised my fist to knock and then lowered it. I imagined Klein. What Klein would do. These men did not know me. I would wear Klein's impenetrable coat, his shield and manner. The millionaire in the sewer. I opened the door and strode in. My bold entrance lost. The barracks empty. Klein's shield to the floor.

Beds. Triple and double bunks. All as narrow as coffins. They were not neat or made. I had expected them to be immaculate, to be able to bounce a coin off their starched surface. But not so. It was a room where children lived. Two sinks, face-cloths laying in them. One wood-burner. Detritus everywhere. Clothing lines strung across almost every space so I had to duck through underwear and shirts to find the door to the kitchen, to my bed, my cot.

A good bolt on the back of the door. Two windows opposite each other with bright yellow curtains decorated with sunflowers. A burner stove as heater for room and water and cook-plate, frying pan still on it. A square sink full of pots. Not a real kitchen. A place for tea and eggs and forked toast cooked from a stool. They would have a mess somewhere else.

I put my bag to the cot. It sank. Little more than a hammock. The same grey blankets that you expect. Warm enough. Everything about the army is just enough. Serve beyond. Endure beyond. Earn and be given just enough to survive. That is the soldier. And men like me are not. And they know it. I bolted the door.

I would make tea. Pretend this was my hotel room and spend the time familiarising myself with its corners and cupboards as Klein was surely doing. There is always some pleasure to find in a new place. Even in a prison. I was not the only person spending their first night here. I thought of the children, of the girl I had seen fall. I hoped she saw it as a grand adventure, as a child should, a first holiday, a different bed. A first morning somewhere else and that brief panic yet exquisite moment when you wake and do not know where you are as if you have been kidnapped by pirates in the night. I hoped that was her experience. I hoped. And I did not feel sorry for myself any more. The kettle whistled, stopped everything with its urgency, as they do, thankfully at times, as telephones do, excepting late at night, as the rap at the door after the sun goes. You and your Jewish wife staring at each other from your chairs across the room in the dark. But that had not happened. It would not happen. I was the one in the camp. And I worked for them. Was one of them. Now.

*

I did not drink my tea. I had lain on the cot and there was something comfortable in its weak softness, like laying on your parents newly laundered bed-linen as a child, before your mother shooed you from it. I fell asleep, exhausted from the road and my afternoon tribulations. Strange how you can sleep in such circumstances. The brain wants to switch off. To forget for a moment what it knows. Paul had once told me that he would often wake up widows waiting for their urns in his mortuary, snoring away in the corridor, sleeping with their spouses one more time under the same roof. He would rouse them, they would apologise, be embarrassed, and then he would hand them the urn and the tears would start again and he would feel cruel. He had deprived them respite. Peace. When their life had become a blur. Except the mothers of young children, Paul said. They never fell asleep. Sometimes they would not even wait. And then they would come back the next day and apologise.

'Those are the worst ones,' he would say. 'But it is the worst and the most important part of my job. It can be the best reward. I have helped them in their despair. If we all did that, if that was everybody's job to each other, the world would have no problems ever again.' He would be drunk when he said such.

I was woken by the door of the kitchen rattling. The bolt. Someone was trying to heave, to kick the door open.

I shot up, unaware of where I was and then it came back. Had no-one told them I would be here? No. There was the cot. Someone had put it here. The banging on the door continued. It was dark outside and in the room. I stood, guessed that the light switch would be by the door, but did not recollect it. Perhaps there were only oil-lamps. I yelled at the banging door, smoothed my hair. Laughter came back to my yell, drunk laughter. I fumbled to the door that was cut out by a frame of light from the barracks. I opened it and with the light rushing in two fellows crashed through with it. They were in underwear and braces, boots and trousers, and in their cups.

'How are you, Company Man?' one of them laughed as they fell into each other. 'It is good to see you!' They had the roughened faces of farm labourers, the shaved heads of schoolboys.

'Good to see you!' the other repeated.

I found the light switch. A weak bulb trickled on. I

straightened my tie, the pin still on it. In the barracks I could see the beds and chairs now full, the room smoky, a table of cards and vodka. An accordion, played badly, a dirging polka. They were all drunk.

I remembered what I had thought about Klein, about his shield. I would only have one chance to cement an impression if I was to have a peaceful night. And they did not know me, know what position I held. But I knew them. And I had Klein's lessons and a flag on my tie that they obeyed.

'Are you permitted to be drinking, soldier?' I was surprised by my own snap. They had bottles that I did not notice and raised them to me, careful not to spill.

'Sure. Sure we are, Company Man. That is all we are "permitted" to do!' He was the tall sinewy type that you see on a Saturday night in the gutter. 'What to you anyway? We just wanted to see your face. Come. Come join us friend. My Company Man.' He held out his open palm.

'I am not your friend. I am here on request of Major Norin. SS work. I require silence and sleep.' I put my hands in my pockets, faced them so they could see the badge, the shield on my front. Both their faces changed, but not in the respectful way I wanted. They were the farm boys again. Their happy drunkenness gone. And the city boy had tried to put them in their place.

The correct way, the only way, to handle such moments is to have no doubts, as Klein would not, as nature would not. You inflate your collar, lizard like, lizard roar. Show your teeth. And hiss.

I put my back to them and walked into the barracks. Kept my hands in my pockets.

'That goes for all of you!' But sure they had not heard.

The accordion stopped with a dying whine. Everything stopped. Only the draw of cigarettes went on. Every cherry-tip pointing at me. The boys behind me stumbling out of the kitchen at my heels.

'My name is *Beck*. Herr *Beck*.' I enunciated my name like a title, like I was pope, walked down the aisle of beds just the same.

'I have come to this shit-hole to make your lives easier.'

Every man in the room could kill me, I was sure, with just the furniture let alone the rifles and bayonets laid on their beds. But they did not know I was the Beck that was without work a few months ago. The Ernst Beck that went hungry one day a week a few months ago and was lucky to have one apple on the day before that hunger. Now I had twenty marks' worth of shoes, a white rich cotton twill shirt and thin black tie with a black and white emblem of their masters. I was blond and blue-eyed and their age. There would have to be a reason, an important reason enough for such an example to not be in uniform. I turned and took them all in again.

'I am here for the SS. I asked to spend the night with the normal men of this camp and not in a hotel. I told Major Norin that I did not want special privilege. I turned down that hotel room. I wanted to be treated as we will all be treated some good day. As equals. I wanted to stay in the camp and be with the brave men of the camp.' I stopped my walk. 'But what do I wake up to after my labour?'

I looked around like a school teacher at a class full of farts and giggles.

'Drink. Gambling. Is this how I am to tell my SS colleagues the German soldier behaves? Kicking at my door when I chose to be here with you? Drove hundreds of miles to witness you, to assist in your work, to improve your task for your better days to come?'

Silence as I walked again. The only sound my soles on their boards still furred with winter mould.

'My work here is top secret. It goes straight to Berlin. And I chose to spend the night here. With you.'

Klein now. Woo them now. As he would.

'Do not make me regret that. I do not wish to deprive you of your kitchen so I will leave the door unlocked but I ask for the importance of my task here, for you, that I be permitted to sleep at least.' I circled them all, caught them all.

'I only wish to make your work easier. More efficient. And to not make me regret my decision to be proud to spend some time with the men who are the backbone of us.'

I was back at my door now.

'Drink. Rest. But let me sleep I ask. I am working. For you.'

I looked to the pair who had disturbed me. Their eyes

away. I closed the door behind me, left the bolt, and took my papers and tobacco from my pocket.

There was a small table and I had to sit to roll. Hands shaking too much. Again. The music did not start up, and despite the tremor running through me I felt myself grinning. Did not think of Etta for a few moments.

This was how it was done. The tanks and the aircraft were the hammers, but the bureaucracy, the lists and the files by the men in smart shoes and ties were the nails to keep everything in place. It was done so easily. Even the salute whittled us down. It was mandatory for all citizens from the beginning and then a few years later only for Aryan Germans. Metal signs on the street lights and wall plaques reminded us to use it. If you did not use it you were treated as suspicious and it was a way of singling out the immigrants who were not permitted. Dividing us instantly. From our neighbours. It made social interaction formal, government controlled. The butcher gave you the salute and you had to return it whether either of you wanted to or not. That had been taken away from you. Our professors greeted us so in class and we responded. I *have* to do this. It is the law. And not the law of fines and chastisement. Camps. Treason. So if every citizen followed the rule what blame on all those desks stamping all those papers, passing all those rules, filling all those trains? If I have to salute my postman how much easier, simpler is it to just do my job? Surely that is more important than saluting a brush-seller? And that was how it was done.

Questioning was treason. Ban smoking in public, ban books, music, film, gatherings. And you abide to appease your neighbour who might report you, and the people police themselves. And that was how it was done. You saluted without thought and beggars saluted the heartiest of all for the change in your pocket. The people would police themselves. We would all become cameras to show the transgressors. Judge each other without being asked to do so. This the future.

I went to the window, my usual habit. Standing beside an open window to blow my smoke away from Etta behind me. It was a clear night. The best stars. The plumes from the chimneys of the furnaces rose up across the moon. I could see the lights from the buildings. I did not have a watch but there was a clock in the kitchen, a tin alarm clock like the type they have in schools to time tests. It was near one in the morning. And the ovens were still going.

Chapter 23

Klein picked me up at eight. He bemoaned that the ash from the camp was in town also. Even with the windows closed. A fine grey dust over every surface in the room. He had complained and had gained a reduction from his bill but still it chagrined with him.

'They should clean the rooms twice a day if they knew that to be a problem. Disgraceful. Did you sleep well, Ernst?'

We were already on the road home. I had risen with the men an hour before. They boiled a pan of eggs, six at a time, and allowed me the first. We used the hot water from the eggs to shave. Four of us around the sink together. There was something happy about it despite the location. Like camping. They laughed at dirty jokes and we shared mugs of tea with goat's milk and spoonfuls of sugar with black specks that I hoped were tea-leaves. I think I preferred this breakfast more than the one I would have had at the hotel. There was a warmth to it that made me forget the day before. A better memory to load on top of it. Keep that one. Push the other aside. How war is lived.

I broached the question of Etta. 'Did you manage to call my wife, sir?'

'There was no answer. I had to go through three exchanges. Took me twenty minutes. I wasn't going to try again. Perhaps she was asleep.' He passed over a piece of paper, headed from his hotel. The number. Erfurt 4703. The number I had requested to the operator. I was right. It had rung. And there had been no reply.

'You can try her again, at luncheon. Once we are into Germany proper. Not this cow-dung outpost.'

Twenty-four hours without her voice. The longest time apart since we had met. I felt like an adulterer. I cannot explain that. You have to be married, and married well to understand.

*

We stopped in Görlitz, which Klein informed was Germany at last, divided from Poland only by a river, but still Germany.

'We have destroyed all the bridges to the other side. If the Allies want Poland they will have to leave that to the red-jackets. They took it for us in '39. I am sure they would love to do so again.'

I got out of the car. 'Surely it is all Germany, sir?'

We were in Peter Street, could park on the street for it

was devoid of cars. Park up right to the sandstone walls of the restaurant like royalty.

'This is Prussia not Saxony. Scratch hard enough here, Ernst, and you will find either a communist or a Jew.'

We walked into the restaurant, all white alcoves and arches, Görlitz as medieval as Erfurt. I spied the telephone at the bar and went to it before Klein could protest.

I was still unsure of my fortune with the device and asked the barman to make the call. His eyes on my suit, fixed on my pin.

'Of course, sir.'

Moments later I was talking to Etta, heard her voice.

'Ernst!' her voice was cracked. 'I was so worried. Is everything all right?'

'Everything is fine. I tried to call. You did not answer. Last night I had to sleep at the camp. Herr Klein called you for me from town. He could not get through either. Are you all right?'

She paused. 'I have not moved. I have been here the whole time.' She said this slowly. 'Perhaps the machine has a fault. It clicks a lot. Can you hear it?'

'No. As long as you are all right.' The barman watching me. The word 'camp' had sprung his ears. I could not say all the things I wanted to in front of his astonished face. The sanity that was her voice. The joy of it even in its electric distortion.

'I'll be home in about three hours. We are just having lunch now.'

'Where are you? You spent the night at the camp? Oh, Ernst.'

'It was fine. We are in Görlitz. I'll tell you about it later. See you soon.' No romantic goodbye. No word on yearning for her. She knew I did not do such in public, would appreciate my not cooing in company. I thanked the barman and found Klein's table. He pointed at my bowl.

'A carrot and pumpkin soup,' he said. 'I'm sure it will remind you of your mother's.'

He did not ask about Etta. I felt like I was home now. That was enough.

Chapter 24

I came back to the house just after six. Klein reluctantly dropped me right outside. Reluctant because he would have to go back on himself to get home. If there had been a bus I am sure he would have put me on it. Would have made me understand how pointless it was for him to sacrifice such waste of his time for us both.

There was a monster of an automobile parked in front of Klein's Opel, the only other car on the street.

'A Mercedes-Benz. W150.' Klein was impressed. To me the car looked like it came from another decade. Dated. Imperial. A rich old man's vehicle.

'There are only maybe eighty of them in the world,' he said. 'Our Party's leaders all have one. It is so exclusive they do not even advertise the price. Do you know someone with such a car, Ernst?' His voice intimated this impossible. I was only grateful that there were no runes on the car's plate.

'No, sir,' I said, but thought otherwise. I got out with my jacket and bag, the plan poking out, and looked at the stately car as Klein crawled off past it respectfully. I could see his head craning at it.

I knew only one man who could afford such and so was not too surprised to find Paul sitting in my chair in the parlour. I had taken in the pipe smoke as I entered the hall. Etta in her chair. Beside the telephone. She stood to greet me home, wrapped me in her arms and that was all I wanted. The stress left me, the tension gone. I did not care to know about Paul, had forgotten Klein and the camp.

I was home.

Etta broke our embrace, stood back, her hands to my shoulders.

'I called Paul to come over last night when you did not call.' This not mentioned on the telephone. 'I did not know what else to do. I was so worried about you. And spending the night alone here.'

Paul scraped his pipe from his teeth. He did not stand.

'I wouldn't have come if I'd known you had no sofa. I would not sleep in your bed, Ernst, separate or not.' The pipe went back to his lips. 'Floor's not so bad though. With enough blankets.'

'Good,' I said. 'Thank you. My boss admired your limousine.'

'Seemed a good idea at the time. Petrol ration does not make it as fun as it was. Good to see you, Ernst. Tea?'

'I need to get the road off me first.'

Etta squeezed my hand, picked up the cups they had been drinking together, and went to the kitchen. I took her seat and began to roll a cigarette. Paul pointed his pipe to my bag by the door. The paper tube of the plan unmistakeable.

'Etta said you were at the camp. At Auschwitz. Are those new oven plans?'

I rolled the cigarette paper across my mouth and watched him.

'She should not say such things. I am not permitted to talk about the plans.'

'Surely you can tell your wife? Why would an oven be so secret?'

'The ovens are for the SS. I do not think they tell the public anything. I do as bid.'

'By them?'

'By my employer.' I struck a match and he waited until I had fixed myself within and blew a blue cloud to hide behind. Some enormous relief went out in the smoke.

'You showed me the plans before. Could I not have a look at these? I am in the trade after all. Use their ovens. I could help. Maybe invest in Topf if they are onto something.'

'That does not sound ethical.'

He laughed.

'You think business is ethical, Ernst? Inside knowledge defines the bankrupts from the ones who drive Mercedes in recessions. In war. Have you seen anything ethical with

Topf? How many German and allied companies do you think work with the SS?'

The chuckle went on, pleased with himself, and the room became cloudy between both our smoke.

'They have no choice.'

'There is always a choice.'

The kettle whistled. I went to help my wife.

*

'Why would you call him?' I asked Etta as she made up a tray. 'Why not one of your friends from the café?'

'Do you think any of my friends can afford a telephone? Your parents do not even have one. The only numbers we have are Paul's and your factory. I had not heard from you and I was worried. I hope I can trust your friends?'

'Yes. I'm sorry I could not get through, Etta. I rang the right number.'

'Perhaps the hook thing, the cradle, was not right. Does it matter now?'

'No. I'm sorry I left you alone.'

'I was not alone.' She took up the tray. 'I missed you so much, Ernst. Isn't that silly? One night and I felt bereaved.'

I followed her out. 'It is not silly at all. That is how it should be.' I watched the back of her head. Imagined her blushing smile.

*

I excused myself as soon as Etta had poured the tea and took mine to the bathroom to wash off the day, the night. I wanted to bathe, looked at the bath, considered it for too long and I heard the radio come on downstairs. Kraus instead of Wagner. It would be rude to bathe. I loosened my tie and rolled off my braces.

Water, soap, mirror, towel. Something human coming back at me from the glass. I buried my face in the cloth and breathed through it. I looked at the water in the basin. A grey sludge, a foam on the surface. I ruffled my hair. More ash. I looked at the mirror again. A film of dust. I wiped my hand over, through the strange grease of it. On my hand again. I emptied the basin and washed again. Again and again. I recalled the rawness of Prüfer's hands. I took the towel, held it out to wipe the mirror. The negative of my face imprinted on it. I threw it to the bath.

Muffled laughter from the parlour. I sat on the bath's edge, drank my tea, thought on Paul. Etta had called him. True, the only number she had. But she had followed me to Weimar, found me at the Party offices. I had to ask Paul where it was. I never questioned if she had done the same, that she might know where his crematoria was. Or had she merely asked a kindly rail conductor at the station? I did not know. Had not thought on it. And should I? One night apart and Paul had driven his yacht of a car to spend the night with my wife. He knew we had separate beds. Had mentioned it. My wife who kept her laundry secret from her husband had shown his friend her bedroom. And I had rung the correct number, even if Klein had only pretended to do so, I had rung the right number. And she did not answer. More laughter from the parlour. The radio barking something in that didactic staccato spittle that announcers use nowadays. News. Always news. Our army always winning. Strategy in withdraw. My tie. I lifted it and looked at the pin. Paul would have seen the pin. Did not mention it. And then I jumped up. Knocked the cup to the tiled floor into pieces.

I had left the plan with him.

Fool. Idiot.

I picked up the china debris. Tried not to rush down the stairs.

*

They were not laughing when the man with the broken cup entered. They were standing, close together, stared at me. They were too close, the radio was shouting. I gripped the broken pieces in my fist. Etta to me before I could speak.

'Ernst! The radio says we have withdrawn from Anzio. From Italy. They say it is for an assault on England. We will give Rome back to the Allies! What does it mean?'

Paul sucked on his pipe. 'It means they are losing. I hear the Soviets have also retaken Sevastopol and Crimea.'

I looked to my bag. The plan untouched.

Etta saw the broken cup.

'Ernst! You are bleeding!'

I touched her hand on mine. Looked only at Paul.

'Don't you mean *we* are losing, Paul?' I ignored the blood. He had stood too close to my Etta. Nobody did that. Not even my father. So I bled.

He smiled. A smile like Klein's.

'Of course,' he said. 'That is what I meant.' He sat to finish his tea. 'We are *all* losing, Ernst.'

The radio went on. The reporter peaking, running out of breath at our glorious stratagem. He reached his crescendo, shouted the salute into the room, the salute that we were all supposed to stand to and return to the ether. We did not. Etta was tending to my hand, the china to the ashtray. Paul sat and watched, half an ear to the radio at the concert announcements.

I wondered how many people still stood and saluted to their light-fittings, men like my father sitting in their armchairs recalling the betrayals of the last war, hoping that a man that had ripped up the terrible treaty would have his retribution for him. Did he just mumble the words to the radio now, save the proud salute for the butcher in the morning, where it could be seen and heard? Like a cloth rabbit that the magician pulls, animated only by his arm raised out majestically. Puts it away before you can see its fraud well.

Chapter 25

I worked hard, dedicated, for the next two months. Dedicated the better word. Everyone works hard; that means nothing. The same oven designs again and again but annotated for different camps. Eastern camps. Northern camps. Places and names I had never heard before.

June into July and Topf produced dozens of triple-muffle ovens, the engineers constantly out for repairs, the mobile oven supply exhausted, not enough brick in Germany to build more.

Our own invasion, we were informed, suspended now the Allies were in France. But no matter. A week later we had begun rocket-bombing London with our 'superior' weapons. We could now save our air-force by destroying enemy nations with unmanned craft launched from our own lands. Now our airmen could protect our borders exclusively. The enemy had made a huge error by landing seaward into France. We could see them now and would not have to travel so far to repel them. Strafe them as they marched. And so the radio went on.

And then in July we assassinated *Him*.

As good as.

When dictators survive such attempts from their own officers, and when you can count the tries on one hand, you must realise how unpopular your leader has become.

One successful attempt and you become a martyr. A bronze statue fifty feet tall. Several failed attempts and you become a black and white cartoon duck quacking away from the oversized shotgun in a Fleischer Talkartoon.

Something was happening. You could feel it. It was summer but it chilled like winter. Not the air. Not the air. Something cold was coming. Erfurt and Weimar were like another country. A land of Oz with mountains keeping the war at bay. But the planes were over us now. Gun batteries in the streets. Our leader's torn trousers from his survival held up for photographic display in the papers. Was this a proud gesture? It returned the cartoon image, looked like he had been blown clean out of them just so. The flapping black and white duck. His own right hand covered by a coat now in photographs and newsreels. Unable to commit to his own salute except with his left. If he himself cannot perform it what for the rest of us ordered to do so?

The consequence of the assassination failure was thousands of executions and the whole of the army having to re-swear loyalty and now they too would have to perform *His* salute, abandon hundreds of years of the traditional, the hand to forehead, the international military hail that connected them to the soldiers they fought, and replace it with something out of one of his beloved cowboy movies, something a greasepaint Indian might do when he met Randolph Scott. The regular soldier must have found it pathetic. A child firing his pop-gun cork at them. It was still beggars in the street who did it the most fervently. That is history. The loudest shout to the mad comes from the gutter. *Hail Caesar! For some alms! God save the King! Shilling, sir? Vive l'Empereur! Livre, Monsieur?* And they hop or limp if they can remember to do so. It is a pity such men do not have the vote. Empires and dictators would never fall if they did. Someone will court them one day, court them like pirates of old. Not the poor. The very homeless. The dissolute. Someone will court them.

*

We bought more furniture. New furniture. I had never had a new sofa. We bought it from a catalogue. Etta telephoned. I was too nervous myself, felt fraudulent somehow. We telephoned and men in brown coats brought a sofa and cushions to us. I walked to my parents and invited them round to see it. That is what it meant to me. Etta found it foolish and she would be right. Her parents probably bought a new sofa whenever the old got dirty. But my mother almost cried and my father inspected the springs and the legs like it was he buying it from us. He shook my hand. Over a sofa.

Etta and I talked about Paul. I would never conceive that she would be unfaithful to me but I had felt something never so before. It was seeing her with another man. A man my age, more successful than I. It was not a jealousy, that is not the emotion, softer than that, less definable than that.

He was our friend. Had come to her when she had not wanted to be alone, when she was worried about her husband. Less definable.

Etta convinced that it was the stress of going to the camps. That my work had come off the paper, into our home, into us. I had told her about the crowd pushing me into the arch, that I got swept away with them, about the night in the barracks. I never told her about the little girl. Just that it was the work, brimming over me. And that would have been fine, if not for the telephone call.

I had cut my hand, my left hand, on a china cup when Paul was in our home. A small cup, a small cut. I had squeezed the broken china between my fist and cut my palm. Etta had dressed it but over the month I was sure it had become infected.

Every night I sat on the edge of the bath and peeled back the bandage to examine. I washed it. Prodded it. Plucked away the dead skin and pressed the pus around my palm. There was something delightful in it. Moving a wound. Pressing it. Feeling it roll and wincing from its pain. I wrapped it back up, looked at myself in the mirror without blinking until my face began to change shape, until my eyes disappeared and my features became someone else's. And then I would blink. And Ernst Beck's face would come back. And then I would go downstairs for supper. I told Etta I was dressing the cut myself. No need for her to attend.

All of this led to Etta leaving the front door open for me after five o'clock. I could work with my hand easily enough but our front door was solid and stiff. I would normally need both hands to open it with my key. She left the door on its latch every evening so I could just push myself in. I would usually call out, put my bag to the floor but today I heard Etta talking from the parlour. Not to another person. Not in the room. It was that loud voice one uses on the telephone, the stressed diction to speak and be heard over the wired crackle.

'Will Ernst be all right after so long? Will he want this?'

My bag stayed on my shoulder. My fist clenched on my wound, my nails pressed into the cut.

'Can we do this, Paul?' she said. 'If Ernst is lost we are all lost.'

I came into the room. Slammed the door to the wall. She held the receiver to her breast open-mouthed. Like a hooked fish. A fish caught.

'What about Ernst?' I asked, dropped my bag as loud as I could. 'Why am I lost, Etta?'

She put the telephone to its cradle before I had crossed the room. I snatched it up, almost clipping her with it as I did so. She flinched. The bony receiver hummed mockingly in my ear. The other voice gone. Etta stepped away as I put it back. Her arms folded, head down.

I did not know what to say. Let her answer my silence.

'Ernst,' she said. Walked the room in small circles. 'You do not understand.'

'What do I not understand? I understand that you are talking to Paul when I am not here. I understand that you are talking about me. To him.' I watched her pace the room not looking at me.

'It was not about you. It is another Ernst.'

I gripped my wound. Felt it bleed cold.

'Who? You expect me to believe that? You are talking to Paul about another Ernst. Is it another Paul also?'

The last to know. The last to know. Bedsits are full of men who were the last to know.

'Sit down, Ernst.' My mother's voice.

'I do not want to sit down.'

'I do.' And she put herself on our new sofa, crossed her legs.

'We did not want you to know because it is dangerous. But Paul and I now need your help. He was going to explain it to you himself. Next month. I did not want you to find out about it like this.'

I went to her. Stood over her.

'Etta?' She was so calm.

'Roll me a cigarette,' she said.

'You do not smoke.' But I gave her the one I had rolled for my home from work coffee. The best one of the day.

'I want to smoke.'

I passed her the matches. My hands shaking too much to help her light. She lit and blew out the match, put it back in the box. A neat wife. She took a deep draw without coughing. She had done this before. How much did I not know about my wife? About the first woman. The only woman in the world.

'Do you know of Ernst Thälmann? That is who we were talking about.'

I had never heard the name.

'We would have been school-children. He was the leader of the KPD. Our communist party. Opposing *Them* in the elections. They banned all other parties when they won and he was imprisoned. He has been in solitary confinement ever since.'

'A *communist*? You were talking about a communist?'

She looked up at me. Put her thoughts into me rather than speak.

'Christ! Etta. Are you a communist as well?'

'As well as *what*, Ernst? I am a German.'

'When it suits you to be!' I turned away. 'So Paul is a communist?'

'Yes.'

'And you?' I faced her.

'Yes.'

I felt sick. My wife. A Jew in their eyes. Now a communist. My work almost every day surrounded by the SS.

I could not speak. Scared to speak to my own wife. She went on.

'When the Party won, Thälmann wanted to join with the SDP to create a general strike to bring them down. The Party rounded them all up and recreated Germany. Would you not want the old Germany back? Back from what we have become? Do you think the Russians are not going to win? Where would we be if we were leaderless when that happens?'

I did not understand. Could not. And it all began to fall out of her, with relief. Her relief. Mine lost.

'I have not been meeting my friends at the café. I never have. We meet up with others in the KPD.'

'We? You mean with Paul?'

'No,' she rubbed her hand, as I was rubbing mine. 'Not always.'

'What are you doing to me! All your life has been a lie!'

'Ernst. You need to calm down.'

'Calm? Etta, you could be killed. *We* could be killed. I have seen the camps. I almost went through the gate, remember? You have no idea what you are doing.'

She stood.

'Exactly, Ernst. You must see it now. That fear you felt. What were you afraid of?'

'Afraid of? I was being pushed into a prison!'

'And you knew you might not get out again. That was it wasn't it? Surely you see now?'

I took the cigarette from her fingers.

'See what?'

'Ernst. That last one you were drawing. The continuous one. Paul says it could—'

I froze.

'*Paul?* How does he know? Did he look at my plans?'

'No.' She looked out of the window. 'He did not have to. I drew them for him. That day I asked you what you were working on.'

My wife. My devious wife. I was dead. Today. Or most assuredly in the coming weeks. The knock on the door coming. She turned her back to me. Head in her hands.

'I copied it. When you were asleep.'

Head still in her hands. Not for me. Not for herself. For betrayal.

I left the room. Went through the kitchen, the kitchen of the house and rooms given us by my employer. I went to the walled garden. Dragged hard the cigarette. I could only look and think on how overgrown the garden. A husband's work. Some spite in me to ignore it. Leave it for her next fool. But if I left her it would not be her house. She would be on the street. Then she would think differently. I threw the smouldering paper to the grass. Hoped it burnt the place down. Her hands came to my back. Head on my shoulder. I stiffened and she retracted. And then I remembered: She had said that Paul needed my help, that *they* needed my help. Help how? Etta took a breath.

'Thälmann is being transferred to Buchenwald. Next month. From Bautzen.'

'What has that got to do with me?'

'If he is at Buchenwald . . . it may be possible to arrange an escape.'

'An *escape*? Are you all insane?'

She went under the door-frame. Crossed her arms.

'Ernst. You can help us. You can get into Buchenwald.'

'I . . . ? What? I would not worry about that, Etta. You, me and Paul will be in there soon enough.' Gallows humour. Understood the phrase now.

I looked to the garden walls, our neighbouring houses, fearful of listening ears, then remembered they were all empty.

She stayed in the doorway.

'It is a month before Thälmann is sent there. We can prepare a plan. They are moving him for execution. We are sure of it. Bautzen prison is not safe now. Now the advance is coming.'

'Who is *we*? Because I can assure you it is not me.' I crossed to her. Held her shoulders. Reasoned against the unreasonable. The ridiculousness of it.

'Etta. I have a good job now. A career in a fine company. A future. Look at our home. Why would we risk all this?'

'Why would Paul? He has more to lose than you. At least he cares for his country.'

I let go of her. Turned away.

'You know who talks like that, Etta? People who can afford to talk like that.'

'Ernst. They tried to blow their great leader up two

weeks ago. They know it is finished. They themselves want rid. They want a new order. The Allies will not deal for surrender while he is still there. You have a chance to help rescue a real leader. A man the Allies would accept.'

'How? How do you know all this?' I squeezed the bandage on my palm, thought of hundreds of thousands packed on cattle trucks from Hungary. The ovens burning all day, all night. I stormed past her, back into my company house. My company. 'I only want what is best for you, Etta. For us.'

She spoke to my back as I went to the parlour, to my bag, to my tobacco that I needed more of each day.

'I want more than that, Ernst Beck!'

I could hear her making coffee as I rolled and lit. I sat and looked at the bandage. The black and the red of it mixed with the white cloth.

Hundreds of thousands. I saw the faces pressing me on through the gates, wondering why I was shouting to the SS. The war that had seemed so far away from our green medieval land now falling on us. And it had come from my own bedroom. I was the young man entrusted to draw up plans for the SS because the floors were riddled with old ties and faiths. Unions and communists. Was that the only reason? Nothing special or promising about Ernst Beck. He was just new and able. Trusted. As Klein had said: 'Scratch hard enough, Ernst.' Out of my own bedroom, my own bed.

She came into the room with coffee, like it was any other

day, like it was yesterday. Her normally pale face red and mottled as she put it down. We looked at each other. And that was enough.

'Ernst,' she said. Said with softness. 'I'm sorry. I am so sorry.'

There is the man you were the last year, and then there is this day. And nothing is the same.

I stood and held her. Breathed her in as she rested into me. Rocked each other. The last couple on the dance floor.

'You smell like me,' I whispered. Cigarette smoke in her red hair. She looked up.

'I am you,' she said.

Chapter 26

He must have thought on it when the telephone went dead. Stuffed his pipe and thought on it. Smoked and walked his elegant rooms and thought on it. My only explanation for what happened the next day.

No sleep the night before. We had lain awake talking, held our voices low as mice. We talked of the jazz club in Fischmarkt we used to go to. The friends that had gone now, how Paul and I never danced and that I really didn't like jazz anyway, but the club was where you went. I told her that when I was boy I was scared of the cathedral. The way it stood on the man-made hill, foreboding as a pyramid, and dominated every quarter of the city, every street you looked down. I used to think it was following me, that it was circling the town on rails, keeping its holy sight on all of us. Waiting for us to sin. Marking boys who did not say their mother's prayers. I had never told anybody this.

She told me how terrified she was when her parents changed

their name and had bought new birth certificates. It was the only crime she had ever done, that her father had ever done. Having to commit a crime to stay safe. To be a criminal to only protect your family that had been born wrong.

Every memory of hers made mine seem small. I didn't tell her about hiding under the arches of the bridge when I had broken one too many glasses for that year and my father had worn his patience out on me. I hadn't had to change my name and run away.

'It's still me, Ernst.' Held my hand. 'It will be a better world without them. Thälmann is a good leader. If we can get him out of Buchenwald his presence will make a difference.'

'Nothing makes a difference. Nothing.'

'One man can make a difference. You can make a difference.'

I said nothing. Weighed all of it. Making patterns of hundreds of faces in the stippled white of the ceiling in the dark and concluded only that I, we, did not deserve this. I could not imagine men like Klein having such problems, such consciences. Loyalty only to themselves, to their company. Work well for both. Step up, step on. Keep up, keep up. Slicked hair, slicked smile. No hundreds of thousands of faces. No bodies in his mind. He had never seen them. No woman in the bed next to him somehow born wrong.

'Remember, Ernst, we are only making ovens . . . We are only pushing and pissing paper.'

That is all you had to do, what a man in a corporation

should do. Sell the ovens. Their use not your concern. The shares, the stockholders your concern. Men with families and portfolios to support, to support your country. But what if you said no? What if every company said no when the SS came to call? What would have happened? My first economics professor, Professor Litt, he who was carried out by his elbows by the SA, told us that the first great companies of the world, some that existed today still, were all founded on slavery. Their diversity into other avenues and the ability to finance other companies based entirely on the profits of slavery. But without that initial success we would have no electricity, no light bulbs, no refrigeration, nothing. Without the profits of slavery we would have no industry. This he said plain:

'If this had not happened, slavery would still exist. And in the countries where this did not happen it still exists. Suffering always births change, births man forward. The only thing to fear is that the rich that control do not have insane men at the helm. And that they answer to the people.'

And then they came through the door and carried him away.

I thought on that all night. Thought on it at my board, staring numbly at the plans for a sub-camp too far east to be real to me, another world. And then Sander's voice came over the speaker at the back of our hall.

'*Ernst Beck to Topf's office. Beck to Topf's office. Immediately.*'

I unclipped and folded my plan, locked it under the ISIS's wheel. My colleague opposite lowered his glasses, stared at my straight face. I pretended not to see. Looked down the aisle expecting to see Klein or Prüfer. No-one. I would walk alone. I could feel the eyes of the floor at my back. My bandaged hand burning.

Before I entered the building that morning I had checked the car park for cars with runes on their plates. You should not start work in such a way. If you start work by noting which cars are present you should not work in such a place. That is how the dishonest and the incompetent start their day. Looking for the men who might catch them. The successful, the incumbent, inspect only their post.

The Topfs' offices were on the third floor. I had never met them, never seen them. Most of their time spent at their villa, the day to day running of the firm handled by Sander. Ludwig and Ernst Topf, one of them with my own name, as Klein had pointed out. When you meet someone with your own name there should be a sense of brother-hood. Already friends. Or is it the other? One namesake judges the other. Are you a better Ernst than I?

I knocked and waited. Still alone. I had expected Klein at least. A new voice called me in. The voice of my pay-cheque.

A double office. Two oak desks like a shipwright's. Drawers and drawers they probably never used, a desktop larger than my bed. I did not know the Topfs shared an office. The surprise of this lost when I saw Paul sitting by the window, his hat resting on his knee. Ludwig Topf stood from his desk and waved me in. Paul stayed seated, tipped two fingers to his forehead in salute.

'Ernst!' Topf declared. 'So pleased to meet you at last. Come in. I am Ludwig. My brother not here today. Take a seat. Here. Before me.'

When you drown it is in pieces. Your feet are swallowed. But you are not drowning. Your knees next, your waist, but you are only in deep water. Only when the water reaches your head does the drowning take place, although you watched it crawl up you. It was not happening then. Pieces. You drown in pieces. You see its inevitability. It is only the head that drowns. The body is immersed but it is only when the water goes over your head that you drown. You were drowning all the time. But it happened only when it went over the part that breathes, the part that speaks. The part that knows. Knew it was coming. And then it is too late.

I took my seat.

'An honour to meet you, Herr Topf,' I said. A chubby face, as angelic as Prüfer, but younger. A well-fed baby producing a well-set man. He had never gone hungry in his life. Confident. The stripe in his suit, the lay of his lapels was a year's savings for me. His jacket swished like a silk curtain. He bowed. To me. Saw the bandage around my hand.

'Whatever have you done there, Ernst?' He sat.

I pressed the wound. Ashamed of it. Assured by it.

'A small cut, sir. It does not affect my work.' I looked at Paul as I pressed it.

'You know Herr Reul of course?' He indicated Paul. 'To think that my new star draughtsman is a friend of one of our finest customers! How provident! Ernst, you should not hide your light so much. You should have mentioned such in your interview. I would have moved you to the third floor by now!'

I blushed this off.

'I considered myself fortunate to be with Herr Klein's department, sir. Earn my position. Help with the war effort.'

I turned my chair to gather Paul into view, as Klein would have done, make a triangle, an equal triangle of us rather than Paul behind me.

'I have mentioned so, sir. To Herrs Klein, Prüfer and Sander.' Mention all the names. 'I do not like to boast. I was happy to be given the privilege.'

'A fine response for a gentleman.' He said this with a true pleasure.

I knew he was making Paul feel special. The ovens were only a third of Topf's business. Maybe Paul did not know this. My power over him. But a good businessman makes every client his best. Everyone gets a Christmas box. A ham for New Year. For that is when they might start looking for new suppliers as the tax year ended. The ham not because they liked you.

Because they wanted to keep you.

'Ernst,' Topf said, 'Paul tells me you have let him know of new oven designs. Particularly for crematoria.' His chin to his palm, elbow to desk. Paul silent. I did not look at him, swallowed hard.

'I asked Herr Reul his professional opinion. When I began, sir.' I looked at Paul. 'I am not sure of what design he refers to?'

Direct. Direct to the man with the fedora on his knee.

Paul shifted in his seat.

'I am in the position, Ernst, to purchase an interest in a third crematoria in Weimar. Turn it to Topf ovens. I only mentioned to Ludwig how proud you were to devote yourself to the designs. That you had asked my opinion. Only as a customer. A future customer.' He brushed his hat. 'I informed him that you were only chasing business. The SS not Topf's only trade.' He grinned at us both. 'A sound business mind, Ludwig, no?'

'Very,' Ludwig said. 'We would be bankrupt if we relied only on the SS. One year rolls into the next chasing bills. Private use is our bread and butter. You have done well, Ernst, to chase business elsewhere.'

I thanked him. And had nothing more to say. Nothing more to want to say. I did not know what had been said before I came into the room. Do not use your tongue to bait your own trap. I was the poor schoolboy footballer again. Heeding my father. Letting the Weimar boys win. So as I would have kit next season.

'Ernst,' Topf said, 'do we *have* any new designs that Herr Reul would be interested to purchase?'

'I do not know if Herr Sander and Herr Prüfer are developing anything commercially, sir. I understand that I am only working on government contracts.'

'And you showed one of these to Herr Reul?'

'I sought a professional opinion. I did not want to make

a mistake. It was for the larger crematoria at Birkenau. For annotation when I first joined.' I did not look at Paul. 'I have shown him nothing since, sir.'

True. It was my wife that had betrayed. Not I.

'But, as you say, I was seeking sales at the same time.'

Ludwig Topf drummed his fingers on the green leather of his desk and we sat in silence other than that solicitous sound. He sniffed, and something went down the back of his throat.

'I could have you fired for that, Ernst. Or worse. But then no business ever proceeded without risk. Thanks to your pursuit of trade Herr Reul wishes to purchase three new Topf ovens for his new premises and replace two in each of his current crematoria. He has placed an order worth three hundred thousand marks. Perhaps the Special Ovens Department is a waste of you! Perhaps salesman is more your line than draughtsman, eh?' He grinned at me. That Klein grin. They always have the same grin. The clown. The disfigured *comprachicos* of Victor Hugo. The smile of the soulless forced to smile.

'I know my position, sir.' I heard myself breathe out. 'I only hope to be competent in my work.'

He relaxed, relaxing me.

'If only I had you here five years ago, Ernst. We would have put Kori of Berlin out of business by now.'

Paul coughed. I imagined him as a raven sitting on my shoulder. Observing. Observing Topf. Watching morsels from my mouth. He cawed at last.

'I have only one request, Ludwig,' he said.

Topf spun his chair to him. Did not ask. Waited.

Paul played with his hat.

'Perhaps – if it would not be too much trouble – I would like to visit Buchenwald. In August. I will be busy this month with my new premises but I would like to see the new trundles and muffles.' He brushed his hair back. 'See how they cope.'

'You would not be permitted to see them in operation, Herr Reul.'

'Of course,' Paul agreed. 'Out of operation naturally. I would like to see how they cope with the stress.'

Topf looked to me, back to Paul.

'Do you expect your own ovens to be so stressed?'

Paul did not even blink. I sat and watched them as if from a stage.

'The British and Americans are in France. The Russians everywhere, Ludwig. I expect that all our country's businesses will be stressed soon enough. Companies expand at the beginning of wars and at their ends. That is why I am expanding now. You know the markets, Ludwig. Topf should be in there also, no?' He waved a hand. 'What is losing a war if it cannot be made an advantage? Would you think the Russians will bring their own ovens?'

This was not a talk for me. I was the boy under the wedding table eavesdropping, my face gobbling stolen cake as bridesmaids giggled over the young men. I would get up and leave if I could. But rooted. Waiting for dismissal.

Paul had uttered the unthinkable, the impermissible.

Germany had lost. He intimated. Inevitably. Make do with that. Move on that.

Topf only nodded.

'Three hundred thousand marks. That is agreed?'

Paul pulled his chequebook.

'May I?' He indicated Topf's desk to write on and stood. Never looked at me.

'Ernst,' Topf's voice went high as the pen moved over the cheque. 'I will inform Herr Klein to arrange a visit to Buchenwald for yourself and Herr Reul. You are dismissed.'

I stood and bowed to them both. Paul ignored.

'Thank you, Herr Topf.'

I was at the door when I heard the cheque tear free.

Topf called to my back.

'Good morning, Ernst. And I was serious about the top floor. And the salesman. You see what a world without unions and socialists can do? How is your house?'

I was at the door, opened it, stood in the frame.

'It is marvellous, sir. I am indebted to be in your service.'

I bowed again, as I went through. Alone in the corridor just as I had entered it. That loneliness when you know that everybody absent is aware of what has gone on. Klein, Prüfer, Sander. Behind their closed doors. Reading their memos. I walked slowly back to my floor. Aware of but one thing. Etta and Paul not insane. You could write a cheque to get into Buchenwald. You could write a cheque for anything now. And I thought on that.

Chapter 27

Tuesday,
22 August 1944

Paul and I waited by the bear-house of the small menagerie at Buchenwald while Klein went inside the camp. He carried a gift for Colonel Pister which Topf had sent to sweeten getting Paul inside. We did not ask what was in the wrapped box.

There were four brown bears walking dully around their concrete pit in view of the parade ground and the chimney of the crematorium. The chimney smoking. The bears would occasionally rear up, sniff at the coarse air, fall down again, sneezing. Every time they did so the white-faced monkeys caged beside the pit skittered and panicked. Paul delighted in this.

'They have a zoo at Treblinka also I hear,' he said. 'Do you think they are Russian bears, Ernst? Would that not be amusing, eh?'

I said I did not know. Not interested. I was looking at the fence fifty feet from the bear-house, by the parade ground where I had seen the morning roll call months before. The prisoners and the bears could see one another. Was that deliberate? How did that seem to each? Which the audience? All of it incongruous. A playground in a graveyard.

*

It was my idea to offer Klein to drive us in Paul's Mercedes. Intimating that Paul was a town driver, would be unfamiliar with the higher gears and rural roads. Klein accepted his superiority in this, had jumped on the prospect of driving the limousine, managing to deflect that the order to visit the camp had come from Ludwig Topf. He was doing me a service, I and one of Topf's best crematoria customers. Public relations. Not work. It had clearly been in his tutelage of me that I had garnered such a sale. The journey had mostly been Klein admiring the car, asking questions, roaring cylinders, and Paul answered all his questions but one.

'How much did she cost, Herr Reul?'

Paul laughed.

'Gentlemen do not ask such, Herr Klein.'

Paul, in the huge rear seat, could not see Klein's face blush, as I could. His lips went narrow. Quiet for the rest of the way.

*

I questioned this to Paul now.

'Why would you not give Klein the price? What difference?'

'Exactly, Ernst. What difference? That man is a phony. I have met his type before. The suits, the shoes, the watch. It is all to proclaim something he is not. He thinks it is about wealth. I tell you the richest people I know, Ernst, all have holes in their sweaters. Not because they cannot afford another one. But because they have a perfectly serviceable comfortable sweater. That man would buy the finest gardening boots he could find to shovel shit. Just to tell you the price of them.

'Money is not a culture, Ernst. Remember that. In fact it is a test of culture. Men like Klein always appear in war, in depressions. They do not need books or music. Only luxury and its pursuit. They will seize any advantage to progress and profit. And they do not understand that others do not have this need.'

A gentle socialist lesson no doubt. Paul the same age as me yet professing and philosophising above me. I wanted to say what I had said to Etta:

'You know who talks like that? People who can afford to talk like that.'

The gate opened in the distance, laughter between a guard and Klein.

'So you think he is hiding something?' I asked.

'Aren't we all?' He put his pipe to his mouth, put a foot on the low wall of the bear-pit as if I were about to photograph him.

Klein came to me. No tell on his face. He did not still have the gift at least.

'We can go in,' he said. 'With escort. An officer.' He addressed us as a group now as he lit a Camel. He offered the case to Paul and then saw the pipe. The case back to his pocket. Not offered to me.

'If we follow the fence we can go in by the east gate. View the Little Camp.'

'What is that?' Paul swung off the pit wall towards us.

'It is for new prisoners. Mostly. It will be safer.'

Paul pointed to the crematorium.

'What about the ovens? Can I not see how they function with new muffles? Those are the muffles I will order?'

'It is in operation,' Klein said. 'It is always in operation. Not possible. But I can explain to you, Herr Reul, how it operates. From morgue to floor. From outside.'

Paul looked at the building.

'You could do that from here, Herr Klein. That would be most dull. Most unrewarding. And I know how an oven works.' He puffed his pipe and considered. A thought rose on his face, as if just occurred. But not a good act. I could see it had been there for days.

'What about the political prisoners? Their barracks? That would be safe, no?'

Klein shook his head.

'That is an isolation barrack. There is some flap going on. They have an Italian princess even. Impossible. No. The Little Camp will suffice. This is not a park, Herr

Reul. And, Ernst – with your hand as it is – don't touch anything.'

Klein gave cigarettes and jokes to the guards at the gate as I watched the shadow of machine-gun barrels pass over ours from the watchtower. The guards did not check our papers. We walked into Buchenwald like a park. Klein had said it was not such.

'Be careful,' a guard called to our back, 'you only leave this place as smoke!' That gallows humour again. The only humour in Germany now. Soldiers do it best. Have the need for it most.

Klein waved his hand to the east.

'Over there you can see the munitions factory. Another over the railway. The quarry just beyond. That is where most of the prisoners work.' He was ahead of us, hurrying. Paul strolled, forced Klein to slow. We were moving past dilapidated wooden buildings, surely older than the camp, barns that had once been for animals, cattle. An SS officer stood waiting for us, hands behind his back. Klein saluted him and he returned without fervour or snap of heels. He never met our eyes. He looked at our shoes, our clothes and his face never lifted from some grim duty beset upon him. A face of nothingness. A portrait in an amateur artist's loft. Perfectly correct, but absent. The artist neglecting the glint of life. I could feel even Paul's confidence shiver away.

We walked on mud, the grass chewed up by the path of endless wheelbarrows and carts. Prisoners worked all around us and I wondered on what Paul was thinking. He had not spoken to me since we entered. We were always within Klein's earshot and I supposed that was the reason. Or I was not part of his intentions. He had wanted to see the ovens, had wanted to see the isolation barracks. Was Thälmann there? He who had my name, the leader of the defunct KPD. What had he intended? Pass wire-cutters to the man? Ludicrous. His plans gone. We were going to see the Little Camp, for new arrivals. That was all. A part of me glad he had been thwarted. My Etta safer with every footstep. Paul stopped constantly, took his breath and looked about, his hands in his overcoat pockets. Klein ushered him on each time and Paul smiled at him like a father to a boy. He had stopped talking. Walked slow. I did not understand his dawdling. I had already spent the limits of the minutes I wanted to be here.

'This is the Little Camp,' Klein said at last and we were at the fence. A fence inside a fence, prison inside a prison. The officer stood away from us. Apart. He kicked mud, stared hard at the workers carrying and clearing, his pistol's holster undone. He let us alone. This not his work. Escorting tourists not his duty.

I had seen the barracks, the other barracks, off the parade ground. Properly constructed buildings fit for purpose if not for quantity. This camp a series of outbuildings suited to farm work. Stables, cowsheds. All the men's eyes to us. They were outside, had made makeshift camps, slept here, not enough room inside the tin-sheeted buildings for them all, and then I no longer paid attention to the buildings.

Their clothes were rags. Their heads shorn badly like sheep. They stared at us like the same. You could divide the hundreds of them in half. Some in good form, only their rough patchy hair and grey cloth conjoining them with the others.

The others.

Half-men. Did not look on them too long. It was like watching the still faces of passengers in the windows of a departing train from the platform. One face gone. Another gone. Faces replacing the others. And then you see they are all looking at you. Stop looking as they stare back.

Some of the fitter stood up. Came towards. Paul moved closer to the fence as Klein pointed out more geographical features, the officer's back to us. One walked right up to the fence from the group. A lye smell. He spoke German to Paul, hurriedly and perfectly.

Paul walked away as if he had heard nothing and then we all heard the wheelbarrow fall over behind us.

The man at the wheelbarrow had stumbled and fell. Potatoes in the mud. He cried out, in Russian I guessed, and Paul ran to him. He was closer than our SS escort but the officer ran also, his pistol free.

I stayed. Looked to Klein. He held a palm to me to remain cemented. As he was.

Do not move when a pistol reveals.

The prisoner was in Paul's arms, they pulled up the wheelbarrow together, their heads side by side, and then a slap from the pistol separated them, the prisoner back to the ground.

Paul held up his hands as the pistol levelled to his waist. He stepped back. The officer's face animated now, red now, cursing at Paul, at the prisoner in the mud, yelling between them. The pistol back in the holster. The man hauled up and then pushed down again to collect the potatoes, nose bleeding. He moved as fast and panicked as a boy learning to swim, apologising all the while, mixing German with Russian in stutters. Paul came back to us. The wheelbarrow went on with a kick to the bearer's hind. The officer ordered, shouted at us, to leave, his hand on his gun-belt. The words cursing. His daily tone.

Paul smoothed his hair, straightened his tie.

'What a place!' he said, grinned at us both. 'Such a place, eh?'

The officer walked us out. I with Klein, right on the heels of the SS. Glad to do so. Paul behind, still strolling. A park in August.

*

In the car Paul gave no disappointment on his short tour, nor the terror of its end. He splayed back on the leather sofa of the rear seat, enjoying Klein as his chauffeur.

'Tell me, Herr Klein? You are not much older than Ernst and myself. We went to school in Erfurt. Did you not? Are you not local?'

'No, sir. I am from Kromsdorf. Outside Weimar. I was privately schooled.'

'Kroms? A farmer's boy! But surely there are no private schools there?'

Klein gripped the wheel. His face hardened. I had never seen it so. No longer the prince at the ball. I, a ghost in the car. Observing. Not party.

'My father is a landowner, Herr Reul. I was privately tutored at home.'

'And what did your father do? I have never heard your family's name locally? Before they were banned I was in the Rotaries and societies. I do not remember a Klein. Perhaps you came after that?'

'A landowner. As I said. And yours?' A deflection. Klein the master of them.

'Just a stonemason. I built my own business. I cannot imagine working for someone else now.'

Klein ground the gears.

'It has its purposes. And its perks.'

Paul leaned forward, his arms over both of our seats.

'Shall I tell you something about Herr Klein, Ernst?'

'No thank you,' I said, looked straight ahead as Klein sped on and Paul went on, disregarded my decline.

'I have always found it prudent,' he gripped both our shoulders, 'to understand the men I do business with. If it is within my ability to do so. It can save time later.' He sat back, spread along his seat. 'To know who to favour.'

232

'The Topfs are my friends. *Actual* friends. You understand this, Hans, eh?' He did not wait for an answer.

'So naturally if I am to spend time with one of their highest employees I should like to know the cut of him. See the future and advantage of our association. Good business, Hans, no? Anyway, Ernst — if you would know — it transpires that Hans here is the son of a drunken farmer. Not even cattle. A crop farmer. A farmer who has sold half the land his family once owned just to keep him in drink. Hans' own mother walked out on them when he was just a boy. His father has disowned him. That was after you joined the Youth was it not, Hans? Your father paid you to leave his house?'

Klein braked hard. A dust cloud all over us. Paul lurched. Klein faced him. The engine running.

'You know a lot about me, Herr Reul. And what do you suppose I know about you?'

Paul relaxed back to his sofa.

'As much as I permit,' he said. Said nothing on the treatment of his car.

Klein gave his grin, turned back to the gears and started off again. Slow.

'As you say, sir.'

I made myself small in my seat. Looked out the window, did not know what was going on. Not my world. I studied my throbbing hand.

Klein breathed deep.

'I am sorry that I have to work for a living, Herr Reul.

But I have risen to become the head of my own department. I see no shame in that.'

'Shame. You do not know the meaning of the word. I work for a living also. But head of the "Special Ovens" department? What exactly are "Special Ovens", Hans? Would they improve my business? That is my interest.'

'I thought you, Herr Reul, understood the nature of the camps? Did not your crematoria handle the ashes for the SS?' Another deflection. Klein dealt them as easy as cards. His tone never changing from anything more than banter over a Martini.

'Ah, yes. But they stopped asking for my assistance years ago. When do you think they will stop asking for yours?'

I watched Klein. I could see his thoughts shuffling the deck. Deal an ace, a witty retort, a blank dismissal. His knuckles white on the wheel. His face straight as ever. He threw out a card from the bottom of the deck.

'When it comes that there is no more room in Hell,' he said. And we were in Erfurt. And Paul stopped asking questions.

Chapter 28

I went home for lunch. Paul and Klein to lunch with the Topfs at their villa. I could tell her that Paul had failed, his morning a failure. I had been there when he went into Buchenwald. No Thälmann. No wire-cutters. My part done. Our part done. Be normal now. Forget about communists, forget about being Jewish. Nothing to do with us. Her husband had done what she asked of him. Sure that it was her turn now. Do as he asked.

The front door was unlatched, as always for my return, our summer lunch of potato salad, beets, poppy-seed bread and half a bottle of Eiswein laid on a blanket in the garden. The last few days tense. Etta would not let our stomachs be so. The tension had come from outside our walls, the worst kind for husband and wife. The world in their bed. But keep it outside if you could. Food a part of that.

We'd had sleepless nights, loveless nights, our new fortunes tinged with dirt and secrets. But the first thing an

Austrian woman packs when the Huns are at the door is the food and pickle jars. Whatever was happening in our lives, whatever was at the door, it would be settled around a plate. A simple plate. If you see a feast before you when you come into an Austrian home something terrible has occurred.

'You are early,' she said, her legs under her knees. She saw my lightened face. 'Did . . .' and she said nothing more as I sat.

'Everything is fine,' I said.

'What about . . . what about Thälmann?'

'That did not happen. Paul never saw him. I think we have done our part now.'

'Is he safe? Is Paul safe?'

I did not mind her concern about another man. She did not ask about me.

'He is lunching with the Topfs. All is fine.'

'It is not fine! What about Thälmann?'

I forked through the food, made a plate. I have a garden. I can eat outside for lunch. It is summer. Bees work around me, her birds waiting for us to leave. My desk a five-minute walk across the street. I could work from home if I wanted. It was fine. A communist imprisoned in Buchenwald the last thing.

'We can relax, Etta. He wanted to get into the camp and that has happened. He can expect no more from us.'

'You think that was all this was about?'

'What else?' I said, popped a pickled beet into my mouth.

'It is about our country, Ernst! Did Paul not see anyone?'

'No.' I did not say about the man at the fence, or the prisoner with the wheelbarrow and I thought on this. On the wheelbarrow. Perhaps not an accident.

'I do not see what Paul hoped to gain. We had an SS escort. There was no way he was going to get close to anyone, let alone this Thälmann.'

'You are wrong. There are communist committees all over the camp. SDP and KDP. A Buchenwald resistance. Christians and Jews with them.' She rocked on her knees. 'He must have achieved something. He must have.' Not a question. Her inner thoughts vocal.

'Is it not better for us that he didn't?' I stopped eating. Her concern for Paul and political prisoners unpalatable. I had become nothing more than her inside man. Her radio news.

'No!' Annoyed, a child scolded. 'What is wrong with you? You think you are safe? That *we* are safe? Ernst, my parents fled the country they were born in, that *their* parents were born in. Your wife had to have a forged life just to stay alive! What world is that? You helped draft an oven that serves no other purpose than to kill hundreds a day!'

'Ovens do not kill,' but knew I was burying myself in her argument as I did, her logic. I used the deflection of all monsters, of the Kleins of the world. I had learned how to use them, how to deal them.

'I only draw them. It is my work. How I pay for this food. Your dress.'

She shot up. Pulled the dress over her head, naked before me. She threw it to me. I could not help but smile. I did not want to, an automatic reaction, a blush. Her statement lost on the husband who only ever sees his wife naked in the dark.

'This is how I would be in one of their showers, Ernst! Take your dress. This is how they would put me in one of your ovens! You will have a wardrobe full of empty dresses soon enough. And not because I would leave you. Or maybe I am just pretty enough that they would keep me alive for a while. What do you think about that? How many wives and daughters have been fated to that?'

She stormed into the house. I heard her run up the stairs. I stayed on the grass. Long enough to drink most of the Eiswein, long enough to let her cool. There was the contradiction in her, in both of us, that I was sympathetic to. We were similar, as I said.

I worked for Topf. I had a career, money, promise. A real home. We had gained much. But she declared guilt when other wives would sigh with relief and I understood this. I had been to Auschwitz and Buchenwald. I helped people in Berlin understand the workings of ovens for their prisons. I got paid to do this. Nothing more. And whereas we survived before, we lived now. Lived in the way that as a student you always imagined you would. A good wife, good work, content. Reward for the studious life you endured. But that was how the corporate world worked, must work. It was its own world. Worked on different rules.

Here is the expense account, here is the company automobile, here is the house, here are the shares.

It is not enough to work and work well. It is to aspire. But the whole world cannot be aspirational. Just the privilege of a select few, and it has to be few, only the illusion that it can be for all. Someone has to sweep the streets. And some of us have to build ovens.

Professor Litt had told us that the Greeks' democracy only worked in the hands of a select few. Not everyone deserves a chance, a vote. When that happens dictatorships follow. And succeed. Always.

'It is flawed,' he said. 'A voter will only vote for that which benefits him, not for the treasury. And the elect work only on this premise. To satisfy the voter. But the elect know they have to work for the treasury. They cannot do both. And then it doesn't work. Eventually you run out of other people's money. And then the dictator emerges telling only his system will correct. And it does. The biggest fraud perpetuated on us all is that we live in a democracy. It does not work. People have no control. Every successful country is run by silent men you did not vote for. Their names not on the paper. That works. Or else you have dictatorships, and the horror to those select men who run us all is that the dictatorship works better.'

I remember him slamming his desk, to wake those of us at the back, or to rage at something he saw coming.

The SA still carried him out by his elbows a month later. It did not matter about his economic theories and his support. He had been born wrong. He had forgot that part of dictatorships.

I did not go back to work that afternoon. I did not want Etta to be alone. Besides, I was only across the street, they could call me if they wished. I worked from home more days than not as far as my floor knew and Prüfer and Sander were away. I was sure the Topfs would not call me directly and Klein was in their company. It seemed a day for an afternoon off work. A prison visit in the morning, an August sun, all the bosses at play or out of the city. Truancy expected.

I made tea for us, and Etta calmed. We talked nothing more on our garden conversation. It had all been said, consigned. That is how marriages work, the chords of dissonance making a compatible tune eventually. You steam. You cool. Touch each other as you pass. And then, a little after five, as we warmed up the radio, the telephone rang.

It was Paul. I was relieved it was not Klein, then decided that Paul a worse call.

'Ernst,' he said. 'Thank you for today. Is Etta well?'

'What do you want?' I was calm. Controlled the telephone in my own house. 'Is there a problem?'

'No. Nothing.' His voice went low, I imagined him looking around his room, peering round his curtains. His home? His office? Topf's office?

'I just wanted to say thank you,' he said. The confidence had gone from his voice. 'And advise.'

I looked over to Etta rigid in her chair. She turned off the radio.

'Advise what?'

'Go to work tomorrow. As normal.'

I needed to be told this? I could feel myself riling. Stood straight, was about to yell down the mouthpiece. He must have sensed my anger. Spoke quickly against it.

'But be sick for Thursday,' he said. 'Or something. Feign something. Say you will not be in for Thursday. Make something up. Please.'

'Why?'

Silence. Again I saw him at his curtains, or covering the telephone from Topf. He had not said where he was calling from.

'It is not safe.' Genuine concern. 'Please. Do not be there, Ernst. And stay indoors. You and Etta. Do not go out. At all.'

'What is this? Have you endangered us?'

'No.' Another pause. 'There is nothing to worry. If I tell you I . . . I would not be confident in your approach to this. Trust me, Ernst. There is probably nothing to be concerned about but I do not have enough information. Do not go out on Thursday. Please, Ernst. As your friend. Trust me on this. And thank you again for today.'

The telephone went dead. No goodbye. No wait for my reply. I held the receiver out, did not put it back. Let Etta hear the tone.

'What did he want?' She leaned forward.

'He told me not to go into work. On Thursday. To stay home. Both of us to stay home.'

'What for? Why?'

'He did not say.' I put the telephone back to its cradle. I had admired it once. Hated it now. What did it ever bring but bad news? It shortened peace. Its prominence in the room not justified. The Pandora's box of the modern. The new insistent knock on the door. The screaming mad aunt in the corner demanding attention just to listen to her admonishment of you. A machine that should never have been put into our homes. As wicked as the post had become. Once a means for news, for the beloved, for the distant, gently sewing together countries and families rent apart. Now for bills, for punishments, for government orders, for telling war widows that they have also lost their sons. The telephone worse for making families jump in their armchairs.

'Ernst?' Etta broke me from my statue. 'What does it mean?'

I put my hands out to her. She took them as if we were about to dance. We hung there just the same. Waiting for the wedding clap to start us moving around the floor.

'I do not know. I will tell Klein tomorrow that I am sick. We will stay in. Thursday.'

She held me. Felt like days since she had done this, and since I had responded.

'Etta?' I whispered to her ear. She said nothing, nuzzled into me. 'I will quit my job. Take a reference and move on. If I can. It was not so bad before. Was it?'

She kissed my cheek. She smelled of a fair. Like our first day.

'It was wonderful,' she said. 'Wonderful.'

That was all I had to do. Etta and I similar again. The husband protecting again. If there would be no ovens on my desk, in my work, there would be no KPD in camps, no SS looking for a Jewess. Just us. Surviving until the end of the war. Like millions. Waiting. That was what the world did, what we all did, the audience, the seats in the theatres. We waited. Popcorn, black and white screen, a bright light in the dark. Waited. For the show to start, and end with us only watching. Not a part of the drama. Safe from it. Looking at your watch. Almost waiting for the movie to end. Hand in hand as they raise the lights, drop the curtain, and you walk out into the light again.

*

I went to Klein's office first thing. He at his window, staring out to the mountain and the smoke from the camp. Eight in the morning. Smoke from the camp. His own Camel smoke rising with it.

'What is it, Ernst?' Did not turn from the glass.

'Sir. With Herr Prüfer not back I am unsure what I am to work on today. I have no oven work. Should I go to the third floor? Help with other projects?'

He still did not turn.

'I have Prüfer's keys,' he said. 'Perhaps you could work on another copy for the continuous oven. I am sure other camps would have need. One copy just for Berlin would slow things down if another is wanted elsewhere. We could pre-empt that. You and I.'

'Would Herr Prüfer not mind?' I deflected instantly. Klein's pupil. 'I would have to work from home as per his instruction, sir.'

'Or his office,' he said. 'He has an ISIS board.' Still only the back of his head and the slow draw of his cigarette.

'I do not think I would be comfortable working in Herr Prüfer's rooms, sir. He may not approve.'

He half-turned.

'I am the head of the Special Ovens Department, Ernst. I am sure he would not mind. You would be under my order.'

'Of course, sir.'

He put out his Camel, returned to his desk.

'Ernst,' he said. 'Your friend. Herr Reul. What he said about me yesterday. In the car. You remember that?'

'I was not paying attention, sir.'

'Thank you, Ernst.' Appeared to mean this. 'And thank you for telling him that you did not wish to hear it.' He smiled at me. Not his puppet smile. 'I will remember that, Ernst. He is your friend after all.'

'Only a school friend,' I said quickly. 'We have barely seen each other since.' Lying easy to me now. Lies as long and empty as the streets.

'Really? Yet you told him about the ovens you were working on?'

He was still, studied me.

I did not flinch.

'For advice. And to bargain a sale. For the company.'

'Yes.' He stood over his desk, still smiling. 'Of course. Well done.' He looked to the files and papers on his desk, rested his hands on the edge of the wood.

'You know, what he said – about me – was true. You know this?'

'No, sir.'

'It is,' he said. Just two words. '*It is.*' Expressed years in them. You dread to hear men speak so. You look down at your feet, smile at corners. Then meet their eyes.

'Yesterday Herr Reul had lunch with Ernst and Ludwig Topf. The widow Topf also there. They ate in the garden. On lawn chairs with gin cocktails. Laughed and talked of things I do not understand. Familiar only to them. I served them. I brought the drinks and the food from the kitchen. They talked and laughed to themselves each time I went into the house carrying my tray. Laughed at my back. They talked of operas and books. I was not even there to them. And you know something, Ernst?'

His face was friendly to me now, as if it was he and not Paul and I that were childhood friends.

'I am glad they did not ask me to join in their talk.' His voice rose. 'I would not have known what to say.' He sat down, pulled another Camel from his personal packet not the chrome orb. Offered me one and his onyx table-lighter. He bid me to sit opposite him.

'When I was a boy my father was drunk every day. I was not educated at home. That was not true. No private schooling. He just did not take me to school. My mother left with my sister when she got fed up of clearing bottles. I did not stay by choice. She just did not take me with her. Our fields would become overgrown and my father would pay locals to do the work for him and take half for their efforts. He was devouring the estate left to him. And you know what I sometimes think? I think that – now that I am older – it was because he never wanted to do this with his life. It had been put upon him. And he paid me to leave because he did not want the same fate to be put to me. Not because he hated me.'

I smoked nervously. Not a conversation. I was a man's audience. Sometimes you do this. Usually you are sober, the other drunk. This was morning. I imagined he had already told this speech to himself in his empty house the night before. In smoking jacket and Martinis. Shouting at his walls.

'Yes, I joined the Youth.' He waved this away. 'You know why? The radio was all I had. Everything *He* said spoke to me. Every problem I had *He* told me was happening all over our country. Dispossessed men like my father, like your father, men who fought for our country, were suffering due to the betrayal of the Bolsheviks and the Jews and laws imposed by those who sided with them. We were the victims. And if we were to succeed, to persevere, it would be through us. From the youth. It was hope, Ernst.'

His look changed, back to the regular Klein, the mannequin, the perfectly suited Klein.

'We had no conscription did we, Ernst? Were we lucky? Do you ever think that?'

I thought I was very lucky. Other students, those in the west and the north spent their summers as medics and orderlies. We still considered ourselves as the Free State of Thuringia, a republic, the place where the Party elect spent their holidays. The war never expected to come this far. When you buy a German calendar it is a picture of our streets, our forests. When I was a child our men still went out in winter to hunt wolves to keep their children safe. Old men still believed in faeries and water nymphs. The anti-aircraft guns on the corners as alien as elephants. I nodded, smoked with a Hans Klein I had never seen before.

'I made myself,' he said, but for his own ears, in his own space. I was no longer in the room. 'But I can never make myself one of *them*. The Party was going to change all that. And then yesterday I see that nothing has changed.' He solidified in his chair. 'But perhaps we can do something worthwhile still. Not by being in service. Work hard. Work well. Make our own fortunes. You, Ernst, are two years behind where I am now. In two years how may we both progress? Think of that. You and I. How Germany was meant to be.'

I put out my Camel, thanked him. For the cigarette only.

'Shall I make a copy of the plan?'

'I think it would help. Yes. Copy it.' He lit another cigarette with the end of his other. 'They are bound to need it. I will get you the plan. I have the SS stamps for it. Wait here.'

'Sir,' I said as he stood. 'I have a problem.'

*

I wanted to tell him not to come into the building tomorrow. Tell him what Paul had said. I saw the little boy listening to the ranting radio in his bedroom while his father ranted drunk downstairs. The boy listening to hope. Then I thought of Etta. Did not think of quitting. I would do that by letter.

'My hand, sir.' I held up my crooked paw like an aged dog. 'I need to see a doctor. In Weimar. I have made an appointment tomorrow. Would ask to be excused for a day. I would expect no wages. I can work on the plan tonight and have a copy for you Friday.'

He looked down at me, the Camel's smoke squinting his eyes.

'Let me see it,' he said.

I held up my bandaged hand. The dirty black of it.

'That looks bad. I had no idea it was so. You should be commended for working with it for so long. I shall use you as a mark for the others. I have a doctor you could see.'

'Thank you. But I have an appointment. Family doctor.'

'A butcher with a dulled spoon no doubt.' The old Klein

returning. 'Not a problem, Ernst. If you work from home, have the plan for Friday and see your quack. Relax with your wife.'

'Thank you, sir.'

He left the room to fetch the plan. I sat and held my hand. Felt the crust breaking beneath as I pressed it and watched the smoke through the window join the clouds of the hills that were not so grey when I was a boy, when Klein was a boy. We had grown up ten miles apart. Saw chimney smoke differently. Knew parents differently. And perhaps that was all it took. How it was done.

Chapter 29

Thursday,
24 August 1944

We could not sleep. When did Wednesday become the Thursday warned against? What time?

Do not go out on Thursday.

In the morning Etta made pastries. German women buy pastries. Austrian women make them. We had coffee in the garden. Breakfast in silence. Waiting.

It started at noon.

The flowers. The beds I had planted. A low sound from them, the hum of bees. Not bees. Not the flowers. The coffee in the cups began to ripple. The birds left.

We ran to the kitchen, shut the glass doors, looked to the sky that started to quake and roar.

Whales appeared in the blue, skimming the roofs. Our walls rumbled. It was like seeing dragons return. The garden plummeted into shade as they came in waves, wings almost touching. It went on forever, our kitchen shaking. And then a different rumbling and Etta buried herself into my chest as I watched the black sky of bombers.

Buchenwald I thought, or Weimar itself. If my kitchen was shaking it had to be close, or not bombs, just the resonance from the aircraft.

The Americans or British coming. The war here. Our Christmas-biscuit-tin city finally a part. A part of the war. At the end of it. What point? What point the planes? You were in France now, Italy. The Russians scraping their feet on our doormats. Why us?

The telephone rang as the drone died. Etta had gone upstairs. Gone to bed with the covers over her. It was Paul on the telephone.

'Thank God you are all right,' he said.

'It went right over us. What was it? Not Weimar?'

'No. The camp. The factories and the quarry. Not meant for the camp itself.'

'But there must have been dozens of them? They must have hit the prison?'

He was silent. I called into the receiver, not sure we had not been cut off.

'Is this what you could not tell me?'

'I can hear them going on now. No. If they could help it I am sure they would not hit the camp. But the munitions factory is close. It would be difficult to not hit some of the prison. I wanted you to keep away. I did not know if they may have intended something on the factory. Is Erfurt safe?'

'I do not know. I think so. But we could hear the bombs.' I took a breath. 'Thank you,' I said.

'Ernst?' A long pause. 'May I come over?'

'No,' said this without hesitation. 'I am done with Topf. I am going to resign. I am done with this. We are done with this.'

'Thälmann is dead,' he said. 'That man with the wheelbarrow? You remember?'

I said nothing, let him go on.

'He told me that Thälmann and the leader of the SDP were executed. Days before. But there is something else. New hope.'

Again I said nothing. Thought of putting the telephone down. He went on as if I was interviewing him.

'That man at the fence I spoke to. He was a British POW. Air-force. There are hundreds of them there. Americans and others. That is illegal, Ernst. If we can get a message to the Luftwaffe that POWs are in a prison camp that could be enough to bring an investigation to the camp from high command. We could—'

I hung up. Illegal he had said. He still thought law mattered. If someone wrote a stern letter it would still matter. He was more naive than I. He called back a minute later. I answered on the first ring.

'I took photographs,' he said. 'I had a button-hole camera.' I remembered his dawdling through the camp, his hands in his pockets. 'If we can get this to the Allies, alert them to Buchenwald, the world will know.'

'*Allies*' he said. They were allies now. Not enemies.

'And you have the plan for that oven. For the other ovens. If the world knew—'

I pressed the bones of the cradle, disconnected the call, laid the receiver on the table. No more calls today.

I went up the stairs and joined Etta in her single bed. We slept. Held each other. I was done. I needed rest. Rest together. Bombs had come to our city. Yet it seemed peaceful. Time to sleep. A nap in August heat. An air-raid siren howled out too late. It was like Vesuvius and Pompeii. People puzzled how couples were found in bed, coupled in bed, under the ash. I understood now. When the end comes we will all hold hands, each other. We lie down and do not run panicked through the streets screaming in horror. We will lie down. Go to bed.

I buried myself in her hair. Relieved at last. It would matter to no-one now that she was Jewish. They would be too busy forging their own passports and papers. I slept.

Surely saved.

Chapter 30

The planes the talk of the factory on Friday. We were assembled to the square outside the factory floor where the prisoners' day-barracks stood. Sander himself delivered a report off a page from his pocket. Klein standing beside him.

The two factories outside the prison had been completely destroyed. The prison had suffered some bombing. The SS barracks had been hit, as had some of the administration buildings. Colonel Pister, the camp commandant, the Father Christmas I had met, lost his wife and daughter.

The isolation barracks where the political prisoners were kept also destroyed. Many of our leader's enemies held there, including the families of the plotters from the failed July assassination. The enemy, Sander declared, had denied them a fair trial under our leader's compassion.

There were no casualties in his speech. The whole disaster

presented as a crime against Topf. The only concern was that we would have no prisoners from the camp to aid us today. He dismissed us. I expected the salute. None offered and we filtered away. Klein weaved his way to me. At my shoulder as I walked.

'Good morning, Ernst. Such a terrible business. I was here when they came overhead. Saw the whole thing from my office. Amazing sight. Shame you were not here.'

'Yes.' The only answer.

'Did you see any of it? Were you in Weimar then?'

'Weimar?'

He stopped walking, the others passing us.

'At your physician?'

'No. I was at home, sir. I saw the planes from the garden. I could not meet my doctor. The air-raid. I shall have to reapply.'

'Of course. Pity.' We walked on. 'I could always get you in to see my man. Here, let me take a look.' He had already taken my arm, my bad hand.

'Tsk. It is so dirty, Ernst. I have bandages in my office, in the medical kit for the floor. Come.'

He led me away by my wrist. I looked up at the white-coats smirking out of our floor window at us, smirking at me being escorted by my father.

'You have completed the copy of the plan I hope? Good. At least something positive from yesterday.'

*

'Does it hurt?' Klein sat on the corner of his desk, I sat before him in the small wooden chair that faced his expansive leather one. He was cutting the new bandage. I thought this happened after the wrap. How my mother had done after childhood scrapes.

'Sometimes it hurts. Not always, sir. I forget about it mostly,' I said. Absently I was thinking about Colonel Pister, the man from Himmler's motor-pool, the commandant at Buchenwald. Yesterday he was commandant at Buchenwald. Now he was a widower. I pictured him crawling through rubble to find his dead daughter.

'Occasionally . . . I appreciate the pain,' I added.

He stopped cutting, stared.

'You *appreciate* it?'

I tried to explain, compared it to a mouth ulcer. How your tongue won't leave it alone. Tried to make a joke of it. He did not smile.

'Take it off. I have iodine. Does your wife not take care of you?'

'It is tender. I prefer to do it myself.'

'It is easier if I do it,' he said. 'Take it off.'

I began to unwind the gauze. Took the time to talk to Klein, just how he had opened to me. Very little that could be more personal than one man changing the dressing of another. It must have happened on battlefields every day, the battlefields that were closing in on us every day. An office not a fair comparison. It would do. Bombers had flown over us yesterday. The relation close enough.

'Herr Klein? Do you not think about the ovens?'

'It is my work, Ernst. I think about them all the time. I have no wife distracting me with the price of cabbage.'

'I mean the nature of them. Their purpose. Do you not think it strange that with the front as it is, the war, that the orders still come? The continuous oven still a project?'

'I know as much as you do about the war. We have cut the cost of our own invasions by forcing the enemy to fight on our conquered lands. Ground they do not know but which we have occupied for years. We will bankrupt them in their boots. And the ovens? I would not be a good businessman if I did not welcome trade.'

I gave him my hand. He had deflected the question about the ovens themselves. Or maybe he had not. It was business. If not Topf it would have been Kori of Berlin, if not them, another. Dozens of companies the same. We were all advantaging on slaves, all accepted SS contracts with SS labour. The greatest, oldest German companies. Not just building plane parts or cutting ball-bearings but furnishing every individual piece for the camps, for plans not for public works. No hospital beds, no new drains. The SS built nothing. Gas pipes, filing systems exclusively for Roma, for Jews, ordered from America. Pesticide in millions of gallons, invented by a Jew. The SS supplied none of this. We did. Got drunk on it. Never thought on the hangover to come. The SS asked. And everyone gave. Everyone.

'Ernst?' Klein still had my hand, a bottle of iodine. Not

used. He put it to his desk, showed me my palm. 'Ernst. There is nothing here? There is no wound on your hand.' He dropped it to my lap. I stared down at the tiny white scar, long healed.

'Ernst?'

Chapter 31

The last week of August a long one. For me. For Germany. We lost Paris. The radio could not deny it. But inevitably, always, painted as redeployment, strategic withdraw, to protect our coastal defences, to keep the war in France. There must have been photographs of it all over the planet. Our papers showed none. A column of text.

Paul had his own victory, versed to me through Etta on Friday as we waited for supper. I did not mind that he had called. Friends can call each other. It is when they ask you to hide this, smuggle this, pass this, that you should worry.

He had contacted a senior-colonel of the Luftwaffe in Berlin. Informed him there were enemy airmen at Buchenwald. I did not see how this would matter to one of our airmen, or how Paul had represented himself, but the day after the bombing the colonel visited the Little Camp, stood down the SS officers there who tried to stop him, and began to get the enemy shifted to a more comfortable

POW camp befitting their status, their right. They were not criminals, not even enemies. To him they were brothers. I did not know enemies could feel that way about each other. Or was it just airmen? Considered themselves somehow special, elite. Above the war in more ways than one. Did soldiers feel that way? Did they look down their rifle's sights, breathe apology before they fired? And what did he make of the others in the camp? The rags of others. Their rights. Not airmen.

To Paul it meant only one thing. A senior officer of the Luftwaffe saw Buchenwald, POW prisoners had seen Buchenwald, experienced Buchenwald. Word would spread. And to me it meant that the KPD spread themselves further than I thought.

Etta stopped going to her meetings. I was to quit my employ. Part of our understanding. She would quit, and I would quit. Be poor again. Back to rented rooms we could not afford, back to subsistence and her waiting off tables. And me to follow, for who would hire a man who voluntarily left Topf and Sons? No-one calls the unemployed noble. There is no such thing as the ethically unemployed.

*

Klein had not understood about my hand. I did not understand about my hand. He dropped the old bandage.

'Are you sick, Ernst?'

'No, sir.'

'Then it is in your mind. And you are sick.' He sat at his desk. 'There is nothing wrong with your hand.' He withdrew from me, the smoke from Buchenwald behind him in his window. 'Maybe it is the camps. Your visits have caused you difficulties. I forget this is your first work. Return to your desk, Ernst.' Disappointment on his face.

I stood as the telephone rang, as if timed for an excuse for him to ignore me. He picked it up as if I were already gone. I was on the door when his voice changed, as the other end of the line imparted something that made his tone rise, quake like a boy's.

'Are you sure? No mistake?' He stood with the handset, gripped the cord. My hand on the door, my good left hand with the insignificant scar. A private call but I could not leave. Something in his stance. Something wanting not to be alone. Both his hands were fists. One around the cord. One around the receiver that we had all begun to hate.

'Of course,' he said to the other end. 'I shall arrange. Thank you. No, I will not require to visit. Thank you. No. No other family. Yes, I understand. That is fine. Thank you.' He put the handle back, gently, not wishing to anger it further. It had done enough to not be angered further.

He sat down, hands through his hair. I could not leave now.

'Herr Klein?' Came closer. 'Is something . . .' I caught my words. You did not talk to your senior so. I wanted to call him by his first name. The grenade of the telephone shattered the suit off his frame, not the Boss suit. Had shattered his coat, his shield. The one I admired of him, hated of him. Aspired to be. The boy sat in the leather chair. Swallowed by a suit too big for him.

'My father,' he said. The boy said. 'He has died.'

I said it. I went to the desk and I said it.

'Hans,' I said. 'Hans, I am sorry.'

'Four hundred prisoner fatalities at the camp yesterday.'

This sentence unconnected to my hearing of his first, as if I had missed another conversation from an invisible person in the room. He did not look at me. He looked at the files and papers on his desk, packed the medical kit away like a jigsaw puzzle, his hands shaking.

'At the camp . . . ? I do not understand.' And then I did, even as I said it, and I stopped edging closer. Stepped back to the door as if covering my tracks in snow.

'It does not matter,' he said. 'I did not think it would be like that. Did not think . . .' He looked up at me. 'You can go, Ernst.'

'Your father was at the camp? But . . . ? Did he work there?'

'No, Ernst.' The old Klein. Tone back as sharp as his suit. 'He was a prisoner. A traitorous criminal. And I put him there.'

He let his words stall me, stall the air in the room.

'My father was employing Jews on his farm. Probably too drunk to even know it. I turned him in. Years ago. When that all mattered. At least that stopped his drinking. So I did that much for him. Now get back to your desk.

Do not think I have forgotten about your malingering injury. You have had a day off work for nothing.'

He picked up a pen, neglected to remove the top before he snatched and slid a sheet of paper under it.

'I am sorry, Herr Klein. For your . . . loss I mean, not my hand . . . I—'

'Out!' He shouted, head down, a wavering arm to the door. 'Get out!' His roar the same as the SS officer with the pistol at the Little Camp.

I shut the door softly. Did not know what I had left in that room. It dragged behind me. Heavier as I moved along the corridor away from it.

The last week of August. Long for us all.

*

Etta was amused about my hand. I explained that I had become so accustomed to bandaging my hand I never noticed it was healed. I was not deceiving her. It was how I felt. I never mentioned about the pain. The pain that was not there.

I did not tell her about Klein's telephone call. I could only think that it might stoke the wrong feelings, her old leanings. I told her I would be in trouble with Klein for arranging a day to see a doctor over it.

'You are leaving anyway.'

'I will have to give four weeks' notice. If I am to be paid.'

She went quiet at this. We were in the parlour, sitting

with the radio on low, a beer each, the smell of supper cooking from the kitchen, telling each other about our day. How it should be.

'I suppose that cannot be helped.'

We did not speak of her getting her old job back. I would not say anything against, but silently we agreed. Too many associations that went with it.

I sat back in my old armchair thinking of Klein, no, not Klein, his father. No name for me to know. I put Colonel Pister's face on him, merged them. Pister pulling bricks off his wife and daughter, finding Klein's father's face, looking into his own face smashed and broken.

He put his own father into Buchenwald.

All I could think of. I looked at Etta. If it came to it, if the other shoe dropped, would he concern himself with us as much. His own father. If he . . .

I got up to serve supper, to distract, did not want to think on it any longer. It was Friday. A week in August with a year's devastation. I would accept with a shrug of mute acceptance, would not be surprised or concerned, if I was given the divine knowledge that by Monday the world would be over.

Chapter 32

I gave my notice in on Monday. Gave the envelope to Klein. Although I did not want to see him I could face Prüfer even less. It would feel like a betrayal to the man who had hired me, even if it was only because I was new, naive, and not because I was of any special talent. I was only local, available. New.

'Why do you want to leave, Ernst?' Klein not looking at me, reading my polite and grateful letter. The letter did not say my true reasons, but it could be detected, its truth hidden in its apology. But lying to Klein would be pointless. We knew each other now. Nothing went past him. In his singularity, his volunteered solitary, he had probably opened up to me more than anyone in his life. Nothing to be proud of. He probably did not have anyone else in his life. And he would not be judged for it. It was his choice, not his fate.

'I do not believe I can work in the Special Ovens Department any more, sir.' I watched the letter hit the desk.

'What about another department? Topf has spoken highly of you. That sale with your friend in Weimar has raised your status. Or is it Topf particularly that you want to leave?'

This. This what he always did. I had begun to measure him over the months and even when I knew his tricks they still worked when other magicians will only show you a trick once. He could imply, innocently, authoritatively, that you were a fool, that you had made the wrong decision and here is a branch for you to reach out to and change your mind and we will say no more about it.

'No,' I said. 'It is not because of Topf. It is for myself. And . . . I do not think I can express why. Not adequately.' If I did not say why I could not attempt to lie.

He watched me. Expressionless. Like listening to a recording of my voice.

'So. You would leave good employ in wartime for reasons you cannot *express*. When your country has enemies on its borders, rather than assist, you would prefer to run. Is there a reason that you cannot tell me? Or am I not permitted to know why you are fleeing? Or does your not telling answer the question?'

Skill. An amazing skill. Marvellous. Unless you are the receiver. I would not stutter and gibber an excuse. Not rattled. I would deflect. As he would.

'Four weeks' notice is not running, sir. I will work on my commitments until then. I know the SS and Topf have been satisfied. I have let no-one down except myself.'

He cooled at this, moved to behind his desk, picked up my letter, folded it back into the envelope as he spoke.

'I cannot accept your resignation, Ernst.' He answered me before I could ask. 'In your own words you have fashioned my reply. Your work is confidential to the SS. Contracts of national importance. If you were working on private concerns I am sure it would not be an issue. But, as it is not, you must remain.' He sat down. Did not pass the envelope back.

'I cannot leave?'

'No. Conditionally illegal to do so. And the SS would need to know why. I'm sure they would be curious. Why a non-party member decided to give up his generous work and his funded home on some unforthcoming whim.' Then lighter now. As he always did. Bees in one hand, honey in the other.

'It is for your own good. Your own protection, Ernst. How would it look if I were forced to admit that my own top man feigned a day off work on the day that Buchenwald was bombed? A faked injury. And then he resigns. What would you think of that? Even if I could let you go that would not be the end of it. My hands are bound as much as yours.' He pointed at my tie. 'You still wear a pin that I gave you. How will that look? And are you not thinking of your wife? You think every man only works pleasantly? Do we not shovel shit to provide? I am sure that if I were married, had dependants, I would not just draft ovens to provide.' He sat back. 'I would *fill* them if I had to.'

I took a step to the desk.

'You *have*.'

I did not think I meant to say such. He could take any meaning he wanted from it. If I meant his father then I meant his father. A flush on his neck. Only the third time I had seen him flare. The first in the limousine with Paul. The next after the call from the camp. I the third.

I took the envelope, went to leave, less nervous than when I entered. The confidence giddying. The next words encouraged by it. A fool's pride.

'That is where we differ, Hans.'

'You will be docked two days' pay for your malingering,' he said to my back. I paused in the doorway. He had stopped fuming.

'My hand did hurt, sir. I wonder what part of you might.'

Not a question. I shut the door. Went to my board. I shivered for an hour. Used to my hands shaking. I expected to see Klein again but he did not show. I expected to see Gestapo appear at the open door of my floor. They did not show.

I walked home half disappointed that they had not.

I would have had some dignity then.

*

The first weeks in September the radio reported nothing but the screaming rant of victories throughout Belgium and Holland. I imagined the announcer standing at his desk, his sweat pouring over the microphone, arms flailing in salute after salute as the room burned about him. Even the most faithful souls, with black, red and white in their hearts must have found it clotting the same heart to map victories with an ever-shrinking defensive border drawing closer, enemies clawing at their chests. You put the map on your wall, drew the lines. And saw.

'This is where we'll make our stand!' A triumphant flatulence. A caged lion's roar.

You take a pin. Stab it in the heart where the lines are circling. Like in all those Westerns *He* loves. When the settlers circle their wagons. Except we were the opposite, the Indians inside the wheeling wagons, the heroes without. A Laurel and Hardy Western. And the pin lands in Berlin.

I should never have gone to university. Would not have such thoughts otherwise. I should be my father now. Whistling across the bridge, buying what he could and only grateful. Grateful for surviving winter. Men like Klein eyeing new cars, old men whistling because they survived the winter. That should have been me. That should have been me whistling and swinging my shopping bag, tipping my hat to the men I went to school with. The ones still alive from the last time. Grateful to be alive. Permitted to live. I had to tell my wife that I could not leave my work because my company worked under SS contract. That sounded pathetic even as I said it. I wanted to be my father. To be simple and ignorant. Honestly ignorant. To celebrate surviving winter with my wife.

'You *have* to stay?' Her voice a whisper, an intimate sound. The sound of lips against ears.

'I have no choice. The SS. Topf works under contract. Apart from the ovens there are the plane parts. Probably a dozen other projects. It is illegal to leave.'

'So *your* Klein says.'

'He is not *my* Klein. And he is right. I will stay until . . . it cannot be long now.'

'People said that last year.' She pulled her shawl around her. Not against the cold.

'On the other hand if I cannot leave then I cannot be fired.'

I did not mean this to be flippant. It just came out. An obvious conclusion. Etta scowled, drew her shawl tighter.

'There are lots of things they could do. If they wanted rid.'

*

September. A warm September. My favourite month. Despite the war. I think you always prefer the month you were born. Not because of your birthday. Just the season you were born *in*. You carry the memory of the moment your skin first felt the air. Uncomfortable in other seasons. Winter children embrace the snow. Spring daughters gather flowers. September sons stand and watch cool setting suns glow across red leaves.

Ash on the leaves. A greasy ash when you plucked them. We did not mark my birthday.

PART THREE

Chapter 33

January 1945

It was rumoured, in whispers, that we had lost more soldiers in the last year than the rest of the war combined. The whole of Europe a cemetery. As it was used to being. New men lay above the bodies of the fallen from the century before, from the last time a would-be emperor marched.

There was no good Christmas for any. Even the Merchants' Bridge conceded. No lights strewn across the buildings which might guide in planes to bomb it. This the first year I had known it without. To not smell the hot chocolate and marzipan from the street sellers, to not hear the tubas and accordions jolly the market. The sounds and smells of my childhood taken, perhaps never to return. This is what prison is. It is not the walls. It is the absence. But a prisoner knows with each day his sentence becomes shorter. We had no calendar to count.

In the months before Christmas the grand idea of the 'People's Militia' sprang up. Old men and invalids called to service, enrolled with an armband and archaic or captured guns with the wrong ammunition to protect their streets. Not unusual to see an old fellow walk the quarter with a medieval crossbow purloined from one of our museums. My father fortunately too old for this foolishness.

Erfurt under the jurisdiction of the Weimar administration, had no Party office for ourselves. Only those previously deemed unfit for service, now cured miraculously by a piece of paper, and those not involved in 'essential' works were called and sworn. Those of us at Topf exempt. Building ovens, maintaining them, essential to the war effort still. Paul Reul also exempt. No-one with pages left in his chequebook was marching anywhere.

Occasionally Paul telephoned, never spoke to Etta, asked how things were in Erfurt, told me about Weimar. He never visited. For whatever his politics he had the quality of manners to respect our wishes. Respect and discretion. Rare now.

Only one time did his tone change to the serious Paul. It was mid-January.

'Maybe Etta and yourself should consider getting out. To Switzerland. Go to her parents.'

'I cannot leave the factory. I told you.'

'Would it matter so much if you just did not turn up? You could be on the train before they noticed.'

'What train? What are you talking about?'

He explained it as if the map was in his hand and he was reading it to me over the telephone. A ticket to Stuttgart. From there a transfer to Zurich. Eight hours to change your life. Buy the tickets as returns and only in those stages. Stuttgart. Zurich.

'I do not think that would be allowed,' I said.

'You said that about my getting into Buchenwald.' And he was right. The chequebook. You could buy anything now. Did not have to beg mercy at the ticket office. A hundred marks could get you to the moon. I had six hundred.

I put down the telephone.

*

Prüfer and Sander were always at Topf now. No more visits to Auschwitz-Birkenau, or any camp. The second and third floor were working together. No more SS ovens. Silos, malting equipment, brewing furnaces. Commercial and private work, Paul's new crematoria. How I expected my work to be when I joined. The normalcy I craved. The factory floor since the bombing of the works at Buchenwald turned over to aircraft parts and munition casings. Anything metal that could be used to assist something to fly or crawl or fire. I was not requested to work from home any more. Nothing secret for Ernst Beck to work on. Finally happy at work. I even began to share jokes with my colleagues and even Klein had stopped seeking me out especially. The shine gone from him. I would sometimes see him from our floor, standing in the car park, smoking slowly, his back to us. One hand in a pocket lifting the back of his jacket, contemplating like Bogart on the number of Johns coming through his nightclub's doors. I would smile to that back. Actually missed talking with him.

On January thirtieth we were ordered to stay late. *He* was giving an address on the people's radio. The twelfth anniversary of his coming. Speakers were wired up from windows to blare over the courtyard and we assembled below, outside the barracks that had been for the camp prisoners. They had all gone now. No-one had questioned this. With the extra work for metal parts we could have used them. No-one questioned this. They had just stopped coming.

It was a good January. Cold, Erfurt cold, which is crisp and dry. We only ever had dusts of snow but always a precipitation in the air, draping the trees and their hills in a perpetual mist that old men believed to be the heated breath of young women anticipating spring.

A screech of electricity before the voice. A whine we were used to. We stared up at the speakers as if they were his eyes, the windows below his moustache and teeth, the roof his black hair. A giant's face.

The voice calm but sounding like an old man's throat. A good speech. No rhetoric. A confidence in us as long as we followed his will. He called on the children to fight, on all of us to fight. The old and the sick. And to work. We must work. Was someone not then? Who was he asking?

The only time I looked to my side, looked quizzically for someone doing the same, was at the mention of the Bolshevik Jew, the Jew Russian. Something contradictory always in his speeches. How can they be capitalists and communists? I never understood that. All these years. I had studied economics but knew nothing about its sociology. Maybe they *could* play both hands and we were just too small to understand. Just accept his word.

Klein was the only one who met my gaze. Standing on the edge of us next to Prüfer, the Topfs and Sander. The cigarette smouldering in one hand, the jacket lifted by the hand in the pocket in his Bogart pose. The look enough to make me salute with the others as the speech ended with the speakers whining like trapped dogs. I slunk home like the same. Not bolstered by the words. Admonished by them. By Klein's stare.

And it was the last time we heard *His* voice.

Chapter 34

A blue cardboard tube no larger than a tin of soup. It sat on Klein's desk, in the centre of it, the columns of papers and files surrounding like seats in the Colosseum, waiting for it to orate.

'My father's ashes.' He pointed his cigarette at the tube.

I said nothing, hands behind my back. He had called me to his office. Not by appearing at my shoulder or crackling from the speaker on the wall. He had positioned himself at the door and bellowed my name down the rows. All heads to me, followed me as I walked out of my row. Klein gone before I reached the door. Walked to his office alone.

Empty save for him behind his desk. A relief at this. He drew on his Camel like pushing a needle into his veins.

'I wondered,' he said, 'if your friend could arrange to have these placed in Weimar. No service. I do not need that. But there are relatives who might be interested in . . .

in where he is. Just keeping them in the crematoria will be enough.'

'If you have names I am sure Paul would contact them for you, sir. That is what he does.'

'No.' Picked up the tube. 'That will not be necessary. Get me a bill for what is required to store them. A cupboard will do.' He came around the desk, gave the tube to me. I took the ashes as softly as I could. Heavier than I imagined. 'I cannot do it myself, Ernst.'

I took that as he said it, not as I might have interpreted it. Nothing in his voice.

'I would appreciate if you could do this for me. Next Friday. February ninth. I will pay for your train. Go there first thing. My warrant. I will forget about docking your pay if you do this service. For me.' He walked back to his desk. The ashes with me. To keep the ashes. 'Thank you, Ernst.'

Maybe he asked because he did not want to see Paul again. That was it. Why he was asking me. As simple as that. I would hold his father's ashes in my home for a week.

'Thank you, Ernst. That is all.'

I left him, walked down the corridor with the grim package. At the stairs came a clack of something unnatural coming up from below. A clack, an accompanying shuffle, a wheeze of breath. I stood and watched a shadow creep up the wall, an oval with a beak for a head, shoulders crooked with the light from the stair. Clack, shuffle, breath. Clack, shuffle, breath. The shadow engulfing the stairwell.

I could turn the corner, make my floor, but could not. I stood, made way for what was coming, gripped the cardboard tube. The figure came into view. Grey cap, black collar. Silver buttons. One booted leg heaved itself to the floor in front of me. There was not another boot that followed.

He wiped a handkerchief across his brow, rested on his crutch, his face glowed in recognition of me.

'Ah. Herr Beck. It is good to see you.' He motioned to the lift. 'I cannot abide those things. No matter the effort. But effort is its own reward, no? I trust you are well?' He moved on without my answer. I watched him sweep along the corridor, the passage I had come from. He stopped when he felt my eyes at his back. Began to turn his neck. I bolted away like a boy caught.

I kept the cardboard tube by my desk for the rest of the day. No-one asked me about it. I walked past an SS car and driver waiting in the yard when I left. I still checked for them.

Eight hours Paul had said. Eight hours and you could be in Zurich.

'Ernst?' Etta met me at the door. She was in that dress with the roses that matched her hair. The roses just blooming. A dress older than our time together.

'What's wrong?' She touched my arm. 'Ernst?'

'I think we should go. Visit your parents.'

She bloomed like the roses on her dress, then saw the cardboard tube in my hand.

'What is that?'

I wanted to say it was Klein's father. Wanted to say that we would keep it somewhere in our house until next Friday. A favour to my employer. Laugh about it somehow. I said it without thinking, like I was drunk. I passed it to her, let her hold it as I spoke. I needed drama if I was to buy a ticket. A ticket to something else. I let it stay in her hands. Passed it on.

'This will be us if we do not go.'

*

We put it by the telephone. That was the end of January. The first week of February. We had last gone to Zurich to marry. That memory soiled. We had grown old already. There was nothing young in Germany any more. All the oldest, the ancient and largest buildings, survived the bombings. In every country they survive. There is a reason for that. And it has nothing to do with reason. They once built things to last the ages. Testaments.

Everything we create now is temporary. That is our message, our testament. Because we know.

What point building monuments to last?

Chapter 35

Friday,
9 February 1945

The ticket office in Erfurt. Busier than I had ever known. Families stood in huddles. Suitcases as if packed for summer holidays. Busy with people not going to work. The soldiers gone. The People's Militia policed the station. That was the importance of the stations now. An old soldier in a Kaiser helm stood at the entrance with a percussion musket. I bought my ticket for Weimar without question, placed the cardboard tube by my hand as I paid. The male clerk eyed it.

'Ashes,' I said. 'My wife's father's. I am taking them to Weimar. They have a remembrance garden there.' I lied for sympathy, to gain favour for my next question.

'My condolences,' he said and passed me my ticket. He was old. Probably walked the streets with a hoe at night like all the others. He was stern and taciturn like all clerks behind glass but I had moved him enough to carry on.

'Could you tell me if the trains to Stuttgart are running? Not today, but generally.' I moved aside my coat so he could see the pin on my tie.

'What would the purpose be?'

I tapped the blue tube.

'More of these. You notice how it always falls to the sons, eh?'

A lightened look, quickly dropped. An empathic stranger's agreement. He had been here also.

'Three times a day. Monday to Friday.' He passed me a timetable. 'Unless the line is bombed of course but . . .' He shrugged. Never thought he would have to say such.

'Can I buy a ticket in advance?'

'No,' he said and then felt sorry for his beloved railway. 'It does not work like that any more.'

I shrugged in apology with him.

'What does, eh?' I took the timetable as we sighed in agreement. Our mutual consolation at our nation's fate. Two strangers agreeing what nations could not. At least he did not say it was impossible.

'*Work*'. So *He* had said on the radio. *Work*. That meant keep the roads open, keep the railways open. Keep working.

'And you would need a travel permit from the Gau for travelling out of state.'

I tipped my hat in thanks. Waited on the platform with whole families crying all around. I was embarrassed for being on my own amongst them. Their stories worse than mine. I looked at my new watch to not look at them. Every time I did so its face said only one thing.

'Remember when you sold your last watch to buy food? Do you want to do that again?'

Every time I looked at its face.

*

Paul greeted me as if our last interactions were nothing but playground bruises. Seeing each other was better than the dead voices down the telephone line. We had hands to shake, better than conveying through mouthpieces and wires. Friends again. Politics for ballots not school friends. That mattered more now. He wore a three-piece tweed. Delighted to tell me that it was from London.

'How is that possible?' I asked.

'Tailors are not at war, Ernst,' he said. 'I still get a catalogue every month from a wine house in Paris. War is stranger than life before it. I cannot buy a loaf of bread without a stamp but the Margaux comes like clockwork. Come. It is midday. Have a glass with me.' He spied the blue tube in my hands that we had discussed on the telephone. 'We will show respect for this. Even if the son does not.'

'He is trying,' I said. He said nothing. Ushered me up his steps.

*

I almost laughed when he put on white gloves and took the cardboard from me. I did not expect such reverence. In my house I had kept it beside the telephone.

'What is required, Ernst?' We sat in his rooms, the blue tube between us, pride of place, resting on a linen cloth on a low table. No wine came.

'Herr Klein would like them stored. No service or notices.'

'He could have done that at home.'

'I think he does not want them . . . around. He said there might be family interested in them.'

'But he is not? Not interested?'

I looked at the plain tube. Why not a box? An urn? Was this it? Hard not to wonder. How I would be finalised.

'I do not know. That is what he said. Bill him for storage. That is all he asked.'

He rummaged for his pipe.

'I will wager you that he is down here to see them soon enough.'

'Not Klein,' I said. Defending him. Defending myself.

Paul watched me as he lit his pipe.

'No,' he said. 'Maybe. Not that one. Who can say? I have a storeroom full. But maybe the ones who would mourn are dead also. Maybe they sit beside each other on my shelves.'

He lit his pipe from a long match. The scent as he waved it out like the smell of Christmas that I missed. 'Have you thought on the conversation we had?'

I sat back, looked out on the market square, breathed in his wondrous pipe smoke that was like burnt apples and cinnamon.

'On leaving? Yes. I was going to give my notice in at Topf. They will not allow it.'

'Ah. You must *know* too much.'

I waited before answering. Watched motorcycles circle the square, their tyres puffing up the dusting of snow. Young men on them. I could only think on why young men were not elsewhere. They grinned at each other across the square. And then I remembered I was young and was not elsewhere also.

'I know nothing,' I said.

'But you do, Ernst.' He leaned forward, I stayed back in the comfort of the chair, kept my eye to the motorcycles and the women with prams stuffed with paper bags of groceries and not babies, or groceries laid on the babies anyway. No men on the street. No soldiers. Just women, boys on motorcycles. Paul stoked on.

'You have that plan for the oven. That continuous oven. They patented it. A mass furnace. For disposal. You showed me a design for a building at the prison that had showers next to the morgue and the ovens. No chutes. Just steps. You, Ernst, have the power to show the world what is going on.'

I rolled myself from the window, looked on his tensing expression, a foolish expression, his eyes wide. The paper tube between us listening.

'What power?' I mocked. 'I am not who you think I am. I have understood your relationship with Etta. Your café politics. But I am not cut to be something just as ridiculous. I will not bring down shit with more shit. Play what you want. You know what I am, Paul?' I sat, mirrored his pose, his hands on his spread knees, as Klein would have done. 'I am every man *not* in this war. I want my wife, I want to work, I want to be paid and live for peace. I want a family. To be done with this. I want it to be the same as when I was at school, when we were at school. I cannot do anything to change anything.'

He did not even pause.

'Then you are a fool. You have that plan. You could change something. Etta's drawing of it is worthless. But the *actual* plan, the SS copy – if you give it to me, Ernst, I can get it to the right people.'

'Then you are the fool. There are no *right* people.' I kicked the table with the ashes. '*That* is the last of a man who died at Buchenwald. The *right* people were supposed to bomb the factories. They hit the camp. Killed prisoners, killed children. A man sent his father's ashes to you. Asked me to bring them. You think a plan for an oven is going to change anything?'

He snapped on his pipe in his teeth, picked up the tube, plucked the top free and poured it over the table.

The contents rattled over the walnut surface. Cinder ash rose in a cloud as he swept his hands though the shards that glistened under it. The ash to cushion the sound should anyone shake it, the ash to hide enough if the tube were opened, for a rudimentary glance. I stared. Paul did not need to see. Knew. Watched my gaze.

Diamonds.

There were dozens of diamonds amid, sparkling under the light from the windows, the roar of the motorcycles the only sound.

'I have been getting parcels like this for weeks,' he said. 'They think I don't know. When I have not been getting ashes delivered for months. Sometimes they don't even bother not to come in uniform. *'Hold my father's, my mother's, my son's ashes for me. No service. Just hold them. I'll pay whatever you want. Just keep them safe.'* That is what it has become, Ernst. That is who you are loyal to.'

I stared at the wealth on the table. I thought Klein had asked me because he could not face Paul. I had given him humanity. Thought he had entrusted me with his father. Passed to me that which he could not. A fellowship. Not so. I would be the one caught with diamonds smuggled. I was the idiot mule walking in chained circle with milk on his hide to churn butter for his master. The master who would take the reward for my labour. Fool. Idiot. He had put his own father into Buchenwald. Keep up, keep up.

Paul scooped them back into the tube.

'Do something yourself,' he said. 'Get to Zurich. Get Etta safe at least. Or give me the plan for the oven and let me do it. I could drive Etta to safety. I could get that plan to where it could expedite the end of this. If the world knew what was happening that would be the end of it. Any nation still in doubt would—' He stopped talking, put the lid back on the tube, stood and listened to the motorcycles outside. They roared louder. I looked out the window. The motorcycles not moving. The young men on them had their feet on the ground. Heads to the sky. The women with prams running. The roar still there. Sirens started, drowned the rumbling. I looked at the clock on the mantel. Twelve twenty-six. I photographed the moment in my mind.

12:26.

I looked at my hands, my shaking hands. Imprinted them in case they were the last I would see of them. I looked at one of the boys on the motorcycles. Imprinted him. His goggles, his mouth and jaw. Took him with me also. He could have looked around for a way out, turned his handle-bars, sped somewhere. He was looking at the sky. I saw a shadow fall across.

'The mortuary,' Paul said, took up the tube, grabbed me. 'It's the safest place.'

We ran like the boys we once were, running from the bell for break, the bell a siren now, holding hands as we ran from his rooms, as the air, the very earth began to rip.

Chapter 36

The bodies shook on their trolley beds as the walls trembled, the dead animated while brick dust fell on our heads. We sat against a wall beneath an arch, Paul suggesting it to be the strongest place, the main wall of the building. It did not feel so.

'Just sit it out,' he said. 'It cannot be much longer.' It had been ten minutes. Explosions every second of it. Sit it out. That is what people did. They never said such things on the radio. Never said families would hold each other in the dark. Sit it out. Sit out the war in cellars. Not our business. No-one trying to kill us. Sit it out. All you could do. The people in the maps.

In Weimar people chose to run to the cherry and apple orchards instead of the crypts of churches, run to the fields, watch the destruction from afar like a cinema screen, their hands in their mouths as they watched an ancient city burn.

'It's not ending!' My hands over my ears, Paul close beside me.

'It will.'

Another barrage, a chunk of ceiling slammed onto a bed, the body beneath gasping with its weight, then still again.

'Why bomb the square?' Paul said. 'Only people live here. The NS square is miles from us.'

'I don't think they care.' And he held my arm as something from the building above gave way with a roar. 'What if we're trapped here?'

'The mortician will come at six.' His answer. Short breath answers between us, between explosions.

'And if *he's* trapped?' My short question. No answer. The lights trickled out. Complete darkness, my hand in front of my face, right at my nose and I could not see it.

Paul cursed then consoled.

'It's the gas we should worry about.'

A greyness came back, lines and shapes in the gloom. Could not decide if it was better to see the dead or not, and still the bombing went on. In the dark it felt like the whole building rose into the air with each rumble or other times rocked side to side like a cakewalk ride at a fair. I did not think of anything. Not of Etta, not of Klein and his diamonds, nothing. My mind numb. Every sense too bombarded by rolling cannonade. I was as mindless as the men in the planes above. This what it must be like for the men at the front, how they could stand up, fire at each other across rubble and fields. Their minds taken by noise and fury, unable to think for themselves. If someone yelled at me now to get up, go outside, stand in a rain of shrapnel I would have. I would have done it just to escape from my own frozen, unthinking state. Grateful for instruction. To have the responsibility for myself held by another.

Gradually it slowed. Like walking away from the roar of a waterfall. We lit matches, assuring each other that we could not smell gas, each doubting the other's ability to discern it like an old couple bickering over an oven left on when they drive from the house.

We crept up, coughed as we did which blew out the matches. We laughed. Actually giggled at our foolishness as we lit another. Laughing in a mortuary like scared boys on a dare to the old witch's house.

'I was going to suggest we should have got out of here and crawled into the ovens. That would have been safer,' Paul whispered. People whisper in the dead dark.

'You would not have got me to do that.' Pragmatic as I brushed the dust from my sleeves, jovial even. Gallows humour again. Trench humour.

'No. I suppose not.' And we stepped through the dark with our tiny torches.

*

In the corridor Paul dragged open the concertina door of the lift. Not a lift for the living. Two shelves across its narrow frame. No need for matches. Light from the narrow glass windows at the street level, you pass these all the time in the street, never know what the small dull squares light. Beer cellars. Mortuaries. The basement homes of those too poor to own real windows.

A winding handle on the outside of the lift. The dead did not care about the bumpy ride.

'The stairs may be dangerous,' he said. 'You go first. I'll raise you then send it down for me.'

I peered into the small long spaces.

'No. I'll try the stairs.'

'Be sensible, Ernst. There could be fires up there. Get in.'

'Exactly. You could be lifting me up into an oven.'

He put his hands over the shelves.

'It does not feel hot.'

'It's been down here.'

'Fine.' He threw off his jacket. Mad at me. 'I will go first. Wind me up if you can manage it.' He clambered in before I could protest. 'You are still like the coward you were at school!' I was left looking at his shoes. Still brilliantly clean.

'Wait,' I said. 'The diamonds.'

'Forget them.' His voice echoed from his coffin. 'I have dozens of urns full.'

'*You* have dozens of urns full. I don't.'

'You are being childish!' His voice from the metal lift sounding like the tin-can telephones tied with string we used to play with as children. I ignored. Not my diamonds. Klein still attached to me.

I ran back, enough light from the corridor to see the blue tube sitting under the wall where we left it, the blue the same colour as the shrouds the corpses were caped in.

I picked it up just as the shriek of metal and masonry came from behind and I ducked as a blast of grit and dust blew me over.

*

My eyes and mouth full of powdered stone. I scratched at it, spat out the cake of it. I had not passed out, just dazed and dizzy as I stood and staggered to the door.

'Paul!' I yelled, balanced myself, pulled myself across the trolleys and their burdens. '*Paul!*'

The corridor a different place now. Only the street wall and part of the ceiling remained. I could see the stone stairs through the collapsed lift shaft, the concertina door flung aside, spiking up through the jigsaw pieces of brick. No shaft left, tendrils of cables swinging from above.

I put the tube in my jacket pocket, pushed through the mess, calling his name. I lifted what I could and thanked god when I saw his tweed jacket, the new London jacket, then remembered he had taken it off in anger of me.

Metal sheets everywhere, as if dumped down the shaft. I slipped on them, scrabbled over stone. *A shoe!*

I reached for it, threw the bricks that smothered, grabbed it and cried for him to hold on.

It came away in my hands and I fell back. Only a shoe.

Not clean and brilliant. Dusty and ancient like the abandoned ones in ghetto streets. I clawed again at the bricks. Only succeeded in making more piles of unending piles. No other shoe and after minutes of this I made the hope go away. You can do that. You can push it aside to make way for the guilt and the shame. It is easier than you think. Not better. Just easier. The people in the maps.

I sat on bricks and listened to the fire bells ringing over the shouts and the howls from the street above. My ears rang, my jaw hurt, my eyes itched with dust and wept without my cause. The blue-grey of them. A cold wind could make them smart. An annoyance all my life.

I tossed the shoe aside. Got up because the sounds outside called me. I moved only because I could. Hand over hand, foot-hold against foot-hold. Because I could.

Chapter 37

The lift door was among the rubble on the floor above, still closed shut in its frame. Perhaps Paul had not thought on that. He would not have been able to get out. The realisation assuaged something. Not my fault. He wou'd not have been able to get out with the door shuttered. Not been able to send the lift down to me. I would have had to roll him back down again. And we would both be dead.

The shaft had gone. Not a bomb. The structure stressed. Part of the street exposed through the wall as if punched in, the jigsaw pieces I had seen below. The roof also hammered through with holes. The sky blue before, hurtling grey waves now. I did not recognise this place.

Did you ever dream about finding a secret door in a place you lived? A room hidden within your walls. It was like that now. I had been here many times. None of it familiar except for objects I had seen in Paul's rooms scattered at my feet. A whole wall gone. The timber of its innards still standing.

I staggered to the half-light, to the ringing bells. A fireman in black canvas filled the hole in the wall.

'Anyone else in here?'

'No,' I coughed. 'There are bodies downstairs. A mortuary. Already dead.'

He fronted me. Axe in hand.

'You robbing them? Who are you?'

'I was visiting my friend. Paul Reul. He owns this place. My name is Ernst Beck. From Erfurt. Please? Is the rail station still open? I must get to my wife. Is Erfurt all right?' I was on him now, could see the hell over his shoulder.

'Where is your friend?' His axe across my body. Holding me back. I pushed it aside.

'In the mortuary. He did not . . . there is no-one alive in here. We were the only two. 'Please? Is the station—'

I froze as the street outside came into me.

Burning cities should only be in paintings. Seen from a distant perspective. An historical view in a gallery. Burning alive in front of you is too large to comprehend. The paintings cannot convey the urgency of fire, the glee of it, the running feet in every direction, the screams of those finding each other, the screams of those not. The realms between them.

I saw a pram burning. A motorcycle wheel spinning merrily. One whole motorcycle on its side screaming in gear round and round like a mad dog, whisking the dust of the snow up and up. The dust and ash a cyclone whirling around the church that still stood, drawn to it. The statues that still stood, heads perpetually bowed, waiting for this moment. I forgot about home. Forgot about Etta. Pushed her aside. Everything small now. Minuscule against this.

I showed my tie to the fireman. The pin. No thief would wear such.

'Let me help,' I said. 'I'm not hurt. I can help.'

He took my shoulder and limped me out. The cobbled street beneath my shoes warm. I have never forgotten it. A street as warm in winter as summer sand.

*

It was late when I got home. Etta in tears. We held each other on the doorstep. No neighbours to see. She kissed the ash from my cheeks and I wiped it off with my own tears.

I had seen rib-cages and screaming skulls on fire. The limbs were charcoal but the ribs burned like braziers. More fat I supposed. The square had filled with hand-drawn wagons full of milk-churns of water as soon as the people returned from their fields of shelter. I had lost my fireman. The bells of the churches rang alongside the fire-wagons, calling people to come for aid. No-one knowing if the planes would reach some destination in the east and turn around like hounds at a hunt. Would come back.

More women than men. They had lost their sons in the years, lost their husbands to the war-maps. Now someone wanted to ease their losses by burning them.

They gripped my lapels, pulled me to them, screaming as if I could be their man or their son come home. I ladled them water from the churns into their cracked cups, called them 'mother' and passed each a diamond from Klein's cardboard tube. No definite reason to do so. Wanted to be rid, to punish, to gift, as if a diamond was better than water, better than their homes back. Most did not notice and I watched them drop from their hands as they walked away only to be snatched up by an urchin in shorts every time. I watched firemen stamp on the rib-cages to put out the flames.

When I ran out of water I walked away. No-one called me back. I did not think on the trains. Not worth trying. Not possible they were running now. Erfurt came back to me. Etta came back to me. Was she safe? Erfurt like this? The market square in Weimar almost gone. The apothecary with the bay window we all used to direct people around the centre gone, disintegrated. The Russian church still standing over all, the statues still there, still pitying. The old stone still standing. As it ever did. The rest like half-finished doll's houses, their front or side walls gone, the timber remaining. You could look into people's homes like a ghost. Their sofas, their bathrooms. All exposed. Privacy not an aspect of war. Wardrobes scattered on the streets. Women gathered up their private clothes and bundled them in their coats. Ashamed that the world could see. They yelled at their children picking up slips and brassieres and waving them like flags. So many children, and that at least a relief. They were laughing. Laughing at their mothers' sobs. No father to admonish.

I thought about Paul's grand car. If I found it could I drive it? Could I get home that way? Then I heard the sound like a wasp trapped in a bottle on the opposite side of the square. The motorcycle still spinning in a circle on its side, trapped in its gears. How difficult could it be? To ride such?

I approached it like it was a wild animal, edged at it and, like the same, kicked my foot at its saddle to calm it and it stopped bucking long enough for me to pull up the starter and switch it off. I stepped back as it died.

You have to push up a fallen motorcycle, not lift. It took me a moment to discover this. It was an old Zundapp, twenty years old but the kids loved them because under the Party they were tax and licence free. Not much more than a bicycle in looks. I could not see the rider. I hoped he had run, got away. I sat and balanced it, pushed the starter and pulled the choke. It was still in gear and went off like a wayward horse. I wobbled for a few yards and then realised why it was named 'the motorcycle for everyone.' Like riding a bicycle downhill. Two gears from a lever on the frame. Point and ride. I mastered it before I left the square. I still had the blue tube in my pocket. One diamond left.

I took the road to Erfurt, kept close to the hedgerows as planes went over, over all the compass. It did not matter whose planes. Just crosses in the sky. Everything in the air the wrong side now.

I was in Etta's arms. Erfurt still the same. Not bombed. I

was the only one on the afternoon streets coated in ash. I have never been as grateful to be home. Nor ever so shamed to be so.

She closed the door behind me, holding onto me.

'I heard the planes,' she said. Enough to say.

We stayed in the hall. Talked low, as if there was a party in the parlour we did not want to be part of.

'Paul is dead.' I said it as it was.

She reacted like women did now. Grief for later.

'Are you all right?'

I said nothing. She ran her hands carefully over me as she spoke. 'Perhaps this could be a good thing. Klein sent you to Weimar. Perhaps we could pretend that you . . . we could get away now.'

'He will telephone to ask. Could you lie? To him?'

'I think I could. We could get away. Tonight.'

I stood back. Of course she could lie.

'I do not want to be dead yet, Etta. And I doubt there is a train after today. And then none until Monday. I have to get our money from the bank. Besides, we need a travel permit from the Gau.'

'Would that be difficult?'

'I would need signed permission from my employer.'

'They won't do that.'

'They might. If I could bargain with them. And I think I know what to do. What I must do.'

She wrapped her arms about herself, sat on the foot of the stairs.

'We are in danger aren't we?'

'No. No more than anyone else.' I took off my dusty jacket. 'Do you think your friends could find out where the Americans are?'

'What for?'

'Paul wanted the plan. Said he could take it to the right people. He can't do that now.' I smiled at my wife. It had been a long time since I had done that proudly. 'I can.'

'But you would have to get it from the factory? Could you not just make a copy?'

'Not proof. The original is designated for the SS. Marked. It will be proof of their plans. I made a copy. Klein asked me to. A stamped copy. I could give them a Topf copy of the same plan they will find in Berlin. Could you find out where the Americans are?'

'There is a meeting tonight. After the café closes. Always on Friday. But I don't know if they will accept me any more. I have not seen them for weeks.'

'I am sure they will listen once they know what I intend to do.'

She got off the step, held me again, as if such an act valuable now.

'How will you get them to give you a travel permit? They said you could not leave?'

I unfurled her from me, took the blue tube from my jacket on the stair. I twisted off the lid and held her hand. Poured the single diamond to her palm. She stared at it. As all do.

'What is this?'

'Leverage.'

And the telephone rang before I could explain. I took the stone back. Etta went white, the colour of the diamond that had been in her hand, stared at the telephone through the wall. I touched her arm.

'Wait here,' I said.

Chapter 38

'Ernst?'

It was Klein. I looked at the mantle clock. After six. Klein still at his office. Late for him on a Friday. Only after six. Felt like I had been gone for days.

'It has been on the radio,' he said. 'The sky is black over there. Are you all right?'

'Yes. Thank you, sir. I am just glad that Erfurt is unharmed. That Etta is fine.'

'And your friend?'

'No. The building was bombed. I was lucky.'

'I see.' He paused enough for grief. 'And the ashes? Are they safe?'

Only two things I could say. Both would be a lie. But if I said I had them he might come to retrieve. I would. He would.

'No,' I said. 'We had already put them away. I'm sorry, sir. The place was destroyed.'

Silence, just the hum of the receiver.

'Will you be at work on Monday, Ernst?'

'Yes, sir. I just need rest. My ears are ringing.'

'I am sorry for Herr Reul. At least Topf has banked his cheque. Goodnight, Ernst.'

I put the receiver down, noticed it did not sit right. One end did not fully connect with the mount. I corrected it, pleased, despite Klein's call, realised that was why Etta had not picked up when I telephoned her all those months ago. Nothing sinister, nothing secret. She said she did not hear it ring. She hadn't. No deception. It had simply not sat home correctly. One thing no longer to concern. I would take a look at it over the weekend. Something to do to distract from today, to distract from the Monday to come.

*

The café owner I supposed also a communist to allow such goings-on in his premises no matter how clandestine they appeared.

We came in the back, through the kitchen, smaller than I had imagined able to serve so many tables. I thought of Etta when she worked here. She would brush past the cooks and the waiters as she worked. I never thought of it before. They probably smiled and blushed at each other all night. I was not jealous as such. No. Only sorry I had removed those blushes.

In the café the chairs were upturned on the tables. Nobody sat. Maybe the owner conceded to their conclave as long as they did not disturb the completeness of the restaurant put to bed. The new height of the chairs made all of them like children. As many women as men. I do not know why that surprised me.

They were as young as us although I felt older in my suit and wing-tips than the other men in caps, shirts and braces, their woollen coats piled up on the bar. I wondered how these youths were not in the war Did they work for essential companies, departments? Is that how the communists infiltrated? Or did they just not turn up with their papers and hid in the cracks which got wider every day?

One of them broke their group to come and smile at Etta, to sniff at me. He had those Bohemian moustaches old men dislike in the youth. I have never liked beards.

'And who is this, Etta?' He spoke to me.

'My husband. Ernst, this is Bernie.'

I put out my hand but he left it there.

'Ah. The one who makes the ovens for the baby-killers.'

My hand back to my pocket.

'I do not make them. I annotate them.'

'Is there a difference?'

He was so assured, convinced he could say anything to anyone. One of those who would smile, cross his arms at the firing squad for the photograph, not realising that the Party had just as many the same, who would do the same. They probably had similar lives behind them. A chip on one shoulder, a braid of entitlement on the other.

'Bernie!' Etta scolded him the same as she would me. I feared for our children. 'Ernst is here to help. How dare you!'

He apologised like scraping shit off his shoes.

'And how is he going to help? Look at him. He has Gestapo written all over.'

I took a step.

'I could help your father's shame by putting you on your arse.'

I said it like Klein would have. Through a promise of smile and eyes that had already settled on the act completed and I was only recalling it fondly. 'We won't be here long. Go stand with your comrades. And listen.'

He looked at Etta's glare, swung away as if bored of me. Slouched on the bar as the others looked between us.

Etta walked with me to the centre of the room of folded arms.

'I am Ernst Beck,' I announced, still with Klein's countenance. I wished for one of his Camels, for the silver lighter. Would not roll a cigarette in front of them.

'I work for Topf and Sons. And if you did not already know, Topf is the prime supplier of ovens for the SS. For the camps. Has been so since before the war.'

A voice chirped.

'Have you come to sell us one? You sound proud.'

'I have come to tell you that Paul Reul died in Weimar this afternoon. I was with him.' I let that whisper around, wished I had kept the smut and dust on me, had not washed it off. 'And that I am done with Topf.'

I walked the room, hands in pockets, as I had at the barracks.

'I do not need to know any of you. I am not here for allegiances. And my wife's politics are her own.'

Bernie came off the bar. Folded his arms with the rest of them.

'So what do you want, Company Man?' The same words a soldier in Auschwitz had said to me. The similar, the dislike of men in suits. If they stood together, the soldier and the communist, I would be the one against the wall as they aimed.

I stopped walking.

'I took a job. Working for one of Erfurt's finest. I wanted to design. I was hired to detail new ovens for the SS. I have come to realise that these ovens were for more than their original intent.'

'Their *only* intent.' Another voice. Did not rise to it. My speech was not practised but it had the sound of it. It was the speech of the sorry drunkard. Interruptions not tolerated, honesty absolute, absolution asked.

'My last work was for what they called a continuous oven for mass use. It was designed on four levels. A single muffle in. The bodies would be put in one by one. They would move down a series of rollers to the furnace at the bottom. The onwards consumption of the bodies below would fuel those burning above. It would save fuel and the necessity to remove waste from the oven. They would burn as fast as you could shovel them in. As many as you could. As many as you wanted.'

Women put their hands to mouths. I did not want to look at the men.

I took a lighted cigarette from a mouth. A protest until he saw the shaking of my hand. I did not even taste it as I dragged. Needed it to drag the last words from my pit.

'Paul wanted me to give him the plan for this oven. He said he could get it to the right people. He cannot do that now. But I can. I can get the plan. Show the world what the SS were doing. What they planned to keep doing. Last summer over five hundred thousand Jews went into Auschwitz. I have been there. None of them were getting out again.' I had drained the cigarette. Another one volunteered, lit for me.

'If you know where the nearest Americans are I promise you I will take this plan to their command. I cannot right anything, I know that now, but you know that the SS will destroy any evidence of anything they can. Wherever they go they leave only fire. But I can do this. And the world will know.'

I stepped back to Etta. She took my hand and we waited as the men of the group counselled. Only Bernie came forward.

'Auschwitz was liberated two weeks ago,' he said. 'By the Russians. You would not know that. I am sure your chiefs do. There'll be paper burning soon enough. Covering their tracks. But if you can get this plan, get to Kassel,' he said. 'Kassel is safe. Wait up in a hotel. A month. The invasion of Germany has begun. They'll cross the Rhine. That's the front now. You'd never make it further west past the road-blocks.' By further west he meant Frankfurt, Wallendorf, anywhere east from

Luxembourg and the Siegfried Line. He took a breath in thought.

'But who knows how long they will take? A month. Two. Maybe not succeed at all.' He touched both our hands. 'They are throwing everything they can at them.'

'I am sorry,' he said. 'But they are not as close as you hope they are.' He looked at me. Understood. 'We know about Etta. Get her out. Before there won't be trains to do so. Take your plan to Kassel and wait. Hide.' He walked back to the group. Etta and I alone.

Kassel. North-west from us. With my small motorcycle, if I could get fuel, I could make it in a day. It did not seem far enough. Hardly worth it. But not Erfurt. Etta safely on a train. I away from Topf and the SS.

They are not as close as you hope they are.

We thanked them and left, hollow inside. Maybe the Americans months away, the red-jackets even further. So it was not over. The radio right. *His* last speech right. We walked home in the blackout without a word.

I had thought I was becoming a hero. Instead no better than them. A boy in a café with grand plans, sentiments only as strong as coffee and cigarettes. There was nothing in my power, my control. Except the one thing every voice agreed on, even the dead. The dead that day. Almost Paul's last words. The woman on my arm.

Get her safe.

They are not as close as you hope they are.

Chapter 39

We did not talk about Weimar. What I had seen. I was fortunate. That was all. Thoughts of Paul's body, his fate, not for us. The authorities would contact his father. In death secrets will out. Papers would be gone through, affiliations discovered. Our distance for our own protection. Mourning only for widows and parents with a world at war. I thought on his headstone, the one he laughed about to break the ice at parties. The last date to be filled now. Waiting. A bomb and a lift shaft. Politics not a part of his end. Death had become ridiculous. You could die lighting an oven because a main leaked miles away, decapitated crossing the street because a bomb hit while you were walking. People hiding in their homes, wiping their children's jam-dried mouths, reading bedtime stories in candlelit cellars. They won't have a day of remembrance for them. The people in the maps. Paul killed in a lift shaft for corpses.

We kept the radio on all the time for warnings, one ear cocked for the sirens. The whole of Erfurt no doubt the same. I told Etta that I wanted to see my parents. I did not have to explain why. You remain children until your parents die. You want to see them when you almost die.

As we walked to the bridge Etta said she had written to her parents with our telephone number, saying she did not know why she had not thought of it before. A telephone still a strange device for us.

She wrote to them every month but we only ever received a handful of replies over the last year, unsure of how many of hers they had read. The postal service mostly for war use now. I told her that the telephone was probably just as limited. That international calls would be non-existent for civilians.

'You don't know that, Ernst,' she said.

'No. Just assuming it's as bad as everything else. Strange how you get used to it. The newspapers still get posted up in the square yet they tell you to reuse envelopes to save paper. The radio preaches victory but you can't even buy an ice-cream.'

'Who wants ice-cream in February?'

The streets quiet. We lowered our voices to not wake the sleeping houses. Talk eventually rowing with one oar round to us getting away from Erfurt.

'Could we not take the plan to Zurich, Ernst? You with me. It would be safer from there.'

'And if something went wrong on the way? Both of us caught with stolen SS plans. Shot in a railway siding.' She squeezed my arm in hers. Not against the cold. 'It would be better for you to go on your own, Etta. No-one knows what you look like. They have my face. As soon as the plan is discovered gone my description will be everywhere.'

This was true, an advantage. In all my months at Topf no-one had met her. I might as well have created her. Fortunate. Lucky idiot. But it meant that one of us could get past the station, on at least one train. Maybe that would be enough, maybe not. She would be resourceful enough, with enough money. She did not need to hold my hand.

'I do not want to leave you.'

'Don't say that. It's not that.' We were at the bridge, on its threshold. On the cusp of time. An AA gun behind us pointing to the sky, the medieval timber and stone in front. Two different worlds. Like the moment I walked into Paul's crematorium, and the moment I staggered out. Two different worlds.

'I want us to go together, Etta. But I must do this alone. No-one will be looking for a single woman on a train, a woman they cannot describe. But they will be looking for me.'

'So we shall sit in different seats. Take different trains. Just hours apart.'

'But then I am not getting the plans out. I am in Zurich. I am running away. Not running *to*. Who am I helping then?'

She took my gloved hands.

'Me, Ernst. You are helping me.'

'You were the one who made me think of *them*. Me, Klein, Sander, Prüfer. Just doing our jobs, our work. Not seeing the end. A hundred German companies, banks, doing the same. Even Zurich doing the same. The Swiss supplying electricity and coal to Berlin. Not seeing. And seeing. But they do not think of the Ernst Becks. I am nothing, Etta.' I walked her onto the bridge. Into a different time.

'That is how I can beat them.'

I felt in her soft touch of me that she believed. Trusted. But I was still the boy. I only wanted my mother to hold me, my father to pour me his Madeira or schnapps. For one more time. And because I had come from the bombing of a town, had lived, when thousands would only have wanted that one thing, two things. Once more. Schnapps with their father. Their mother's hot stew too hot. No son should say goodbye to their parents. The millions who never got to do so. Lucky idiot.

'Besides. I do not have a vanity seat for the motorcycle. My backside is raw from it. Even with a saddle. It's for picnics, not distance.' I swung her along. 'I like your hide as it is.'

Gallows humour. Trench humour. Humour of those waiting to be bombed.

*

My father was bent almost double as I told him, as if I had put a wagon's load on his back.

'Paul Reul? Your friend from school? Aker Reul's boy?' This is how Germans remembered sons and daughters. By remembering their fathers' names or their fathers' scandals.

'Yes, Papa.' I coaxed him into his armchair. 'It was a terrible thing.'

'What about Weimar? What does it look like? Why bomb such? Homes and churches.'

'There is an NS square. But they did not bomb that.'

He sat, scratched his head and the arms of the chair.

'So. They wanted to kill people?'

I sat on the sofa. Said nothing on this and he waved me to remain quiet.

'I am glad you got out, Ernst. This family. Never with the luck. From my father to his. God is changing his mind on us at last.'

He never asked why I was there and I would not have known what to say. I had a diamond in my pocket as small as an October peach pit, weighted like a millstone.

There was almost an annoyance from them both when we first arrived. It was Saturday evening. Their supper was sandwiches and pickles and the radio and a private time for them. Old people become like that. Even when you are their children Saturday is still like it was when your father used to work.

'I have seen people all week. I will see you all in church on Sunday and work with all of you on Monday. Saturday is when I undo the top button of my trouser and wear a vest and I have no meat for you.'

'There was no mention of it in the paper?' he said.

The 'paper' to my father was *Der Sturmer*, 'The Attack'. A rag, but the only one still regularly pinned up in the street notices. These were glass-fronted frames that held the sheets of the paper in a long line so that anyone could have access to the 'news'. It was anti everything and appealed to the basest reader and the young boy seeking a pencil-sketched frilly glimpse of cleavage. Our leader read it religiously.

My mother was crying in the kitchen while Etta consoled. Crying because I had been at the bombing, crying gladly because I had survived. Great racking sobs that men do not understand because they swallow them with schnapps and roll their eyes at the wails, convinced that the world would stop spinning if they did the same.

'So,' my father reaching for pipe and tobacco bag, 'perhaps it is not so long before we are bombed.' The end of his conversation on it. 'Is your job still safe, Ernst?'

'I am leaving,' I said. It came natural to say so. Decision made. I was not judging or weighing it any more and he did not need to understand. He forgot about the loading of his pipe.

'What for? Your first work? Are you mad?' His conclusion made in one sentence. One exasperation tumbling over another, the pipe-loading resumed like a task begrudged.

'Things have changed,' I said. 'With the work Topf has been doing. Etta and I are not comfortable with it.'

'Pah! Who is "comfortable" with their work? Work is work. Nothing would happen if everyone thought like that,

Ernst. What have they been doing that makes a young man quit his job?'

'I am not quitting. They won't allow that. I am leaving without their say. It is the ovens, Papa.'

My mother had stopped wailing, Etta hushing her into her bosom.

'What ovens? Almost a year now you have worked for them. What difference?' His voice a beat, as fathers do when they can no longer beat you with their open hand. Angry at his fool of a son. The son who was cutting away his years with foolishness. The son who might have kept him furnished for old age.

'They kill Jews, Papa. Poles, Roma, Russians. They need the ovens to dispose.'

'Yes. For the typhus.' Still that beat. Delivered with hand-strokes and pipe-puffs.

'No, Papa.' I rubbed my nose against the harshness of the pine cones mixed with coke in the burner. The habits of the old in winter. He probably still broke ice on the river to store for water. 'I have been in Auschwitz. They have more ovens than water tanks. Yet they build showers for hundreds. For water tanks that cannot feed them.'

'Nonsense.' He slapped away the air of my words. 'And for what matter anyway? Jews. Roma. Parasites all. You are too young to understand.'

I stood. Looked down over my father for the first time since I was sixteen and had declared that I disliked the pipe smoke in our house.

'Etta is Jewish,' I said. 'I am married to a Jew.'

The muffled sobbing from the kitchen stopped.

'They would take away our marriage. Take her away.' I let that hang. My mother in the kitchen doorway. It never had a door. There were still hinge marks where one had stood. Painted over. The nicks of a penknife that charted my growth chipping the paint.

'My wife – your daughter – would be on a cattle truck to prison.'

I sat back down, looked to the window, through the lace curtain to the timbered house over. Wondered what conversations went on within. Done with mine. Etta behind my mother in the kitchen, her eyes on me, my mother moving into the room. Away from Etta, to my father's chair.

My father said nothing, took his pipe from his mouth and reached to his shoulder for my mother's hand. They were still. As I was. As Etta was. She had been holding my mother to her bosom moments before. I could not read her face. A laugh came up from the bridge below, broke our statues.

'Get out of my house,' my father said. Then repeated it louder when I stared back at him, as if I had not heard, as if he were answering an echo with a louder call.

'*Get out of my house!*'

My mother said nothing, her tears brimming. She gripped my father's hand. He would speak.

'How dare you!' His face red. 'How dare you. My own son! Wed to a Jew!'

He dropped my mother's hand, struggled from his chair.

I did not expect this. I had hoped that if all went wrong with getting Etta on a train she might stay here. Here in the house I was born. Where we all come back to. I stood with him, over him, no longer the giant of my childhood. But still his boy. Spittle on his lip.

'We would all be taken! How dare you do this to your mother. What I have sacrificed for you. The years, the money I have spent on raising. On your education. And this is how you repay in my old age! My son. Married to a whore!'

I did not understand his anger. I could reason. Say I did not know she was a Jew when I married her. But then I would be him. As Etta had said. An old man shouting at the dark. His affairs of the world came from newspapers of the gutter. The press extolled that Jews would marry German women for their money. Eager German youth would marry Jewesses for their easy virtue, the paper carrying a cartoon to prove it. Always a cartoon. Always letters to the editor to prove.

Etta closed her arms about her in the kitchen, her head down, making herself smaller, crawling into herself. My mother tried to touch me as I passed, withdrew as if I were made of flame. I swept Etta out of there. She kept her head down. My father shouting all the while.

'Out! Out! No son have I!' His arms waving, my mother sunk into her corner chair wailing into her sleeve. 'Take your whore! Try to kill your parents why not? I would rather a soldier for a son. Look at your mother. See what you have done!'

We were at the door, the door to the stairs above a camera shop. The stairs I had ascended thousands of times. Never again. Not while I breathed. Not while they breathed. And maybe not even after. Let rats have them.

I held the door open, looked back into the room. If I said something it would only empower him more, hurt my mother more. The look was enough. He saw it. The last look from his son. I went to close the door behind us but Etta stayed my hand.

She straightened her dress, picked up our coats and hats from behind the door. Addressed them together.

'Father.' She bowed. 'Mother.' Her goodbye. I was not there. Only Etta. And she left with me. A thousand times I had clicked that door closed. The last time.

We went down the stairs, left the door open to the street. Let *him* crawl down and shut out the wind.

'I am sorry, Etta. I did not know.'

She took my hand.

'I did.' Her face away from me, watching the river under the bridge. Both of us getting used to just us, used to walking empty streets in silence. The only shadows in a city.

Chapter 40

I was up before the dawn on Sunday. I percolated coffee, burned toast, cursed at it and our pale butter. But you cannot waste bread and so coughed on the dust of it. I sat in the garden, smoked and drank coffee until the sun crept over the tiles of the houses beyond.

We made love last night. The kind that comes from sadness; when you know it might be the last, are thankful for the first, when you could see the future of it, the different beds you would own, the different walls watching. All before you. And then someday, this day. All behind you.

We had a plan that we did not speak of. A plan of stages. Each stage could be the final one, the rest never coming, so we did not speak of them, only the first. I would get our money from the bank during my lunch on Monday, give the money to Etta and then try to get a travel permit from Klein. *Try.* Try. A word only slightly larger than 'No'. The smallest words the heaviest.

I doubted I could get the permit stamped from the Gau even if I got it. But maybe that could be bluffed at the station, chaos everywhere, the rules were for yesterday, and, as Paul had said, demonstrated, you could buy anything now. I was sure that a good number of ticket officers and policemen's wives owned good jewellery collections lately. And I had a diamond. A diamond that would do or not do. As I said. Stages. Each one needed a plan B, and almost every one of those came down to the motorcycle I had set in the hall. Running. Running away. I had a petrol ration that I never used but the tank on the motorcycle only good for eighty kilometres at best. Work on that when it came to it. As I said. Stages. Get Etta to Stuttgart. Get the plan and get to Kassel. Stages. Thinking beyond that pointless. Getting past Monday and Tuesday would be difficult enough. Dwelling on further days pointless. And what was the point of any of it anyway? What point running?

I could just as well carry on working for Topf, forget it all. That KPD bearded pup said that the Russians had liberated Auschwitz. I could not imagine that 'liberation' was the word. A winter in Erfurt a pleasant season. In Poland I imagined fingers froze black. But if that city of a prison was gone surely all of our enemies knew. What difference would one plan for an oven make? They would find enough in Berlin. I was deluding myself that the little efforts of Ernst Beck able to enlighten anybody to anything.

Etta's movements in the kitchen broke my haze. I went and drank the last of the coffee with her. Sunday morning small talk a past thing. Only possible to talk of the war that was once distant.

'They would not bomb on a Sunday would they?' she asked. 'Not Sunday? We can relax today can't we?'

I agreed, but didn't know. We were all Christian weren't we? And that thought amused. The definition of Christian, even the definition of religion an oddment of another time, for another time, a peculiarity of a childish mind, as when you saw a group of nuns walking the streets for the first time and gripped your mother's hand and asked her what the strange wraiths were. And the answer didn't help your fear.

My thoughts of the morning, of my doubts, needed Etta's validation. She had taken Paul's death like women in war endured everything, absorbed everything. Men write poetry about it. But the women make sure there is a place to sit and write the poetry. There was nothing that could be bombed that could not be loaded onto anything with wheels and rebuilt somewhere else and biscuits and apples would appear from coat pockets while men carried only brandy, tobacco and woe. Paul's death as ridiculous as everything else.

'Of course it is worth it, Ernst,' she said. 'Do you think that plan would survive the war? They will burn all. Everything they have done is criminal. And you talk as if it is all over already. How many times have we thought that? And then another year gets pulled out of a hat.' The rattling and washing of the percolator and its pieces, another pot prepared as she chided me. No. Not that. Not chiding. A debating campaigner. Campaigning for reason and for what her man needed to be told on a Sunday morning when just about everything else to him seemed a better idea.

'If you think it is done what point to send me to my parents? Or are you suggesting that is not important now? That we stay here like mice and keep quiet, work as normal, pretend they did not ask you to clarify monsters' ovens that could kill thousands? Or that perhaps they do not concern themselves with Jews any more?' The whistling kettle did not stall. 'You know what, Ernst? The only thing I ever truly understood in the KPD, the only thing I learnt, was that the Jew was the only thing they ever concerned themselves with. Trains, slaves, camps, pits and ovens. That is all they ever dreamed of.'

She caught the kettle before it screamed.

'And they will not want the world to know. And if you think it does not matter then go tell your Klein tomorrow that your wife is a Jew. See what happens. I am sure they will spare the time!'

Always 'my Klein'.

'And what if your plan for that monstrosity is the only one that survives their purge? What if no-one ever knows because Ernst Beck never told anybody that Topf built ovens for the SS and not just that but that they wanted to build one taller than a house that could burn hundreds an hour?'

She busied with the percolator, her back to me, last

night's love forgotten. 'Maybe Bernie was right. Maybe you are as much a baby-killer as them.'

I rolled a cigarette. I wanted confidence from her. To give me some virtue I was lacking.

Sometimes talking to your partner is like climbing to the top of a helter-skelter with your piece of carpet. Five exhausting minutes to climb round and round, wondering the worth of it as your legs and chest burn. Five seconds to come down again, out of breath with carpet burns, and the boy behind you kicks you in the back.

'The telephone needs adjusting,' I said, walked to the parlour, sat and smoked in my armchair for time enough to calm then shuffled the chair to the telephone's table.

I concentrated on the contraption, my hands cooling my anger. She was right. And damn that. I had wanted a virtue, her to tell me I was doing the right thing or even some thing. One person in the maps they lorded over doing something. Instead I was a monster for thinking otherwise. I was not Paul. Not even Bernie KPD. Maybe she wanted the romantic end. Maybe we were supposed to end up in a ditch with bullet holes and a piece of paper in my pocket for an oven design never built. I had no father now. I could only picture hers cupping his cognac, listening to jazz on his long-wave radio, picking her up from the station in his Mercedes and shaking his head. *I told you to never marry that boy.*

The mouthpiece unscrewed easily enough, its own thread, no screws. I figured this was the offending piece, pulling the other end up somehow, breaking the connection.

I was childishly pleased at seeing the inside. The soldering, the magnet and microphone. I had taken the back off my parents' radio as a boy, looked and prodded inside as if I was journeying into space. The delicate complication of it. The magic. The endless world of a boy with a screwdriver and prying hands. Then the endless red beat of your father's palm on your backside.

Such a simple device, the Bakelite just a decoration to conceal only a corded wire running inside to the receiver and the discs of magnet and speaker in the other end. Perhaps the base held the magic. I plied out the speaker, confident I could understand it, sure that it sat wrong, that was all. The machine had to be balanced correctly. The fitting slightly off. I would put it back firmer. Announce it was fixed. Regain some pride.

Putting it back together I noticed a smaller copper and rubber wire attached to the others. Not soldered. Clipped to the others. I held the speaker and the Bakelite in my hand. Two wires I could understand. Voice, receiver. The working of the third lost. Then perhaps I did not know telephones enough.

I screwed the mouthpiece back, put the bone to the cradle. And then the child poking inside the radio followed the bite of curiosity.

The third wire travelled with the braided cords to the rear of the telephone. It wound round them as tightly as a tapeworm, innocuous in daily use, hiding with its brothers. Hiding. Hiding to the fool who had never owned a telephone before. One wire to hear, one to speak. A third wire.

I stood and stepped away from the black of the telephone, backed away from the thought forming. A third wire. A neighbour with a glass to the wall. Invisible behind the wall.

Etta came in with coffee, began to apologise for her speech then questioned the ridiculousness of the man horrified in an empty room. She put the coffee down gently, gently to not shock the maniac backing from a telephone.

'Ernst?'

I gave her my dismay. In a look. From her, to the device on the little table. The device they had put in our home. Put there before we moved in. Not there when we looked at the house.

'Etta?' I whispered. Instinctive to do so. 'Etta, do you think they can record telephones? I think there is a wire in the phone that shouldn't—'

It rang. In reply to me.

It rang. On a Sunday.

Chapter 41

It rang five times before the bell finally echoed off while we stared at it. When they made these things did they intend for the ring to be so aggressive, a deliberate thought?

Make it loud and assertive. It is what they are used to. They will answer and do what it says. Germany embraced the telephone like no other country.

Before we could speak it started again. We held each other. Foolish. Held each other as if the thing were about to spit bullets.

'I'll get it,' Etta said, pulled away.

'No,' I said. A terror in me. I could only think that they knew I had tampered. The dial on the base an all-seeing eye. A voice on the other end about to yell at me, call me in, admonish me for touching, for questioning. But if we did not answer? Would the rap on the door follow, the jackboot to the frame, the rifles and helmets, the cap with the skull? We lived in a country that feared men who walked in pairs with leather coats and fedoras. Caps and badges at least meant arrest, records. You disappeared when the others came.

'I will get it,' she said. 'You do not have to be home. I'll say you are not here. But we have to know.'

The fourth ring, louder I was sure, but I knew she was right. Always right. Her husband ready to hide behind curtains. A telephone. I was afraid of a telephone. My plan for the next few days a fantasy. I had imagined myself. The worst trick a man can play to his mirror. Paul was the man for it. Bernie the man for it. Ernst Beck would put his head down as if he were in a barber's chair. Thank them for the striped suit. Build his own oven. His wife picked up the telephone.

'Hello? Etta Beck speaking.'

I watched her relax, a handkerchief I did not know she was clutching fell to the floor and she looked brightly at me as she spoke.

'Yes, Papa!' she said. 'We have a telephone. You got my letter! How are you?'

Of course. She had given her parents our number. Who else on a Sunday?

I fell into my chair. Relieved, but something had gone from me. I did not listen to her conversation. I had come to a wall I did not know was in front of me. I was Ernst Beck. Only Ernst Beck. I was good in school. I went to university. I craved a good job, a life where I could have a good woman, security, and a country to look after me. I did not see Ernst Beck riding through snow on a motorcycle to an American general with a posse on his tail, bullets over his shoulder. I was the man Randolph Scott punched, not even the man that followed him. I was the townsman they did not make the movies about. A background player. The man in the apron with no lines to speak. The man who held the horse. Waved the hero on.

'Yes, Papa.'

I listened as Etta faced me.

'I am coming to see you and Mama. Erfurt is not as safe as it was. Did you hear that Weimar was bombed? Ernst was there. No he is fine. He is leaving work and—'

I jumped up, mouthed a curse. Had I not told her? Not clear? They were listening. Had been listening for months. I had only ever answered the telephone. Etta used it. God knows what conversations she had conspired and now why not tell your father everything.

She waved me down, ended the call, the way children end telephone calls. Yes Papa, no Papa, I will see you soon, Papa.

'What is wrong with you, Ernst?'

'The telephone! They are listening! And you tell them I am leaving. That you are going to Zurich. What are you thinking?'

She went to the coffee as if nothing had happened.

'Ernst. I can see it now even if you can't. Forget the telephone. They gave us this house. If they can listen on that thing there is probably a device in every light-fitting.' She passed me coffee. 'What does it matter now?'

There is a sane man in every madhouse. And he becomes the maddest of them.

'How many conversations have you had on it? With your little group? Are you trying to kill us?'

She took her coffee cup, took it from the room, left me with the telephone and the light-fittings, spoke over her shoulder in the doorway.

'Yes, Ernst. I am trying to kill us. Again. And save our country. Maybe I should put you on a train? Give me the plan. Or what do you want to do?'

Sunday. The day when as a boy I played quietly with my trucks beneath the table with the cherry tablecloth decoration while my father cursed Monday. The Sunday I promised I would not have when I became a man.

Ernst Beck alone with the light-fittings and the telephone. Could they listen to the telephone? You knew the operator could if she wished but for your government to do such? Ridiculous. Paul's death. A third wire in a telephone. Me riding into the sunset. Everything ridiculous now.

I went for a walk. Did not look across to the factory. The park just a doleful path past the old ghetto. I left my coat and hat. Needed the sting of the cold, the wreath of tobacco about as I smoked, the halo of my breath. Tried not to understand the part of me that wished for planes to come, to return. To remove.

Chapter 42

Monday,
12 February 1945

No cars with runes and pennants in the yard. That to be
thankful for. A weekend like a month but I did not expect
such sympathy and interest from all of those around. From
the reception to the third floor, everyone had an ear and
an eye for Ernst Beck. Handshakes as if I was brave for just
being alive. Brave. I put on my white-coat and Klein found
me in the cloakroom.

'Glad to see you back, Ernst.' Hands in pockets, leaning
on the wall. 'Back Ernst Beck! A joke, eh? No? Anyway,
good for you. I admire your ethic. A lesser man would have
used such for a week off at least.'

I thanked him, even if I did not know what for. An
automatic reaction.

'I am just glad I got out, sir.'

'Of course. A tragedy. A crime. Those monsters will be hung when we win. Killing women and children. Come. To my office, Ernst.'

I followed him. Nothing in his tone to suggest anything. Just my usual awkward morning moments in his office. I think he liked to have these talks before I had taken coffee. A power thing. As the professor with the dullest class keeps the most dulled students after hours.

'Ernst,' he took his seat, did not offer mine. 'I am afraid there may be a question in the future about your keeping of the house.'

Not the avenue of conversation I was expecting. I was thrown. I thought some discussion of his father's 'ashes', or of worse. My concern only for my lunch hour. The walk into town, to the bank. The first stage.

'Sir?'

'It was discussed Friday. Sander and I. It seems there will be a drying up of SS contracts. Temporarily. Hopefully. Your work has moved to more "normal" operations. There may be some resentment. On the floors. About your keeping of the house. It is not of immediate concern. I have vouched for you. In your interest. Based on the fact there could well be a resurrection of the SS work, we have agreed not to take your home from you. For the present. You understand, Ernst?'

He was telling me that my home was in jeopardy. That he had spoken up for me. Even without coffee I could see through it. With his tutelage of me he either forgot how he had taught me to discern or still labelled me the Ernst

Beck in short trousers, the boy who knew nothing about automobiles, could not even drive or realise the importance. Even if I had the same car he would still mock me for cleaning it myself, to not pay a man to do it for me. But I read this, saw through this. There had been a cheque after all. A cheque from a dead man for thousands of marks for work that now would not need to be carried out. The cheque banked. The paperwork lost in the mess that was Weimar. Perhaps years before anyone questioned, decades.

Do you want to keep your house, your home, your future, Ernst Beck? To be a conspirator, if even a low one?

It struck me then. Too few of these moments. Some never to be seen. Never taken up if you were not quick enough. I became him. Saw how it was done. How *this* world turned. Against the turning of the other. Keep up, keep up.

I would not need the leverage I had stumbled on, that Paul Reul had poured across a table, that I had poured into Etta's palm. Nothing so vulgar. I would not have to threaten going to Gestapo leather coats with tales of a dead man's ashes full of diamonds. Two cards up my sleeve. One he had dealt to me. The audience could fool the magician.

'Of course, sir. I understand.' I took a seat without invite. 'But may I make a request?'

He sat back. His next words unsettled the confidence I thought I had.

'Do I need a witness?'

'No.' My incredulity not false. 'No. It is a personal request.'

He sprang his chrome orb of cigarettes, offered me first, lit mine for me as he rose to sit on the edge of his desk.

I drew deep, exhaled away from me, absently looked to the windows. The smoke from Buchenwald still visible.

'What with Weimar so close I would think it safer – prefer it – if my wife could go to her parents. They are in Zurich.'

I explained it all. A travel permit, for Etta, not I. Ernst Beck would stay and work. But please afford him the chance to get his wife to safety.

'She does not work for Topf, Ernst,' he said. 'And I doubt we could get it signed off in Weimar. Their desks are covered in rubble. More important things to concern than getting your wife to her mother's skirts.'

I went to speak, he swung off the desk to ignore me.

'However, let me talk to Sander and the Topfs. In light of your work over the year – and with my praise for you – it may not be so impossible. After all . . .' He went to a desk drawer, pulled out a wad of travel permits. 'It is not as if they are rare.' He dropped them back to the drawer. Locked it. Key to his pocket. 'There would of course be the concern that your wife also knows something of the Topf trade with the SS. That she knows something that would perhaps not be . . . "safe" to know.' He took his seat. 'Only in innocence of course, Ernst. What a husband might say to his wife. You agree?'

'I have never spoken untoward about my work.' The same tone as his. I thought of the telephone, the third wire, tried to recall every conversation I had taken on the thing, had thought on it all night, sure that nothing I had said to the device was against me.

'I understand that my wife does not work for Topf. But a permit is a permit. She might at least get on a train with one. To Stuttgart at least. She could make her own way from there. Buy her own way from there. Just to get her out of Erfurt. That is all.'

He put out his cigarette and I rubbed out mine on top of it. Better than a handshake.

'I will see what I can do for you, Ernst. Come see me at the end of the day.'

The teacher with the dullest class.

*

The bank was in the Anger, the Reichsbank. I took a tram for speed. Even so, out of breath when I got there.

A bank from the last century. An image they wanted to maintain. Old. Established. Safe. All dark wood and wide desks, red ropes and brass so that you would think that everyone who worked there was richer because they worked there. Richer than you, that they washed their hands after handing you your money, that they had these grand desks and chandeliers because they knew what they were doing, never urgent until you are at the counter wasting their time. And then they disappoint like second dates.

'I am sorry, Herr Beck. You may only withdraw

two hundred marks a week.' He was not sorry, and explained before I could ask. 'There is a shortage of paper marks. You can have coin. Or stamps of course.'

'But it is my money.' The stupidest words you can say in a bank. There was a woman crying and being herded into a corner by shushing tail-coats. She was screaming that her house had been bombed, Weimar I assumed. She needed ten thousand marks, cash, her money, for a new place. The landlord demanded cash, they all did now. Not a poor woman. No husband with her. This would not be a Jewish landlord, not a Jewish bank. They did not have her money. This was Germans together. This was Germany.

'*Work*', *He* had said on the radio. *Work*. But do not expect your money when you have need of it.

'There will be a charge for such a withdrawal, Herr Beck. Fifteen percent.'

I wrote the slip. 'And you'll take that from the money that I cannot have, yes? The money that doesn't exist?' A queue behind me awaiting the same bad easily explained news. Still, two hundred marks. That should do. And a diamond. Rely on that. Do not try to think on where it may have come from. A tiny stone that could open doors like a crowbar when called upon. But just once, just one door. But not an oven door.

February, but by the time I got back to Etta I was sweating. I gave her the notes. The first stage. We had money. With the cash in my wallet and change we had two hundred and thirty-five marks. It is surprising how money can bring hope. It should not be so.

I patted the motorcycle as I left. I had a page of petrol rations not used. An exit to use. I did not let Etta hold me before I left. I would be back in a few hours. Back with a travel permit. Second stage. I waved to her from the gate, distracted by an accordion player on our lonely street. He had chosen the wrong spot. Most likely picked for the wealthy-looking homes, not knowing they were empty save ours. A lambskin waistcoat with beaded stars, a happy curled moustache and happy stout belly. At Christmas he probably would have worked on the bridge with all the others. Christmas never happened so he gave February music, something French, not a polka. I gave him the last pfennigs in my pocket.

'Good luck to you, sir,' he waved his cap. Then he gave the salute and the call as I walked to the factory. I pretended not to hear.

Chapter 43

An afternoon of inking line drawings for malt burners. Dull, but with the satisfying rule of neatness over creativity, to concentrate and be delicate, comfort in the patience and intricacy. Devoid of thought other than the nib of the pen and the steadiness of hand. Its reward in its distraction. Of me. If this was not my work it would be my hobby. The solitude of detail. As such I went to Klein's office with a hangman's calm. Not the shivering of the condemned. He had a roll of permits. I was not asking payment for my silence. A gentleman's handshake. A businessman's hand-shake. The walls of a factory, of industry, designed to keep secrets in. One cheque cashed from a dead man, one permit given. Fair trade. I had become as Klein now. Or just grown up now. These subjects not taught at university. You just go out into the world and they come.

I knocked on the door, the call to enter instant.

'Take a seat, Ernst.' Klein stood by his window. His pallor

of one who had smoked all day, as newspapermen or detectives do in the American movies. All stress and snappy talk.

'I cannot grant you a permit.'

My chair weakened. I held its arms as if a pitching boat. I had no questions. He would answer them for me.

'It is a security matter. Anyone associated with Topf not permitted to travel. This comes from the SS.' His first look to me. 'I am sorry.'

'But Etta does not work for Topf. You said so yourself. This is for my wife. Not for me. Have I ever asked for anything?'

'All travel is restricted. Regardless.' He lit another cigarette. 'The trains run, but only with permits signed from Weimar. You would never get that. Not for months. You know this. It would just be a useless piece of paper.'

'Then give it to me. If it is useless. I could bribe Etta onto a train. They queue at the station all day. I have seen them. But a permit would help. I'm sure.'

'I understand, Ernst. But if you work for Topf so does your wife. By proxy. Do not offend me. Do not suggest I am ignorant enough to not consider that she has knowledge. It would be harmful for the company.'

This was not him talking. I could tell. Maybe he had tried, maybe not. He had appeased me in the morning because that is what bosses do. At the close of business, after five, is when they drop the guillotine.

I stood up, would not let my second stage be thwarted so easily. Could not go home with this. Mirrored his pose.

'I need that permit, Hans.'

He flushed at my use of his name. Looked me up and down. Our suits the same, mine under white-coat. The wing-tips the same. I had cuff-links now, not buttons. Almost a year I had been here. I was a dull pin in comparison, not shiny but still sharp. Grown sharper. And he grinned, his circus grin, the one of Victor Hugo's *comprachicos'* mutilations. The Man Who Laughs.

'And what, Ernst, would you do. Without a permit.' Not a question. He never questioned. Only put his thoughts into the room. Blew a veil of smoke at me.

I pushed open his orb of cigarettes. Plucked one and sat down. Used my matches instead of his table-lighter. Respected that at least.

'I would be forced to do two things. And be fired for both.'

He went behind his chair and I wished I had not sat. He was above me, framed in the window. Commanded the room.

'Do what? Exactly?'

Something of pride in his voice. Wondering what his pupil considered. What he had constructed.

'I could go to the Gestapo. Tell them that Topf and Sons have cashed a cheque for thousands of marks from a dead man. For work they would never do.'

He blew this off like cooling soup.

'Just business. We would return the monies. If occasioned. We did not know he was dead. Apologise and move on. Anything else?'

'A cardboard tube of diamonds.'

He moved from the chair. Leaned on the edge of his desk in his perfected fatherly manner. Smoked and watched me sweat.

This was not the stage I wanted. One. Get the money. Two. Get the permit. Or not. My plan ripped from my notes. One, two, three. The third stage. Etta on a train. Anything past that just the foolishness of a boy sticking a plan down his trousers and running. He saw it all in my face. The cigarette paper stuck to my dry lip.

'Ah,' he said.

Just that. An apologetic sigh. For both of us.

He leaned across his desk and pressed the box beside his telephone. A white light came on. Stayed on.

'You must love your wife very much, Ernst.'

I watched the light blink out. Forgot to smoke. I sat as in a dentist's chair. Waited to be addressed. I thought I had thrown the winning card to the table. Wondered on what I had not done correctly. I had threatened. He had a drawer full of travel permits. I had missed something, misjudged something. Sweat on my face. In February. I remembered the first day I saw the factory, the chimney in the centre of the roof, when I imagined the oven in the basement fuelling the floors. It must've been firing now. Pictured Etta at the window, waiting for me, watching the smoke rise from the chimney.

The door opened. A one-legged man eased himself into the room. Did not shut the door. The uniform. The cap.

I had almost forgotten him, forgotten they existed, that surely they were too busy. But what would a one-legged colonel do in Berlin? Terror enough here.

'Helmut,' Klein said. 'Ernst here would like to explain what has happened to your diamonds.'

'Ah,' he had said. A thousand words.

Klein's hand to my shoulder.

'Come, Ernst,' he said. Softly. A dragon's wing. 'We will discuss this in Prüfer's office.'

I rose with his hand like a marionette, dropped the cigarette to the floor.

The colonel said nothing, waited in the door-frame. He followed us out, the clack of his crutch the only sound as we walked.

There had been no car with runes when I had returned from lunch. It had come while I worked.

They always come when you are not watching.

That is how it is done.

Chapter 44

Prüfer's office absent of him and the ISIS board. It had been cleared away to make room for a new machine, the desk also moved to accommodate, to nest beside the curious thing sat on its own trolley.

The colonel took Prüfer's leather chair, I the wooden, Klein the window. That would be our setting for however long this took. It was long after five. Etta expecting me.

The colonel removed his cap, his crutch resting against him. He had a half-eaten plate of grapes and cheese on the desk. I could only think that they would be the fat late harvest grapes. Frozen. Used for the sweet wines. Ignorant to eat them with cheese. I thought on that wine, on if I would ever taste anything again. Did not want to hear. To answer the questions. I did not hear the first time it came.

'Ernst?' the colonel asked again. 'Where are the diamonds?'

I looked up from the plate. Could not answer. He eased back into the chair.

'You see, Ernst, there comes a time in war when men must make, how you might say . . . securities . . . for themselves. You wish to make your wife secure. So surely you can see how those of us without families, without wives, those who must stay and fight, need to secure for themselves a contingency that no-one else will provide.' He opened his arms. 'And you know there is no faith in paper, Ernst. It always falls to diamonds and gold. Always.'

I spoke then. I was the jester to the king. I could say what I wanted.

'And where did they come from?'

'From the ground. And after that the terrible truth about gems is the tragedies that come from owning them. All diamonds look like tears for a reason.'

I did not expect such poetry from a man with so much silver and braid. He was relaxed, patient, trying to relax me with his philosophy. A man of reason. He smiled away my question. Moved on.

'I am a colonel, Ernst. But I am not a *real* colonel. A paper colonel they say. Behind my back.' He slapped his thigh, the thigh where his leg ended. 'Do you know how I lost this? It was in the last war. And not how you might expect.'

I was glad for the story, for the pause, the delay, my eyes drawn to the ominous machine beside us. The size of a writing desk, two wheels on the front of it the size of a child's bicycle. It looked like some industrial tool for sewing or spinning.

Wheels always spin. Spin to make something. I had missed the story, came in on the end.

'My own brother! Can you believe that, Ernst? He shot me in the trench so I could not go over the top! Tried to save his little brother. But I lost my leg because of it, and he his life. And they made me a captain. And then when this war began I was made a colonel. For the SS. You know why the SS, Ernst?'

'No, Colonel,' I said and looked at the back of Klein at the window. I had let him down. Ashamed to look at me. That back more terrifying than the bald cripple in front of me. My shame his shame. He would not be my ally.

'Because *He* had need of colonels. He needed ranks. Most of the true army did not approve of His actions, His demands. So he rose His own colonels, majors, His and Himmler's own divisions. Legitimacy. Yet still the old ones resist. Attempt coups and assassinations year after year. And you know why?'

I was not expected to reply. I was being lulled, softened. I was sure this was how he began all questionings. Confusion and beguilement. I would answer because I was not sure what a question was. He talked slow and deliberate. Until I thought I knew him. Until I felt sorry for him and our leader.

'It was because *He* was not one of them. Just a foot soldier. The little corporal. The army is a class unto itself. Its echelons are privileged sons. And the air-force? God in Heaven! Even worse. They think themselves out of Siegfried legends. They shake hands with our enemies when they get the chance. Send each other food parcels when they are prisoners. Like they are in some gentlemen's club. They think war is an occupation. A union. And so the SS came. And I sit at a desk in front of people like you. Because they would not even care that you exist. You are not the war.' He took a breath, took a grape. '*He* knows differently.'

The pistol came to the desk with a rattle, broke the hypnotic speech.

'You know what this is, Ernst? It is an Erfurt Luger.' He touched the odd bevelled wheels at the back of the pistol, caressed the etching.

'You see that? The Erfurt crown. I had this pistol in the first war. My brother shot me with his. I'll wager you did not even know there used to be an arms factory in Erfurt, eh? Our enemies took that from us. Their treaty forbade us to make weapons. Hundreds of thousands of men and women became unemployed within a year. They forbade us to have our own industries. Yet they all wanted to come in and sell us what we were not allowed to make for ourselves. Came and stole our industries. Our inventions.' He picked up the telephone.

'You know what the Americans and British did with this? Used it to call their servants downstairs. We had a network of exchanges before they even knew what an exchange was.' He dropped it back to its cradle with a chime of the bell, swivelled his chair to look on the strange machine. 'And this? This you should know.'

Enough. Just stand up and walk out. I did not have his diamonds, did not have a travel permit. So what? Just get up and leave. I am not a soldier, I do not work for the SS. I am free. A citizen. Do they shoot German civilians? They guillotined students. A bullet less work, less meaning.

But we sit. We always do. And then cannot explain why we did so. But they know us. Know their people. We only stand and roar disapproval at football matches and bad actors.

Klein still looked out the window. I wondered where Prüfer was, where Sander was, wondered what would happen if I walked out of the room and straight to Topf's office? Informed him that a one-legged man with an old Luger was holding his employee in his factory. Whose factory was it? Whose country was it? Who paid this old man's wage?

But we do not get out of our chairs. We sit. Always. And they have always relied upon it.

'It is called a Magnetophon.' Scoffed. 'What a name! How they come up with such, eh?'

And then the diamonds forgotten.

'It was quite a coincidence,' he said. 'You see, you chose to take tea at the Elephant Hotel in Weimar. Last year. And although I am sure you would have known it to be our leader's favourite hotel in the state, you could not have realised that we have wire recordings set up throughout.' A gleeful eye.

'Wire recordings are of course not very sophisticated,

even if our enemies are still decades behind us. But your recording was most interesting. Not only because we had been observing your friend Herr Reul for some time . . .' He dropped his eyes from me, began squaring a notepad and pencil on the desk. 'But because it was revealed to us that you had decided to not legally declare you were married to a Jewess.'

Klein turned his head from the window.

'Helmut? You never mentioned this?'

The colonel ignored.

'So, naturally, given your predilection for deviancy, we arranged with Topf and the Gestapo to afford you a house where we could monitor your activities.' He tapped the machine proudly.

'The enemy has always wondered how we are able to broadcast speeches simultaneously across the empire. Regardless of time-zone. Iron oxide recordings. Those morons record on wax with needles. Like some kid in his box room with his Negro music. This device enables us to record hours of conversation, replicate it endlessly. The future of security will be the removal of privacy. All governments know this.'

He sat back, let it all sink in. The pistol left on the desk.

'The surprising thing – and in your favour, Ernst – is that with some limitations it appears that your conversations reveal that you acted under duress. You have been a good German. If anything you seemed to oppose both Herr Reul and your whore.' Whore. My father's word, the voice almost the same. 'It is apparent that your actions were as one under threat. A man protecting his treacherous false wife and himself. Forced. Would I be correct? You had to collaborate for fear of reprisal from their group, yes?'

You know these times when they come. I had seen many of them. Probably not the last citizen to be in a dock without a dock. You know why they call it a dock? It is the end of your journey. Your ship has come in, and not in the good sense. I had always been wrong. There was never going to be a knock on the door late at night. No leather coats and fedoras. It would be a hand on your shoulder in the bright of day, in the street, in the baker's while you were buying bread, while you were at work. How it was done. They knew the truth before you said it. They had written it for you.

'I wanted nothing to do with it,' I said. 'And Etta is no longer a part. Of any of it.'

I went for my papers and tobacco and his hand lighted on the pistol. As if I needed to be reminded of it. I smirked at the drama, his thought that I was reaching for a gun. Like one of our leader's favoured cowboy movies.

Maybe that was it. Maybe that was the whole war. Zane Grey not *Mein Kampf*. *He* imagined himself in a Western. We the frontiersmen. He our bold law-man in white hat who the townsfolk followed against the cattle barons, against the 'Vons' that ruled. Maybe it was just that dumb. I glanced at Klein, his face more perturbed than I expected. I rolled a cigarette on my knee. An image our leader would approve.

'And my wife is not a whore. Her parents are Jewish by birth. They were all born in Germany. As Germans. I did not find out about my wife until that day. You know I am not a communist. My only intention is to "resettle" my wife in another country. Where she can do no harm. And be out of here. Is that not what the Party would demand? Would it not be cheaper for me to do it for you?'

I lit my paper, took the longest draw on it that I have ever done, my blue eyes watered with it. An annoyance all my life. People think I care, am sentimental or gentle because my eyes water. That something has moved me. It is the pale blueness of them. Nothing more.

'What harm? I am staying. She will be gone.'

'You do not understand the law, Ernst.' His philosophy professor smile that he had given when we first met.

'The law works backwards, not forwards. Let us say that your whore stole and cracked open a walnut. She ate the contents. That is gone. But the shell remains for all to see. Are we to forget that she stole it because the nut is gone? When we can all still look upon the shell?'

I said it without care. It was done now. I had my cigarette, he had his pistol, was probably recording our one-sided debate so I said it for a court somewhere.

'The only "nut" in this room, Helmut, is you.' And I knew why men smiled at their photograph for the firing squad.

He sprang forward, struggled to reach for me, for my cigarette, and I drew back as the cripple flailed.

'I did not give you permission to smoke!'

'Helmut! Colonel!' Klein came from the window, pulled back the colonel's shoulder. 'This was to investigate the KPD. That was my understanding. Ernst knows that now. You only need to know what he knows. I cannot allow this to continue under Topf's roof. The diamonds were our interest. Not this interrogation. Ask him about those or take him and his wife to Weimar and arrest them there. This is a place of work.'

Voss glared, threw Klein's hand from him.

'I do not give a shit about the diamonds. Your share is *shit* to me. I want a Bolshevik Jewess married to a German!' He switched between us both, his face red. 'Do not think that I cannot have her removed from you tonight. Do not think that she will not be dead tomorrow.'

Klein stepped back.

'That is his wife, Colonel. You never said anything about her being Jewish. I thought this a political investigation, as we have helped before, with the other groups working in the factory. You want the KPD. That is what we agreed.'

Voss took up his pistol, wiped the sweat from his head with his gun hand. Amputees sweat more, their blood pressure higher. They are not as agitated as they look. The room warm despite the season. The furnace in the basement. The pistol hand hit the desk. The slam of the gun worse than the shot that might come from it.

'She is a Jewess witch! Bolshevik whore! I have heard her speak for months. This is not Topf's or your concern, Klein.' He holstered the pistol. 'I will remove him to

Buchenwald. And the whore.' He took his crutch, raised himself. 'I will send for my driver and my guard from downstairs.'

The telephone rang. Klein and I looked at each other. His expression looser than his normal tight constrained confidence. I had seen his face like this only once before. The day of the telephone call from Buchenwald. When he learned of his father's death. He fumbled at his pockets for cigarettes. Not there. In the orb in his office, his silver case left there. I offered him my rolled pittance. He took it as he answered the telephone. Voss waited for the other end to say its piece.

'It is for you, Colonel.' Klein passed it over.

Voss snapped his uniform, smartened the cloth before speaking into the telephone. Klein came to my side, to my chair. I rolled another cigarette for myself. My hands steadier than I had known them for a year. The calmness of the prisoner caught. I could not think on Etta. She was across the street. Within my grasp and theirs. But this afternoon not foreseen. Not even stage two. Just the coincidence of Ernst Beck asking for a travel permit and Voss at the factory with his recording device. Ernst Beck with his diamonds, the diamonds he had given away. All but one. Still that card to play, up my sleeve. War the time for magicians, for sleight of hand. Slight. Everything slight. Time yet.

They would need to organise something to get us both arrested and to the camp. Something official, something stamped. They loved their stamps. I was in Topf's factory,

Hans Klein beside me. He had thought this was about the diamonds, about the KPD. I could work on that. He had not known my wife was a Jew. His father gone. Etta the colonel's greatest concern. I was in a seat in Topf's factory, still felt safe. Even if it was only a seat in an aeroplane with both wings gone. But still a seat. Not against a wall.

The colonel put his back to us, answered steadily to every question from the telephone, put it down without farewell and swung back to Klein.

'Hans.' A demand in his voice. 'I must report back to Weimar. Something has come up. I am ordered to withdraw with the machine to a safer site.' He picked up the telephone again, dialled as he spoke.

'I will have a detail sent from Weimar to collect Herr Beck and his Jewess.' He broke off as the call was answered, barked his orders and hung up, spoke too fast for me to comprehend. He put back his cap, never looked at me, passed his pistol to Klein.

'Hold him here until they arrive.'

Klein took the weapon as if it were venomous, swapped his cigarette to his other hand awkwardly, resumed his position by the window.

'Colonel? Helmut? What is this?' Bewildered by the steel in his hand.

'Keep him here. I am ordering you as a Party member to observe an instruction. My driver will be up to take the machine.'

I smoked, blew my tobacco cloud at him. The colonel

leaving, fleeing. A call for him to leave us here. The Jew lover, the communist collaborator. So important minutes before. Fuck him and his uniform.

'Is it a raid, Colonel?' I said. 'Are you afraid of bombs, Helmut? I thought my wife was the danger?'

He hobbled around the desk, pressed his empty leg against mine. Spoke low like a lover.

'I am looking at you for the last time, Herr Beck. I have never seen your wife. And no-one — mark me now — will see either of you ever again. I am going because I have use. Worth preserving. This machine worth more than you and your whore. You should be thankful that — when you are no more — your and your whore's voices will be used to destroy the irrelevancy of your communist colleagues.'

He limped to the door, looked to Klein, nodded at the pistol. I spoke over his order as his mouth opened.

'Auschwitz has fallen, Helmut. Did you know that?' I wanted Klein to hear it. 'The red-jackets know. Know what you have done.'

'Hold him,' Voss said. 'I authorise you to shoot him if he attempts to leave. Be faithful to your Party.'

The door closed. I looked at the clock. Six. The night coming. Etta waiting. Klein leaned against the window, drew the last of my cigarette given.

'Ernst,' he said, looked at the gun, rested it on his knee. 'Ernst? How is this happening?'

Chapter 45

When I was a boy, in winter, the men would still go out with their rifles to hunt wolves. Into the hills, through the snow, through the pines and the beech. Sometimes they would take us, take their boys. Rites, as they say. And sometimes we would see. See a dead wolf, see young wolves watching.

Maybe thirty men, maybe more, less. It seemed a lot. And a lot of drinking, and jokes I did not understand. All to kill one wolf. Never any more. Just one. And then they would trudge down from the hills again. The season ended. Arguing over who had made the shot. All buying one man drinks to fill his legs when it was agreed.

I asked my father the point. The point, what success, in killing just one wolf.

'We are only allowed to hunt one, Ernst. It is the law.' And he would draw me close to him and his horrible breath that fathers have, the smell of tobacco in the teeth, of old meat in the teeth.

'But think on this. That is one animal that will not breed this summer. He will make no seven litters. Take no wife. And next year we will kill another. And no more litters from him. And that way we keep them back.'

'But why not just kill them all? Then they would be gone for good.'

He laughed. His friends laughed, slapped my back.

'Then the rabbits would starve us out, Ernst!'

I still did not understand.

*

'Hans. This is happening because of what we have done. But I am not chained to this chair.' I stood. He took the gun from his knee, levelled it at me. 'Hans?'

The door opened. A man in box-cap and grey uniform looked on me, looked on Klein with the pistol. Said nothing. Walked to the device and its trolley. Pulled it from the room and closed the door on us. We heard the lift at the end of the corridor before we spoke again.

'Who else is here?' I asked. 'Could we not tell someone? Hans? This is where we work. This is crazy.'

'There is no-one here. They wanted it this way. I told Helmut you wanted a travel permit and he came here at once. Brought his machine. Played it to me. I thought this was a communist thing, Ernst. I knew they were recording you.'

'You put it in didn't you? You put the telephone in.'

'Yes.' The gun back to his knee. 'I didn't know such a thing was capable. It's like magic. If they can do such a thing what else can they do? But I was assured you were innocent. It was to catch that rat Reul. His friends.'

'And my wife? Is she a rat?'

He came off the window, weighed the pistol, threw down his cigarette.

'I had no idea. Ernst. Believe me. I am sorry. You really did not know she was a Jew?'

'What difference? You set up that device to catch her as well as Paul. Probably hoped to catch me. How disappointed you must have been. When you heard. When I was not like him.'

'No,' he said. 'No. I was proud. As for your wife . . . I thought only of protecting my country. Is that wrong? Could you blame me for that?'

'In a few months we will all be blamed.' I sat down. Pulled out my tobacco pouch. Two papers left. Tobacco dust. Had not picked up my ration. I rolled anyway. Mumbled more than spoke.

'You heard his telephone call. Must be important to take him away. A raid heading this way maybe. Is this how you want it to end? You with a gun on me? An Erfurt gun?'

He put it to the desk.

'No,' he said, pointed to my tobacco pouch. 'Can I have one of those?'

I rolled it. Lit them together.

'It is my last,' I said, and we even found a humour to

share in my saying it. A shared irony. 'And now you know my Etta is Jewish. What on that?'

'Do not make me say sorry again, Ernst.' The old Klein returning with the waft of tobacco. We dragged together. 'I thought only that she might be a political matter. A lead to bigger fish. I was doing my job.'

'A fish rots from the head down, Hans. Have you heard that phrase before? It is not true. But it fits. Their head is rotting. And your job is head of the Special Ovens Department for Topf. When did we work for the SS?'

'Every company works for the SS, Ernst.'

'But now my wife is a Jew as well. What does that mean, Hans?'

He deflected, as always, or maybe not. Maybe thinking on something. Maybe on the killing of one wolf so he cannot breed.

'You say Auschwitz has fallen? You know this?'

'Liberated by the Russians. They might only be fifty miles away by now.'

'So Buchenwald might be ended soon?'

He looked hard at me. I saw the boy Klein again. The boy who had put his father into a camp.

I thought on Bernie's words, Bernie KPD, his apologetic words.

They are not as close as you hope they are.

'Yes. That is what will happen.'

He smoked fast. Put his hand to my shoulder.

'They want to burn the plans. This week. Hide every

contact with them and Topf. But you heard him. Even now all he cares about is that you are a German married to a Jew. That both of you would be in the Gau tonight. How did this happen, Ernst?'

'Because I wanted to be like you. Aspired to be. As you didn't want to be a farmer's boy. All against each other. What they relied on.'

He sat back in the window, looked at the smoke in the distance grey against the black sky. The smoke that never stopped.

'I killed my father,' he said. Not to me. To the smoke. Dark now, dark outside.

The diamonds, tear-shaped Voss had said. There is a reason they are shaped so.

Chapter 46

Etta was at the gate, waiting for me. I ran towards, and she knew. Knew it had happened, was time, in the hallway with her bag as I came through the door, dropped it, held me.

'I'm going aren't I?' Her voice not hers. A new voice.

'Now,' I said, let go of her, got hold of the motorcycle. 'Now.'

I wheeled the bike out, set it on its stand on the pavement as she followed in her coat.

We did not speak, only my instruction when I told her to place her feet on the frame when I pushed off, only a parcel shelf for her to sit on.

She tucked her skirt to avoid the wheel, put her suitcase in the back of me. Never said a word. Held me as tight as she could. I started up. Rode the pavement as a black car sped past, out of the factory.

I took the corner to avoid following it.
And we were gone.

*

'We haven't much time,' Hans said. He had made a decision,
refused protest. 'Take off your white-coat. Give it to me.'
'Hans?'
'Don't argue, Ernst. I'm still your chief.'
He put on the coat, pulled me to the window, pushed
the gun into my hand.
'You want to be me?' he said. Insisted. 'Then be me.'
'Hans?'
'It will be hours before they know. I have no wife, Ernst.
No-one to miss me. Get her out of here.' He sat in the
wooden chair.
'Now hold that gun on me. Speak if spoken to.' We heard
the lift reach the floor. 'Let me do this.'
'You do not owe me this, Hans. You don't know what
you're doing.'
'It's dark, Ernst. Late. It's just one night. They'll realise
their mistake and blame each other and let me go. Don't
let me think on this any longer than I have to.' The sound
of boots along the corridor. 'I won't say anything. Now be
the best Hans Klein you can be.'
'I don't think I could be that.'
He ignored, sat in the wooden chair. And we said no more.
The door opened.

*

I propped the bike against the station wall and we walked into the concourse, full as always despite the hour, despite the dusty snow falling. The train leaving at 7:18. It would reach Stuttgart after midnight. No uniforms here other than the armbands of old men. I set Etta to the first pillar of the platform. Looked at the clock.

7:06.

'Wait here,' I said. 'Give me the money. I'll get the ticket.'

She handed over her purse.

'What about the travel permit?'

'I have it,' I said. 'Wait here.'

*

'Is this the prisoner?'

Helmets. I did not expect helmets. You see them on posters, in newsreels. Two actual soldiers standing in the doorway. I was used to caps, those square box hats like boy scouts. They had automatic weapons on slings. I had never seen such guns. Imagined they could destroy walls if they chose.

'Yes,' I said, waved the Luger to Hans as they came.

'Herr Klein?' The taller of them asked.

I nodded.

And that was it.

They pulled him from the chair, together, slammed him

363

to the wall, a forearm across his throat. No anger, no emotion. Like moving furniture.

'And his Jew?'

I had the gun. Looked at Klein.

I had a gun.

He read my thoughts, shook his head as best he could.

I walked over. Passed the pistol to them.

'I will get you the address,' I said. 'From my office. One minute.'

Klein said nothing, his throat held against the wall. The look between us not enough. I hoped to convey something. Not enough. But he grinned at me. His grin. That would do.

And probably for the first time in his life someone slapped it off him. Slapped the grin off the face of the director of operations. The Special Ovens Department. Department D IV of Topf and Sons.

I strode from the room, as Klein would, a conviction that one of them might follow. A breath when they did not.

I went to Klein's office first, the lock on his desk drawer snapped like a chicken bone when I took his letter-knife to it. I pocketed the knife and peeled a travel permit from the roll of them. I saw his cigarette case and lighter, picked them up. Hated myself for doing so. I wasn't thinking of the tobacco. Thinking of the months ahead. The little things I could trade for bread. My coat and hat from the cloakroom and then realised I could have taken the whole roll of permits, probably as good as silver for trading. No time. Forget that. I went to the long drawers where we kept our plans and took out my copy of the oven, my duplicate, a photo-carbon of the original. It had the eagles, the runes, the right date. Good enough. And I tucked it down the seat of my trousers, against my back, as foolishly as I had ever imagined doing. I hit the stairs. Ran from the building.

Left him.

*

'It is a travel permit!' I pleaded to the ticket clerk. 'What difference does it make if it is stamped? How could I get it stamped from Weimar? The whole place is broken!'

7:10.

Eight minutes. I heard the steam and the whistle.

'I'm sorry, sir.' Not the same man I had seen last week. The same expression, the same tolerance. He had heard it all before. A hundred times today. 'It must be stamped from the Gau.'

'One ticket,' I said. 'One ticket to Stuttgart. Just for my wife. Please.'

'You have a permit. Do better. You are halfway there. Get it stamped and come back tomorrow.' He called over my shoulder. '*Next!*'

'Wait,' I said, hid the man behind me with my body, filled the window with my Party tie-pin and the roll of money. 'Let me buy ten tickets,' I said. 'For the price of one.' Began to peel off the notes. 'How much would that be?'

Another whistle from the train stopping.

'I cannot do that,' he said. His voice lower now. The voice of the streets, of the alleys. The new voice of Germany.

I passed the small stone from my pocket to his brass change drawer.

'What about now?' I said. 'One single to Stuttgart.'

He looked at the brass tray shaped like a seashell, the white stone. He no longer looked at me, ripped a ticket and the drawer emptied. A stone the shape of a tear vanished. As it had probably done a dozen times before.

'Standing ticket only,' he said. '*Next!*'

I ran to Etta, the train there, the train guards carried clubs instead of flags. I gave her the ticket, had to beat others from the door just to get her aboard, passed her one hundred marks.

7:16.

'Buy a ticket from Stuttgart to Zurich. A return if you can. It will not draw as much attention as a single.' No travel permit for that journey. But she would cope, she would do something. Women could bribe better than their fool husbands. Enough money for a taxi even. And she could cope without me. Didn't even need me.

'Ernst?' Her voice choking.

'Don't worry.' I shut the door. A whistle. Wheels rolling. 'I'll get to Kassel. I'll call. I have your father's telephone.'

No real goodbye. No kiss. What point in a sad kiss? We did not show in public. Held hands only if no-one could see.

The train eased out. Her face gone from the door as others elbowed their way through the carriage.

No movie farewell. No palms pressed against glass, no misty eyes and longing waves from the window. Guards were throwing cases from the doors. People tried to hang off the carriage and crashed to the platform or were swatted away by guards and passengers.

But she was safe. Safer now.

A diamond to get on a train. The way the world was now.

I walked away.

Almost got outside.

Saw the black cars before they saw me.

I turned from the front entrance, arrowed to a side exit. I swapped my hat with one of the old militia men, slapping his shoulder in faked inebriated gratitude, took his holed woollen cap in exchange for my sixty-mark fedora, thanked him for his service, called him father.

It took two trash cans for me to find a bottle, a soda bottle but it would do. I pulled down my tie and staggered out of the station, feigned drunkenness, sat on the stone beside my motorcycle, drank from an empty bottle and watched the raincoats step out of the cars shadowed by uniforms and slung weapons. They went past without a look, the falling snow helping to blur me with the rest of the world. Two cars. They had brought two cars. A thousand bullets.

I took up the bike. Hundreds of kilometres in front of me. And a little two-stroke engine puttered away from Erfurt.

No wife now. No Hans Klein, no work, no family. No choice but to go forwards.

What choice should there ever be for a good man? For heroes?

PART FOUR

Chapter 47

Civilian vehicles had almost vanished from the streets in the last two years. The destruction of our reserves and of our synthetic production the chief aim of our enemies. A war machine cannot roll without fuel. That's the real reason we invaded Russia when we did instead of finishing the West first. We needed their oil. Simple as that. It was as Klein had said. It is always about the East. Where it leads. For a thousand years. The Silk Road now an oil slick. Only medical personnel, the police and Party officials had access to fuel. Unless you were wealthy of course. The world had not changed that much.

Vehicles were converted to run on liquid gas or anything that burned, wood chips even. Motorcycles did not have this ruling, exempt, which is why there were tens of thousands of them on our streets. It did not mean you could get petrol. This I found just outside of Waldkappel when the tank showed empty two hours away from Erfurt, a few miles out of Thuringia, the first time I had left the state of my birth. I did not even know if these people would have a different accent to mine. Hessians known to speak a low German, some as coarse as sailors. Goethe spoke and wrote the same.

Cold, after ten, but thankfully stopped snowing. I braked the bike as I reached the sign for the town. The dynamo light died, I warmed my hands close to her little engine and put down the stand to stretch my legs.

An empty straight road in a forest. I had seen no other vehicle, but still I paced the road ready to duck to the trees.

My hands were red, numb, the temperature just above freezing, grateful that the bike could not go faster to freeze me more.

I stamped, hugged my arms, watched my clouds of breath then went for the false warmth of a cigarette.

The lighter flashed, lit the trees by the roadside and I glimpsed shadows of things moving that were not there. The low branches were rifles, the knots of the trunks all stalking faces. The tobacco steadied. I did not think on the silver case and lighter, their owner, hurried them back to my pocket. A coat and wool hat. I was probably doing better than most. But not much. I drew on the Camel, mapped what I knew as I would a patent stretched before me on my ISIS board.

Not enough fuel to go back, that much settled. I had to get into town, get more. Go on, Ernst Beck. Keep on. Is this not what you wanted? What you imagined a hero does?

No good place would be open now. Find a hole for the night. I needed food and water. Shelter. I had run as if from a burning building. But I had money, a chequebook, ration pages. I threw the cigarette to the snow, fuelled by the confidence of it, its banishment of emptiness.

I had a motorcycle, money, cigarettes. I was a king. Not running. I had a mission. I was at the bike, emboldened by it.

Then I saw the yellow lights crawling along the road high behind me. No point in starting; they would be going twice as fast. I rolled the bike off the stand and tried to take her down the bank into the trees. She ran down it, took me with her. We crashed together beside the trees like drunks, every part of her that stuck out punched into me.

I waited on top of her. She was still warm, oddly comforting as my chest beat. No comfort if the car stopped.

The lights rolled above me, a sweeping roar, a spattering of slushed snow as they careened past. I looked up, the red lights from the rear falling down the trees, gone, took up the bike again. Wing-tip shoes are not suited for pushing a motorcycle up a bank. I was on my knees for the most of it.

I had to play the choke and starter like an instrument before she conceded. I had expected to see lights in Waldkappel. There were none. And even in the dark, as I got closer, I could see there was almost no Waldkappel either.

*

The buildings like gingerbread houses crumbling after New Year, the snow the nibbled icing. Drawn in moonlight, against the dark, only skeletons of homes, rib-cages of roofs, shelled bullet-wound walls. I had seen Weimar freshly burnt, living, coursing with flame, this a town of giants' gravestones, my engine disturbing their slumber. I stopped in the middle of the street, feet to the cobbled ground.

This was kept from us. No notion that this was the state of our country. It was like reading a book that changed its story halfway through. The main character a prince switched to beggar without a paragraph narrating the exchange. All the story changed. I shut off the engine, to not disturb the tomb, wheeled the bike and felt ashamed to walk the streets. I cannot explain that.

Always head for the church in a new town, always the largest building, everything gathers around it, life gathers around it. I saw its stepped Gothic roofs against the moon.

The ancient buildings always stand, as I said. Testaments. The only thing that marked the roads were the unlit streetlamps stretching away from me like Calvary crosses. I followed them.

*

Nothing around the church but the remains of houses. So I walked on with my machine burden, my Quixotic ass. At a crossroad I saw a swinging sign on what might have been the main road. Only bars and butchers have swinging signs high on their walls. All the signs a German needs. I pushed towards it.

A good square white-washed building, the iron sign proclaiming it to be the 'Hof Kassel'. Maybe that meant this was the road to Kassel. Better. I had done better. I hoped. I set the bike on its stand and knocked on the double oak doors as quietly as you can to still gain attention within and stepped back to the street to wait for a light.

An old woman opened a shutter. A real Mother Hulder in glasses and headscarf berated me from above, her words a mystery of vulgarity.

'A room,' I called. 'I just want a room, mother. I have travelled from Erfurt.'

She shut the window with a curse but I saw the light travel the room. I sheltered in the alcoved doorway, pretended to be colder for pity. The door unlocked.

'What are you?' she asked. 'A duck or a goose?'

I did not understand this. They have different tongues out here.

'Only cold, mother,' I said and hammed it up with foot-stamps and rubbing hands. She stood aside, misery all over her face as I tramped in.

'We are closed,' she said. 'Ten marks if you want a bed.' I had heard these people often spoke contradictory in the same sentence.

'Ten? A day's wage?'

'Free outside,' she flapped her shawl over her headscarf and walked to the bar with me behind her.

'Ten,' I agreed. 'And some bread and cheese. Water.'

'Ah,' she held out her hand. 'A queer from Erfurt. In Hesse you drink your apple wine. Draw your own water why don't you? What else would you do?' Her hand still out. I gave her the ten.

'Where can I get some fuel for my motorcycle?'

'I have cheese under that dish,' she indicated a porcelain cow on the bar. 'I will bring you some bread. It is grainy but good. The wine is also grainy and it will come sometime with the bread. The fuel is on the moon so fair travel to you.'

I dared not ask for anything hot. Out on my heels else. I sat at the bar and she scowled. It is their way.

'Is there no fuel in town?'

'It has been almost a month since we have been bombed. How blessed you are. Erfurt queers.' She shuffled to the kitchen and I lifted the porcelain cow, took out Klein's letter-knife and cut a good chunk for my ten marks.

A tankard of cider in her generosity, a doorstep of bread as she came back.

'The cow says she has no butter so late.' She slapped the plate to me.

'Thank you, mother. Is there a farm or somewhere I could get fuel? I am going on to Kassel. Is this the road?'

'Oh,' she bemoaned. 'I am questioned in my sleep? In my dreams? I am going up the stairs still asleep. Take the first door. I will be up at seven if we are not burned awake, Erfurt. Try not to play your piano too late.' She took the lamp and I was left in the dark.

Food. Cider. A bed. Glad in the dark. I relished the sound of my jaws working. And Etta. I looked for a clock. Past ten now. Midnight when she would get into Stuttgart. We were further apart than we had ever been. Even before we met there were only scant miles between us as we grew up. I felt stretched thin. Could not remember her last words to me. What stage now? Fuel. Get fuel. Work on that. I took the oven plan from my back, stretched it over the bar in the dark. Saluted my cider to it, life coming back to my hands. A church and a bar still stood. The best cider and cheese I have ever had in my life, a bed fit for angels waiting for me above surely. Tomorrow I would find fuel, a telephone, speak to Etta. I folded up the plan and crawled to bed. No running water. A bowl and a chamber pot, a mattress without sheets or pillow.

I slept like a prince.

Awoke like a thief.

Chapter 48

It was like the night I had spent at Auschwitz. Woke without knowing where I was — as I said, like a thief waiting to be snatched, jumped awake, caught my breath and remembered.

I went to the bowl and the mirror. Red nose and unshaven face. I did not even have a comb, ran my hands through my hair with the water, stared into the speckled mirror, the black gaps like galaxies to be lost in, and thought on the little girl I had run to at the camp.

I tried to save her from being crushed. Let her be carried under the arch instead. Had hoped she imagined it like a holiday. A new bed, a new room. She could have sat on the parcel shelf of my bike. She would have fitted, like Etta had. She would have fitted.

I washed my face, looked down to the chamber pot. I could not use it and leave it for Mother Hulder. Wait for the road. Too shy to let someone else see my piss. To be judged for my piss. I thought of Etta. Her days an endless search for privacy. She would have walked a mile out of her way to not let anyone hear her toilet. I smiled. Fuel and a telephone. And all would be right again. She would be home now. I could not think otherwise. Quilts wrapped around her and her mother's hot chocolate. Reading books by the fireside and an album of jazz records to flick through. You used to buy them like photograph albums. The recordings so short you bought a concert like a book. A lost pleasure. It is the little things you miss in wartime. Etta had not understood about the ice-cream.

'*Who wants ice-cream in February?*' she said.

I did not mean the ice-cream. I meant the simplicity. That was taken from us. The seconds of the clock were taken from us. We only had the hours, the calendars, the months. These shoes will do for another month, these pickles will last for another month, these tyres, this coffee, this ink, this coin. These people.

A war is the vanishing of tiny things. A thimble for a pail. That is how they kill us. The people in the maps.

I left the face in the mirror, put on my cold clothes and went downstairs.

Mother Hulder had not wiped clean her scowl. I asked if this was the Kassel road and she at least gave me that.

'If you go under the viaduct that is the road. That's what they've been trying to bomb. Killing us a pastime.' She gave me a mug of buttermilk and bread-crust for breakfast then presented some sandwiches wrapped in greaseproof paper.

The crinkle of the paper in my hand the nicest sound I ever heard.

'Thank you, mother,' I said.

'Two marks,' she said. 'Ham in them.'

I gave her the money and asked about fuel.

'What are you doing here?' she asked.

'I am a journalist,' I said. Lied. Easy. Getting easier. 'Recording what I see. But I need fuel for my bike, mother.'

'A queer paper man from Erfurt. I thought as much. You write a symphony for me.'

She went to her kitchen before I could answer, returned with a crock bottle.

'This should get you to Kassel. Your pretty green girl's bike will run on this. Farmer's red fuel for the boiler. It will smoke but it will run.'

I took out my wallet again.

She raised her arms, hailed the empty room.

'And now I am just awake and am insulted. God bless me.' She passed the bottle. 'I made myself happy by selling you pig-fat sandwiches with paper sauerkraut. If there's anything pink in them I will marry a poor widow.'

'Thank you, mother,' I said. Hugged her, and she did not prise herself from it.

'Go, paper man,' she said, brushed me from her. 'I will gamble that I and a blind man write better than you. Kassel indeed.'

'Would you like my ration for the fuel?'

'I'll give it to the king of the moon shall I? Leave the bottle on the street. I will shut my door against Erfurt queers.'

And we were done.

Behind the parcel shelf of the bike sat a small metal box. I put the sandwiches in it. I had never checked it before. A small leather pouch of spanners inside. A young man had bought them, put them to the back of his bike. He would tighten every bolt of his old machine religiously every week. He had seen the pouch in a window. Saved his money to buy them, thought of the girl he would take into the fields on his bike and placed his spanners proudly in the little box. I unwrapped it and against the cold of the morning tightened every bolt on his machine. For him. Good boy. Good alive boy I hoped. The smallest thing I could do was appreciate his machine that had saved me.

The tank glugged the fuel, started like it was her adventure. Mother Hulder locked back in her rooms hoarding her marks taken from an Erfurt queer. Tuesday. Could adventures start on Tuesday?

The viaduct came soon enough. Arches like the plinths of old gods over harbours, grand as we always do them, did them. Our nineteenth-century architects imagining a future. I went under them like Jason chasing his fleece. Only one thought. If Waldkappel was almost tinder what else was west, was left of us?

Kassel safe Bernie had said. Wait there.

Wait. Or find.

Which to be?

The sun at my back. Cold clothes warming up, refreshed. The streets empty. Forty kilometres, straight road. Just over an hour. The sun, and everything, everything else, at my back.

Chapter 49

Every school-child knew this place. Knew Kassel to be the home of the Brothers Grimm. A heritage of children's folk tales honoured in one place forever. A place of palaces, of legends. The palaces stood. The legends irremovable. The homes and streets not so.

Not a wall without some scorch-mark bruise as its smallest injury, as if the buildings had fought each other like boxers, the losers on their backs, the winners displaying their broken teeth. Not a roof complete. I felt a burning on my face to cry, too cold to do so, only the ever-watering of my blue eyes as usual. An annoyance all my life.

Dirty, ragged children chased the bike down the street, boys with sticks, their sisters watching from the pavement with doll-sized prams or actual prams with wails within.

I rolled on like watching a newsreel. Left and right of me no better view. The same as Waldkappel, the street-lamps and the road signs as mournful as scarecrows, their arms east and west, pretending, assuring that the town still existed beneath the snow and rubble.

We pulled up at a sandstone building, still intact, most of the street still there. The boys descended on my bike with their chair-leg sticks. Screaming local insults or just screaming as they slammed at the guards of the bike for no reason other than it was there, newly there, was not destroyed and so should be. I shooed them away like geese and they ran off laughing, threw stones at me.

Could not be angry at them. Pitied them. Did not know what they had seen, had endured. Most wore the coats of their fathers, their older brothers, holes in their trousers and their knees. Not one of them shouted in a whole sentence. Fragments. Fragments of speech. The barking of dogs. They were probably growing tails just the same, gnawed on bones. We were killing our children. And they relished it. Two of them flashed the nubs of their penises at me.

The old philosophy was that you could measure a country by the way it treated its old and its prisoners. I knew now that you should look at the children. How many inches of dirt you could wipe from their faces or cut from matted hair. Measure the dirt for how many years it would take to repair them.

I whistled to the tallest and brought the sandwiches from the metal box and shook them at him. He loped to me like an animal.

I gave him half of one and told him he would get the rest of it if he looked after the bike until I returned. His cheeks filled with the bread in one gulp, nodded because he could not speak with the girth of it and I put the rest to my pocket as he watched so he could see the treasure waiting for his reward. I took the bag of spanners. The boy who owned them did not deserve such a purchase to be stolen, even if I had done so.

I chose the building for its size, that it still stood, that it must be a hotel or apartment block. Kassel had a Gau, was a military district, had prison sub-camps. It would still have hotels. Even if the old ones were gone someone would set up another out of their private homes. The officers would need somewhere to stay.

I removed the woollen cap, smoothed my hair, opened the door and went to the desk. Always a mother now, always a mother behind the desks or at the bars. I had no pleasantries left in me and neither did she.

'I need a room.'

She rotated the register to me.

'Ten marks a night.' Her hand open.

'How much for a week?' Put my real name to the page. What difference?

'No weekly rate.' She blew the ink on the book in the same motion as she took my money, did not read my name or my home. 'We have hot running water. Good water. No meals. Go left, Esten's place. Food there. He closes at three.'

'Where can I find a telephone? And I need somewhere to put my motorcycle.'

'No telephone. People's telephone at the Gau. I have a yard round back. Put your thing there. I lock every night.'

'Thank you, mother.'

She kissed her lips, tugged at her shawl. I waited for my key and she remembered that was how things used to be and something of the old landlady returned, blushed at how it used to be when gentlemen walked into her premises.

'Sorry. No key. Room fifteen. No single rooms so no key. You share with officer.'

I tried not to react on the word, turned it to an affront.

'Ten marks to share a room?'

'The SS have taken all my rooms. Do better why don't you. I am glad that I have men with guns here.'

'I'll move my bike,' I said, went for the door.

'I have no-one to carry your bags,' she called after.

'I don't have any.' Dolefully.

She must have taken a glance at the book.

'Erfurt? Why would you leave there?'

'I am still wondering on that,' and went outside to pay a ten-year-old in sandwiches.

He stood like a soldier over the bike. The others throwing stones but ran when I appeared at his side.

I gave him all Mother Hulder's bread. As she would have done.

'Give one to your mother, eh?'

'She was bombed.' His eyes only on my paper-wrapped sandwiches. 'I live with my aunt. She doesn't like me. I

have to shit outside. She's old. I've had a birthday since.'
He snatched the sandwiches from me.

'Don't swear. Give a sandwich to your aunt.' He missed
my words, his feet gone, vanished around a corner. What
children did now. Appeared and vanished like ghosts. Only
their heels. Flashes of them out of the corner of your eyes.

I wheeled the bike into the walled yard. Went to telephone Etta with a pocket full of some boy's spanners. Walk.
Save petrol. Telephone Etta, do not think it will not happen,
that her voice is not there, then eat and then see what
manner of man, of officer, I was to share a room with.

*

A twenty-minute walk to the Gau on Wilhelmshöhe, my
first time crossing the Fulda, the canal-barges and punts
probably more in use now than ever this century. The old
virtues always return. We had thought horses limited to
parades, rivers and canals for pleasure. They came back
like they never went away. Horses and rivers. Our first
things. The forever things. The horses always come back.
Even for the army. They pulled guns as much as they did
potato carts. Did not care for the nature of the burden.
Never did. Posters showed tanks roaring over mud mounds.
The machine supreme over all. It might have done us better
to show the most faithful, plodding cannon through fields
like ploughs. A sureness to inspire. The gas giants rotting
in sheds. The horse, head down, going on. Never not needed.

Failed when his heart did. Better inspiration. Tanks stopped by stones.

Along the wide emptiness of Wilhelmshöhe you could almost be blown down by the wind. With the buildings gone it ran round the half-walls and rushed, bit cold from all sides, the dust cascading towards the Bergpark and the Hercules statue in the distance. You could see him from everywhere now, no structures to block his vision, but Wilhelmshöhe lead straight to him, calling you to him.

Directions to the Gau gladly given by the first man I came across but he did not warn about the queues, probably thought he would not have to. You get used to queuing in war. This one skirted the whole of the building. All old. Grandmothers with bundles, grey men in caps and holed overcoats and waistcoats with watch-chains without watches. This was victorious Germany. Cold starving people who had spat on and sent their neighbours to rot in ghettoes, burned their temples. Victorious people.

Today you. Tomorrow me.

Not what it was supposed to mean. Depends what end you are standing on when you said it.

He thought we were going to be the cowboys, the settlers. Could not have foreseen we would become the Indians on the reservations, the paintings of cold huddled figures straggling through snow.

I asked the line if I had to stand here to make a telephone call. No-one answered, maybe not cared to answer. My accent wrong. I walked to the front, queried the first rifle and greatcoat I saw. Asked him the same question.

'Where to?' he said.

'Zurich.'

'No Zurich. Germany only. Back in line.'

I walked away. Glad not to have wasted my time in line, hollowed out that I still had not spoken to her.

*

At the eatery I had an old sausage and beer. The sausage not old because of the war, just the way they ate them, hung for a week and always served with beer. Sixty pfennigs. A fair price for a place with a tarpaulin for a roof. A radio on rope hung from the wall, the announcer's never-pausing voice the only one in the place, the slurp of soup the dominant sound. An old man in leather jacket and box-cap tried to talk to me but his stammer and cough made him give up and I smiled and shrugged until he turned back to his plate, frustrated with himself, assuring me with slurs and waving hands that he could speak two years ago.

We had studied this city at university. We had books and even film. All to learn how a medieval city had grown modern without swallowing the architecture, with remembering its heritage, its heart. Now stepped on, gone. People lived amongst their furniture on the streets, replicating their parlours. An electric tram wheeled past my window pulled by a horse. Coal wagons from the bombed station everywhere and utilised for clearing rubble, salvaging bricks, rescuing slate to repair roofs. The women and children collected, the men pulled. Fruitless to me. Not to them.

Everywhere I looked an odd mix of picture-books of Roman or Greek ruins, old towers without Gothic spires, churches of huge stubborn blocks that bombs had only managed to chip and then the devastation of an inferno that had flattened the future that Kassel had tried to build for the next century. Blown away like straw from months of blanket bombing. Only the statue of Hercules, the monument high in the hills, looked down unharmed over his city, sure that there was inspiration in his survival. He had watched over them for more than two hundred years. This just a blink of his eye. He had not stepped on them.

I wondered on two things as I ate my first hot meal since Sunday, my first since I had left Etta, each spoonful reminding. I even waited for it to cool and closed my eyes and imagined the man at the table next to me was the sound of her eating before me. I wondered how it must feel to be these rags of people listening to our 'victories' on a radio swinging from a wall you could see through, to survive here listening to more tripe than on your plate, and wondered on the other thing. Wondered on what type of officer I would find in my room when I returned.

There was not much of him in the room. A razor and cracked dish with a different hotel logo on it. A trio of crude health magazines held in place under the lamp, a nightshirt on his bed. The shelf in the wardrobe with two apples and a water canteen. One hanger, a zipped-up suit bag. I felt the cloth within then pulled back from it, closed the wardrobe. Privacy still a thing.

Nothing evidenced a bad man, but then I did not know what did, what to expect. Not any more. A gun, a flag, a crutch. What would he display? I took the plan from my back and put it under my mattress. Sat on the bed and listened to the nothingness outside. Could hear myself breathe.

Chapter 50

I imagined him young, my age at least, if only because the bathroom was not full of pills and creams, and the covers of his magazines expressed an interest in women's bathing suits.

I was not disappointed. Corporal Franz Werra an image of me. We could have been brothers with our blond hair and blue eyes, a sliver of a year between us, except I his picture of Dorian Gray. Two days' beard, greasy hair, wind-chapped face, my clothes reeking of petrol and road. I was sure there was a moment before his hand went out to me that he suspected that a Jew in hiding had slid himself under his door. His concern gone, joy on his face when my accent was not Bavarian or Hesse.

'Ah,' he said. 'Good to hear a decent voice at last. Gotha University. Yourself?'

'Erfurt graduate. Ernst Beck.'

He shook my hand exuberantly, his speech just as vigorous.

'We are probably the youngest men in this shitty hotel.

I have not had a room-mate yet. You look a terrible fellow. The witch has hot water here until six. Take a bath. Do you need to borrow a blade?'

'I do not even have a razor. I left in a hurry. After Weimar was bombed.'

'Really?' He took off his holster, put it to the wardrobe, then the distinctive jacket to the chair, the cap to the bed. 'Is it as bad as this?' He sat on our only chair.

'I do not think anything could be as bad as this.' I went to the bathroom, started the water, only feet away so we could still talk. 'I would appreciate a loan of your razor. Thank you. Where can I buy some wares?'

'A fellow on a wagon comes in tomorrow and Saturdays from the better villages. Or there is always an old boy with a handcart on Konigstor who sharpens. He might have something. What do you need?'

I stepped back into the room.

'What you see is what I have.'

'You really left in a hurry didn't you?'

'I only had my motorcycle. I could not carry much else.'

He stretched for the table, took up my case and lighter.

'I'll trade you a use of my soap and razor for a cigarette.' He turned the case in his hand. 'Silver. Very nice.' He took a cigarette from the band, sniffed at it. 'A Camel? A man of means. Who is HK?'

'Sorry?'

He struck the lighter. Took a cool drag, sighed out a grateful cloud. Watched me.

'HK. The monogram on the case.' He looked at the lighter. 'And on this.' He put them back to the night-stand. 'You said your name was Ernst Beck?'

'I bought them like that. Pawnbrokers. I am afraid I do not have that much means to buy my own silver.' I went back into the bathroom. 'These are not your towels as well are they? I cannot impose that much.' Deflect. Deflect like Klein. Tried not to recall him. Yet. Too soon.

'No. The witch at least provides linen. Why would you come to this shit-hole?'

'I did not know it was so bad. Everyone said it was safe here. I might go back now.'

'Quite a risk to get here. For nothing. Travel is restricted. How did you manage it?'

I busied with the bath and taking off my cuff-links, spoke as if that my only interest.

'The Erfurt roads were open. I never came across any blocked.' I put my head around the wall. 'You do not mind do you? After all I did not know I would be sharing with an SS officer.' I came fully in, went for the cigarettes.

'No.' And he meant it. 'As long as you are not running from something. Good luck to you. Most people shy from the SS. It is refreshing to see someone so relaxed.'

The cigarette to my lips. I noticed my hands did not tremble any more.

'I work with the SS every day. I work in the design departments for Topf and Sons. Work at the camps now and then.'

394

'Ah.' His expression genuinely relieved. 'I was wondering why you were not signed up. Vital work. Lucky bastard. Me, I've been in the shit since '41. Only in the SS since August. My degree brings me to this shit-hole for administration.' He held the cigarette out admiringly. 'This shit is good.'

'You say shit a lot.' I thought of the boy I had told not to swear.

He laughed, wagged his cigarette at me.

'So will you. Soon enough. How is it you are not at work now?'

Questions. All that uniforms know how to do. Keep asking until something trips, until something slips.

'Work has slowed. I might not be permitted to talk about that now I say it. You understand? Confidential work. Sorry. My mistake.' As Klein would, grinned as Klein would. He nodded approvingly. 'So I took some time off. My first in a year. I thought Erfurt might be next, after Weimar was bombed. I will admit I was afraid. Now I think I have made a mistake.'

'We all have. But at least my day has improved now I have a room-mate with Camels. You won't see those again around here. We get navy shit if we're lucky. You can get some branded ones from that chap tomorrow.' He snapped his fingers. 'Hey! Could you pick me up some? We can't shop outside. Can't even drink with these people. Can only mess in the Gau. We're only in this witch's shit-hole because our quarters is a hospital – why are you laughing?'

I liked him. Liked an SS officer. Maybe it was his age. Maybe it was the relief of talking to someone who did not look half-dead, still had life and talked about cigarettes and drink, not ovens and putting your wife on a train.

'Sorry.' I was giggling, actually giggling, held my chest. 'It was what you said. I was just picturing a witch's shit-hole.'

He broke out with me, choked on our cigarettes. A knock came on the door and the crone's voice screeched through the wood.

'Hoy!' She rapped faster. 'No women in here! What are you doing?'

A waved dismissal from Franz.

'Go bring us some schnapps and beer, mother!'

The door went silent, our laughter grew as she departed for her orders, both of us wiping our eyes.

'See,' he said, stepping to the wardrobe and his holster. 'She knows I'll shoot her if she doesn't bring it.' He took out the gun, saw my face drop but shushed me as he held it out for me to see, continued to laugh when I saw it up close.

'It's carved of wood!' he howled. 'Can you believe that shit? I work in an office! They don't even give us real guns! I'll have to throw it at the Americans!' He fake shot me and the lamp before putting it back and tossed me one of his apples, the other for himself.

We sat on our beds, opposite each other like a university dorm, as we had both done once, not so long ago. Two young men hiccup laughing. Laughing like schoolboys at swear words and old ladies as we chomped on scrumped apples. Nothing in any of it to laugh so. But it came. And I did not recognise my own laugh.

I had tried to make Etta understand about the ice-cream, about the little things, the thimble for the pail.

A rotten room without a key in a flattened city. An SS officer. A man running from them.

He might have stamped chits for transports, filed IBM cards for the marked. I helped build ovens for the end of the line. A night of schnapps and cigarettes to come. Always conscious of the last cigarette. Leave one for morning. The way it should be for young men. The dissonance of laughter when the dispossessed recognise each other.

I had my bath and shave, became Ernst Beck again. Mother brought our schnapps. We drank and smoked slow, talked of university and professors, swore we had the same bad ones and the same morons that ruined every class. I did not talk of Etta. Did not say I was married. Kept that close. Here might be a man who could help me make a telephone call. Thought like Klein.

And then the sirens came. And then the planes drowned them.

And we stopped laughing.

Franz turned off the light by its fragile beaded chain. I asked if the building had a cellar. He hissed me quiet, hand on my forearm, his head at the window. I thought he had quietened me lest the pilots heard us. No. He was listening *to* them, not for them.

'This place has been targeted forty times since I've been here,' he said. 'I know the sound. They're too high, too slow. Hundreds of them. Not for us. Heading east.' He turned the light back on, stood and drank high.

'Ernst. You did not make a mistake.' Drank again. 'You won't be going back.' He passed me the bottle. 'Here. Drink.' He watched me swallow. No mirth on his face. Just approval that the schnapps sank in my belly.

'I think that some place east of us will not be there tomorrow.'

Chapter 51

Franz gone before dawn on the Wednesday. I supposed the planes meant he would have to attend early or maybe these were his normal hours. Either way he did not disturb and I awoke more leisurely than I had for weeks despite, or perhaps for the threat above.

I needed money. After my rent for Wednesday, which allowed me access to a communal chicory coffee pot and oat biscuits, I was down to eighty marks and change. And there is nothing like war for inflation and advantage. And I needed news. Needed to know if there was any word on Americans near, or at least what had happened to some poor souls last night.

Our landlady deigned to tell that there was a bank in Vellmar, a district town a good walk away, across the river again. She did not know or even wonder if there would be a working exchange there. I set off thinking only on the calling of Etta, but in a stronger way now. My need to assure her and not myself. Maybe you could not make calls to other countries. Maybe Etta knew this, would understand, and as I walked through mere stones of streets, the bricks as if trying to return to their quarry birth, I thought that maybe this was what Bernie of the KDP had meant when he said it would be safe here. Not safe from the war. Safe only because who would look for anyone, any rat, in a place of dust and rats.

A cold hour-and-a-half walk to Vellmar, saving the bike for emergencies, but their bank limited to one hundred marks per customer. And they knew nothing about calling Zurich. I discovered a horse-drawn charabanc back to the city but even so it took almost an hour and I missed the fellow with the wagon and his wares. Cursed a beggar's luck, trudged my way to the eatery and then discovered fortune, glad to have missed the errant gypsy and his black goods. A man of destiny had set up a tented barber-shop, as large as a newspaper stand, one stool on the street, hot water from a small milk-churn heated on a brazier. A two-pfenning shave, five for a cut. Even if I came here every day, even with his long line, I would save money over buying my own razor. And more than that. Who better to tell you the world than a barber?

*

It was Dresden that had been bombed, so the barber informed. No. Not the right word. Not bombed. Furnace burned. Reduced down to the homes of insects. Scorched so even the nests and eggs of birds in the gables were ash. The trees and bodies charcoal.

First, a blanket of fire, small incendiaries to set timber frames and roofs, all the roofs, alight for hours. Then when the people came out from hiding to fight the flames, crept from their holes thinking it was over, the heavy bombers came. The flame their markers. Again and again. All through the night. The ground white with heat. The February moon blacked out by wings and fuselage.

'It was on the radio,' my barber said. 'I had the chap here who puts up the papers at the Gau.' He nodded as if this was our secret. 'There's nothing at Dresden to bomb. This is personal. They are animals. Here, yes. The station, the factories. Why not? I have a fellow tells me they can make twenty Tiger tanks a week. No fuel to run them more than a hundred yards. Who would have guessed it would come down to oil, eh? Tsk, tsk.' Tsk tsk. Mimicking the sound of his scissors, as rude mechanicals do. Their irritations and vocal clicks become the sounds of their tools.

He paused his blade on my throat and I looked up at his face squinting to the skies. No siren this time, just black crucifixes against the blue. Hundreds of them again. A sense they were mocking us with their slow hum. As if they had all the time in the world. Nothing to stop them. Parading. In front of us. Practising their victory parade. Training day over Germany.

'Those bastards.' He wiped his blade. 'Look at them. They are going back for seconds.' He wiped my face with a hot towel as if it was two years ago, as if we were normal again and not doing this on the street. We retained even the slight awkwardness of paying him for his service as if by our closeness we had become friends and this was the vulgar act of exchange as ever it was and he was not in a tent and I not sat on a stool in the road. We thanked each other. We still did that. Something odd in it. We should apologise to each other for the cheapness of it all, the degradation of it all, or congratulate each other that we could still do this. The people in the maps. You could still see the tails of the planes in a black line across the sky long after the sound had gone.

'Do you have any cigarettes to buy?' I asked. 'Or tobacco and papers? Two if you have. I promised a friend.'

He went to a box under his towels. Two packets of Atikahs, Greek tobacco pretending to be Turkish, twenty-five in each, ten marks for the pair. Everything had become under the counter, even a pleasure in it, the nod and the wink, the conjoined conspiracy, but you had to pay much for the counter that wasn't there. But even he knew nothing about telephoning across borders.

That evening I promised myself I would ask Franz for his help. There had to be some advantage in sharing with an SS, even if only a corporal. A couple of bottles of schnapps from the eatery would help grease.

Just walking the streets had cost me thirty marks in one day. Get five back from Franz for the cigarettes, and perhaps I did not need schnapps, but still I would be broke with just food and rent in a fortnight if I was not careful and that thought inspired me to press for Franz's help with an international call. Say it was to get my father to wire me some funds. Not *my* father. That avenue closed.

He came in with a copy of the *Attack*, printed only twice a week now, his body heavy as he read.

'Have you seen this, Ernst? It was Dresden last night. Obliterated. And the planes today – did you hear them? – the same course. Dresden. Disgraceful. You might as well blow up the Pantheon.'

'I found a barber,' I said. 'He told me. I had no idea they had such a force in the air.'

'They have our Russian oilfields, and Africa's, and their Arabs and Muslims wishing to be Jews. We have the planes. Not the fuel. Then there would be a fight.' He threw the paper to my bed. 'We would kick them to shit. But mark me: this will become an infantry war. Man against man. *Us* against gum-chewing masturbators. Piece of shit bastards!'

I tossed him the cigarettes. He clapped them in the air, face lit up like a Christmas child's.

'For me? Good man. How much do I owe?' He somehow managed to remove his coat and pipe a cigarette in his mouth like Houdini escaping a strait-jacket.

'Five,' I said. 'I will stump for the wine,' indicated the bottles on the night-stand.

'A saint you are. I should have wrote you to come a month ago. It must be hard for you to stay here, now you are stuck here. This town will bust you broke.'

'I wondered if you might help on that, Franz. If it is not trouble for you?'

We lit up together, sat on our beds. His bit his lip and sighed. I laughed. To loosen the woe on his face.

'Not money! I could probably buy and sell you this month! I would not ask a Gotha man for money. I would find more in a river.'

'That is true.' He exhaled gratefully. 'Before I forget, there is a story about you in the paper.'

I felt the blood run from my face. He almost melted in glee.

'Not you! About Erfurt. You think they'd announce your arrival in Kassel in the paper?' He splayed his hands. '*Great skinny Topf designer arrives to save us all.* No. Something about a communist leader killed at Weimar. No names, but he had links in Erfurt and at Topf. They've arrested the ringleader there.'

I leafed over the paper. Pretended to not be fascinated, to not be terrified.

'Topf has a long problem with communists,' I said. 'Part of why I was hired. New blood.'

'Well, if he's been arrested I know it's not you. But – on that – you should present yourself at the Gau tomorrow. I had to tell my commander I had a room-mate. Rules. Everyone's a spy now. I'll take you in. It won't take more than an hour. Sorry to trouble. But you understand?'

'Yes,' I said, took the cork from the wine. Needed a drink. 'An hour? That long?'

'A call to check your ID. Call to Topf I would guess. You know how administration works. We love to stamp everything. Give me a swig of that.'

'I could stay somewhere else,' I said, passed over the bottle, thinking of the bike, thinking of running again. 'After yesterday and today I'm sure they are too busy. I don't want to trouble you, Franz.'

'Shit, no. Don't worry about that. You'd be getting me away from my desk. What did you want me to help you with?'

'It doesn't matter,' I said. 'It was just about getting stamps. Wanted to write to my father for money. Not important.'

'Good. I'll get some sandwiches from the witch for dinner. She doesn't spit that much in them.'

I smoked and read the story as he washed, singing his Youth anthems in a derisive tone, changing words for whatever he felt most offensive.

The newspaper thin, one page bleeding into the other, the print like a typewriter on its third run of the ribbon.

A Topf employee had been arrested as an enemy of the state. Arrested based on information gathered by the police and from secret papers recovered from the death of a head member of the KPD in Weimar. Topf and Sons were continuing to aid the police.

I closed the paper, took a drink, listened to Franz's songs and sat on the bed and wondered how far my fuel would take me. And what an SS officer would make of his room-mate running.

Chapter 52

There were no names in the paper, and Franz explained from his bath.

'Because they would make them martyrs – is that a Jewish word? – it would warn the others. Just let them know we're on to them. You know this war would've been won years ago if it wasn't for shitting communists. I would be a working man with a pretty ex-wife and kids by now if it wasn't for this war. Maybe you could get me a job at Topf. Why the hell did I join the Youth? Why didn't you? Oh, right. Erfurt. You chaps didn't even know there was a war until this month.'

After his bath we ate turkey sandwiches and pickles, drank both bottles together. Franz a big drinker, gulped, narrowed his eyes as he did so. You recognise people that drink to black things out. They don't even like the taste so they drink fast. He reminded of the young men I had seen at the barracks at Auschwitz, only with less farm in him.

He smoked as if each cigarette was the last. I did not want to talk any more of tomorrow, to pretend that it did not bother me. Could convince myself that it did not.

'Do you know where I could get some fuel, Franz? For my motorcycle?'

He did not even have to think about it.

'Find a cattle farmer. Whatever the farm they all get the same ration. So you'll get a wheat farmer with not enough and a pig farmer drinking the stuff. Ask around. Someone will have a tank or two. Best be quick. They'll be raiding the farms for the tanks soon enough.' He went quiet after this, drank harder, then jumped to the wardrobe.

'Hey, have you seen this?' He unzipped the bag on the rail. A black suit with silver buttons and braid. 'My dress suit! Would you believe such! It has tails.' He flapped them at me. It was that black suit from the old days, the red armband still on it. *There are many people who will fall ill when they see this black,* Himmler had said. They still did, even when only flashed from a wardrobe.

'I will get to wear it when we win!' Franz danced with it, one circle, before hanging it back in one swoop. 'When all the girls in hiding come out again and I find me a "von" widow to keep me. You have a girl, Ernst?'

'No.' I said this too flatly, like I spoke of lost love and he ended the subject, went back to the cigarettes and wine as if his hands could never be empty lest they might run through his hair and pluck it out, make fists against walls or beat someone. Why the dispossessed drink and smoke, why soldiers drink and smoke. Keep the hands from the razor blade.

'I could arrange for you to make a telephone call to your father. If you wished,' he offered. 'Quicker than writing. He could make a wire transfer. The Gau has an office for the Reichsbank. They could cut you a cheque and cash it.'

My spine went too rigid, my face too hopeful.

'You really want to speak to your old man, eh?'

The danger forgotten. The risk worth it. Prisons not full of those who got caught when they returned to the scene of the crime, as paperbacks sold in train stations would have it. Prisons full of those who would say goodbye to their lovers. The chance of the voice and embrace worth it. Only single men evade. Every police force knows. Hang around the women long enough. The skulker will return.

'Can I make a call to Zurich?'

'Your father lives *there*? You should have joined him. Well. It can be done. If I explain to them why. They'd rather that to having another beggar. They're all my friends anyhow. All of us admin chaps are from the Youth. All corporals with no chance of promotion and wooden guns.' He stubbed out on the paper of the turkey sandwiches, a terrible smell, lit another in the same move. 'You know how it's done? We tap into the Atlantic cables and go through there. Berlin has been listening to the Americans for years. They think we have no international access, wiped out our communications by clipping telegraph poles. They think we are idiots.

Then they wonder why our tanks appear beside them. And you know how we record them?'

'Magnetic recordings. Iron on paper. I know. They do it at Topf. The SS I mean.'

'You know everything. I thought you just built ovens.' He went solemn. 'I'm talking too much. I shouldn't have said any of that. It's the drink. I shouldn't tell such things to you. I'm sorry, Ernst.'

'I know. We don't know each other. And this is not the time.'

He sat on his bed.

'It shouldn't be like that. I'm glad you understand. You haven't asked me anything. But we can talk like men in a bar can't we?' He took a drink to illustrate. 'You know what we should do? If they asked me? Blow up the fucking auto-bahns. We're blowing up our own old railways but the Americans don't give a shit about them. We're leaving them our roads to travel by. They're rolling in on their shitty tanks because we've the best roads in the world. Take them out and they'd have to shovel their tanks along. They're reaching us because of the roads. But we're too proud of them. Might as well give them a fucking carpet to walk on.'

He stopped talking, took three drinks to my one. I saw his workday there.

'Do you think they'll bomb again tonight?' I asked. Not a light question, something to break his mood. He lay out on the bed, cigarette aimed to the ceiling.

'Who gives a shit,' he said, rolled over to the wall. Like

he was already in prison. And the planes went overhead again.

*

We left at eight the next day. I kept my holed wool cap in my pocket despite the cold, for shame, embarrassed to wear it in front of him. I asked Franz to wait for me on the corner, wait for me while I checked on my bike. I had the folded plan against my back again, the spanners and letter-knife in my coat.

It had not snowed and but for a frost in the shade her green frame was fine and waiting. I stood at her for a few seconds, rolled the accelerator. I could be gone from Kassel. Head west. Find a new town and cash a cheque. I checked the tank, a dipstick gauge on the cap. Three-quarters full. Eighty kilometres of road at least. But to talk to her. Perhaps for the last time. I needed it probably more than my pragmatic Etta.

'*You fool,*' she would say. '*Where are you?*' And I would tell her I was calling from the SS office in Kassel and she would hang up. But I was cold, hungry. In need of comfort. And that is how you get caught.

Get on the bike. Go. Run. But there would be her voice. A telephone call offered. I could speak to her before they spoke to Topf. What I did know and what I did not could fill the back of a stamp. But I could rely on chaos. Dresden bombed, maybe Erfurt. Maybe they could not get through to Topf or maybe the telephone answered by reception only. 'Yes,' she would say. 'Herr Beck works here. I'm sorry? You are breaking up caller.' *Kaw, Kawler, Kaw.*

'What are you doing?' Franz at the door of the yard, uniform snapped to the collar. His greatcoat and cap, the black gloves, making that image of photographs we had seen for years. The handsome SS officer in control of everything and everyone. You could not help but obey. It had become ingrained. You see them and you pick up your suitcase, move along with your head down and tip your cap. Did our enemies know that? That even we feared them? We have a culture for uniforms. Expect to be questioned by them. Respect uniforms. Even ice-cream sellers wear peaked caps and silver buttons.

'What are you doing?'

And then the gun would come out.

'Nothing,' I said. 'Just checking she was not frozen.' And I went with him, left the bike. In an hour it would be too late to regret. Hoped her next owner would be a good one.

Chapter 53

We breezed into the Gau, no queue for us, a four-storey building of pillars and those massive red banners on flagpoles that declared the Party louder than a marching band. The line of the people outside turning their shoulders from me, from us.

'You know Rundstedt is here,' Franz said. 'The field marshall. In charge of the whole shitting West. This is his headquarters. He has a whole floor. So I sleep in that witch's hole. It fits they would send an old man to a hospital.'

Franz became a foot taller as we entered. Took off his cap and put his gloves inside, saluted and snapped his heels to the desk.

He signed in, chatted to grey uniforms back and forth as I stood aside, stood back on the marble floor. A dread upon me. Franz not my room-mate any more. Speech changed, stance changed. A uniform. One of them.

His hand came out and I gave my identification and

watched it disappear from me. He smiled swiftly, blocked my gaze to my card walking away to another room.

'Come back with me, Ernst.' He took my arm, took me to a corridor. 'Let's make your call while we wait. Don't worry. They'll check your worker's pass and call Topf. It will be back for you when we return. We might have to wait to access the telephone, that is all.'

The building still the hospital it once was. Long corridors, junctions to other long corridors until eventually you come to an unrewarding tiny room, dazed and nauseated from your walk of hundreds of light bulbs and bleached floors which you expected to end at a throne instead of the windowless alcove of flickering lights and moths.

A starched young woman at her station, lit by the type of green-shaded lamp that I dreamed would accompany my work at home. Franz's cap to her desk. Quiet words exchanged, close to her blushing face, her smile, his cocked head to me, signalling me to come on. I gave a look down the corridor behind. Empty. No-one coming for me. Followed Franz to a radio room not much bigger than the barber's tent from yesterday.

A wall of lights and switches. Nine in the morning and the fellow at the bank of machines already exhausted in vest and braces, his small round glasses smeared and steamed, fruit flies swirling about his head, or dead, fried to the single twitching bulb above him.

'Eisel,' Franz said. 'Can my friend here make a call to his father? To Zurich?'

The chair swung and rocked.

'He can.' He sized me up. 'Who is he?'

'Works for Topf and Sons, in Erfurt. He needs his father to wire him money.'

'Who doesn't.' He rolled his chair to his machines, filled with the same spools as Voss's device. 'What's the number?'

I reeled it off from the paper in my wallet, brushed the fruit flies from the front of my face.

Eisel picked up an enormous green receiver, a rotary inside its handle. I watched his finger dial at every third number I gave. He seemed to guess the last.

'It's ringing,' he said, passed it to me.

'An operator?' I took the strange heavy handle. 'What shall I say?'

Eisel rolled his eyes.

'That's your father on the end of the line. You have one minute. I'll log it as a test. I have work to do.'

I needed both hands to hold the thing to my ear, a large bowl like an oversized pipe to speak into. A closing in my throat as it rang. Rang and rang.

Please let this be worth it. Let me hear her.

A click as someone picked up.

'Kirch residence?'

Her.

'Etta!' I said this too loud. 'Sister! Hello, sister! It's Ernst. I am on someone else's telephone. He's with me now. I can't be long. How are you?'

'Oh, Ernst! Ernst! I am very well. How . . . how are you?'

'Good, good, sister. I am in Kassel. How is father?'

'Fine, fine.' I could hear the tears. 'Everything is fine. Father's not here. Can . . . can I pass a message?'

In the cupboard of a room both men's eyes were on me. I had not expected this would be the way I would be with her. Watched. Listened to. I should be used to that. At least she understood. Knew others were listening. In the cramped room she could probably hear their breaths. My smart Etta. My good wife.

Eisel began to wind his hand to me, signalling me to finish up.

'I need money. The rent is crazy here. It will be all right when I get back to work but I need six hundred marks to see me. Father can telegram it to the Gau here. They can frank a cheque. You'll tell him, Etta? The Kassel Gau.'

'Yes, yes, of course.'

'And how is your husband, Etta?'

The line quiet.

'I miss him so much, Ernst. I wish . . . but I'm sure he knows. As long as you are well, Ernst.'

'I'm fine.' I looked up at Franz. 'I'm in good company. Once I get back to work—'

'That's it,' Eisel said.

'I have to go now, Etta. I love you.'

'Oh, Ernst—' The line dead. I hesitated to give back the telephone. Felt it still warm with her voice. My hand upon it. Her hand on hers. Holding hands.

'Thank you, Eisel,' I said. 'Thank you, Franz. This means a lot to me.'

'Maybe I won't pay you for the cigarettes now, eh?' He gave two of them to Eisel and pushed me from the room, back to the antechamber with the woman.

'Your father's name is Kirch?' Franz asked. Had heard the voice on the other end.

I was getting used to thinking on my feet. A fine liar.

'My stepfather.'

Franz satisfied. 'We'll go wait for your ID. Come. See how long you can keep me from my desk. At least you get to leave.'

We went back along the corridor. My heart too light. My step quickening. I had forgotten about my worker's pass, about the call to Topf. No longer cared. Forgot even about the plan rubbing against my back. I had heard her voice. Was dead and buried before that. I had sensed spring again. She was safe. No matter for me.

*

The reception crowded. An urgency to every boot and cap. Something had happened, was happening. Only one group of officers not in a hurry. A circle of them. Laughing and slapping each other's backs. I looked away as Franz pulled me to a seat.

'Great,' he said. 'I'm going to have to leave you, Ernst. Find out what this shit is. Probably Dresden again. It was

Ash Wednesday yesterday. They'll call it Ash Dresden at this rate. Go to the desk, Ernst. See if they've got your identification back. I'll see you tonight.'

He left me sitting on a bench against the wall. The only civilian in the place. Sitting like a naked boy in church, believing every eye on me. I watched the group of caps and grey still laughing, talking loud as high ranks do. Something about them drawing me. Something odd I could not place. An optical illusion about them my brain would not let me see. I blinked them away and went to the desk, asked about my card.

The woman went through her pigeon-holes and papers.

'No,' she said. 'It is not here. Do you know what it is about? We're very busy.'

This my way out. Escape in chaos. Why should I ask her? *'Please, madam, have I been caught yet? Where do I surrender myself?'*

'No,' I said. 'It's fine. I'll come back tomorrow.' War a wonderful place to get lost. Fate had already given me one glorious moment so why not another? I thanked her.

I went to leave, watched the laughing group of caps and boots separate and saw in their dispersement the optical illusion that my eye could not close on.

Seven men. Seven caps. But not enough legs for them all.

I saw the crutch, not the face, put my head down as the body swung forwards and I tried not to bolt across the floor to the doors.

Too many bodies, too many uniforms pressing me back and sideways, taking me to him like a magnet as I tried to press my way through. Like before. The camp. Going under the arch. The same horror.

He was only three bodies from me. I was treading on toes and apologising as I pushed. Then only an ear between us as he changed direction to escape the same crowd and I reacted as only a child might.

I crouched, pretended to tie a shoe as the crutch brushed past me. I saw a gap and the bright light through the glass doors and almost rolled my way towards it. And I was up, pushed the doors free, met the air and stumbled down the steps to the street.

No voice called. No call to stop. I wouldn't know what a bullet would sound like if I heard it. You couldn't rely on the movies for these sounds. They make everything up. Even noise. The speed of the shot faster than its sound. You would be dead before you heard it.

I tried not to run the road. Not hurry. Counted my steps in time with my heart. Only Hercules on his hill watching my receding back.

Chapter 54

I vomited at the first corner I came to. Still civilised enough
to do it in a drain. Urchins laughing at me, miming my
heave in a chorus line one at a time. I staggered the half-
mile back to the house, always looking over my shoulder,
contemplating all the horrors that the crutch entailed.
Imagination is mostly terror. But so is instinct. Fate had
given me Etta's voice. It had given me the chance to get
away without my identification, without a call to Topf and,
as fee for its goodness, it had shown me Voss. And so follow
your instinct Ernst Beck.

At the house, motorcycles and side-cars. Helmeted
adjutants astride the bikes eyeing me enter. I had not seen
any officers here other than Franz. Did not worry about it
to show. The witch and Franz had told me all the rooms
were let out to them. Fitting to see them now. I forced my
anxiety to be more from the cold than of the square jaws
watching. Hugged myself and rushed inside.

I stamped off the cold, waited at the desk to pay my rent, heard the talking, could not help but look along the hall, to the open door. The parlour full of them, full of their loud voices, always belonging to a bar. Talking over each other like drunks. Attention only on each other. The peasant in the wool cap and summer coat not worth an eye.

I needed to wash up, had vomit on my coat, stank of it. The witch not there. A pot of coffee and a plate of fried bread on the front desk. Her ten marks of breakfast and bed. No stomach for it. Nausea still. The thought of coffee, her coffee on an empty stomach too much. Rest a while, settle down. Eat later. I walked past the parlour and to the stairs, pretended to search for something in my wallet to not meet anyone's eye. Slow. Walk slow Ernst. Twenty steps to the room. The longest I have walked.

Bolted the door behind me, back to it, holding the world from it. Thoughts of Etta and the doors she would always close to keep her mystery. Her bathroom sanctum. Would give my life to hear her running a tap now.

I took my first breath of the morning. Laughed. No. Not a laugh. A hand over mouth simpleton's relief. Misplaced glee at where I had come to hide. An acorn in a pile of almonds. Who would look for Ernst Beck in a hotel full of SS? The fool genius. Idiot. Fool.

Perhaps he is sharing a room with one of us? Did he really put his own name in the register? Our hotel?

I washed and smoked, took out the plan and put it to

the bed. Talked to it. My only friend. The only player in my conspiracy. Let it judge me. Blew my smoke in its face. Dog-eared. Aged years in days. The ink already fading. A well made forgery. My own Turin shroud. Too good to be real.

What are you? What are we doing?

There were the sig-runes, the signatures, my pen-strokes.

Will anyone care? Why am I doing this? What's the manner of it?

Empty stomach. Light head. Cold. February cold. The hum of planes high above. Etta's voice from the paper.

They were going to build me.

*

Perhaps they have.

You do not know.

And what if they win?

How will they continue then? They would ask you back. To do more. If they win no-one could stop them. Meat grinders next. You will draw giant meat grinders. For them.

You drew me. You helped them. You could see what I was. It is your amends.

Who will know if you do not show me?

You might have the one plan not burned.

Could show that which burned within.

I worked for Topf and Sons. We built ovens. Designed them. That's all. All that we did. I didn't do anything.

You could have put that girl from the camp on your bike.

Could. If you had it then. Or if you could drive a car. If you weren't such a boy. If time were a line you could ride. And would you?

You freed yourself from the arch. Begged an officer to save you. Left them. Left her.

I am paper thin.

What are you, Ernst Beck, but cold and lonely? How thin?

What did you imagine? Want? Your wife on a train. What did she hope?

Why did you take me? Paper thin.

Every oven began paper thin.

Hundreds and thousands within lines on paper. The people in the maps. Who are you saving? Hoping to save?

What point?

Paul Reul without ashes.

Hans Klein.

What was his last look? Last.

Fool.

Idiot.

I saw myself fold onto the bed. Made sure the chattering paper was beneath my chest before I passed out.

*

A rapping on the door woke me. Woke like a thief again. Jumped, slapped myself awake in a sweat.

Because I am a thief.

Getting dark outside. Late afternoon. The knock came again, this time a voice. Franz. Swearing at me through the door. I folded the plan back under the mattress.

'Why did you bolt the door?' This maddened him more than it should, I thought. He came into the room still in coat and cap, still in uniform, his back to me, looked about the room as if disgusted, as if it were not his.

'I was taking a nap. Longer than I wanted. Sorry.'

He faced me.

'You don't look well, Ernst.'

I sat on our chair.

'I was sick this morning. I should eat more hot meals. Not these sandwiches all the time. The only damned place to eat closes at three.'

He took off his cap and coat. At last. Franz again. Not one of them.

'You need to find a widow with a chicken and a pot.' The holster came off, back to the wardrobe. 'You should have gone back to Erfurt when you had the chance. Too late now.'

'It's not bombed is it?'

'I don't know. But the roads are closed. By Monday anyone in this city is staying here. Did you get your worker's pass back?'

I pictured Voss pocketing my card, hobbling into a car, pointing a black-gloved finger down the road through the windscreen.

'No,' I said. 'I'll get it tomorrow. I'll have to pick up the telegram from my father.'

'I'll get them. Get the cheque cut for you. You'll be hours if you go.'

Some relief in this. Not wanting to go back to that place. A child again, hiding among the crevices and stonework of the Merchants' Bridge from my father's belt.

'Thank you, Franz.'

'No problem. Naturally you'll lend me sixty marks for the privilege, old boy. Listen. I'll get some apple wine and see if the witch can make you up some soup. She has some books in the parlour. I'll find you something racy.'

I thanked him again. All I ever did now it seemed. Thanked Franz. Thanked an SS officer. I gave him my rent money to pass to her. That would surely grace her to turn a spoon with some potatoes.

I should run. Get on the bike and go. The colonel here in Kassel. Probably not for me, surely not for me. Who would care about Ernst Beck? But get him to get to his wife. You could not trust the newspapers to tell truth. A liar like the rest of us, like the radio. The report the newspaper gave probably did not refer to Hans. He was in his home with a Martini in one hand and a Camel in the other. Topf too busy burning plans to answer the telephone. The lines already down. The Gau in chaos with more important things to concern than Ernst Beck and his wife. The heart of Germany was being bombed. One line written somewhere about Ernst Beck and his Jewish communist wife. A million lines written above it. A fish rots from its head down. Told this to Hans. A philosopher above Hans. Not true. A metaphor for a country's failure. A dog cannot get rid of its own fleas. Better. Truer. You are a flea, Ernst Beck. Run. Go. But you need that cheque. You will brunt the fall because you need that money and your pass. And the roads closed. So sit and wait to get caught.

It started to snow again, went to the window and watched it coating the ruins, building them up again, painting them white. Everything looks better in snow. Of all I had to concern me there was the strange numbness in my pit that Franz Werra would be disappointed in Ernst Beck.

My parents, Etta, Hans and the Topfs, Prüfer and Sander, yet all I could think of was Franz judging me. Shaking his head as they carted me away. I could not reconcile except with a cigarette as I watched the snow. He was going to wangle me soup because I said I was sick. I had bought him cigarettes. We shared a room in a bombed-out city, had only known him three days. Maybe it was a male thing. That way you can make best friends in one drunken night, like people used to before this. Spend years meeting without knowing their second name. Or maybe just a liar's thing, a war thing. Any day dead. Any day.

He came into the room with a tray. A bottle. A bowl covered with cloth, a paperback book. The waft of chicken soup. The room became a home. I ate, wished we had a radio. Franz watched me eat, pleased, as if he could see my strength returning with each spoonful. I faked revival, like you might with your mother. I was weak with something more than lack of food. We did not talk. It was

Thursday evening. I had been in Kassel three days. Or three years. Franz and I old men. But soup. And Etta's voice. She had made it. Was safe. All that might go wrong was a journey to be, and might never be. This was good. Today. Tonight. This was good. Franz uncorked the wine. Drink the only thing left for young men. Barely a war for us now.

Machines rolled and flew. Automatons were at war. Buttons were pressed. Faces did not look on faces from across a field. No trenches. A war on paper now, end any day now, and no-one would care about Ernst Beck and his lapsed loyalties. It was all about the maps. The young men still living would live, go home to their wives, find wives. I could not imagine what would come. But they did. They knew. *He* knew.

A knock on the door. I put the tray to the bed, expected this. Franz answered the door. Expected it also.

A soldier in helmet. Such a helmet. Designed so well. Somehow it removed the wearer from the world. They looked like machines.

He saluted Franz in the doorway. I stood. Waited. Had always waited for the knock.

'Your rifle, Corporal Werra.' The helmet passed over a gun and bag. Saluted again as Franz took them. Franz waved him away, closed the door. Not a door for me. No longer my door. I was furniture in a barracks.

He dropped the bag to the floor, checked the bolt, the action of the weapon. Did not look the same man.

'This,' he said, put the weapon to his bed, sat with it behind him. 'This it comes to.'

Silence for a moment. Drank wine. Spoke again. The last time for the night.

'You know all wars come to streets. Always town to town. House to house. Why don't they just start like that? If that's how they end?' He lit a cigarette, dragged long. 'It's shit. All shit. If they knew it would end like this . . . this should have been day one. Then we could all go home.'

'It's snowing,' I said, did not know what else to say. There was now a rifle in our room, a bag of ammunition. I went back to my soup.

Franz to the window, struggled with the clasp.

'Best check how far I can open this. See if I can watch the corner from it.'

Chapter 55

I had my hair cut. Shorn. At the barber on the street. My head in his mirror like the prisoners I had seen at the camps. Cut for spring. Perhaps cut for disguise. Certainly had never worn it so short. Wondered if Etta had trimmed hers, changed hers. The red curls gone. Hair long about her shoulders. It was almost the end of March. Near seven weeks since last seen, last touched by me. Her hair would be at her shoulders. I fiddled with the wedding band in my waistcoat more and more.

The weeks since Franz first brought a rifle into our room had become a monotonous parade of washing the same clothes in the bath, suppers of stews and potatoes, bread and cheese, and stronger and stronger drink as apple wine was locally remade as vodka then to gin and even the children drank. A weak beer or cider still common for a child's breakfast, but gin? My mother would wail if she knew.

The newspapers reduced to only a weekly edition, the

radio broadcasting only three hours of an evening. The eatery forced to extend his opening hours so crowds could gather and listen to the reports from where the radio still hung from a string and nail on his broken wall. Something appropriate in its fragile hold from crashing to the floor. Only occasionally did I see the same faces. A smile from the old man who had struggled to speak to me. Then one week I did not see him at all and never again. Did not know his name to ask after.

Franz spent more and more time out of the room. Days and nights away. He was always late in getting paid and I would lend him money. It was not a favour. It was regular enough to not even be mentioned or asked for. I would offer, he would accept; we shared wine and cigarettes, shared a toothbrush like overnight lovers, so what matter. We knew I owed him for getting the money in the first. He had franked a cheque and had cashed it at the Gau. The roads were closed, I could not have got to a bank and would not have got six hundred marks from them. My worker's pass came back without question. Relief in fate for that. Bureaucracy in war probably as broken as everything else, despite the Party's proud efficiency for it. The Americans were driving tanks through its cracks, so why not little Ernst Beck? Senior-Colonel Voss in Kassel nothing to do with me. My name not even in his thoughts. Forgotten. After all, only Hans Klein and I knew I copied the plan, hidden it in my work drawer amongst dozens of others. Topf had probably spent days burning papers, shook hands with the SS officers supervising, never knowing that a pathetic motorcycle had puttered off into the night with their worst. The one that even they would shame to confess. And then there was Hans.

In the quietness of the days it was impossible that he did not come to me. Again and again I pictured conversations between Sander and Prüfer, with the Topfs, with the SS, with Voss.

The talk was always blurred, changed direction and outcome, like trying to listen to two dinner parties at opposite tables, and when I thought I had found the outcome, found the fear that led to me, it would change and another round of wine would go round and round with it.

Hans a communist? Surely not? A traitor? Never! But he let Ernst Beck escape. His Jew wife escape. He was in on it. No. He has explained it all. Then where is Ernst Beck? Where is Hans? Why is he in prison? No. He has given everything up. Told us it was all Ernst. But he is in prison? No. He is at home. I had dinner with him last night. He says he knows nothing about Ernst. A moment of compassion. He has told us everything. Never mind. Nothing is missing. The Jewess and her communist husband have gone to Zurich. Here is Hans now. He will tell you.

I brushed flies from my face. March. Flies. Thousands of them. Did not want to think what they were attracted to. In the first nine days of March we were bombed four times. Every day you found shoes in the streets, white shirts and pink negligees stuck in trees like kites where they had blown from a broken suitcase or a broken room where someone had tried to pack in a hurry. Every day the flat resonance of guns, distant like storm waves on rocks, like thunder never bringing rain, and planes replaced birds, sometimes singular and as low as swifts just above the telegraph poles or in formation as high as returning geese. You did not even look up any more. They plodded the sky as we plodded the streets, as if they no longer cared either.

I rode the motorcycle around the squares of the town once a week, to keep the battery charged, to see what was selling from a blanket stall today. My escape still mine I believed. Eighty kilometres. With the fuel in her I still had eighty kilometres I could distance. Could still run. And I was a citizen now. People waved at me as I rode by. And the children only half-heartedly threw their stones.

The ragged streets had become like the corridors of my hotel, my hostel. I used to use dozens of doors, dozens of corridors. In the factory of my work. Now the same cracked sights all the time. The door into the hotel, the door of my room, again and again. The streets just an extension of the hotel, a longer corridor with no door at the other end. Just one big loop to bring me back to the same two doors. Excepting for my wedding I had travelled further in these months than I had ever done in my life. Yet had gone nowhere.

Then it finally happened. The last Thursday in March.

The people came first. The refugees. In wagons, in

handcarts. Asses and horses. The people's faces all the same. Either wailing or empty. Nothing in between. Crying or nothing. The faces of nothing the worst. They looked like they were made of glass, that one more nudge off the edge and they would fall. Shatter to the floor.

Napoleon had come again. An army had crossed the Rhine. The Americans in Frankfurt.

I ran back to the room, somehow knowing that Franz was there. Our door open and I rushed in, calling him.

'I know,' he said before I could speak. He was sat on his bed, cigarette in mouth, oiling his rifle, rolling the bolt back and forth. 'At least they will stop bombing us for a time. Stop them shitting rockets on the farms for a change.' He looked up at me. 'You look pleased, Ernst.'

It was true. I was breathless, the boyhood run had flushed my face, but more than this. It felt like the end. I had lost sight of it. Become just another ghost in the city. More doors in my future now. One of them with Etta behind.

I flopped to my bed, dismissed Franz's comment. He raised the weapon to shoulder, to the window, his eye along the sight. A soldier. Not Franz. His face in stone.

'They say it's Patton,' he said. 'It's been Patton since Italy. But they say he's as short of fuel as we are. You know we're training pilots in one hour then sending them up? All the fuel we can afford. Jesus.' He fired the empty bolt, clicked it back instantly. 'I suppose I'd better load this thing. I won't be going anywhere tomorrow.'

'Tomorrow?'

'They'll be here tomorrow. You could go to the old brewery. Or the Bergpark. It will be safe there.'

I could not do that. This event my hope. I imagined walking up to a general. Handing him my evidence of what our leaders had been doing, had been planning to do. Did they know? Did anyone have any idea? The red-jackets found Auschwitz. Would a Yankee general pat me on the back and say, 'We know, son. We always knew. You run along.'

But I needed them. This had been my whole. Hide behind them. Was running to them. Had convinced myself that I was doing right. Not saving myself. Saving the future from its present. A four-storey oven. An oven fuelled by corpses. Hundreds a day. Thousands a week. Surely they could not imagine such a thing? Not imagine what had been planned, what had been done. Or maybe I expected too much from them. Maybe they would look at the plan, judge it differently. A good thing. A thing for them. For their own camps.

'I'll stay here,' I said. 'With you.' Not noble. I needed to be near. To run to the first starred man I saw. To the sheriff's badge. But I did not want to think of Franz Werra alone in this room. Pictured shell casings on the floor. Down to his last cigarette. I had left Hans Klein alone. 'Maybe it will not come to that, Franz.'

'If we win it won't. They bomb the shit out of the city and still miss the tank factory. We will meet them with Tigers. Their pieces of shit can't match a Tiger. Maybe you could help. Run ammo between the rooms, across the street. Just about every window's got a rifle in it.' He reached for the night-stand, gave me an envelope. 'Keep that for me. That's my parents' address on the front. If . . . you know. Post it for me.' He fed a clip into the magazine, slammed it in. 'I'll owe you the stamp.'

Chapter 56

We were woken by the rumbling of tracked wheels along the streets. Not tanks. Armoured vehicles with gun barrels and machine-guns. Looked as if they were trying to be part bus and part tank, difficulty in being both.

I went out for breakfast, left Franz in full uniform with coffee and cigarettes for food. He did not talk. I understood that.

On the streets men wore overcoats in warm spring. They hid sticks beneath wrapped with white handkerchiefs. Readied to stand on corners with their hands up and the sticks and cloth high above. Germans. Not Jews or Roma, not Poles. Germans. What goes around comes around. The cheapest platitudes are the most enduring and accurate. Given jocosely, off the cuff. And true every time. That is why they endure. Simple people say them. Perhaps because simple people experience them. Simple people do not speak

Latin, do not have quality quotes for their lives. They have three walls and no roof.

From the south you could hear the shelling. From the villages, from the farms. Tanks met tanks. Every day for weeks you could look up into the sky and see the wild corkscrew trail of our great rockets snaking over to England. Even today they went. Even today when you ducked at the sound of a shell in a field only a walk away. Our leader still fighting a war over channels of water, planning with telescopes, the enemy only needing to clean their spectacles for a closer look.

Two days later they were in the city.

April Fool's Day.

Ernst Beck the fool. The idiot. Fitting.

*

You only ever see one rat. You know, are told, they are there, within feet of you. That there are whole colonies of them living alongside. You only ever see one. And maybe it's the same one. That each of us has his own. You point it out, scurrying under cars and park benches and the girl at your side never sees it. It's gone. She has her own rat. Her own herald.

We'd never accept that. Our importance in the world, in the scheme, heralded by rats, not lions. But I think it is almost true. From what I have seen, what we have known. No trumpets or fanfare. Just a rat for each of us. Makes more sense to imagine a God that would do that. His joke. And us too arrogant to perceive his disdain.

He runs from you when you spy him. Runs ahead and past when your ship sinks. He freezes before he runs, when you see him. I saw him. And then he ran. His act done.

And the tanks and mortars came.

*

You look at your feet, watch the smut dance off the kerb into the gutter like fleas jumping. A hum coming off the walls shivering dust. Then the groan and creak of metal against metal. Huge metal. The sound of an iron ship launching painfully to the sea, and then the enormous eye appears from around the corner, roams on its stalk with a grinding shriek, looks on you. And you run as the cobbled street quakes. See a rat doing the same.

I could only run to the familiar door, run to Franz, heavy dust blowing into the room through the open window, Franz sat on the chair in front of it, watching the tanks roll, rifle barrel resting on the sill.

'Tigers,' he said. 'What did I tell you. Tigers. Straight off the line.'

I said nothing, still catching breath.

'Better stay here for now, Ernst.'

'Where else would I go.' Statement. No body left for questions. Sank on my bed.

He stayed at the window, head up and down the street,

hand to the gun. 'They're going west. Probably go south along the river. The Americans are coming south. I don't think it will reach us today.'

He still had his head to the street. His eyes off me, I felt under the mattress for the plan. Should keep it on me now.

'It's still there,' he called back.

I withdrew my hand.

'What is?' Thinking he meant something in the street, some machine.

'That paper of yours. It's still there.'

I went cold.

'I saw it weeks ago, Ernst.' He turned from the window. 'If you're going to hide something, old boy, don't choose a place where a witch changes the bed sometimes.'

'You've seen it?'

'We all have secrets, Ernst. Your record at Topf checked out. Not from them. Couldn't get through. From Berlin. You are quite famous. So I don't need to know that you're keeping a plan safe for Topf. Or delivering it wherever. I'm sure it's good work. Maybe I'll get a medal for protecting you.' He went back to the window.

I took the plan out, unfolded it to the bed.

'Do you know what this is, Franz?' Said this slowly, a professor questioning a cheater on an exam.

'No. Don't need to know.'

'Yes. Yes you do. You need to know.' Felt the hero return. My purpose, after so many weeks. Fruition. Needed to tell someone. After so long. Needed to convince myself, rebuild myself. Ernst Beck not a ghost.

He came back from the window.

'Is this going to take a cigarette?'

'It might.'

*

I explained it to him, watched him react. Left out the intention of me taking it to the Americans. He still wore his colours. A gun, a uniform. But human.

'Hundreds?' His voice muted. 'Every day?'

'Maybe thousands. The ovens break from overuse of coal. This design negates that. It fuels itself.'

'But from the bodies? Why would we need this?'

I folded back the plan. Put it aside only. No need to hide it.

'We don't. No-one does. It was designed three years ago. They had not thought it necessary then. But I was asked to annotate it last year. To be built.'

He lit another cigarette.

'You have a horrible task, Ernst. This is like something from a farm. A butcher. This was for the camps?'

'I measured it for Auschwitz.'

He looked over to the rifle.

'I thought *I* had a bad job.' A near smile, a close acknowledgement of something. 'If you keep this safe, Ernst, you'll be a hero. One day. If our enemies got hold of such a thing . . .'

My face must have changed, another thought on it, for Franz sprang his hand to grab the paper. I the faster, his hand on the back of mine. I gathered it up, to my back, and he drew away. A street between us. Wider than the dust avenue below our window.

'My work, Franz. My plan. My duty. You said we had secrets. This is mine.'

He leaned back on his bed, a mordant look, a comment coming. Drowned by the sound of mortar fire a street from us.

The corporal, not Franz, went to the window, grabbed his rifle, held it out the window as the explosions hit.

They were not a day from us. Today. Now. He closed the window, locked the clasp.

'You better go see what the witch might have for us to eat. You won't be going out today.' He watched me tuck the plan under the back of my shirt.

'Don't worry, Ernst.' He sat on the chair, gun slumped against him. 'I do not really care, old boy. And tomorrow it won't even matter.'

Chapter 57

It went on for three more days. The water spluttered from the taps, dust in it. I was grey; plaster and grit coated to my skin. Sandpaper when I washed.

The witch had gone. Run. So we had full use of her kitchen, marvelled at what she had been squirrelling away. Tins of peaches and fermented apples, powdered milk and eggs, and pickles that you only saw at Christmas and usually left until next Christmas.

She had her own cannery and even canned whole chickens. You could roast them and they tasted as terrible as you would imagine. Swallowed them with sauerkraut and pickles in the same gulp to keep them down.

Not one man among us knew how to make bread. We took her flour and used it to batter the canned chickens. The subtleties of different foods at different times of day lost. You had dry-fried chicken for breakfast, when you could take time, when the shelling paused – all soldiers take breakfast. Peach and watered oats for lunch. Scrambled eggs and kidney beans for supper. The water, only good for boiling, filtered through muslin squares. Dandelion coffee all that was left. Brought a mug of it to Franz and watched out the window with him.

It was not a battle, not as you might write of one. The tanks were nested around the city, far around. Away from us. A perimeter. The streets a child's game of hide and seek, of cowboys and Indians. As *He* would have wanted. Forgot that the cowboys always won.

Shooting from corners, from windows and doorways. Mortar shells whistled into buildings, shots into the falling dust, then either people running out, in nightdresses or overcoats, or those with uniforms and guns shooting back, stumbling, falling. Echoes off the walls. Cursing and gunfire. A shot. Echo. A curse. Echo. Again and again, like a record stuck at its end. Reverberating around the walls that still remained, recorded into the brick. To be played in another time. If time still a thing after all this. Hear what we heard from our window which once only brought in the sound of morning, the call of the mother for her children to come in from play. The record at its end, rubbing against the label. Shot, curse, plea. Echo. Then someone lifted up the needle. A few minutes of silence, of repositioning of the mortar, of the bazooka, of the needle, and then back to it. The next record placed. Franz and I, drinking dandelion coffee and watching a woman in her nightdress cling to a lamp-post while her husband tried to drag her away as a bazooka on the corner was set. A helmet tap, ears covered, trigger pulled. And they would both be gone. Shoes. Coats. Shoes in the gutter, nightdresses on the street. Every day. Not a battle. Not as you might write of one.

*

It was still morning and I was in the kitchen making oats when it began.

There was a burst of gunfire from outside, as if right outside, under the high windows of the kitchen, so close it made me duck to the kitchen table. I was alone there. Crawled out to not be.

The kitchen behind the reception, in front of the main door, and I kept my head below the desk as another burst hit the building. Rapid stuttering fire. Weapons that sounded like they spewed bullets from a wood-chipper. Faster than breath, faster than the blood or the blink of eye that accompanies.

The spew of them following as I moved from space to covered space. Sunlight and smoke from perfect holes along the walls and I went under the streaking rays, would burn at their touch.

At the stairs the hail followed and I went flat, slithered up. If I was alone so was Franz. Pushed images out of my mind about that. Franz. Not Hans. Franz. Only the names similar. My deed not. He would not be alone.

Upstairs the crack of rifles came from every room. No

voices, just the accent of guns, stoic German accents of guns. Fire, pull, snap, fire. Elegant and controlled. From the streets the brash gangster laugh of the automatic-gun, chomping bullets like chewing gum. Ungraceful, loose.

Our door the first in the corridor.

'Get down!' Franz at the window, rifle firing.

He was in a cloud of smoke and sun. Concentration blazing off him like a light. A concert violinist bathed in spotlight. His practised movements reminiscent of such, the same dedicated fury and passion. Not like my father's half-drunken wolf hunts. He looked beautiful. Jarring to imagine such.

I pulled up the mattresses and put them either side of the windows. Franz said nothing, I took this as approval and knelt behind him. Wanted so strongly to look at the street. Compelled. A devil's finger beckoning me to take a look.

I peered past Franz's hip at the sill, crept my head just above it like a boy slowly pushing open the drawer of a forbidden box of matches to the dangerous wonders within.

All I could see was the window opposite, a mirror of Franz in it, another firing to the corner, and then that burst again, a puff of dust as I ducked. I crept up again. The window empty.

A chime as Franz's clip emptied, slapped my shoulder to hand him another from the bag at his feet but I stopped moving as the rumble of geared metal came from both ends of the street.

'Shit,' Franz spat and I could not help but stand up to see as I passed him the clip.

The huge telegraph-pole barrel of a Tiger heaving up over a pile of rubble to our right. Left, a smaller tank faced him off, in shadow, the sun at his back. Squaring against each other like two gunfighters in the final act of one of our leader's favoured movies, but not the image he would have wanted to see, not as manicured and noble. Clumsy and laboured like two tortoises about to battle for a square of basking rock. A battle for a rock, for rubble.

'Shit.'

Franz fired like an archer at the smaller tank, like my father at a wolf that was not allowed to breed that year. I saw the buildings tremble as the machines went at each other. In all my life I have never heard such a sound. It was not the sound of the end of the world. That came after. With the silence and the dust. You could hear the dust fall.

Franz fired through the smoke, less shooting from the other rooms. I could hear boots running, yelling from street corners. The random burst again, closer still. Then something bit a chunk out of the window frame and Franz fell to the naked wire mesh of his bed, slapped his hand to his neck.

'Shit! *Shit!*' Hand and wrist red. I pulled him to sit. Red on me, his neck dripping to his lap. I ran to the bathroom, grabbed a towel. My body awkward as I tried to press it on him and he snatched it from me and I stood like a fool. Apologised. Watched him dying.

A ricochet. Not even an aimed shot. A dumb bullet flying off a dumb window frame. I saw all his teeth as he grimaced, a grin like Hans, like in the movie from my youth, the mutilated Victor Hugo clown. I pulled a mattress from the wall, threw it to my bed, his breath behind me like a raging animal, a dying wolf.

I took him, a rag-doll, put him on the bed, to bed, his grey uniform black, the white towel shrunk and red as it sucked at him, only his face as white as the towel had been seconds before. His eyes not with me. Ridiculous. Like Paul's death. Ridiculous. I knew this now, how death, violent death comes. Clumsy. Nothing noble. A child walking around in his father's boots. Stumbles and breaks his teeth on a table while you're still amused at the image of him.

Nothing stopped outside. The tanks rolled and fired. The stuttering guns went on. Franz Werra's breath stopped coming and I waited for my own.

And he left.

Sat on his bed's wire frame and watched him. He might still be there somewhere. Would not leave him alone. Until I was sure. I would wait with him for one cigarette. I did not have that luxury with Paul, with Hans, with Etta. I needed it. Found myself smiling on him. Could not help but find something still amusing in him. His last words.

'*Shit.*' His last words. All he said.

'*Shit.*'

The simple platitudes.

Chapter 58

Far from now, someone will be in this room. The beds will not be here, the wardrobe gone, the room empty, the room gone. Someone will stand at the window, repainting the wood or fitting new casements, and they will tut at the gouge in the wood, the chip of the stone on the outside, and think on the work and cost required to prise out the frame just to replace one piece. Or ignore it, pretend they never saw it. Cover it with curtains. Never concern how the hole got there. And no-one but me will know. Just a split in a window frame, just an argument between husband and wife about replacing or ignoring. And maybe they have a boy, maybe he comes to the room to remove himself from the shouting, to see what the fuss is about, and he sees the cracked wood and the crescent shape left by something hitting and leaving the wood fast. And he knows. He goes to the *kino* on Saturday mornings and sees the cowboys shoot at each other from windows and rooftops, sees the glass break and the wood fly. He knows what happened here. He turns and sees it. Runs from room to room, looks for and finds the smart round holes in the ceilings, the pock marks on the outside walls of the building opposite. And he knows what happened here.

And the unfortunate thing, far from now, when the room has gone, the unfortunate thing will be.

The boy will smile. Be joyed that this thing happened in his house.

*

I took up my coat, checked the pockets. Letter-knife, silver case and lighter, envelope for Franz's parents, wallet and worker's pass. Paper plan. Wedding band. Put it on. For the first time in weeks.

The shooting lessened, but not the noise. Grenades. Mortars. I took his dress uniform from the wardrobe, put it with him and went downstairs. They would know it was his if I did that. He would wear it in his grave. Not at a ball. Something.

I left through the back door. To the yard. Looked long and hard at the motorcycle. All motorcycles look impatient. Waiting to move. They look like the skeletons of animals in museums, like dinosaurs where they pose them as if in action. Head turned, jaws open, tail whipping. But that's not how they died. They dropped dead from age, from sickness, from hunger, from predator. They died like us. But if we posed them like that no-one would go to see. No-one wants to be reminded. And it is a reminder, a memory. The strangest memory. For it hasn't happened yet. We despair to be reminded. Prefer to believe it does not happen.

Leave the bike. Riding it would look aggressive. It was never mine. And I didn't need it. Not now. Ernst Beck no longer running. I opened the metal box and gave back its pouch of spanners.

I could hear the machines roaring, grinding, walked to the sound, to the corner, and it was like walking out onto a stage from the shelter of the wings. A louder, brighter world. I ignored it all, strode to the centre of the street, wide berth to the deafening Tiger, then regained my path of heading straight to the smaller tank, to the green uniforms already waving me away as I raised my arms and still came on.

The Tiger's turret squealed, imagined it over my shoulder, aiming at the other tank staring straight back at me, my body between them both, still walking.

Any one of those watching could cut me down, grey or green, and it wouldn't matter to me now. I had someone else's blood on me. A friend's. And that had a strange numbness. Removed from what you might and might not do on any normal day. But I had a wedding band on me as well. And I had not had a normal day for a year. Craved one. Would make one.

I began shouting. My English capable.

'I am people!' I yelled. 'People! Not soldier!' The people in the maps.

The Tiger fired.

The sound threw me to the ground. The shell high. A hole in a building another scene away. The smaller one shot back. Hit its mark and the Tiger reared, rolled backwards. I stood up in the falling dust as if nothing had occurred around me, my ears whistling, my hands raised again. The green jackets stopped waving me away, waved me on, beckoned me to the corner.

The shooting from the windows stopped.

Not for me. Ernst Beck not that valued.

I stood against a wall, arms above my head as a soldier in green patted me down with one hand, his weapon away from me. They all looked so young. The first thing I noticed. Younger than me. You expect your invading army to be older.

He found the letter-knife and the silver case and lighter. Took only the knife, tossed it aside. I went to fetch it up, did not think otherwise. It was not mine.

'*Nicht,*' he said. '*Nicht.* Leave it.'

Such a strange voice. It did not even sound like English. The German did not sound like German.

I bent for the knife.

'Not mine,' I said, arms still up, then lowered one and leaned to the knife. 'A friend's.' I picked it up. 'A friend's. I will return it to him. Please.' Went back to the wall with it, back to my pocket, the gun never threatening.

'Stay there,' he said, stepped backwards into the road, called someone over, someone named Tenenbaum.

Tenenbaum! Almost like 'Christmas tree'. No-one with such a name could be a bad one.

German soldiers walked from the avenues and buildings, no helmets or caps, hands up, heads low. They walked in threes or fives. Not wishing to look massed.

First-Lieutenant Edward Tenenbaum introduced himself to me. He spoke understandable German, reassured me that all was well and asked for my identification. He scanned it and, of all the information on there, of all the questions he could have asked, his first was a good one, a right one.

'Where is your wife?'

I spoke English first, apologised.

'Zurich, sir. She is safe. Thank you.'

'For what?'

'Asking about my Etta. My wife.'

'Are you all right? What are you doing here?'

'Waiting for you,' I said.

'For *me*?'

'For Americans.' I nodded my head to the German soldiers walking. Not marching. 'What is happening, please?'

He handed back my card.

'Command surrendered at noon. These guys holding out. You, sir, should make your way to the Gau, yes? You understand? We're aiding civilians there. You understand? It's not safe here.'

I had stopped listening. Noon he had said. Surrendered at noon. Half an hour ago at least. Franz dead for only minutes. They had surrendered at noon. I saw Franz's grin full of blood. An irony in it now, an irony that he did not know, or he had seen it a moment after. As he left. As all becomes known.

The lieutenant must have judged my glaze as one of an imbecile. Must have seen many such faces. War faces. The sight of his back moving away woke me.

Now Ernst. Now.

'Lieutenant Tenenbaum,' I called, and he paused just enough. 'I need to speak to someone in command.'

'What?'

He was my age I guessed, maybe even younger. Young enough to still listen to men his age. Old enough to discern what to listen to.

'I am no regular civilian, sir.' I straightened my shabby coat, pulled down my frayed cuffs, still with good brass cuff-links.

'I have important information. I have come from Erfurt to find Americans.'

Stand like Hans, Ernst Beck. Speak like him, frame his pose. But I could not. The air out of me, ears still ringing. My shoulders would no longer go back, hair full of dust and without pomade, my wing-tips scuffed like boots. I could not. Not Hans Klein. Saw him in front of me, before I left him. Telling me to be the best Hans Klein I could be. The Hans Klein I would never be.

'I have worked with the SS. Came here to find you. Give information.'

'What information?' He came back.

I pulled the plan from behind me, too fast, his hand to his holster and I slowed as I carried the paper free, handed it to him. Kept my fingertips fraily dancing on its edges as he opened it out. Mine. So long mine. Fragile in my eye like a papyrus script. The sunlight would break it.

'What the hell is this? A building?'

'It is an oven. I worked for Topf and Sons. In Erfurt. We made ovens for the SS. For the Party. I need to speak to someone. Someone in command, sir.'

'An oven? It's enormous. What . . .'

I answered for him, answered for his eyes that I could see perceiving. At the dates, at the SS stamps, the eagle, the sig-runes. He was looking at something significant, something stolen. Something that belonged on an important desk and not a Kassel street.

'For the camps,' I said. 'Those levels running down that you see are grated conveyors. You have seen the camps, yes?'

'We know of them,' he said. 'We all got camps.'

'Not like this. Not like this. This is what they wanted to do,' I said, nodding like a madman and I bit my lip to stop it. My hands tentatively pulled the paper from him. Mine. My work. He let me take it back. Brushed his hands.

'It can incinerate thousands of corpses,' I said. 'It is fuelled by the motion of the bodies. Their fat. I would like to speak to someone in command, please, lieutenant. I can show you camps. I can help. I know where they are.'

He withdrew from me. Not actually. As Franz had done.

453

A space between us. His face no longer the helpful German interpreter. I saw the face that all might have for Ernst Beck when this was done.

'You better come with me.' Hand clamped to my shoulder. I could not keep up with his pace. Understood that. Understood that he did not want me to.

*

I was in an office building opposite the Gau. A makeshift command until the Gau had been cleared fully, until all the papers had been signed, until one general had capitulated on paper to another. Swords were not passed, crowns not given. A signature on paper. Wars began and ended with signatures when once they had opened and closed with emperors and citadel walls. Now generals signed on the line. A contract. Civilised. Business.

I rode there in a 'jeep'. They called it that. Half a car. A ride like a wooden carousel at a fair. Jeep. A strange army. They called our stick-grenades 'potato-mashers', their own they called 'pineapples'. It was like children playing at war. Perhaps how they got through it. Childish names, connotations to everything, for everything. Even the badges on their arms were bright, like pictures cut from a comic-book. Ours were black. Diamonds, the occasional leaf, simple pips for rank. Not reds, not yellows, no coloured piping, no stars like fireworks. But we both had the eagle. The same standard.

'What the hell am I looking at?' This from a captain. This usage of 'hell' common to them. Tenenbaum's first words when he saw the plan. The driver of the jeep had said similar: 'Who the hell is this?' Maybe they believed they were in Hell. They did not talk like this in the movies; perhaps not permitted to do so.

Surprised by how tall they were, how well fed. Not as we imagined them. And they were calm. Confident. That was it. Assurance. There was an acceptance through them that everything was opening exactly as it should. The lieutenant who escorted me had rode through streets of ash and fire, whistling, one foot resting outside the car. Soldiers waved to us as we passed, not saluted, waved 'Hi'. This brag of theirs did not inspire. They might not understand after all, might not care. Not take me in. Not help. Put me back on the street with my funny drawing and carry on with their circus army and their whistles and waves.

The man Tenenbaum explained to the captain as best he could. I watched, listened, tried to interject but my nose running and I sneezed into my hand. I could feel myself waning, my hands paling even through the dried blood, Franz's blood, still on them.

'May I sit, please?' Even my voice pale. They looked at me blankly. I did not know if I had spoke English or German. They did not respond. I sought my own chair, limped to it so they might understand. I sat and gathered.

The captain made notes. I assumed of the names attached to the documents. But he did not understand the document.

'Why would they want a machine like this? This is the SS. Is it for meat? He says it does hundreds a day? What for?'

I coughed. The same blank look back at me. *Now Ernst. Now.*

'You don't understand,' I said. In English. If I spoke slow I was sure I could manage. 'You don't know, do you?' I think I smiled.

'This "machine" was patented by my company for the SS. My role was to make our designs clearer for Berlin. I draft ovens. Designs for the camps. They get larger. They burn all day. All night. They burn so much that they break. And we go fix them. We bring them portable units while we fix so they can keep burning. This one – this oven – is almost automated. Needs only two men. Very little fuel. It fuels itself. By the bodies consuming each other. They go in and go down on conveyors moved by the motion of them. By the mass of them. And they all mix together at the bottom.' I paused to sneeze again. I was punctuating my speech with my hands, conducting it with my hands so they could follow.

'It was patented in '42. Then forgotten. Not used. Then last summer they remembered. Last summer they asked me to draw it again. For Berlin. For the camps. Last summer they moved half a million Jews from Hungary. To the camps. They wanted this oven for those camps. Do you see? Please?'

I sat back, exhausted from it, from trying to explain to children an adult's world, the perspective of a piece of paper and a travelling fool.

The captain studied me. My clothes, my waning.

'We're not as ignorant as you think, Mr Beck.' He indicated Tenenbaum. 'Ed here has a man attached to him. An ex-prisoner. We know what we need to. Ed, why don't you tell him what you do.' The captain sat, held up my plan like reading a newspaper and the lieutenant spoke in German.

He was not part of the infantry, he said. His unit involved in psychological warfare. They were the ones who printed the red leaflets dropped all over the front lines that promised surrendering soldiers food and protection under the Geneva rules. The rules that we and the red-jackets did not accept. They even had their own printing press. Edward Tenenbaum's position in Kassel was to drive with a loud-hailer around the streets and villages assuring resisting soldiers they would be fairly treated. His American German invaluable for such. Invaluable to me that Edward realised the magnitude of my schematic.

'They'll destroy everything they can,' he said. 'If they haven't already. Unfortunately that probably also means . . . anybody in . . .'

I did not need him to finish.

'Not if you were quick,' I said. 'You can get to Buchenwald in a few days. A week if you are going north. I got here in two days coming west from Erfurt.'

'Buchenwald?'

'Outside Weimar. A camp. I have been there. I can take you, show you.' I saw the captain folding my plan.

457

My plan. My paper. My fingers on it before I knew what I was doing.

'Please, sir,' I said, dragging it back. 'It is mine. I should keep it. Make sure it gets to proper place.'

'Are you kidding me, Kraut?' Veins in his neck purple. 'I'm a god-damn US captain under General Bradley! You have a god-damn military secret there!'

'It is mine. Sir. I will hand it over when we reach Buchenwald. I must get there.'

'Where the hell is Buchenwald?'

Edward defused.

'Outside Weimar. Patton plans to get to Weimar by the thirteenth. That's ten days. This guy says he can get us there in a week.'

'And Erfurt,' I added. 'If you help me get to Buchenwald.'

Edward rubbed his neck.

'Man, you sure want to get to that camp. What the hell's in it for you?'

I put the plan inside my coat.

'I . . . I have a friend there.' Limped to my chair again. Repeated slowly in case my English was not as capable.

'I have a friend.'

Chapter 59

I woke up in hospital, in the Gau. Tenenbaum in a chair watching me, speculating on me, his hands resting on his lap, legs crossed. The bedside lamp on. Night. I could see lumps of bodies in the other beds around me.

'You're sweating,' he said. 'You were having a nightmare. Do you remember passing out?'

I had slumped off the chair in front of him and the captain apparently. I must have been out for hours, it was dark, I was starving.

'I'll bring you some soup. You're going to need your strength to come on the road with me.'

He gave little importance to it, explained casually that his unit were 'peeps', that this word was what the jeeps were originally 'monikered' because they could nip in and out, 'peep' at the enemy and get back to base at thirty miles per hour across a field of rocks or a river. Peeps. Jeeps. The strangest army.

We would head out tomorrow, himself and another civilian with us. He had no contemplation, hesitation, of riding into his enemy's country. The war already over. We would radio back every afternoon and the tanks and others would follow.

'Do you need to fetch any personal stuff?'

'Could I bring my motorcycle? It is only small.'

He laughed.

'I meant clothes, but, sure. Why not. If you can get it on the back it's yours. Why do you want it?'

I said it frankly. Could not tell in his German where his humour was.

'In case I have to get away. In case *they* come.'

'Sure. Sure.' He stood up. 'Whatever you want. I'll get your soup.'

'Lieutenant?' I almost whispered, looked around the other beds. 'Are there other . . . Germans here? Any . . . officers I mean?' Sure he could see the anxiety on me. His levity lifted.

'No. No officers. We wouldn't put you in with soldiers. Why?'

'I am a betrayer, no? A traitor.'

'Ernst.' He put his smile back on. 'You're only a traitor if the bad guys win. And we're the United States Army. The bad guys never win. Someday you'll be a hero.' He left. I only noticed then that they did not screw their caps to their heads, did not wear them at all. Even his captain in his office did not need the formality. A strange army.

It did not seem possible that they could be victors. Not with such an attitude. Maybe the British and the others were the formal ones. Maybe they were like our soldiers, our leaders. This army their cannon fodder. Or maybe I just did not understand. We the archaic force. Fighting in the old ways. And that is why we were now the retreated, the vanquished.

Edward Tenenbaum returned with a potato soup, watched me eat. Nourishment brought my senses back, my concerns.

'My plan? Where are my clothes? My plan?'

'I hope you can trust your plan to me, Ernst. Temporarily. You'll travel with me tomorrow. I'll come for you at six. With your clothes. Could have left today if you hadn't fainted on us.' He got up, wagged his finger at me. 'Don't let me down now, Ernst. Get me to that camp.' Winked at me, left without a care in the world. The strangest army.

*

I could not sleep. Would not sleep. I kept my feet out of the bed. You cannot sleep fully if your feet are exposed. You just drift, never fully rest. A caveman memory I guess. Animals go for feet first.

I said her name over and over, and when I was too tired to speak it I said it in my head. Slept like that. With her beside. And no nightmare came.

*

Real scrambled eggs for breakfast, real coffee. Felt normal again. That's all you need to feel human again. Pathetic. Food. Not books, not words or love. Just food.

The stir of April light in the early morning outside. The concrete of the building shimmering eggshell blue. The red banners gone. A less intimidating building now. The same dishevelled queue forming outside already.

Edward Tenenbaum waiting in the jeep, drinking coffee straight from a flask. Another fellow beside him in greatcoat and fedora, older than us, introduced to me as Egon Fleck. The pale look of all of us, but I only guessed him as German. He had been at Buchenwald. That was enough to not question further. We drove to my hotel, the building different from yesterday. Battered and exhausted.

The little motorcycle fitted on the back of the jeep as if made for it. Webbing straps held it on. The jeep's designer had imagined such jury-rigging, hooks and anchors all over. The only compromise was for me to sit with the petrol can, the 'jerry-can' Edward called it. A German invention they had utilised. The insult of the name lost. Jeep, Jerry, a dozen other phrases that did not belong in war. Everything a euphemism in their speech. A series of beeps and whistles for real words. 'Bazooka'. I have written this word myself. A ridiculous word. Proper words for our weapons, our vehicles. Yet we were losing. Bazooka. Jeep. Peeps. Pineapples. Potato-mashers. These were not soldiers of old wars. They played games with words. Playground names for dreadful things. And I could only think that there might be something to fear in them for that. In the future.

There were no road-blocks when we left Kassel. I watched the city vanish in the early-morning mist as if my entirety within her had been a dream. I was sorry. Felt sorry for a city. For a body I had left on a bed.

But heroes move forward.

Chapter 60

24 April 1945
Personal File

Alfred Toombs
Chief of Intelligence

BUCHENWALD

A <u>Preliminary Report</u>
by EGON W. FLECK, Civ.
and
1st Lt. EDWARD A. TENENBAUM.

NOTE: Special distribution is being made of this report because preliminary evaluation indicates that it is one of the most significant accounts yet written on an aspect of life in Nazi Germany.

464

It is NOT just another report on a concentration camp. It does not deal exclusively with the horror of life in Buchenwald, nor with the brutalities of the Nazi perverts.

The report is obviously controversial. It has not been possible in so short a time to cross-check and weigh every detail. But independent investigation leads to the tentative conclusion that the basic story can be accepted. Later study and interrogation may lead to modification of this picture – one way or the other.

A fortnight later I sat on the balcony of a villa in Vienna's mountains under a warm April sun drinking coffee from a porcelain cup, smoking real American Camels. The previous occupant of the villa, the district governor, arrested and removed. We were the new residents. Edward, Egon and I, and eleven communist survivors from Buchenwald.

The head of the PWD, the psychological war department which Edward was attached to, was an American-German Jew. Edward the son of Polish Jews. The outgoing governor who had deported sixty-five thousand Jews to the camps as a 'contribution to European culture' now had two sleeping in his beds.

They were here to write a report. Document Buchenwald for Washington. I tagging along, using Vienna as a stepping stone for Switzerland, grateful for the

Americans' protection, their food and shelter. And the governor had a fine collection of suits.

The war not over, just vast countries returned to themselves, dusting themselves down and starting again. But the fighting over enough for reports on the discovered camps to be written.

On the road, after Kassel, Lieutenant Tenenbaum had shown no possibility that what we were doing had any danger attached. Maybe that was controlled. Maybe just to pacify Egon and I. To him it was simple. The army would maintain a north–south invasion, roll a line across Germany to meet up with the Russians. Forget getting to Berlin, the red-jackets would get there first. His role was to 'peep' ahead, stop, let the armoured division catch up if all was well and then carry on. He wore his helmet only if he had a feeling to wear it. Nothing for Egon and I.

Egon was mostly quiet. He only spoke openly when he prayed before he ate. Never talked about family or his past. He was there for one reason. He had been in Buchenwald. I could show them where it was, how to get there, but he could show 'it'. And I imagined that was part of his silence. We were taking him back to that place. What would a man talk about if that his object of being?

Edward spoke a lot. He was a Yale graduate, the highest grade. *Summa cum laude*. An economist. He had already been chosen as someone who would help rebuild the mark for Europe when this was all done. He said it as a matter of fact. With all of this around us, with Franz Werra dead in a hotel room, Hans Klein in a camp or dead, my wife in another country, my parents' fate unknown, the displacement and reduction of races, someone somewhere had contemplated on the future of the mark and sent Edward Tenenbaum to do so. I never imagined that other nations would concern themselves, were concerning themselves, with our currency. There are sides to war that does not make sense except on bank ledgers. Our enemies would need only Germany. Not its people.

It was 11 April when we saw them. Seven days out of Kassel. I said it would take a week.

Our jeep gone ahead as always, to wait for the tanks and armoured cars to follow. We were north of Weimar. That had been our action. Go round, go north, and then back on ourselves. The US Army moving up from the south, the German army concentrated in Berlin. The countryside not of interest.

We came across hamlets untouched by the war. Their farming, their season carrying on as if of another world. We met labourers more interested in the jeep than the American escorting us. Gave us potatoes and apple wine. Planes were all they knew of it. They pointed to the sky and mimed the planes for Edward, marvelled at the star painted on the jeep's bonnet, laughed at Edward's German accent, wondered what Egon and I were doing with this alien and his odd vehicle. And then, on a gravel road lined with beech forest, we saw them.

They marched. Thousands of men in striped uniforms

marching along the side of the road. They carried German guns, waved at us as we drove past, and Edward stopped the jeep. He ordered us to stay in the car, to stand and tell them to go back. Back because the tanks were behind us, that it was not safe.

They saluted us like walking to a football match, were friendly, because we had a star on our car and an American, but they all said the same thing.

They were going to kill Germans. Said this to me and Egon. They were going to Weimar. They were going to kill Germans. There were SS hiding in the forest. They had taken prison clothes to disguise themselves. They were hunting them.

Edward convinced, ordered, most of them to go back and we followed their trail. By then the armoured division caught up and the tanks made them turn back. We were ahead. Just after five we reached the turn in the road over the railway where I had been with Hans Klein a year before. I tapped Edward's shoulder, told him to go on, that there was another gate east.

'What the hell are those bears doing there?' He had seen the zoo. I explained as best I could, odd even as I said it. Egon said nothing. We were at the gate, his eyes fixed to it.

There were armed guards. Not SS guards.

Edward swung out of the jeep, introduced himself, gave cigarettes through the wire of the gate. They told him that the last of the SS had run off after hearing tank and small-arms fire from the hills, although they had captured over eighty which were held within. Since the first of the month the SS had been marching out large groups of prisoners, the fittest prisoners, thousands of them every day. Today the communist factions in the camp had taken it over. All undesirables and criminals were herded into the 'Little Camp'.

I called Edward back, told him I knew the Little Camp. That it was a barbed-wire square of wooden and sheet-metal rotting huts in the centre of the prison. Told him we have to go there. I had to go there.

'Ernst. This could be dangerous.' The first time he had used this word. 'This is a prison taken over by inmates. I can't think of anything worse right now.'

I got out of the car.

'I can,' I said, and Egon followed. I ordered the gates to be opened. Faced them. Stood like I owned the place. As Klein would have done.

'We are translators for the Americans. They are behind us. But they do not know where you are. We can show them. Protect you. I have been here before,' indicated Egon, 'we have been here before, know what you have suffered. Trucks will come with food and medicines. But we need to see. And I may have a friend here. I need to find him. Who is in command?'

'Comrade Eiden runs the camp now.' A military response from a communist German in rags.

'Inform him the United States Army is here to assist. Let me in to find my friend.'

'What about him?' Their eyes to Egon.

'I have no friends left,' he said, gave them the look of the camp. The unfocussed glaze of one looking past barbed wire to the woods beyond. They opened the gate.

Edward walked by my shoulder, whispered, a new experience for him. His voice always loud.

'This is crazy, Ernst.'

'Then wait outside for your tanks. You're lucky. You're not looking for a man who saved your life, your wife's life. Look around. Your army will find Germans here. We did this to ourselves.'

I walked ahead, left Edward and Egon, went straight for the Little Camp. The place where they put the undesirables, the unclean, the near-dead.

It was guarded also. Expected that. I smoothed my short hair, not much longer than theirs, straightened my coat. Became the best Hans Klein that I could as they puffed up their chests and closed together in front of the gate.

'I'm with the US Army,' I lied. The strong lie. Shoulders back. 'Twelfth Army under General Bradley.' I took out the silver case, the silver lighter. Lit up slow. Their eyes never leaving the silver. Offered them a cigarette each.

'I'm looking for a civilian. Would have been here two months. Hans Klein. Do you . . .'

I stopped talking. Saw beyond them. And Egon stepped back.

Shapes moved from the twilight over the guard's shoulders. Not men. Shapes. Angles for bodies, spheres for heads. Not people.

They shuffled from the tents and stables. White and blue ghouls. Hair gone, cheeks shrunken with missing teeth, sucking on their gums, their heads enlarged by their sunk temples. You could see the cracks of bone that made up their skulls. They crawled or hobbled on spindle legs like spiders or on branches for crutches. They moved to the sound of my voice. A healthy voice. That meant food. Even if I had only eaten it myself. The memory of food about me. Maybe something in my pockets. An apple I might have been gifting for a horse, a toffee from my car, for my children, forgotten in my pocket.

'You want to go in there?' The guard's thick voice, a Russian voice. A communist sneer. Some, as always in such places, better fed than others. 'My guest.' He pulled back the bolt on the gate. I stood at his face.

'Half an hour behind us are generals. You have heard of Patton? Bradley? They are coming right here. How you act in the next half-hour will be the remainder of your war. Lieutenant Tenenbaum is speaking with your leader. This is an American camp from today. Thank you for your assistance. You will be commended, comrades.' That's how Klein would have done it. 'When I come back to this gate make sure you let me out.'

'Typhus,' one of them said.

'Don't worry. I won't lick anybody.' I looked back at Egon. Rooted. He shook his head. And I was alone.

'Anyone I come back with you let us both out. Understand? I have to report to General Patton in an hour.'

I marked my words with a stab of my cigarette, put it to the ground. Went inside the gate.

I moved through the bodies, a fairground maze of distorting mirrors. Crashed into them, sidled round skins of bones, breathed only when I had to.

I repeated his name to all of them, repeated that help and food was coming. I was a raft to the drowning, all of them clinging to me. Fingers missing, feet gnarled or lost, stumps dragging. Dripping sores of flesh. Remnants of men, and I had not noticed the multitude of them that were naked. Not noticed because their genitals, as hairless as their heads, had begun to shrink back into their bodies. They were cheap puppets of men. Wood too expensive to make them fully. Keep them light for the strings that would lift them. I was moving through the under-earth of a cemetery. And children. There were children. Do not make me recall that. And still I called his name, did not run back to the gate. I thought of Paul. Thought of what he burned. Once it had been fat men with watch-chains and widows. Then it had become these. Then the camps decided they could do it for themselves. And I drew the ovens for them.

I was in the barracks. Rows of shelves to the ceiling. Could not imagine that this was where humans slept. Suited more for a place where lost post would be abandoned. Pigeon-holes of a post-office.

Called his name. Some heads moved in the shelves, eyes swivelled on me like the heads of dolls tipped back. I had to fight not to run, did not want to go further. And I had no hope then. The stench too strong, the symbolism of the flies too evident. Fifty-nine days since I saw him. Since I left him. I hoped they had shot him on his first dawn. Not this. Not this. Almost did not want to meet him.

I walked out of there, back to the clamouring ghouls. Maybe he had done better. Hans Klein after all. This small place for new arrivals, Hans had said so himself when we came here together. A place for traitors, for diseased, the old and weak. But Hans Klein would light a Camel, straighten his tie, convince them he belonged in the main camp, the political barracks, that he was a personal friend of Colonel Pister, worked closely with the SS. Then he had walked out the next day, went back to the Topfs who had complained to our leader himself about the internment of such a faithful Party member.

I walked with a wake of ghosts behind, saw Edward at the gate. The guards smiling and meek to the tall American. Another man with him, Eiden I assumed, the man now in charge, who allowed this to continue.

I turned once more to the Little Camp, to the crowd. Would try one more thing. I cupped my hands to my mouth, bellowed as hard as I could.

'I am Ernst Beck! Ernst Beck!' I moved further in. 'From Topf. From Erfurt. You saved my wife, Hans!' Nothing. 'Thank you. Thank you, Hans! Thank you, Herr Klein!'

Nothing.

I brushed the hands off me. Told them everything was going to be better now. Not all right. I could not promise that. Just better. Just different. Maybe never better. But it would be different. I made my way to the gate. Passed through it alone.

'Any luck?' Edward asked.

'No. He is not here.'

The man Eiden piped up. 'Who are you looking for? I was in the commissary and records. I know most. Was he recent?'

'A couple of months ago,' I said. 'His name was Hans Klein. His name is Hans Klein.'

'From Topf?'

I stepped closer. 'Yes. You know him? That is him.'

'He was never in the Little Camp.'

I knew it. Knew that Klein would not allow such. He would have had supper with Colonel Pister, the colonel from Himmler's motor-pool. The Topfs would have called. The one-legged monster would have barked down a telephone. Klein out before he loosed his tie, went home and loosed the top off a bottle of vermouth.

Eiden snorted. Put a finger to his nose, hacked a shot of phlegm to the mud.

'They shot him the morning after he arrived. Burned in the pits. The ovens broken. How did you know him?'

I walked past Edward, past them. Clenched my fist against the old scar that was never there.

'He was my boss.'

Eiden sniffed, put his hands in his pockets. 'Then he probably deserved it.'

I slipped in the mud as I punched his jaw. The last violent act of my war.

*

My name is Ernst Beck. I grew up in Erfurt on the medieval bridge that you see in postcards. I studied at Erfurt University. Martin Luther went there.

The first job I had in my life was drafting ovens for concentration camps. The second job I had was helping construct a report on the camp at Buchenwald.

We brought eleven former inmates of the camp to Vienna to assist. Hans Klein not one of them. I am smoking Camels from his case and using his lighter, wearing a suit of the former head of our leader's Youth regiments. He is in prison. The Geneva rules he ignored ensuring his food and treatment.

I drew an oven that could burn hundreds a day. Not enough time for it to happen, and the newsreels showed the pits and the piles of corpses instead. Patton ordered movie cameras before ambulances. Knew no-one would believe otherwise. And I can only give the cruellest observation on that.

Footage of a pile of ash would not have horrified the world for eternity.

I know – know it in my own history – that our instinct is to deny. We sleep bad enough as is.

This the year of my war.

Chapter 61

A fine house in a rural suburb of Gotha. Detached. Garden in front. A magnolia tree shading the porch. June now. The tree would have been budding in April.

The surrender done. June and normality. Regaining normality. Bending things back into shape. Twisting the circles back to squares. Forming countries again as if nothing had happened, shaping new ones to suit the red-jackets, the Americans, the British.

Roosevelt died the day after we entered Buchenwald, before Patton and Bradley got there, before the official liberation. Our leader and Mussolini and Roosevelt all gone within thirty days of each other, in one month. Three from the first war. Ended when the game they had started playing as youths rolled its last dice. The first war ended now. The board put away. Until the next throw. The spider of the first only a husk. It had eggs to hatch. And they had died now also. Eggs of their own.

I pulled the doorbell, stood back. My hair had grown back to its strong blond, pomade smooth. I wore a suit and tie despite the Saturday. Felt it fitting. For delivering such a letter.

The woman answering the door was not a maid. Somehow I had expected one. I took off my hat.

'Frau Werra?' I asked. She opened the door wider.

'My name is Ernst Beck, Frau Werra.' I did not need to say much else, she saw the letter in my hand. An official one sat behind her mantle clock or in a box atop the ward-robe, or in her son's room, or in the attic for all I knew. Mine had more weight, she saw it hung heavy in my hand.

'I was with Franz when he died,' I said. Could not say it better than that. It was to be expected. Everything said plain now, understood to be so. Franz probably knew I could not post it. Knew his mother would need to see the last person who knew him, and I never thought otherwise. He would owe me the stamp.

She almost did not take it. Her hand reached and drew away. She said what she had to.

'Won't . . . will you come in?'

I put the letter to her hand.

'I cannot stay. Franz gave me this. For you.'

'His father is inside. He would . . .'

I knew she wanted this. If I came into the house, walked his floors, somehow he would walk them. He was in the air about me, in my youth, in the blond hair and blue eyes. And I could stay. And that was the very reason I could not.

'No. Thank you, mother. Would you come to the car for me, Frau Werra?' I held out my hand to the path of her garden gate, to the car. She removed her apron, no-one in the street should see it.

I took her to the car. Etta's father had taught her to drive in our absence from each other. Considered it part of survival now. Should anything go against the neutrality of Zurich. And I had kept the little motorcycle that had saved me for the same. For the knock on the door.

'This is my wife, Etta.' They shook hands through the open window. 'Franz helped me speak to her. When she could not stay with me. When . . . when she had to leave.'

'Oh,' she said. 'Oh.' Read what she was not told.

'Pleased to meet you, Frau Werra,' Etta beamed. 'Ernst has told me much about your son.'

I took the mother's hands. The letter between.

'Your son was a friend of mine.' I spoke only to her eyes. 'He defended to the end. When generals had surrendered like cowards he did not. Thank you. Thank you for raising a good German son.'

She held me, and I let it. The last to know him. Wanted to breathe something from him.

A moment of this, then she eased me away, hid her face as she walked back up her path.

Every general should have to parade themselves in front of mothers.

I got in the car.

'What now?' Etta asked, started the engine. The car, a

small saloon loaned to us from the young lieutenant. Part of his reward. He had no need for it. Edward Tenenbaum now in Berlin. Reconstructing the mark. A banker now. A business not in the business of improving the world. Only concerned with saving the mark. Dividing a country.

What now?

Ludwig Topf killed himself when the Russians came to Erfurt. He would have stood over his huge desk as the beating came at his door, wondered at the plans they knew of that had not been burnt, the ovens not destroyed. Wondered how they knew.

He did not shoot himself over what he had been complicit with. Wrote a note denying. He just did not want to meet the brothers and fathers of the Russians that knew. Put a pistol to his mouth. I hoped it was an Erfurt Luger.

Ernst Topf fled to the West. They let him come. He came with enough money after all. Prüfer, Sander and the other engineers were imprisoned by the Russians. The end for them. For all the horrors of our prison camps you did not want to be a German in a Russian one.

No-one called for me. I had given them the plan for an oven that might have never been built. But it showed intention. The foresight of a great plan. Something other than just controlling disease. A machine. That was enough to let me go free. Let me hold my wife again. I was only doing my job. As the men who planned to incinerate Dresden had only done theirs. But still, a job I would be shamed to deny being part of for the rest of my life.

'*I was only doing my job, my duty. Only following orders.*' But we lost. So they were the wrong orders. But there were those that said no, said, '*I shall not*'. Thousands of them. Their last words. But empathy for them lost in horror.

A new Germany. Albeit one to be split in two, one that faced the same restrictions that had brought us to this. Another treaty against us. So no real matter, no real problem. The same problem. I had lived almost my whole life under it.

You get older, and life is not about change, as you expected, not about adventure or aspiration, as you hoped. It is about asking *please*.

Please let everything be the same, or please let everything be different. Just please let it not get harder. Harder or worse. This much money and no more. Or maybe more if it comes. And that will be the world from now on.

The stones in your shoes.

When you are a child and forced to go on a walk with your father on a Sunday. And you whine and can't put on your shoes and there are stones in your shoes, little stones, chips of pebbles only, and you whine about them also. And your father stands above.

'You are coming for a walk,' he says. 'Shake out the stones. Don't complain,' he says. 'You will always get stones in your shoes.'

I know that now. Know that I don't want *fewer* stones in my shoes. I want no *more* stones. I am fine with the stones I have. Can walk with them. I can feel them, accept them.

You get stones in your shoes. You don't get them if you never walk.

Etta shut off the engine, thought I had not heard her above it.

'Ernst?' she asked again. 'What now?'

Author's Note

It's over two decades since I read an interview with one of the Topf descendants. After the unification of Germany many families and companies who had lost property in the years after the war were interested in reclaiming it or ensuring that business continued after unification. The only reason Dagmar Topf made the papers was because the factory and family villa she was interested in holding on to was now labelled as the workplace where the 'engineers of the Final Solution' designed the ovens for the concentration camps of the SS.

The perspective of the article followed the vein of veiled disgust. Why would you want to retain that? Why wouldn't you raze it to the ground?

Dagmar Topf's attitude was one that still rings around the world whenever those complicit with the Nazi regime appeal.

They were only doing their jobs. They had to. What choice did they have?

And it's the same argument we hear today, still reeling from the aftershocks of fiscal and corporate irresponsibility which only aspired to one goal: to make as much money as possible out of deliberately making others poor and consciously, by economic model, creating generations yet to come forced to live in a precariat society where stability and constancy will be cultural relics.

'I didn't do anything that wasn't in the rules.' 'I have done nothing illegal.'

I was only doing my job.

This is not a holocaust story, and only in its setting and circumstance is it intended to be an historical story. I wanted to ask, 'What would you do?'

Since the rise of technology and its erosion of borders and instant commerce, moral decisions can be distanced because we never have to visit the consequences of trade and cost, and increasingly the business of failure is a preferred model. We see companies bought and sold for single figures, assets stripped, pensions revoked, government backing of failure, whole towns bankrupted, and a handful of people walk off with millions. There is money in deliberate failure which no idealistic economist could ever have predicted or even dreamed of as something to aspire to for any society. Many of the world's largest companies no longer make anything. The concept of production, of supporting the economy while still profiting, is not the model that modern capitalism requires. They make money by moving money, by devaluing the economy. Credit agencies now factor in the price of the inevitable government bailout for company schemes designed to fail as the bailout becomes part of the projected profits.

The prominence of such practice leads all of us to the possibility that by merely working and consuming we can sometimes, to many degrees, be a part of a system which not only profits from exploitation, misery, conflict and failure but also actively encourages such by its reward, and to resist is to be told that you aren't 'aspirational' enough. We only object because we are envious. So it is such with Ernst Beck.

Solomon Asch, and especially Stanley Milgram's experiments (the war still in their living memories) demonstrated that obedience, conformity, could be manufactured. Milgram's infamous electric-shock experiments had their origins in two seemingly contradictory observations. One had been Hannah Arendt's coverage of the Eichmann trial where she was vilified for suggesting that Eichmann represented 'the banality of evil'; a man simply doing his job, and that this is what we should fear. He was not the Devil doing the Devil's work. The other was the TV show *Candid Camera* which in its American heyday would take its laughs from demonstrating the frailty of individuality against the easier state, even desire, of conformity and obedience. Laughed-at weakness.

I wondered what it might be like to have worked in a company that laboured under SS contract, more specifically those that supplied and worked for the camps themselves.

The ovens are a powerful reminder of the nature of the extreme; they still stand, are exhibited in silent abjectness, but someone was paid to design and build them. There is nothing guilty in building an oven, nothing evil with needing ovens for prisons, yet the ovens are a unifying symbol of what remains. Only what remains reminds. And we have learnt from this. Corporations and governments have learnt from this.

Should we be horrified that companies competed to supply them? Should we have expected the companies to question the quantity of ovens required? What corporation would question such today? I wonder if it is only with relief for the Allies that it was a German company that supplied; but wonder if that was simply down to logistics.

We often hear that the modern corporate system appeals to a psychopathic personality, that its traits and methods warrant such and its electronic nature further removes any possibility of empathy. As such Hans Klein in the story represents this. It is only when the world encroaches on him personally that he questions, and Ernst Beck's admiration of him, his aspiration is not misplaced today.

Many companies, institutions, domestic and foreign, took payment and assisted the Nazi regime. From filing systems and their machines, to electricity and coal, gold belonging to governments in exile given up willingly, to motor engines and gas jets, to the refusal of countries to take Jewish refugees, but the thing that abhors the most are the ovens and what they represent. The others are unseen, smaller horrors. And companies and institutions remembered, learnt from this. And, after all, the doctrine, the dictatorship, did not fail because of the people objecting. To call Topf and Sons the engineers of the Final Solution is just as narrow as we insist things should be.

Historically this is a work of fiction. I chose the name Ernst Beck in reference to the anthropologist Ernest Becker, and apart from the chief directors of the Topf factory and various camp commanders all other characters and situations are fictional. The timeline of the story however does follow the last year of the war in respect of the camps, the bombings and Ernst's time in Waldkappel and Kassel. The continuous oven for mass use is not a work of fiction. It was never put into production, but they wanted it to exist. The horror of its possibility the starkest concept behind the story I could imagine. And I didn't imagine it.

When I started the story the question I wanted to ask was, 'What would you do?' During the work this gradually became, 'What should you do? Now. Today.' And I think this became the better, still relevant question in any modern parallel you wish for conjecture. There is no clear moment in the story for Ernst Beck to realise the implications of his work. There never is. It is, for all of us, only ever gradual and dawning, and only with hindsight do we pontificate on our own ethics and bravado. But if such an oven had come to exist, had been put to use, if the war had not closed as it did, if the conquerors had not brought the film cameras to the camps and the men and women that filmed, I don't think I could have written this story. I don't think I would want to write anything.

*

'To live fully is to live with an awareness of the rumble of terror that underlies everything.'

Ernest Becker

Acknowledgements

I'd like to thank my agent, James Gill, through what turned out to be a long path to publication. During that time there were shifts and changes of supporters and editors and I was sorry to see them go and move on but I'm grateful to them all especially Katie Espiner and Cassie Browne. Many thanks to Charlotte Cray at the Borough Press and Holly Ainley for taking the helm through to the end.

I'm glad that I can look back on this work a couple of years since writing as at the time there had to be a detachment to the narrative that did not prove to be an easy one to research and it was impossible to not trawl through a wide amount of unsettling material to try and pin down facts and story possibilities without becoming affected by it but I'm grateful to the following (and others too numerous) for their information:

The Buchenwald and Mittelbau-Dora Memorial Foundation, The Tiergarten 4 Association, and The Engineers of "The Final Solution". Topf and Sons – Builders of The Auschwitz Ovens exhibition, Erfurt.

Robert Lautner
October 2016